JAMES McGEE

The Reckoning

HarperCollins*Publishers*

HarperCollins*Publishers*
1 London Bridge Street,
London SE1 9GF

www.harpercollins.co.uk

Published by HarperCollins*Publishers* 2017

1

A catalogue record for this book is available from the British Library

ISBN: 978-0-00-750766-5 (HB)

Set in Sabon LT Std 11.25/14.5 pt by
Palimpsest Book Production Limited, Falkirk, Stirlingshire

Printed and bound in Great Britain by Clays Ltd, St Ives plc

MIX
Paper from
responsible sources
FSC C007454
www.fsc.org

FSC™ is a non-profit international organisation established to promote
the responsible management of the world's forests. Products carrying the
FSC label are independently certified to assure consumers that they come
from forests that are managed to meet the social, economic and
ecological needs of present and future generations,
and other controlled sources.

Find out more about HarperCollins and the environment at
www.harpercollins.co.uk/green

THE RECKONING

1

It was late evening and in the Hanged Man trade was brisk, which wasn't surprising, given the weather outside. Rain had been falling on and off most of the day and there was nothing more welcoming on a wet winter's night than a crackling fire to warm the bones, a swig of brandy to comfort the soul and perhaps a wager or two to while away the time.

The tavern was situated – some would say hidden – in an alleyway behind Buckbridge Street and thus it did not cater for what other, more salubrious, establishments might have termed a passing trade. The Hanged Man was for locals. It wasn't somewhere you stumbled upon by accident.

The western end of Buckbridge Street was only a stone's throw from Oxford Street; not in itself a notorious address, but it was the area that lay beyond the street's eastern border, trapped between Broad Street to the south and Great Russell Street to the north, which deterred those citizens of a more upstanding character from venturing uninvited into its shadowy maw.

Covering close to ten acres, the St Giles Rookery was a fetid maze of crumbling tenements, roofless hovels, dank cellars, crooked passageways and rat-infested sewers. To law-abiding Londoners it was a filthy, festering sore; a canker eating away at the city's heart. To its inhabitants – those who were seen as living on the more disreputable fringes of society – it was home. The Hanged Man was a refuge within a refuge.

On the ground floor, dense tobacco fumes rising from the tables had merged with the smoke from the hearth to form an opaque layer of fog which sat suspended between windowsill and ceiling. A hubbub of conversation and coarse laughter filled the room. In one corner, close to the fire, a fiddler – blind in one eye and seemingly oblivious to the din around him – was attempting to scrape out a tune on an instrument in dire need of a new set of strings. At his feet, a small wire-coated terrier rested its head on its paws, while his immediate neighbour, a drunken moll, sprawled half in and half out of her chair, her large, blue-veined breasts spilling like opened sacks of lard from her part-fastened bodice.

Reached by a staircase leading up from the back of the taproom, the first floor was noticeably quieter. At a table next to the rear window, a game of dominoes was in progress. Relaxed and unbothered by the sounds filtering from below, the four players studied the pattern of tiles laid out on the table before them; each man ruminating over his hand and the move he was about to make.

"Jesus, Del, you've been lookin' at those bloody bones for 'alf an hour. How long's it goin' to take?"

The speaker, a balding, morose-looking individual with stubbled jowls and a silver ring in his right ear, rolled his eyes towards his other two companions in exaggerated disbelief.

"I'm thinkin', ain't I?" the player to his left protested. Of a similar age to the speaker, but with a fuller face and salt-and-pepper hair, he wrinkled his brow as he contemplated his remaining tiles and scratched his chin with the edge of a stubby thumb.

"Well, think faster. God knows, I ain't gettin' any younger."

"You take your time, my son." It was the bearded player to the speaker's right who spoke. "Jasper's only narked 'cos he's down a bob. If he was up, he wouldn't be botherin'."

"Plus he wants us to forget it's 'is round," the player opposite Jasper murmured without raising his head. "Mine's another brandy, when you're ready."

"Heard that," the first speaker responded. "I'll get 'em in soon as Del here makes up 'is mind."

"You catch that, Del?" the bearded man said. "Best get a move on."

"There," Del said, as he slid his tile across the table and deposited it at the end of the row. "How's that?"

Jasper stared down at Del's contribution and then at his own instantly redundant counters. "Double three? Double *three*?"

"Make that *two* bob." The bearded man – whose name was Ned – grinned as he added his own tile to the opposite end of the row. "I were you, I'd get the drinks in afore Del cleans you out. Mine's a porter."

As the player opposite him – stocky, broad-shouldered, with a craggy face and close-cropped, pewter-coloured hair – relinquished his remaining tile, Jasper snorted in disgust, regarded the man to his left with exasperation and muttered darkly, "One of these days. One of these bloody days . . ."

Placing his leftover tiles on the table he rose from his chair. "Right, I'm off to the pisser. Get 'em in. I'll settle up when I get back."

"Heard that one before," Del chuckled as he totted up the score on a ragged scrap of paper. Calculations made, he began to spread the tiles face down in preparation for another game.

By which time Jasper was already out of earshot and heading for the back stairs.

"You want to watch it," Ned warned. "You wind him up too hard and the bugger'll snap. Seen Jasper when he snaps. Not a pretty sight. Last time it 'appened, he chewed a watchman's ear off. He was spittin' gristle for a week."

"Nah," Del said confidently. "Bark's worse than 'is bite."

"Tell that to the poor sod who lost 'is ear."

As the two men traded quips, their companion, seated with his back to the window, remained silent, his right hand curved around his glass. From his posture and calm expression, he looked at ease with his surroundings, though as he surveyed the floor his watchful eyes told a different story. Raising his glass to his lips, his attention moved towards the table at the top of the stairs and the man seated there alone, reading a book.

Sensing he was under observation, the reader looked up and

met the grey-haired man's study with an even gaze. The connection lasted perhaps a second before the grey-haired man's eyes moved on, scanning the room.

Forger Jimmy Radd was in his usual corner, one hand on his glass of rum, the other resting on the arm of a stick-thin moll with a strawberry birthmark just visible along the curve of her throat. At the counter, hunched in seats made from empty Madeira casks, cracksman Willy Mellows was in deep conversation with Abel McSwain, the local fence, while two tables away a bespectacled, scholarly dressed individual, known to all as The Padre – in reality a physician struck off for gross misconduct – was making notes in the margin of a well-thumbed, leather-bound copy of the Book of Common Prayer, interspersing his scribbles by taking measured sips from the glass of gin resting by his right elbow. Glancing sideways over the rim of his spectacles, he acknowledged the grey-haired man's perusal with a small nod before returning to his jottings.

Tiles arranged to his satisfaction, Del sat back. "All set." Frowning, he looked around. "Bugger not back yet? Got a nerve, tellin' me *I'm* takin' my time. All he 'as to do is shake it dry."

"It was his round, don't forget," Ned said.

"Tight sod," Del said. "In that case, mine's a large one. That'll teach him." Del paused as he glanced over Ned's shoulder. "'Old up, 'e's here."

Jasper's head had reappeared at the top of the stairs.

"He don't look too happy," Ned observed.

It didn't need a genius to see that Jasper did indeed look, if not in the best of spirits then certainly more than a little distracted. His ascent from the passageway leading to the outdoor privy was slow, almost hesitant.

"God's sake," Del muttered sotto voce, "now, what?"

As two men rose into view beyond Jasper's left shoulder.

At which point Jasper was propelled forward by a hard shove in the back and the duo behind him stepped into plain sight.

Both were dressed for the weather, in wide-brimmed hats and long, calf-length riding coats, the collars turned up. Both coats hung open, revealing a pistol stuck in each man's belt. The pistols

4

were clearly back-up weapons, as each man hefted a thirty-inch-long Barbar blunderbuss which, prior to that moment, they had been concealing beneath the rainwear. As Jasper went sprawling, chairs toppled and customers scattered, only to become rooted as the gunmen brought their weapons to bear.

"Ah, shite," Del said, the blood draining from his face.

The grey-haired man started to rise.

"Don't you bloody move, Jago."

The room fell silent, while from downstairs came the incongruous sounds of continued merriment and the rasping groan of a badly tuned fiddle.

The warning had carried a distinct Irish brogue. As his partner covered the room, the gunman who'd spoken stepped forward.

The grey-haired man looked quickly towards the table at the top of the taproom stairs. The lone customer was still seated, but this time his hands were palm down on the table beside his book and his jaw was clenched. The business end of a third Barbar nuzzled the back of his head. The weapon-holder stood behind him. He was dressed in similar fashion to his companions, in a long coat and a hat which cast his face in shadow. Above his clamped lips, the seated man's eyes expressed silent apology. The grey-haired man's gaze returned to the threat in hand.

"Told you I'd be back," the first rain-coated man announced.

"So you did," Nathaniel Jago said calmly.

"And that there'd be a reckoning."

"As I recall."

The gunman frowned. Tall, with a cadaverous face, a faint bruise was visible below his left eye.

"God save us, Shaughnessy," Jago said softly. "I might have grey hairs but they ain't affected my memory. Talking o'which, you remember what I said to *you* last time?"

A thin smile formed on the Irishman's face. "Said you'd kill me if I showed my face."

"Offer still stands."

The gunman's eyes flickered. The grin faded. "Think you're king of the castle, don't you?"

"An' you got plans to the contrary, I take it?"

"Do it, Patrick," the second gunman urged; the brogue as strong as his companion's. "Bloody do it now."

"What's up, Declan?" Jago's gaze flickered to the speaker. "Arms gettin' tired?" He moved his gaze back. In the second it had taken to divert the first gunman's attention, he'd already braced himself. His hands cupped the edge of the table.

"Going to enjoy this," Shaughnessy gloated.

Made for close-quarter combat, the blunderbuss was a fearsome weapon and capable of inflicting appalling damage. From where Jago was standing, the muzzle looked as big as a howitzer. He wondered if the table top would absorb any of the gun's load and if he'd be able to move in time. Unlikely, but it was worth a try. At this stage, anything was worth a try, to avoid the murderous hail that was about to be unleashed in his direction.

But it wasn't Shaughnessy who opened the bidding.

As the Irishman's trigger finger tightened, a sharp grunt and a clatter from the direction of the taproom stairs drew everyone's attention. Shaughnessy pivoted, in time to see his companion sinking to the ground, hands clasped about his throat, blood spurting from between his fingers. As the body toppled, another figure moved into view. The Barbar, Shaughnessy saw, had changed hands.

With a curse, he turned back and fired.

The roar from the gun was deafening. A woman screamed. Downstairs, the music trailed off and the fiddler's dog let out a shrill bark of alarm.

But by then Jago was already hurling himself aside.

Having anticipated the move, Del and Ned were also flinging themselves backwards. As the table went over, dominoes, coins of the realm, alcohol and broken glass flew in all directions. The table top did absorb a lot of the charge but it wasn't enough. Jago, still travelling, felt the impact as shot scored across his right shoulder. The window took the rest. He heard the panes shatter as he hit the floor. And then he was rolling, or trying to.

Around him, panicking customers, undeterred by the second gunman's threatening stance, were throwing themselves behind tables or towards the back stairs and sanctuary.

Jago's legs were caught up in Ned's abandoned chair. He kicked it away. His shoulder felt as if it was on fire. He looked up. Shaughnessy stood over him. The Irishman had drawn the back-up pistol from his belt. He levelled it, eyes black with rage.

Christ, Jago thought wildly.

The second gunshot was as loud as a whip crack.

Jago flinched and then watched in disbelief as Patrick Shaughnessy's head snapped back, the air misting red as the body fell away.

Declan, who'd already turned to face the new threat, bellowed an obscenity at seeing his comrade cut down and brought his own gun to bear.

Which was when Jasper, who was still half-prone, rammed the edge of his boot heel into Declan's left knee. It was enough to send Declan's aim wide. Shot slammed into the rafters and then there was another ferocious roar and Declan went over backwards, the discharged weapon falling from his grip. Something warm and viscous landed across Jago's left cheek. Wiping it off hurriedly, he stared down at his hand and the ragged piece of flesh adhering to it. His sleeves, he saw, were flecked with blood. Flicking the offending gobbet on to the floor, he raised his head cautiously as the echo from the guns died away.

It was hard to make out details. The room was filled with dissipating powder smoke and the sulphurous stench of rotten eggs, while the scene was more reminiscent of an abattoir than a public house. Around the room, people were slowly regaining their feet, transfixed by the carnage. Astonishingly, from below there came the screech of a fiddle starting up, indicating that, to the downstairs clientele, who'd only heard the gunshots and not witnessed the effects, it had sounded like just another drunken night in the Hanged Man.

Jago stood groggily, ears ringing. He stared down at the bodies and then at the two men who'd come to a halt beside him.

One was the former occupant of the far table who now held a discharged pistol. The second man, whose hands gripped the still-smoking Barbar, was taller and might have been mistaken

7

for an associate of the dead men, for he, too, was dressed in a long military greatcoat. The difference was that he wore no hat, which, now that he had drawn closer, rendered his features visible, in particular the powder burn below his right eye and the two ragged scars that ran across his left cheek.

Jago stared at him. The other man gazed back, a grim smile on his face.

"Can't leave you alone for a minute, can I?" he said.

Several seconds passed before Jago found his voice.

"Nice to see you, too, Officer Hawkwood. It's been a while."

2

"So who were they?"

Hawkwood looked down at the body being hauled unceremoniously towards the back stairs by the boot heels, Del and Ned having taken a leg each. A trail of blood, black in the candlelight, marked their passage across the uneven floorboards.

Jago followed his gaze. "That one's Patrick Shaughnessy. The one missin' half 'is brains – good shot, by the way; those things have quite a kick – is his younger brother, Declan, who didn't have that much reasonin' power to begin with. The one who had the drop on Micah, I don't know; never seen him before. Ne'er-do-well cousin, I expect. They tend to hunt in packs. Christ, go easy, Padre!"

The former physician's name was Roper. His manner and the way in which Jago had summoned him to tend to his wounds indicated to Hawkwood that this probably wasn't the first time his services had been called upon. There had been a faint tremor in the man's hands as he'd helped Jago remove his bloodied shirt, which either suggested he was fearful of his patient or else he had an over-fondness for the Genever, which might have gone some way to explain why he was reduced to performing crudely lit examinations on the floor of the Hanged Man rather than by chandelier in a set of well-appointed consulting rooms in Berkley Square.

Jago winced as a pea-sized nub of black gravel was prised from the meat of his shoulder and deposited with a plunk on to a tin plate by his elbow. The physician was extracting the projectiles using a pair of tweezers he'd taken from a black bag that had been resting beneath the table he'd recently vacated. Some pieces of shrapnel had gone in deeper than others and among the paraphernalia set down were several rolls of lint bandage, two scalpels, scissors and a collection of vials with indecipherable labels which could have contained anything from laudanum to cold elderberry tea. If Hawkwood hadn't known any better, it looked as though the former doctor had come prepared for surgery.

The room was gradually coming to order. Chairs and tables had been righted and free drinks dispensed. Conversations had resumed, albeit warily and with startled glances whenever somebody coughed or scraped a chair leg inadvertently. It was plain that around some tables nerves were still a tad jittery.

Despite the air of jumpiness, Hawkwood couldn't help but consider the way in which most of those present seemed to have recovered from the shock of having had their evening's drinking so startlingly interrupted. He knew the ways of the capital's rookeries, of which there were several – nurseries of crime, as the authorities had christened them – and had meted out his own form of justice in their diseased enclaves often enough. Even so, the speed with which equilibrium had been restored in this particular hostelry spoke volumes for the manner in which the inhabitants of the rookeries went about their daily lives: their casual attitude towards death and summary justice, and their complete lack of faith in anything approaching legitimate authority; not one person had suggested calling the police. In this place, any support there might once have been for the forces of law and order had evaporated a long time ago.

Hawkwood studied the body of the second Shaughnessy brother, which wasn't yet on the move. The shot from the Barbar – also loaded with gravel, he guessed – had torn into the dead man's upper torso as effectively as grape cutting through a square of infantry. Death would have been close to instantaneous. If the brothers had just woken up together, either in Hell or Purgatory, they'd be wondering what had hit them.

"They seemed a tad annoyed," Hawkwood said.

Jago grunted as another piece of gravel was levered out. "*They* were annoyed? State of my shirt; I'm bloody livid. Ruined my game, too; 'specially as I was up."

"What were they mad about?"

"Idiots had ideas above their station. Thought they could work their way around the natural peckin' order. I had to set them straight. They didn't like being chastised. Patrick in particular."

"Newcomers, I take it?"

St Giles was often the first port of call for the poorest of the Irish immigrants who came looking for a new start in a new city. Those inhabitants who'd failed to welcome the influx with open arms referred to it as Little Dublin.

Jago nodded. "They were warned. They didn't listen."

"There could be more of them."

"Wouldn't surprise me. The buggers breed like rats. I'll cross that bridge when I come to it."

"Be interesting to know how they came by the guns," Hawkwood said, eyeing the three blunderbusses that were taking up space at the other end of the table. "These look like Post Office issue."

"You askin' as a police officer or a concerned citizen?"

"Both."

The blunderbuss was the weapon of choice for mail coach guards, who were the only Post Office employees allowed to carry firearms. Designed to protect the cargo from interception by highwaymen, they had served their purpose well. There hadn't been a serious attack on a mail coach for more than two decades.

"Money talks," Jago said. "How many villains you know have been caught carryin' an army- or navy-issue pistol? Bloody 'undreds, I should think. Scatterguns ain't that hard to get hold of, you know the right person."

"And *you'd* know that how?" Hawkwood said.

Jago grinned and tapped his nose with his left forefinger and then said, "Shit!" as another bit of gravel was extracted and dropped on to the plate.

Hawkwood counted them up. Five tiny olive-pit-sized fragments occupied the platter, while a couple of puncture wounds had yet to be probed.

Still, he thought, Jago had been lucky.

"You were lucky," Hawkwood said.

Jago looked up at him. "Really? An' how do you work that out?"

"You're still here. You should be as dead as Shaughnessy, the range he fired from. I'm wondering if his powder was damp. Either that or it was low quality."

"Tell that to the bloody window," Jago said. "From where I was standin', I'd say it was dry enough."

"Nah, your man's right. The bastard should've taken your head off. Good job you moved when you did." Del, who'd arrived back with Ned, jabbed a thumb at Declan Shaughnessy's lifeless corpse. "Else you'd've ended up like 'is nibs."

"You're a real comfort, Del," Ned said. "Anyone ever tell you that?"

"Only your missus," Del retorted, grinning.

"There," the physician announced. "Done – or as far as I can tell." Putting down the tweezers, he cut off a length of lint. Taking one of the vials, he removed the stopper, soaked the lint with the contents and proceeded to dab the wounds, much to his patient's further discomfort.

"Keep the area as clean as possible. If the wounds become inflamed, you know where to find me or else get another doctor to take a look. I've done the best I can but I may not have got them all."

Using the rest of the lint, the physician began to fashion a bandage around Jago's shoulder. His hands, Hawkwood saw, were now perfectly steady and the dressing was expertly applied. Roper was clearly no quack. The man may have lost his standing among his former peers and patients and been ostracized by the more reputable areas of society, but from what Hawkwood had seen, if he was now using his medical skills to aid the less fortunate in

London's back streets, the people of the rookery were lucky to have him.

Hawkwood watched as the physician restored his equipment to his bag before moving to attend to those customers who'd been caught in the crossfire. Thankfully, there weren't many. Serious peripheral wounds had been prevented as most people had used the tables and furniture as cover. The majority of the injured were suffering from the effects of flying splinters and glass fragments rather than gravel pellets.

The landlord, a dour-looking character whom Jago had addressed as Bram, was already nailing boards over the broken window. He'd looked ready to take someone's head off when he'd first inspected the damage, but a look from Jago and a promise of financial restitution had cooled his ire, as had an immediate contribution to the restoration fund following a search of the dead men's pockets.

Jago grimaced as he eased his shirt back over his shoulder. "Wounds, my arse. Pin pricks more like. Typical bloody bog trotter. Had me in his sights and he still cocked it up."

"Got the drop on Jasper, though," Ned said, grinning. He lifted his chin. "Come on, Del. It's Declan's turn for the cart, and don't forget his bloody hat."

"Like you'd've fared any better," Jasper countered. "Bastard crept up on me when I was takin' a piss. I was distracted." He watched as Del and Ned rearranged Declan's ragged corpse into a manageable position for carriage before looking contritely towards Jago. "Sorry, big man; my fault they got up here."

Jago shook his head. "Could've happened to any of us."

"Not you," Del said as he took hold of Declan's right ankle. "If it'd been you in the pisser, he'd've shot you where you stood. *You'd* be dead and *we'd* be none the wiser as to who'd done it."

"An' you'd have split my winnings between you," Jago said. "Right?"

Del grinned. "Too right. No sense in letting all that spare change go to waste."

"Bastards," Jago said, but without malice, as Ned and Del

began to manhandle the second Shaughnessy brother towards the back stairwell.

"What'll you do with the bodies?" Hawkwood asked.

Jago shrugged. "Give 'em to the night-soil men. Either that or feed 'em to Reilly's hogs."

Jago wasn't joking about the hogs. Even though they sounded like something out of a children's fairy tale, along with wicked witches, ogres and fire-breathing dragons, the animals were real. Reilly, a slaughterman with premises off Hosier Lane, housed the things in a pen at the rear of his yard, where, it was said, they were kept infrequently fed in anticipation of a time when their services might be required.

It was a prime, albeit extreme, example of the type of self-efficiency employed by the denizens of the rookery who over the years had devised their own unique methods for settling disputes and disposing of their dead. Admittedly, it was a practice frowned upon by law, but on this occasion, looking on the positive side, it did eliminate the need for an official report on the altercation.

A dull thudding sound came from the stairs. Hawkwood presumed it was what was left of Declan's skull making contact with the treads as his remains were transported down.

Micah returned to the table. "Night-soil men said they'll take them. They wanted the money up front."

"You took care of it?"

Micah nodded. "They're waiting on the last one."

As if on cue, Del and Ned reappeared and moved to the third body, which was still lying at the top of the taproom stairs.

"Hope Bram's got plenty of shavings," Del muttered. "Makin' a hell of a mess of 'is floor."

Ned looked at him askance. "How can you tell? Years I've been coming 'ere, it always looks like this."

"Just makin' conversation," Del said. "You ready?"

"Wait," Hawkwood said. Kneeling, he withdrew the stiletto from the ruined throat.

"Wouldn't want to forget that, would we?" Jago said sardonically as Hawkwood wiped the blade on the corpse's sleeve before returning the knife to his right boot. "All right, lads. Carry on."

Ned nodded to his companion and then caught Jasper's eye as they set off towards the stairs, the body sagging between them. "Get 'em in, old son. We're going to need something strong after this. And don't give me that look. It's still your bloody round. We ain't forgotten."

"Should've got the night-soil lads to do the liftin' and carryin'," Jasper grated.

"Then what'd the smell be like?" Del said, over his shoulder. "Don't want them tramping *their* shit all over the floor as well. It's bad enough as it is."

"Jesus, it's like listenin' to a bunch of bloody fishwives," said Jago. "If I'd wanted this much witterin', I'd've gone to Billingsgate. Just load the damned things on to the cart. The sooner they're off the premises and headin' downriver, the better I'll feel. And you, Jasper, get the drinks in; else I may decide they can take you with them. You'd make good ballast."

Turning to Hawkwood, he shook his head in resignation. "Swear to God, it's like herdin' cats." Buttoning his shirt, he eased himself into a comfortable position. "Right, that's the formalities over. I take it you're ready for a wet?"

"Brandy," Hawkwood said.

Jago relayed the order to Jasper before turning back. "So, what can I do you for?"

It was such an incongruous question, coming in the aftermath of all that had ensued, that Hawkwood hesitated before answering, wondering if he'd dreamt the entire sequence of events.

"I need your help."

Jago sat back, wincing as his injured shoulder made contact with the chair. "Jesus, you've got a bloody nerve. What's it been? Three months without a word, and then you swan back in without so much as a heads-up to tell me you need a favour? Is that any way to treat your friends?"

"I just saved your life," Hawkwood pointed out.

"Aye, well there is that, I suppose," Jago conceded with a wry grin. "So, how was France? Heard you had a spot of bother."

Hawkwood stared at him. "How in the hell . . .?"

Jago's grin widened. "Went to see Magistrate Read, didn't I?"

"And he *told* you?"

"Well, not in so many words. Would've been easier gettin' blood from a stone. But seeing as I've helped you and him out now and again in the pursuit of your official duties, he did let slip you were abroad on the king's business."

"In France?"

Jago shook his head. "Guessed that bit, seeing as you speak Frog like a native and the last time *I* was involved you were hanging around with our privateer pal, Lasseur. Thought there might be a connection."

Jago studied Hawkwood's face. "Though, seeing as they ain't declared peace and you've a couple more scars on your noggin, I'm guessing things might not have gone according to plan."

Hawkwood looked back at him.

"Well?" Jago asked.

"Maybe later."

"Which is a polite way of sayin' I should mind my own business. All right, so how long have you been home?"

"Not long."

"And what? This the first time you thought to drop by?"

"No. I tried to reach you a week back, but I was told you were away sorting out some business."

Partially mollified by Hawkwood's response, Jago eased himself into a more comfortable position and made a face. "That's one way of puttin' it."

Hawkwood waited.

"A spot of bother with one of my suppliers. Had to make a visit to the coast to sort it out."

"And did you?"

"Sort it?" Jago smiled grimly. "Oh, aye."

Hawkwood bit back a smile of his own. In Jago's language, "a spot of bother" could cover a multitude of sins, most of which, Hawkwood knew, stemmed from activities that were, if not strictly illegal then certainly open to interpretation when based upon the authorities' understanding of the term. As for the remainder; they were entirely unlawful.

In the years since the two of them had returned from the Peninsula, Nathaniel Jago had made a point of steering his own unconventional career path. His experiences as a sergeant in the British Army had served him well, providing him with an understanding of both discipline and the need for organization, two factors which had proved essential in expediting his rise through the London underworld, a fraternity not known for its tolerance of transgressors, as had just been illustrated.

As a peace officer, Hawkwood had never sought to influence or curb his former sergeant's more dubious pursuits. He owed him too much. Jago had guarded his back and saved his life more times than he could remember. That truth alone outweighed any consideration he might have for curtailing the man's efforts to make a livelihood, even if that did tend to border on the questionable. Besides, it helped having someone on the other side of the fence to keep him abreast of what was happening in the murkier realms of the country's sprawling capital. Providing, that is, they didn't encroach upon a certain former army sergeant's sphere of operations.

Not having met Del, Ned or Jasper before, Hawkwood assumed they were part of Jago's inner circle. In the normal scheme of things, therefore, it was unlikely their paths would have crossed. Jago referring to him as *Officer* would have resonated, though, so it said much for Jago's status that none of them had raised an objection or even registered shock at his presence. That said, it was equally possible that their equanimity was due to the fact that he was alone and on their turf and at their mercy, should they decide to turn belligerent. For any law officer, the Rookery was, to all intents and purposes, foreign ground. There might as well have been a sign at the entrance to the street proclaiming *Abandon hope, all ye who enter here*; despite the authority his Runner's warrant gave him, Hawkwood knew it held as much sway here as on the far side of the moon. But while he was here, he remained under Jago's protection. Had that not been the case, his safety would not have been assured.

Unless Micah came to his aid.

Hawkwood didn't know a lot about Jago's lieutenant, other than the former sergeant trusted him with his life. He'd been a soldier, Jago had once let that slip, but as to where and when he'd served, Jago didn't know, or else he knew but had decided that was Micah's own business and therefore exempt from discussion, unless Micah chose to make it so.

He was younger than Hawkwood, probably by a decade, and, from what Hawkwood did know of him, a man of few words. There had been two occasions when, in company with Jago, Micah had stood at Hawkwood's shoulder and both times he'd shown himself to be resourceful, calm in a crisis, and good with weapons; characteristics which had been even more evident this evening. What more was required from a right-hand man?

Jago's voice broke into Hawkwood's thoughts.

"All right, so what's this all about?"

A shadow appeared at the table and Jago paused. It was Jasper, bearing the drinks, which coincided with Ned and Del's return from their downstairs delivery.

"Good lad," Del said, reaching for a glass. "All that totin', I'm bloody parched."

They might have been a couple of draymen dropping off casks of ale, Hawkwood mused, rather than drinking pals who'd just deposited three dead bodies on to a cart loaded with barrels of human waste.

Glancing around, it occurred to him that anyone walking into the room afresh wouldn't have the slightest notion that anything untoward had taken place, save, perhaps, for noticing a few more dark stains on the floor that hadn't been there before. Though, even as he pondered on the matter, these were being wiped away with wet rags and a fresh layer of sawdust applied.

It was uncanny, Hawkwood thought, how men and women, when surrounded by the most appalling squalor, swiftly become immune to the worst excesses of human nature. Here, where only the strongest survived, in a welter of gunfire, three men had died in as many seconds and yet, even before their bodies had been removed, the world, such as it was, had returned to normal, or as normal as it could be in a place like this.

18

He wondered what that said about his own actions. He was a peace officer, supposedly on the side of justice, and yet in the blink of an eye he'd knifed one man to death and shot the head off another. But then the Shaughnessys and their cohort had been prepared to murder in cold blood. Hawkwood had been a witness to that and he had acted without any thought as to the consequences. So had killing now become second nature? Was life really that cheap?

Micah reappeared.

"It's done," he said quietly.

Jago nodded. "That case, me an' 'is lordship here need a bit of privacy, which means we're commandeerin' the table. Del, you, Ned and Jasper take a look around. See if any more Shaughnessys are loiterin' with intent. Don't want to be caught with our pants down again, do we?"

A pointed look towards Jasper prompted a quick emptying of glasses while three pairs of eyes swivelled in Hawkwood's direction. Del, somewhat inevitably, was the first to speak, though his face was unexpectedly serious.

"Any friend of Nathaniel's is a friend of ours. What you did tonight . . . you'll always be welcome here . . ." And then the irrepressible grin returned. ". . . *Officer*."

Jago shook his head. "God save us. All right, bugger off. I'll see you at the Ark."

The three men turned away.

"Oi!"

They looked back.

"You can take those with you. Don't want 'em givin' the place a bad name." Jago indicated the Barbars, but then turned to Hawkwood. "Unless you want a souvenir?"

The offer was tempting. They were fine weapons; man stoppers.

"They're all yours," Hawkwood said.

The guns were collected and the trio headed towards the exit. Jago addressed Micah: "No more excitement tonight, all right?"

Micah nodded.

Jago winked. "Best reload, though, just in case."

19

Micah's mouth twitched. He looked off as Del, Jasper and Ned left by the back stairs and then his eyes returned to Jago and he nodded once more. Returning to his table, he took his seat, moved his discarded book to one side, and began to clean the pistol.

Jago turned to Hawkwood. "He scares me sometimes, too."

Hawkwood took a sip of brandy, savouring the taste. He suspected it was from Jago's private stock that the landlord kept under the counter, which meant it was French, not Spanish. He wondered if Jago's trip to the coast had anything to do with his supply routes. Best not to enquire too deeply into that.

"Right," Jago said. "Where were we?"

Hawkwood placed his glass on the table. "There's been a murder."

"In this town? There's a novelty."

"Any other night and I'd think it was funny, too."

"But it ain't?"

"Not by a long shot."

"Which'd also be funny by itself, right?"

"Not this time," Hawkwood said. "This one's different."

3

It occurred to Hawkwood, as he stared down at the body, that the last grave he'd looked into had been his own.

That had been in a forest clearing on the far side of the world. There had been snow on the ground and frost on the trees and the chilled night air had been made rank by the sour smell of a latrine ditch because that was what lye smelled like when used to render down bodies. The bodies in question should have been his and that of Major Douglas Lawrence, courtesy of an American execution detail. In the end, it had been Hawkwood and Lawrence who'd stumbled away, leaving four dead Yankee troopers in their wake and an American army in hot pursuit. It was strange how things worked out and how a vivid memory could be triggered by the sight of a corpse in a pit.

This particular pit occupied the south-west corner of St George the Martyr's burying ground. Situated in the parish of St Pancras, the burying ground was unusual in that it was nowhere near the church to which it was dedicated. That lay a third of a mile away to the south, on the other side of Queen Square; not a huge distance but markedly inconvenient when it came to conducting funeral and burial services.

Also unique was the fact that, along its northern aspect, the graveyard shared a dividing wall with a neighbouring cemetery, that of St George's Church, Bloomsbury, which made Hawkwood wonder, in a moment of inappropriate whimsy, if any funeral processions had inadvertently found themselves on the wrong side of the wall. There were no convenient gates linking the two burial grounds, meaning that any funeral party which turned left instead of right would have to reverse all the way back to the entrances on Grays Inn Lane and start all over again.

The burying ground's southern perimeter was also determined by a wall, though of a greater height than the dividing one for it had been built to separate the cemetery from the grounds of the Foundling Hospital, a vast, grey building which dwarfed its surroundings like a man-o'-war towering above a fleet of rowboats. The rear of the chapel roof was just visible above the ivy-covered parapet, as were the chimneys and upper storeys of the hospital's forbidding west wing.

The grave had been dug close to the wall, in the lee of a pointed stone obelisk, one of many memorials that had been erected among the trees. An inscription, weathered by rain and frost, was barely legible, save for the surname of the deceased – *Falconer* – but even those letters had begun to fade, a state which mirrored the burying ground's general air of decay.

The overcast sky did little to enhance the wintry setting. It had been raining hard all morning and while the rain had eased to a thin, misty drizzle, leaving the grass and what remained of the winter foliage to shine and glisten; the same could not be said for the pathways and the rectangular patches of earth which showed where fresh plots had been excavated and the soil recently filled in. They had all turned to cloying mud, though, if it hadn't been for the rain, it was doubtful the body would have been discovered.

The grave was the intended resting place of one Isaiah Ballard, a local drayman who'd had the misfortune to have been trampled to death by one of his own mules. The funeral service had been scheduled for late morning, after which the body was to be transported in dignified procession from church to burial plot, making use, somewhat ironically, of his soon-to-be equally redundant wagon.

It was a sexton's responsibility to supervise the maintenance of the burying ground, including the digging of the graves; this particular one having been prepared the previous afternoon. The sexton, whose small stone cottage was tucked into the corner of the graveyard, had risen earlier and, in the company of two gravediggers, been making his final inspection to ensure that the interment ran smoothly.

The three men had arrived at the site to find that the mound of excavated soil by the side of the pit had been transformed into a heavy sludge. The deluge had also eaten away the edge of the grave and formed runnels in the sod down which small rivulets of rainwater were still dribbling like miniature cataracts.

On the point of directing the gravediggers to shore up the sides of the hole, the sexton's eyes had been drawn to the bottom of the pit and a disturbance in the soil caused by the run-off. It had taken several seconds for him to realize what he was looking at. When the truth dawned, he'd raised the alarm.

When Hawkwood arrived, his first thought had been to wonder why the sexton had gone to all the bother. This was not because he viewed the examination of an unexpected dead body in a graveyard as an inconvenience, but because London's burying grounds were notoriously overcrowded and, in the normal course of events, it wasn't unheard of for the dead to be piled atop one another like stacks of kindling. Indeed, where the poor of the parish were concerned – to whom coffins were considered a luxury – the practice had become commonplace, which said a lot for the sexton's integrity. It would have been easy for the gravediggers to have shovelled mud back over the body to hide it. No one would have been any the wiser.

Judging by the expression on the face of the constable standing alongside him, who'd been the first functionary called to the scene, Hawkwood wasn't the only one harbouring reservations as to whether this was really the sort of incident that demanded the attention of a Principal Officer.

A constable's duties rarely ventured beyond those carried out by the average nightwatchman, which in most cases involved patrolling a regular beat and discouraging the activities of petty thieves and prostitutes. So it wasn't hard to imagine what was going through this particular constable's mind. Uppermost,

Hawkwood suspected, was likely to be the question: *Why me?* Followed closely by the thought: *Oh, God, please not again.*

The constable's name was Hopkins. A year ago, the young recruit's probationary period had come to an abrupt end on the night he'd accompanied Hawkwood and Nathaniel Jago in their pursuit of a crew of body-snatchers who'd turned to murder in order to top up their earnings. The chase had ended in a ferocious close-quarter gunfight. Throughout the confrontation the constable had proved brave and capable. He'd also displayed a commendable ability to look the other way when it came to interpreting how best to dispense summary justice to a gang of cold-blooded killers.

He'd filled out his uniform since Hawkwood had last seen him, though the shock of red hair was still there, poking defiantly from beneath the brim of the black felt hat, as was the pair of jug ears which would have put the handles of a milk churn to shame.

When Hawkwood arrived on the scene, the constable's face had brightened in recognition. It was a light soon extinguished, however, for while he could be considered as still being relatively damp behind the ears, Hopkins was wise enough to know that in this situation, to smile at being greeted by name by a senior officer without the need for prompting would have been viewed as singularly inappropriate.

Squatting at the side of the trench, Hawkwood stared bleakly into its sodden depths. One good thing about the rain: it did help to dampen the smells; or at least some of them. Hawkwood didn't know the burial practices followed in St George the Martyr's parish. If it was like most others within the city, there would be a section reserved for poor holes: pits which were deep enough to hold up to seven tiers of burial sacks. Left open until they were filled to the brim, they allowed the stench of putrefaction to permeate the surrounding air. Nearby buildings were not immune and it wasn't unknown for churches to be abandoned due to the smells rising from the decaying corpses stored in the crypts below them and for clergy to conduct funeral services from a comfortable distance. Hawkwood wondered if that was the reason for the burying ground's estranged location. At the moment, the odours rising to meet him were of mud, loam, leaf mould and, curiously, fermenting apples. It could have been a lot worse.

The mud and the layer of dead leaves made it hard to distinguish details but then, gradually, as his eyes grew accustomed to the lumpy contours at the bottom of the trench he saw what had captured the sexton's and, as a consequence, the constable's attention. Sticking out of the ooze was the torn edge of a piece of sacking. Poking out from beneath the sacking was not a stone, as he had first thought, but the back of a human hand. Close to it was what appeared to be a scrap of folded parchment. Concentrating his gaze further, he saw that it wasn't parchment at all, but the edge of a cheekbone which had been washed by the rain. Following the line of the bone, the ridge of an eye socket came into view.

A child, he thought, straightening. Someone had placed a child's body in a sack and tossed it into the trench. He gazed up at the Foundling Hospital's wall and considered the permutations offered by its proximity. He turned back to the pit. Suddenly, the sack and the shape of the contents contained within it became more pronounced. Clumps of what he had thought were clotted leaves had materialized into what were clearly thick strands of long matted hair.

A female.

He addressed the sexton. "You're sure it's recent?"

The sexton, whose name was Stubbs, nodded grimly. "'T'weren't there yesterday."

A spare, slim-built man and not that old, despite a receding hairline, the sexton was using a stick to support his left leg. The stick probably explained the gravediggers' presence. Traditionally, the sexton was the one who more often than not did the digging.

And they would have noticed a body in a sack, Hawkwood thought. Otherwise they'd have trodden all over it.

He turned to the two gravediggers, who confirmed the sexton's words with one sullen and one nervous nod. Their names, Hawkwood had learned, were Gulley and Dobbs. Gulley, round-shouldered with a moody cast to his features, was the older of the two. Dobbs, his apprentice, looked sixteen going on sixty. Hawkwood assumed the premature ageing was due to him having seen the contents of the trench.

Not the most promising start to a career, Hawkwood mused. Then again, it was one way of preparing the lad for what the job was likely to entail, assuming he managed to see out the rest of the day. Not that he was the only one present who'd lost colour. Constable Hopkins was looking a bit pale about the gills, too.

"Why?" Hawkwood asked.

The sexton, realizing he was the one being addressed, frowned.

"You could have got them to cover it up," Hawkwood said. "No one would have known."

"*I'd* know. Seen enough poor beggars tossed in pits without it 'appenin' on my own bloody doorstep. It ain't right. It ain't bloody Christian."

Eyeing the cane, Hawkwood took an educated guess. "What regiment?"

The sexton's chin lifted. "Thirty-sixth." The reply came quickly, proudly.

"You served under Burne?" Hawkwood said.

The sexton looked surprised and drew himself up further. "That I did." He threw Hawkwood a speculative glance, as if taking in the greatcoat for the first time. Though it had a military cut, it was American, not British made. "You?"

"The ninety-fifth."

A new understanding showed in the sexton's eyes. He studied Hawkwood's face and the scars that were upon it. "Then you know what it was like. You'll have seen it, too."

Hawkwood nodded. "I have."

The sexton brandished his stick. "Got this at Corunna. So, like I said, seen a lot of folk die before their time." He stared down into the trench. "That ain't how it's supposed to be. She didn't deserve this."

"No," Hawkwood said heavily. "She didn't."

The sexton fell silent. Then he enquired softly, "So?"

Hawkwood studied the lay of the body and took a calming breath.

Don't think about it; just do it.

As if reading his mind, Constable Hopkins took a tentative pace forward.

Hawkwood stopped him with a look. "Any idea what you plan to do when you're down there?"

Hopkins flushed and shook his head. "Er, no, s—, er, Captain," the constable amended hurriedly, clearly remembering their previous association when he'd been warned by Hawkwood not to address him as "sir".

"Me neither. So there's no need for us both to get our boots wet, is there? We're officers of the law. One of us should still look presentable." As he spoke, Hawkwood removed his coat and held it out.

Managing to look chastened and yet relieved at the same time, the constable took the garment and stepped back.

The trench was around eight feet in length and wasn't that deep, as Hawkwood found out when he landed at the bottom and felt the surface give slightly beneath him. The height of the trench should have been the giveaway. Most graves were close to six or seven feet deep. This one was shallower than that, which meant there was, in all probability, an earlier burial in the plot. And if there was one, the chances were there had been others before that.

The burial ground had been in use for at least a century and there wasn't much acreage. That meant a lot of bodies had been buried in an ever-diminishing space. A vision of putting his boot through a rotting coffin lid or, worse, long-fermented remains, flashed through his mind, dispelled when he reasoned that Gulley – or more likely his apprentice – wouldn't have been able to dig the later grave as the ground wouldn't have supported his weight while he worked. Even so, it was a precarious sensation. As it was, the mud was already pulling at his boots as if it wanted to drag him under.

Planting his feet close to the corners of the trench, still not entirely sure what he expected to find, he bent down. The smell was worse at the bottom, a lot worse. He could feel the sickly-sweet scent clogging his nostrils and reaching into the back of his throat. Trapped by the earthen walls, the smell was impossible to ignore and would have been impossible to describe. Holding his breath wasn't a viable option. Instead, he tried not to swallow. He looked up and saw four faces staring back at him. Bowing his head and adjusting his feet for balance, he eased the edge of the sacking away from the skull and used his fingers to scrape mud from the face. As more waxen flesh came to light the gender of the corpse was confirmed.

And it was a woman, not a child.

Plastered to the face, the original hair colour was hard to determine. Lifting it away from the cold, damp flesh was like trying to remove seaweed from a stone. The smell around him was growing more rank. He tried not to think of the fluids and other substances which, over the years, must have been leaching into the soil from the surrounding graves.

Lying on her left side, mouth partly open, it was as if she were asleep. The position of the hand added to the illusion. Unsettlingly, as he brushed another strand of hair from her brow, he saw that her right eye was staring blankly back at him. It reminded Hawkwood of a fish on a slab, though fish eyes were usually brighter. Removing the mud from her face had left dark streaks, like greasy tear tracks. There was a tight look to the skin but as his fingers wiped more slime away from the exposed flesh he felt it give beneath his fingertips.

Hawkwood was familiar with the effect of death on the human body. He'd seen it often enough on battlefields and in hospital tents and mortuary rooms. There was a period, he knew, beginning shortly after life had been extinguished, during which a corpse went through a transformation. It began with the contraction of the smaller muscles, around the eyes and the mouth, before spreading through the rest of the body, into the neck and shoulders and through into the extremities. Thereafter, as the body stiffened, feet started to curl inwards and fingers formed into talons. With time, however, the stiffness left the body, returning it to a relaxed state. From the texture of the skin, Hawkwood had the feeling that latter process was already well advanced. She had been dead for a while.

Using the edge of his hand, he continued to heel the mud away gently, gradually revealing the rest of the features. The dark blotches were instantly apparent, as were the indentations in the cheekbone, which beneath the mottled skin looked misshapen and, when he ran the ends of his fingers across them, felt uneven to the touch. Tiny specks in the corners of the eye were either tiny grains of dirt or a sign that the first flies had laid their eggs.

Hawkwood let go a quiet curse. There had always been the chance that the body had been left in the grave out of desperation and the worry – probably by a relative – of not being able to afford even the most meagre of funeral expenses. Had that been the likely scenario, Hawkwood would have been willing, if there had been no visible signs of hurt, to have left the corpse in the sexton's charge with an instruction to place the body in the most convenient poor hole. But the bruising and the obvious fracture of the facial bones prevented him from pursuing that charitable, if unethical, course of action.

He probed the earth at the back of the skull on the off-chance that a rock or a large stone had caused the damage post-mortem but, as he'd suspected, there was nothing save for more mud.

He was on the point of rising when what looked like a small twig jutting from the mud caught his eye. He paused. There was something about it that didn't look right, but he couldn't see what it was. Curious, angling his head for a better look, he went to pick it up. And then his hand stilled. It wasn't a broken twig, he realized. It was the end of a knotted cord. Her wrists had been bound together.

"What is it?" the sexton enquired from above.

Hawkwood sighed and stood. "We're going to need a cart."

"A cart?" It was Gulley who spoke. The question was posed without enthusiasm.

"It's a wooden box on wheels."

Hawkwood's response was rewarded with a venomous look. It was clear the gravedigger had been resentful of the sexton's act of civic duty from the start. Hawkwood's sarcasm wasn't helping.

"You do *have* a cart?" Hawkwood said.

"It's in the lean-to." Sexton Stubbs pointed helpfully with his cane towards the cottage and the ramshackle wooden structure set off to one side of it.

"One of you, then," Hawkwood said, pointedly.

The directive was met with a disgruntled scowl. Mouthing an oath, Gulley turned to his protégé. "All right, you 'eard."

Looking relieved to have been delegated, the young gravedigger turned to go, anxious to put distance between him and the pit's contents. His commitment to the job looked to be disappearing by the second.

"Leave the shovel," Hawkwood said. "You'll get it back."

The apprentice hesitated then thrust the tool blade-first into the mound of dirt.

"And bring more sacking," Hawkwood instructed. "Dry, if you have it."

He glanced towards the sexton, who nodded and said, "There's some on a shelf inside the door. You'll see it."

With a wary nod the youth about-turned and hurried off through the drizzle and the puddles.

Hawkwood addressed the older man. "You have something to say?"

The gravedigger jerked his chin at the open trench. "Don't see why we can't leave the bloody thing down there. We throw in some soil, we can cover it up."

"*Her*," Hawkwood snapped. "Not *it*. And no, we can't. Unless you've a particular reason you don't want her brought up?"

The gravedigger's jaw flexed.

Hawkwood felt his anger rise. "Had the idea you might make a few pounds, maybe? Got an arrangement with the sack-'em-up men for the one on top? Throw in this one and you'd make a bit extra? That it?"

It could also account for the shallowness of the trench, he thought, because it made the task of exhuming the bodies that much easier.

The look on the man's face told Hawkwood he'd struck a nerve, but he felt no satisfaction, merely increasing repugnance.

Gulley wouldn't be the first graveyard worker who earned extra spending money by passing information on upcoming funerals to the resurrection gangs, to whom freshly buried corpses were regarded as regular income, and he wouldn't be the last. Interesting, too, that Gulley had referred to the body as the "thing", which was what the resurrection men called their hauls.

The expression on Hopkins' face told Hawkwood that he wasn't the only one recalling the run-in with the carrion hunters. Some of the darker memories from that experience had evidently been awakened in the constable's brain; images that were best left undisturbed.

For a moment it looked as though the gravedigger was about to offer further protest, but Hawkwood's expression and tone of voice must have warned him that an argument was futile and might prove detrimental to his own health.

It was then that the wisdom of what he was about to do struck Hawkwood forcibly and he cursed his rashness. It was too late now, though, for he had no intention of giving Gulley the satisfaction of knowing he might be dealing with a police officer who'd just made what could well turn out be a very unwise decision. But as he caught the sexton's eye, he was rewarded with a small, almost imperceptible nod of acknowledgement, or it might have been gratitude.

Over the constable's shoulder, he saw that Dobbs was on his way back, pushing a flat, two-wheeled cart before him, the sacking folded on top. The cart's wheels had become clogged with mud, making progress difficult. The older gravedigger, Hawkwood noted, could see that his assistant was struggling but made no attempt to assist. By the time the cart rolled to a halt, the apprentice was perspiring heavily.

Hawkwood addressed Gulley. "Your turn. Get down here – and mind where you step."

The gravedigger's knuckles whitened against the handle of his shovel.

"You won't need that," Hawkwood told him.

Sensing tension in the air, the constable went to step forward again.

Hawkwood, wondering what assistance Hopkins intended to offer while still holding his coat, waved him away.

It took a further ten minutes to scrape away the mud and, with Gulley taking the feet and Hawkwood the torso, and with the apprentice Dobbs helping to take the weight, lift the sack and its contents up and out of the grave, though it seemed more like a lifetime. The mud was reluctant to release its grip and by the time Hawkwood and the gravedigger were helped out of the pit, their boots and breeches were wet to the thigh and caked in clay. Hawkwood had also been uncomfortably aware of the ominous creaking sounds that had come from beneath his and the gravedigger's feet as they'd taken the weight of the corpse between them. It had been with great relief that he had stepped back on to solid ground.

"I want her delivered to the dead house at Christ's Hospital," Hawkwood instructed as the cadaver was placed on the cart and covered with the dry sacking.

"You know it?"

The constable nodded.

"For the attention of Surgeon Quill. He's to expect me later."

"Yes, Captain."

"Good." Hawkwood took back his coat, but did not put it on. "Dobbs can assist. Make sure the body's covered at all times. I'm probably in enough trouble as it is; God forbid an arm should come loose and frighten the horses."

Hawkwood knew that wasn't likely to happen, but having the two men watch over their gruesome load was one way of ensuring it would arrive safely. The other reason for the precaution was that during the excavation it had become obvious that inside the sack the corpse was naked. A clothed cadaver being carted through the streets was bad enough. The ramifications, if the state of this one ever came to light, didn't bear thinking about.

"You can't do that!" Gulley protested.

Hawkwood spun back. "Of course I bloody can! I can do anything I want. I can even leave you in the damned hole if you don't stop whining."

Gulley bristled. "But there's graves to dig!"

"Then do your own bloody digging! You've got a shovel. It's not hard. You hold it at the thin end and use the other end to move the dirt."

Gulley coloured under the onslaught.

Ignoring him, Hawkwood addressed the constable. "What the hell are you waiting for? Go."

Jerked into activity, Hopkins swallowed and called Dobbs to him. As the cart trundled away, Hawkwood turned to the sexton. "When's the funeral party due?"

The sexton drew a pocket watch from his jacket. "Not for an hour, yet."

"Then you've time to make the site presentable?"

The sexton gazed about him. "Aye, reckon so." He looked down at Hawkwood's muddy forearms and clay-covered boots and breeches, and jerked his chin towards the cottage and the smoke curling up above the black-slate roof. "Got hot water on the fire, if'n you want to clean up."

Hawkwood considered the filth on his hands and the activity they'd been engaged in. "It's a kind offer, Mr Stubbs. I'm obliged."

The sexton nodded. To the hovering Gulley, who'd retrieved his shovel and was holding it across his chest as if he was about to defend an attack on a bridge, he said, "I'll be back soon as me and the officer here have concluded our business. Smartly now, Solomon, if you please. Don't want to keep the widow waitin'."

Before Gulley could reply, the sexton gestured to Hawkwood. "This way."

Hawkwood was not surprised to find the interior of the cottage was as tidy as a barracks. Not that there was much to it. The ground floor consisted of a single room which served as both parlour and kitchen. The furniture was plain and functional. There was an oak table, a bench and small dresser in the cooking area and a settle that faced the open hearth, which was protected by a metal guard. The wall at the back of the hearth and the ceiling immediately above it was black with soot. Cord had been strung across the ceiling from which several threadbare shirts had been hung to dry. A set of stairs in one corner led to the first floor and the sexton's no doubt equally neat sleeping quarters. Incongruously, a small writing desk sat against the wall opposite the fire. Above it was a shelf bearing half a dozen leather-bound volumes.

Asking Hawkwood to take a seat, the sexton poured hot water into a jug from a pot on the hearth and emptied the jug into a blue enamel basin which he placed on the table. A drying cloth and scrubbing brush were produced from a table drawer.

The basin had to be replenished twice, by which time Hawkwood had removed most of the dirt from his hands and arms and his skin was pink from the scrubbing. Cleaning the mud from his breeches and boots would have to wait.

The sexton took the basin outside and emptied it on to the ground. Returning, he set it on the dresser and from a cupboard beneath produced a flask and two battered tin mugs. Without asking, he poured a measure into each mug and handed one to Hawkwood.

"It'll take away the taste of the pit."

Hawkwood drank. Brandy: definitely not the good stuff, but the sexton was right. The smell of the grave had been so strong that by the time the body had been loaded on to the cart it did feel as though the back of his throat had become coated with the trench's contents. Two swallows of the sexton's brew and it felt as if his entire larynx had been cauterized. As cures went, it was eye-wateringly effective.

When his vocal cords had recovered from the shock, he asked the sexton if he'd heard or seen anything during the night.

Predictably, Stubbs shook his head. "Not a bloody thing. I tends to sleep right through. Might stir if a field battery was to open up by my ear, but that ain't likely round these parts."

And the rain would have covered most sounds, anyway, Hawkwood thought, as well as every other sign that might have pointed to whoever dumped the body in the pit. As for the place of entry, in retrospect it was ludicrous to think the corpse might have come from over the hospital wall, which meant access had either been made via the main gate or else the body had been carried over the dividing wall from the adjacent burial ground.

Which left him where? Maybe the body would provide the answer. Suddenly, Gulley's argument was starting to make sense. Perhaps it would have been easier to have left the thing where it was.

The thing.

Dammit, he thought. Now I'm calling her that. He drained the mug.

Sexton Stubbs, he saw, was throwing him a speculative look.

"You've a question?" Hawkwood said.

The sexton hesitated then said, "Back there, the constable called you 'Captain'. If'n you don't mind me askin', that mean you were an officer when you was in the Rifles?"

"Eventually," Hawkwood said. "It didn't last."

The sexton turned the statement over in his mind. Emboldened by the cynical half-smile on Hawkwood's face, he enquired cautiously, "You miss it?"

"The army?"

The sexton nodded.

"Sometimes," Hawkwood admitted. "You?"

Hawkwood thought about the sexton's admission when they were standing by the graveside. Stubbs had received his wound at Corunna. Hawkwood remembered Corunna; the epic retreat across northern Spain in appalling winter weather. Discipline had broken down, food had been scarce and the dead and wounded had been left by the roadside. When Moore's army eventually reached the port, there was no sign of the transports that should have been there to carry them home. By the time the ships arrived, four days later, the French, under Marshal Soult, had caught up and the town was surrounded, forcing the British to take to the field.

While Hawkwood had been leading skirmish parties against French forward positions, the 36th Regiment, along with others, had been engaged in a decisive rear-guard action on the opposite flank. Moore's army had saved the day, albeit at the cost of his own life, and the evacuation had been completed. The 95th and the 36th had been among the last troops to embark.

The sexton took his time answering. Swirling the dregs of the brandy around the inside of his mug, he tipped the drink back and placed the empty receptacle on the table. Drawing a sleeve across his lips, he looked Hawkwood full in the eye.

"Every bleedin' day."

4

Rumour had it that Quill had once served in the Royal Navy and that he'd been wounded in action at the Battle of Lissa while serving aboard HMS *Volage* under Phipps Hornby. Hawkwood had no idea if the rumours were true. From his own limited experiences of life on board a man-o'-war, he thought Quill did have the look of someone who might be at home between decks, though not as a surgeon; more likely as the captain of a gun crew. He had a bruiser's stature. The shaven, bullet-shaped skull added to the mystique. It wasn't hard to imagine him screaming orders, surrounded by sweaty, hard-pressed men ramming powder and shot down the barrel of a 32-pounder while enveloped in a world of fire, flame and flying splinters.

And yet, on the occasions that Hawkwood had visited him, there had been no visible sign of a wounding and he'd always appeared remarkably affable, which, given the nature of his work and the environment in which he laboured, was something of a miracle. Quill was the surgeon appointed by the Coroner to perform necropsies, usually whenever the circumstances of death were outside the ordinary. His place of work was a dead house.

Quill's dead house was located in a dark and gloomy cellar – formerly a crypt – situated beneath an annexe of Christ's Hospital. With St Bartholomew's just around the corner, it was a convenient staging post for transferring bodies from hospital to grave. The authorities had been using it for decades, mostly because they hadn't had to make any structural alterations.

Sleeves rolled up above his elbows, Quill was bent over one of his examination tables when Hawkwood arrived.

"Door!" he commanded with his customary opening brusqueness. He did not turn immediately, but when he did, he smiled upon recognizing his visitor. In the gloom, his breath misted as he spoke. "Officer Hawkwood! Hah! I was warned you'd be along."

It was a macabre vision, for the surgeon's hands were red with gore, as was the apron he was wearing. Hawkwood couldn't recall a time when he hadn't seen Quill in his bloody apron and didn't like to think what the rest of the stains might be. Beneath the examination table, the flagstone floor was slick with dark fluids.

"Warned?" It was all Hawkwood could do not to clamp a hand over his nose and mouth, for the smell was appalling; worse than anything at the burying ground.

Quill grinned. Clearly unmoved by the reek coming off the bodies around him, he also seemed unaffected by the cold. Beads of sweat shone across his bald pate and Hawkwood could have sworn there was steam rising from the apron. He'd seen similar sights when heat appeared to ascend from the innards of wounded and just-killed soldiers; and in Smithfield slaughterhouses, too, on market day. But these bodies weren't warm; they were anything but. He decided it had to be a trick of the light.

"Good to see you again," Quill said. "I take it you're here for the St George's cadaver?"

Hawkwood realized the surgeon was clasping a scalpel in his right hand. His stomach turned.

"I am."

"I couldn't have examined it where it was?"

"If you had," Hawkwood said, "you'd have ended up like me."

The surgeon studied the gap in Hawkwood's coat and beneath it the stained breeches and boots to which the mud was still clinging.

"You think that would have made a difference?" Spreading his arms, the surgeon invited Hawkwood to inspect his apron.

"It was a burying ground. It was in the wet and I didn't think it was a proper place to perform an examination."

"There wasn't convenient shelter nearby?"

Hawkwood thought about Sexton Stubbs' cottage. "No."

"And, in any case," Quill said wryly, "you wanted it done directly."

Hawkwood nodded. "Yes."

Quill fixed him with an accusing eye. "You thought I would move *your* find to the front of the queue?"

The inference was clear. There were procedures when it came to performing necropsies. Surgeons like Quill worked for the Coroner, but the latter couldn't act without permission from a justice of the peace. Since inquests were expensive, they were ordered only when there was evidence of violence or the cause of death was suspicious. However, if the death involved someone from the impoverished layers of society, many justices would rule an inquest unnecessary; thus there would be no crime to investigate. Hawkwood was relying on his past association with Quill in a bid to circumvent the system.

Hawkwood glanced around the room. It looked as though the surgeon was behind in his work. Below the curved roof, the walls were lined with bodies, awaiting either examination or dispatch to their place of interment. It wasn't hard to see why Quill, despite their past dealings, might be irked by another one turning up unannounced.

But when he turned, the smile was back, which could only mean one thing.

"You've already taken a look," Hawkwood said. "Haven't you?"

Placing the scalpel on the examination table and removing a blood-stained cloth from behind his apron string, Quill wiped his hands. "As it's you, I have – and it's not pretty, though she was once, I think, poor mite."

The surgeon moved to an adjacent table and then stepped aside to provide Hawkwood with a better view.

Covered to the neck by a grubby sheet, the body was lying on its side in almost the same position in which it had been found. Hawkwood thought about the dead woman's naked state and the pit she'd been lifted from and how many bodies there might have been buried beneath her. Tied, thrust into a sack, cast down into a stranger's grave and then covered with a filthy shroud that would have been used on God knew how many other remains; if ever proof were needed that the dispossessed were robbed of all dignity, even in death, this was it. The one redeeming feature, if it could be called such, was that the corpse's eyes were no longer wide and staring, but half-closed. Presumably, Quill had taken advantage of the rigor leaving the body to make the adjustment. The cord, Hawkwood saw, had been cut from her wrists.

"You'll appreciate it's been only a short time since I took delivery," Quill said, "and that my initial examination was somewhat cursory."

"I'll take whatever you've got."

"As you wish." Tucking the cloth back into his apron, Quill placed both hands on the table and gazed down at the remains. "We have a young female – eighteen to twenty-five years of age or thereabouts. Cause of death: asphyxia . . . strangulation." The surgeon paused, as if mulling over his diagnosis. "Probably."

"Probably?"

"There is noticeable bruising under the throat, caused by some sort of ligature." Quill pointed towards the corpse's jawline. "Possibly the same cord that was used to bind her wrists and ankles."

"Her ankles were tied *as well*?"

Quill shrugged philosophically. "Easier to fit her in the sack."

There was less engrained dirt than Hawkwood remembered as he gazed down upon the remains. From the state of the water in a tin bowl placed by the corpse's feet, Quill had already made a token effort to wipe the body down prior to his examination. As a result, the discoloration in the skin was even more pronounced than it had been when Hawkwood had observed it at the bottom of the pit.

"And if it wasn't . . . strangulation?"

"There are several contusions, a fracture of the zygomatic – the cheekbone – as well as dislocation of the mandible. There is also damage to the left side of the skull. Here, you see?"

40

"She was beaten?"

"Severely, I'd say."

"Beaten *and* throttled?"

"Yes. But then you'd already guessed that before you brought her up, am I right?" The surgeon eyed him perceptively.

"I thought it was a possibility, from the parts of her I could see."

"Which is why you referred her to me."

"Guilty as charged."

"The constable described the circumstances in which she was found. Clearly she was not meant to be discovered."

"Clearly," Hawkwood repeated softly.

"If you're wondering about the constable, by the way, I did ask him if he wanted to wait, but he declined; said he had to make his report. I believe this was his first visit to a dead house. He did well, considering, which is more than can be said for his companion. The poor boy had to be helped out."

He meant Dobbs. At this rate, Hawkwood thought, the apprentice's first day was likely to be his last.

"There is more," Quill said.

Without ceremony, the surgeon folded the sheet back to reveal the top half of the body. There was a mottled tint to the pale dead flesh. Hawkwood wondered if it was due to the candle glow. The most noticeable aberration was the dark area of what looked like bruising along the left side of the torso. Hawkwood had to bend slightly to study it. "She was hit that hard?"

Quill shook his head. "It's called lividity. When the heart stops beating, the blood settles into the lowest parts of the body. This indicates she was lying on her left side as she is now; as she was when they found her, yes?"

"Yes." Struck by a thought, Hawkwood turned. "Might she have been alive when she was put down there?"

Quill considered the question. "From the state of her, I'd say whoever was responsible made sure she was dead before they put her in the hole." The surgeon sighed. "A small mercy, I fear."

Hawkwood stared down at the body.

"There are other injuries," Quill said, and pointed to the area below the breasts.

Hawkwood looked. Because of the way the body was lying all he could see was the discoloration caused by the blood settlement. And then he saw the lesions.

"What are those?"

"Stab wounds."

"Throttled, beaten *and* stabbed?"

"She died hard," Quill said heavily. "I'll have a better idea of their cause when the rigor's left her completely. That will allow me a closer examination. Otherwise I'd have to break bones. I'd prefer not to do that if it can be helped. We're almost there. An hour or two and I'll have her properly laid out."

Hawkwood couldn't think of a single appropriate reply. He looked down at the body. "Was she violated?"

"As I said, I've yet to make a full examination. I will check, though." The surgeon frowned. "Forgive me asking, but why this one?"

"*This* one?"

"Most would have left her there."

Hawkwood turned. "Because a brave soldier didn't think it right that someone tossed her into a hole without due ceremony, and I didn't want the bloody resurrection men getting to her."

Though they still might.

Quill grunted non-committally and then Hawkwood saw the surgeon's eyes narrow. Taking the rag from his apron, Quill wetted it in the bowl and used it to gently rub the skin on the corpse's right upper arm. "Now, what . . ." he murmured softly ". . . do you suppose this is?"

Hawkwood moved closer.

The pigment in the skin could easily have been mistaken for a consequence of what Quill had termed the lividity process, but as the damp cloth did its work and the dirt was wiped away, Hawkwood saw that it was something else. There was pigmentation but it had been there before the body had settled.

"I declare," Quill said, straightening. "She has a tattoo. Looks

42

like a flower; a rose, unless I miss my guess. Nicely wrought, too. See how the petals are drawn?"

Quill's admiration for the ink-work made Hawkwood wonder again about the surgeon's background and if he had indeed seen naval service. He eyed the man's forearms. There didn't appear to be any anchors or sea-serpents or salutes to Mother, though they could have been high up on Quill's arms and hidden by the sleeves of his shirt. Maybe he had a large one on his back – HMS *Volage* under full sail, surrounded by mermaids.

"Intriguing," Quill murmured, appearing not to have noticed Hawkwood's surreptitious perusal of his anatomy.

"You mean, what sort of woman gets herself tattooed?" Hawkwood said.

"Indeed."

"And what happened to her clothes?"

"Ah," Quill said. "Now, that one I can answer. They were buried with her, at the bottom of the bag." The surgeon jerked his head. "Over there, the small table in the corner."

Crossing the room, Hawkwood found it hard to avert his eyes from some of the horrors on show. The space was not well lit and shadows were playing across the intervening tables, revealing a stomach-churning vista of part-opened chests, excised ribcages, and basins and weighing scales containing items of viscera that would have looked more at home on a butcher's block. From the condition of the bodies on display, Quill liked to work on more than one at a time. Hawkwood couldn't think of a single conceivable reason why that should be.

Arriving at the opposite wall, mercifully without losing the contents of his own stomach, Hawkwood examined the items to which Quill had referred. The bundle did not consist of much: a thin muslin dress, a cotton chemise, a pair of stockings and a pair of half-boots. The sacking had not protected them from the wet. All were soaked and heavily stained. The stench of the pit rose from them, though it was more than likely they had also absorbed some of the odours seeping from the walls and tables in Quill's dead house.

Placing the clothing to one side, Hawkwood picked up the boots. They appeared to be of good quality, or at least they had been before the water had got to them; made from some kind of velvet material, with a small heel, not for walking but for evening wear.

"I don't think she was a vagrant," Hawkwood said, re-joining Quill at the examination table, one of the boots in his hand.

Quill looked down at the footwear and nodded in agreement. "I thought that, too. The clothes do not strike me as hand-me-downs. Indeed, the stockings would appear to be silk. Also, as you'll have noticed, other than the water damage, all are intact, which suggests they were not removed from her by force. She disrobed prior to being attacked."

He turned back to the body. "Notwithstanding her current condition, there's no evidence that she was malnourished."

Hawkwood did not reply. He focused his eyes on the tattoo. Quill followed his gaze. "The rose is significant, you think?"

"Maybe," Hawkwood said, as a thought struck him.

Quill looked at him. "You're asking yourself what sort of woman who's young and pretty and who wears expensive clothes and removes them voluntarily, might carry a tattoo on her shoulder."

Hawkwood considered the boot he was holding.

"I think we can both hazard a guess, don't you?" Quill said.

Hawkwood nodded. "It'd be a place to start."

Quill held out his hand. "Then I think you have your work cut out. Don't let me detain you."

Hawkwood passed the boot over. "I don't suppose you can tell me when she might have been killed?"

Quill shook his head. "Not with any certainty. Rigor's not a precise measure. It can take between two and twelve hours to take hold fully, but the process can also be slowed or accelerated depending on location and temperature."

Hawkwood thought about the rain and the cold and the mud she'd been buried under. Mud had remarkable properties. It could both protect and preserve. He recalled the times on campaign when on cold nights he and Jago had smeared their blankets with clay; with straw bedding for a base, the mud had provided extra insulation against the cold and they'd generally passed the night in relative comfort.

He realized Quill was still talking.

"A body returns to its flaccid state after a further eighteen hours or thereabouts. I note the flies have started their work, but the eggs have yet to reach the larvae stage, which could be down to the temperature of the ground. Given that, and from her current condition and from what you and the constable have told me, I'd estimate she's been dead for between twenty-four and thirty-six hours."

Hawkwood absorbed the information.

"You really do end up with the most interesting ones, don't you?" Quill murmured.

"It's a curse," Hawkwood said as he turned to go.

Quill smiled grimly. "You should have my job."

"I'm sorry, but can you explain to me again why this is Bow Street's case," Hawkwood said, "and not the Garden's?"

The "Garden" was Hatton Garden. St George the Martyr's burying ground fell within the Hatton Garden Public Office's area of jurisdiction, though only by the width of a few streets.

Chief Magistrate James Read turned away from the rain-spattered window, clasped his hands behind his back and raised his coat-tails to the fire. Late middle-aged and trimly built, with aquiline features and swept-back silver hair, the magistrate's fastidious appearance exuded quiet authority. If he was irritated by the lack of grace in Hawkwood's enquiry, he gave no outward sign.

"It was at Hatton Garden's request."

"Request?" Hawkwood said cautiously.

"For assistance; from Magistrate Turton."

"Magistrate Turton has his own Principal Officers," Hawkwood said, still unconvinced. "Why does he need us?"

"It would appear he has a shortage."

"Of Principal Officers."

"Correct," Read said patiently. "He has six at his disposal. Four are engaged in investigations of their own and thus cannot be spared. The other two are confined to their beds because of illness; hence the request. And before you say anything, I confess that I, too, was somewhat surprised. However, as we are on Magistrate Turton's doorstep, I saw no reason why we could not offer him assistance, on this occasion."

Excluding Bow Street, there were seven other Public Offices located across the metropolis. Autonomous save in matters of staffing and the setting of annual budgets – for which the Home Department was responsible – each one operated independently from its neighbours. So much so, that it was almost a point of honour for offices not to exchange information. Requests for help, therefore, were rare. Requests for help from Bow Street were exceedingly rare.

"Besides," Read continued, "an initiative has been issued; from the Home Department, from Mr Callum Day, the official conduit between this office and Whitehall."

Hawkwood groaned inwardly. He'd never met Day, but the last time the Home Department had used its initiative, he'd ended up in France and, as a consequence, the other side of the Atlantic, an endeavour from which he was still smarting.

Leaving the fire and returning to his desk, the Chief Magistrate took his seat. "It has long been felt among certain circles that the fight against the criminal element would be better served if there was more cooperation between the Public Offices."

James Read smiled thinly at Hawkwood's less than overjoyed expression. "I can tell what you're thinking. Nevertheless, I'm inclined to agree that there is merit in the idea and, in times of adversity, I see no reason why the parishes should not combine their resources. We are, in case you've forgotten, supposed to be on the same side."

Read's eyes flickered to the paperwork on his desk. One of the communiqués, Hawkwood saw, was affixed with a broken wax seal, upon which the indentation of the Home Minister's office was plainly visible.

"Also . . ." Read said, ". . . it will give you something to do after your adventures abroad."

Placing the Home Department correspondence to one side,

the Chief Magistrate looked up. "And now that your curiosity has been satisfied, what can you tell me – besides the fact that we have a body . . . in a grave?"

Ignoring the Chief Magistrate's mordant comment, Hawkwood nodded. "The burial plot was adjacent to the Foundling Hospital. I thought it might be a child, a cast-off."

"But it wasn't and you have another theory?"

"In as much as it's not a child but a woman. Surgeon Quill and I think she may have been a working girl."

Read frowned and listened as Hawkwood described the tattoo.

"You're suggesting that if we can identify the victim through the ink-work, we may have a lead to her killer?"

"Yes."

Lowering his forearms on to his desk, his fingers still laced, Read appeared sceptical. "If she *is* a working girl, I put it to you that you'll have more than *a* lead, you'll likely have scores of them."

"There is that," Hawkwood admitted.

"You have a means of establishing her identity?"

"I'm working on it."

Read looked thoughtful.

Hawkwood recognized the look. "Sir?"

Read let out a sigh. "Murder's a foul business, though, sadly, a far from uncommon occurrence, especially among the more – how shall I put it? – socially disadvantaged. And our resources are not infinite. Truth be told, they are anything but. So, given what we know, this could be a fruitless exercise. While the young woman's death is undoubtedly a heinous crime, if I were to assign an officer of your experience to the case for a significant length of time it would seriously deplete our own resources. In short, therefore, while I'm willing for this office to render assistance to Magistrate Turton, I do not intend it to become our life's work. It will be for a few days at the most. So use them well. I take it your strategy is to cultivate your informers who have access to the more shadowy areas of our city?"

He means Jago.

"It is."

47

"Very well. But if nothing is forthcoming after what I consider to be an appropriate period, know that I will reassign you to more pressing duties and a lower-ranked officer will be delegated to continue the enquiry; that is, if Magistrate Turton remains short-staffed. Young Hopkins is proving to be a most capable individual and has, in fact, expressed a desire to become a Principal Officer. It would be a shame to discourage him from pursuing that ambition."

"Indeed it would, sir."

Hawkwood was rewarded with a sharp look. Then the Chief Magistrate nodded. "Keep me informed and do try not to tread on too many toes."

"I'll do my best."

But if all else fails . . .

Reaching the door, he was about to let himself out when Read's voice sounded again.

"Officer Hawkwood."

Hawkwood turned.

"Regarding Surgeon Quill; I assume it was on *your* authority that the body was delivered to his dead house?"

"It was."

"Rather presumptuous, was it not? You do *know* there are coroners and rules governing investigations into wrongful deaths?"

"I've always thought of them more as a set of recommendations than hard rules."

The Chief Magistrate fixed Hawkwood with a flinty gaze. "Only when they suit you, you mean."

"I used my judgement. If we'd gone by the book, by the time we'd found a coroner willing to drag himself from his bed, there would have been two bodies in the pit. There's nothing worse than a confused coroner, sir. Take it from me."

"By two, you are referring to the plot's intended occupant."

"The funeral party was already on its way. It would have been a bit crowded down there."

Pinching the bridge of his nose, the Chief Magistrate closed his eyes. Then, after letting go a sigh, he re-opened them and nodded in weary acceptance.

A knock sounded. Before Read could respond and Hawkwood move aside, the door opened and Bow Street's Chief Clerk, Ezra Twigg, entered, bearing a note.

"My apologies, sir." Twigg blinked owlishly. "I've a message for Officer Hawkwood, from Surgeon Quill. It's marked 'urgent'."

"Speak of the devil," Read murmured. He nodded at Twigg. "Very well."

Twigg handed Hawkwood the note. Hawkwood opened it. The message was concise.

There is more,
Quill

Hawkwood folded the paper without speaking.

"Will there be a reply?" Twigg enquired.

"No," Hawkwood said.

Read frowned.

"Quill's completed his examination," Hawkwood said. "I should go."

"Oh, by all means," Read said drily. "Don't let us detain you."

Ezra Twigg glanced towards the Chief Magistrate; when no further directive was forthcoming, he turned for the door. Hawkwood followed.

"Officer Hawkwood," Read called again.

Curbing his irritation, Hawkwood turned and saw that the Chief Magistrate had left the sanctuary of his desk and resumed his pose in front of the fire.

The magistrate raised his chin. "There is one thing I neglected to mention."

"Sir?"

James Read held Hawkwood's gaze for perhaps three or four seconds. Then the corner of his mouth twisted to form an oblique smile.

"Welcome back."

5

When Hawkwood re-entered the dead room, there was no shouted order to close the door and this time, when Quill turned to greet him, there was no humour in the surgeon's expression, either. Instead, Quill's face looked as if it had been carved from stone. The cellar appeared darker than it had before; colder, too, perhaps because of Quill's less than welcoming disposition. The smell, though, was as bad as ever.

Taking his cue from the room's chilly atmosphere, Hawkwood did not speak as he took the note from his pocket and held it up. Quill crooked a finger and, with a rising sense of dread, Hawkwood followed him across to the examination table.

The body was there, covered by the sheet. Wordlessly, Quill drew the material aside.

The corpse now lay on its back in the prone position, hands by its sides. This time the eyes were fully closed but it was not to her eyes that Hawkwood's attention was drawn. It was to the dead woman's abdomen and the trauma that had been inflicted upon it.

"They're not stab wounds," Hawkwood said cautiously. "They don't look deep enough."

"No," Quill said. "I was mistaken. She was not stabbed."

"Scratched, then."

"In a manner of speaking."

"I'm not with you."

Quill reached for a candle. "Take this."

Hawkwood took the light and held it above the body. Caught in a sudden draught, the candle flame fluttered and then steadied. He stared down at the wounds, which still looked nothing more than a series of random score marks angled across the surface of the skin. While they were not deep, they were not that shallow, either. They were the sort of cuts which, suffered singly, might have been caused by catching the skin on a rusty nail; quick to bleed but, by the same token, quick to close and form a scab. Lowering the flame, Hawkwood allowed his eyes to follow the progression of the wounds across the width of the body. Only then was he able to take in what Quill had seen.

The first letter that had been carved into the flesh was a sharp-angled ⟨. It had been made by two distinct strokes of a blade, as if the perpetrator had been trying to form a triangle and given up. The second letter had been made using the same principle, with the addition of a horizontal incision linking the two cuts to form an A. The next was an R, followed by a single vertical slash to represent an I. There were three more letters, all rendered using a minimal number of strokes.

"C-A-R-I-T-A-S," Quill said, "in case you were wondering."

"I can spell, damn it!" Hawkwood stared at the cuts. "What I don't know is what the hell it's doing there. Is it even a word?"

Quill said calmly, "I believe it's Latin."

"Latin?"

"It means charity."

Hawkwood turned.

Quill gave what could have been interpreted as an apologetic shrug. "Latin studies; one of the consequences of a classical education, though a necessity when considering a career in medicine."

Hawkwood returned his attention to the body.

"This is not something I've come across before," Quill said. "You?"

Hawkwood found his voice. "Not like this."

"Like *this?*" Quill countered sharply.

51

"When I was in Spain, the *guerrillero*s used to mutilate the bodies of dead French soldiers as a warning to others."

"They wrote messages in the *flesh*?"

"No, usually they'd cut something off. Noses, fingers, cocks. It scared the Frogs shitless."

"I can imagine," Quill said, adding pointedly, "Not quite the same though."

"No," Hawkwood agreed. "Not quite."

Quill let out a sigh. "But bad enough."

"Yes."

Quill held Hawkwood's gaze. His expression was even darker than it had been before.

"Did you find anything else?" Hawkwood asked, wondering what other horrors might be lurking.

"No," Quill said. "Mercifully. She was not violated – not as we understand the term, at any rate, though my examination did reveal that she was no stranger to coition."

There followed a moment's pause then Quill chewed his lip and said pointedly, "Fore and aft."

Offering a contrite shrug for having used the phrase, the surgeon made a face. "Your suspicions regarding her likely profession would, therefore, appear to have merit."

"Then cover her up, for Christ's sake." Hawkwood stepped away from the table, allowing Quill to draw the sheet over the body. He. turned back. "Forgive me, I didn't mean to snap."

"No apology required," Quill said.

"I want him," Hawkwood said. "I want the bastard who did this."

"*Him?*" Quill said.

"Him. Them."

God help us if it's a "her". What kind of woman would do this to another?

"Ah, but it's not just the 'who' though, is it?" Quill said. "It's the rest of it. And I'm afraid I can't help you with that conundrum. My responsibility extends only as far as determining the cause of death, not the persons or reasoning behind it. My domain is the 'how'. The 'who' and the 'why' are your department."

Thanks to Magistrate bloody Turton, and a sexton with a conscience, Hawkwood thought bitterly.

"That's not to say I'm not intrigued, of course," Quill added, "as a medical man. But it ain't my field. You want an answer as to why someone should carve anything into some poor woman's belly, you don't need a surgeon; you need a mind doctor." The surgeon cocked his head. "Know any mind doctors?"

Hawkwood stared at Quill. Quill stared back at him. "What?"

"As a matter of fact," Hawkwood said. "I believe I do."

It had been winter when Hawkwood had last visited the building and there had been a heavy frost on the ground. It was winter once again, or at least the tail end of it, and while the weather was not as harsh, it was immediately apparent that the intervening months had not been kind, for the place appeared even more decrepit and run down than it had before.

Segments of the surrounding wall looked as if they were about to collapse, while the trees, which, during the summer, would have formed a natural screen, appeared to be suffering from some form of incurable blight, with many of their lower branches having been lopped off by the neighbouring residents for use as domestic kindling. Moorfields, the area of open ground which fronted the building, had all the characteristics of a freshly ploughed pasture. Subsidence, having bedevilled the site for decades, had taken a more drastic toll of late and the ponds which had formed in the resulting depressions had almost doubled in size. Most of the iron railings that had once ringed the common land had disappeared.

The twin statues were still there, guarding the entry gates: both male – one wearing shackles, head drawn back; the other reclining as if having just awoken from a troubled sleep. Their naked torsos, stained black over the years, were splattered with ash and pigeon droppings. Steeling himself, Hawkwood ducked beneath them, crossed the courtyard and headed for the main door. Tugging on the bell pull, he waited. The eye-hatch slid aside and a pale, unshaven face appeared in the opening.

"Officer Hawkwood, Bow Street Public Office; here to see Apothecary Locke."

"You expected?" a gravelly voice wheezed.

Hawkwood had anticipated the question and raised his tipstaff so that the brass crown was displayed. "I don't need an appointment."

After a moment's hesitation, the hatch scraped shut. The sound of several large bolts being withdrawn was followed by the rasp of wood on stone as the door was hauled back. Hawkwood took a quick gulp of air and stepped through the gap. The door closed ominously behind him.

Welcome to Bedlam . . . again.

The last time he'd called upon Robert Locke, the apothecary's office had been on the first floor. To get there, he'd been escorted through the main gallery, past cell doors that had opened on to scenes more suited to a travelling freak show than a hospital wing. The sight of distressed patients – male and female – chained to walls, many squatting in their own filth, and the pitiful looks they'd given him as he'd gone past, had stayed in the mind for a long time afterwards, as had their cries of distress at spying a stranger in their midst. He was considerably relieved, therefore, when, this time, the unsmiling, blue-coated attendant avoided the central staircase and led him down a dank and draughty ground-floor corridor towards the rear of the building, the uneven floorboards creaking beneath their combined tread.

While the route might have altered, the smells had not. The combination of rotting timbers, damp straw, stale cabbage and human sewage were as bad as he remembered and easily equalled the odours at the bottom of the grave-pit and the stench in Quill's dead house. It was further indication – as if the exterior signs had not been proof enough – that Bethlem Hospital had reached its final stage of decomposition.

This time, there was no brass plate beside the door. There was only the word *Apothecary* scrawled on a piece of torn card looped over the doorknob. The attendant knocked and Hawkwood was announced. Hearing a small grunt of surprise, Hawkwood pushed past the attendant and very nearly went sprawling arse over elbow due to a metal pail that had been placed on the floor two feet inside the door. As entrances went, it wasn't the most dignified he'd ever made.

Recovering his footing, he saw that the pail was one of several mis-matched receptacles that had been placed around the room in order to catch the rainwater that was dripping from the ceiling. An assortment of buckets, basins, pots and jugs had been pressed into service. Even as he took in the sight, there came the sound of a droplet hitting the surface of the water in one of the make-shift reservoirs, more than half of which were ready for emptying. A quick glance above his head at the spots of mould high in the corners of the walls and the dark, damp patches radiating out from the ceiling rose told their own depressing story.

"Officer Hawkwood?"

The bespectacled, studious-looking man who rose from behind his desk could have been mistaken for a bank clerk or a school-teacher rather than an apothecary in a madhouse, though it was plain that, like the building in which he worked, Robert Locke looked as though he had seen better days. He appeared thinner than Hawkwood remembered and older, too, for there were lines on his face that had not been there before.

"Doctor," Hawkwood said, as the apothecary advanced towards him, looking both flustered and, Hawkwood thought, more than a tad apprehensive.

Removing his spectacles – an affectation which Hawkwood had come to know well from their previous encounters – Locke wiped them on a handkerchief, slid them back on to his nose and turned to the hovering attendant. "Thank you, Mr O'Brien; that will be all."

Dismissed, the attendant left the room. Locke, despite his obvious concern as to why Hawkwood might have returned, extended his hand. The apothecary's grip was firm, though cold to the touch. Hawkwood wondered if it was a sign that Locke's health was failing or a reflection of the state of the building which was disintegrating brick by brick around him.

"Come in, sir, come in," Locke said. "Please forgive the accom-modation. As you can see, there's been little improvement since your last visit." The apothecary offered an apologetic smile. "That is to say, there has been no improvement whatsoever."

"You've changed offices," Hawkwood pointed out.

"Well, yes, but that was a matter of necessity – the ceiling fell in upstairs." Locke indicated the state of the decor above his head and the crockery at his feet. "I fear it's only a matter of time before the same thing happens again. Mind where you step."

"I thought you were moving to new premises," Hawkwood said.

Locke sighed wearily. "Oh, indeed we were; or rather, we will be: St George's Fields. The first stone was laid back in April, though God knows when it will be finished. In the meantime, you find us thus. Still sinking, but making do as best we can. Come, stand by the fire. It's one of the few comforts I have left, though that might alter when we run out of wood, unless I start burning the furniture."

Rubbing his hands together, Locke crossed to the fireplace and picked up a poker. Crouching down, the apothecary took two small logs from a stack at the side of the hearth and added them to the embers, allowing Hawkwood a bird's-eye view of his frayed collar and the specks of dandruff adhering to it.

Stoking life into the flames, he laid the poker down and stood up. "So," he said, turning. "What brings you back to our door? It seems only five minutes, but it must be . . . what? – a year or thereabouts since the affair with Colonel Hyde?" He threw Hawkwood a worried look. "I'm assuming this has nothing to do with those appalling events?"

"No," Hawkwood said.

Strange, he thought, how previous cases came back to haunt you. It had been Hyde, a former army surgeon, whose escape from Bedlam and demand for bodies upon which to practise his skills had led to the confrontation with the murderous resurrection gang, an encounter from which no one had emerged untarnished.

Clearly relieved, Locke nodded. "I followed it all in the news sheets, of course; a foul business. When his crimes were finally brought to light, I did ask myself if there was anything I could

56

have done differently that might have deterred him from his actions."

"There was nothing anyone could have done," Hawkwood said. "He was insane and he was clever. And now he's dead and the world's the better for it."

"According to the newspapers, he died while resisting arrest."

"Yes," Hawkwood said.

After I ran the bastard through.

He found that Locke was regarding him closely. When he'd first called upon the apothecary, Hawkwood had thought Locke to be nothing more than a lickspittle, a petty official harbouring resentment towards his superiors for having left him in sole charge of a shambles of a hospital and a largely incompetent and uncaring workforce. Subsequent events had altered Hawkwood's perception of the man, for it had been Locke's knowledge of his former patient's mental condition that had enabled Hawkwood to eventually track down the lunatic Colonel Hyde, and dispatch him to a place where he was no longer a threat to humanity: to wit, the fires of hell and damnation. A rapier thrust had been the method of execution, though that was just one of many details that had been omitted from the official report.

"So," the apothecary prompted as his gaze fell away. "How may I be of service?"

"I'm looking for someone," Hawkwood said, "and I need your advice in narrowing my search."

Locke frowned. "Really? How so?"

"I'm investigating a murder."

Taken aback, Locke's eyes widened.

"A woman's been killed. At the moment, she's nameless."

Locke blinked. "And what? You think she may have a connection with the hospital; a former patient, perhaps?"

"I don't believe so."

Locke looked even more nonplussed. "Then, forgive me, but why . . .?"

"The circumstances of her death are . . . unusual."

The apothecary opened his mouth as if to speak and then closed it abruptly. Clearly confused, he gestured to the chair in

57

front of his desk. "We should make ourselves more comfortable." Returning to his former position behind the desk, he settled himself and said, "Why don't you start at the beginning?"

Locke remained silent as Hawkwood related the circumstances surrounding the finding of the body and its delivery to Quill's necropsy room. When it came to a description of the mutilations that had been performed upon the corpse, the apothecary's head lifted and he sat back. Taking out his handkerchief, he removed his spectacles and began to clean the lenses, his face still; his movements slow and deliberate.

Hawkwood waited. Several seconds passed before Locke tucked the handkerchief away and used both hands to position his spectacles back on the bridge of his nose. Blinking, he searched Hawkwood's face. "I don't know what to say."

"Say you'll help me," Hawkwood said.

"But of course. I'll assist in any way I can, though I'm not sure how. What do you require?"

"When we were dealing with Hyde, I asked you what circumstances might have driven him to commit murder."

Locke nodded. "I remember."

"I'm hoping you can do the same again. I need to know what sort of person I'm looking for this time. I'm assuming it's a 'he'. If you can give me some idea of what might be going through the bastard's mind, then maybe I can use the information to hunt him down."

"*Hunt?*" Locke said cautiously. "You make him sound like some kind of wild animal."

"He killed a woman and carved a word into her flesh. How would *you* describe him?"

Locke blinked. "From what I know, animals usually have a valid reason for killing: to survive; to acquire food or a mate; to establish their territory; or to protect their offspring. I think you'll find that men kill for a far greater variety of reasons, most of them trivial – excluding war, of course . . . though even then, I wouldn't swear to it." Tilting his head, Locke fixed Hawkwood with a pointed look. "But I suspect that is something you are well aware of."

The apothecary knew that Hawkwood had served as an officer in the Rifles and was, therefore, intimately familiar with the horrors of the battlefield.

"I was a soldier. It wasn't my place to question the why. My duty was to take care of the how and the when." Hawkwood smiled thinly at Locke's bemused expression. "Forgive me; I had a similar conversation recently with the Coroner's surgeon."

Locke said nothing.

"With Hyde," Hawkwood said, "I was sure we were dealing with a madman because he'd been locked up in this place, but you convinced me it wasn't that simple. For a start, even though he was a patient here, Hyde did not consider himself to be mad."

Locke spread his hands. "That is the nature of the sickness. I told you at the time, while other doctors consider madness to be a spiritual malaise, I believe it to be a physical disease, an organic disorder within the brain. It can affect anyone, from a soldier to a surgeon, from a kitchen maid to a—"

"King?" Hawkwood finished.

"Indeed." Locke smiled faintly. "And while their behaviour may be unfathomable to others, within their own minds, they are being perfectly rational."

"And Hyde didn't think of himself as either sane or insane, because that was the nature of his delusion."

"Correct."

"When I asked you what made Hyde commit murder, you told me it was necessary to know how his delusion arose in the first place."

"But of course. Without knowledge of a person's history there is no way of determining what makes them commit irrational acts, which is why I'm unable to provide you with the information you require. You forget; Hyde was already known to us. We had both his medical and his army records, thus we were able to chart the course of his delusions. His crimes were not committed in isolation. They were part of a natural progression, stemming from his experiences during the war. There was a purpose to his actions; validity, if you will; at least in *his* mind.

With regards to the individual you are now seeking, we have no point of reference, therefore I have nothing to chart."

"We have *caritas*," Hawkwood said, clutching at his remaining straw. "Does that tell us anything?"

Locke considered the question. "It implies the author is an educated man."

"And?"

"His education may prompt him to believe he is of a superior intellect to those around him, which could mean he holds a position of authority. Alternatively, he could occupy a more modest position but believes he has been held back by those above him who, in his opinion, are his inferiors. Jealousy turns to resentment. Resentment turns to anger, anger to rage . . ."

"And rage to murder," Hawkwood said softly.

"A simplistic rendering, but yes. Though, murder is not always born of anger. It is also an illustration of the control one person wields over another; a way of the killer showing that he has the power over life and death."

"Like Hyde?"

The apothecary nodded. "Like Colonel Hyde. He decides who lives and who dies. In his own mind, he is the one before whom all others should bow down."

"You're not telling me he thinks he's God?"

As Hawkwood absorbed that thought, Locke said, "Clearly, the word *caritas* holds a particular significance."

"You mean why not 'whore' or 'Jezebel'," Hawkwood said.

Locke made a face. "Perhaps we should be thankful for small mercies. If I remember my scriptures, Jezebel was consumed by a pack of stray dogs. Had your murderer chosen that as his means of disposal, I doubt she'd have been found at all."

Hawkwood was digesting that morbid titbit and wondering if it was the apothecary's attempt at wit when Locke said, "From your description of the wounds, he is clearly prone to rage; yet methodical, too; capable of deliberation."

"How can you tell that?"

The apothecary paused and then said, "Because it took thought to choose that particular word and it would have taken time to carve it into her flesh."

Reaching for a pencil, Locke took a sheet of paper from the detritus on his desk and, employing a series of single strokes of the pencil, began to write. When he had finished, he held up the paper. Upon it was etched the word CARITAS.

"From your description of the wounds, he would have had to employ some eighteen separate cuts. Therefore he took his time. Ergo, he was not afraid of being interrupted." Locke paused and then said, "As a matter of interest, were there any other similar cuts on the body, close to the same area?"

Hawkwood thought back. "One or two, yes, now you mention it."

"More than likely they were practice cuts, to allow him to perfect his calligraphy." The apothecary laid the paper on the desk and studied his penmanship. "One has to wonder who the message was for."

"For?" Hawkwood said, still trying to come to terms with the fact that the killer had perfected his technique before committing himself to the final indignation.

"We must assume it was meant to be read. Otherwise, why take the trouble?" Locke looked up. "You are aware that *caritas* can have other meanings besides 'charity'?"

"No," Hawkwood said. "I wasn't."

"It can also mean 'esteem' or 'virtue'. If she was a working girl, as you suspect, then the latter interpretation would be more apposite."

"Because she'd be considered a woman without virtue? So this was what? Some kind of punishment?"

"Possibly, or a warning to those who would ply a similar trade. The killer is giving notice that this is the fate that will befall them if they do not change their immoral ways."

"Well, if that's his goal," Hawkwood said, "he'll have his work cut out, given the number of molls in this city."

"So will you," Locke observed. "Seeing as you'll be the one trying to stop him."

A faint, far-off scream made the apothecary cock his head.

As he did so, a water droplet splashed on to his sleeve from the ceiling above. Cursing, he dabbed the offending spot with his handkerchief while a cacophony of hoarse cries began to spread through the building. It was as if the first scream had been a prompt. It sounded, Hawkwood thought, as though a pack of wolves had been loosed from a cage.

Taking the interruption as his cue, and struck by a sudden and overwhelming desire to escape the hospital's oppressive atmosphere, Hawkwood got to his feet.

Locke rose with him. As he did so, the apothecary reached for the bell pull on the wall behind his desk and gave the cord a short tug. "I'm sorry I could not be of more help."

Hawkwood shook his head. "On the contrary, you've confirmed what I'd already half suspected."

Somewhere in the depths, he presumed a bell had rung and he wondered if the sound of it had been drowned by the noises that were beginning to echo through the corridors, among them the clatter of running feet.

At that moment, however, the door opened to admit the attendant who'd delivered him to Locke's inner sanctum, causing Hawkwood to wonder if the man had been hovering outside throughout the entire course of his and Locke's conversation.

"Second opinions are my speciality," Locke said, smiling. "Should any further information come to light, my door will still be open."

"If it hasn't been consigned to the flames," Hawkwood said.

Locke chuckled. "I'll make sure it's the last thing to go." He held out his hand. "Mr O'Brien will show you out. It was a pleasure seeing you again . . . despite the circumstances."

The smile was replaced suddenly by a more thoughtful expression. "I hope you catch him." There was the merest pause then Locke said, "When you do run him down, it will be interesting to see if he also tries to resist arrest."

Before Hawkwood could respond, the apothecary gave a quick, wry smile, nodded and turned for his desk, his hands clasped behind his back.

The attendant moved aside to allow Hawkwood to exit. It

was as the door was closing behind him that the thought struck. Sticking out a hand to stop the door's swing, he stepped back into the room. Locke was back behind his desk. He glanced up.

"There is one thing," Hawkwood said.

Locke half rose.

"Something I forgot to ask."

The apothecary nodded sombrely. "I know."

"You *know*?"

Locke lowered himself into his chair. "It's just occurred to you that the question you should have asked is not: will he kill again? The question is: has he killed before?"

"Yes."

"Because if you are to prevent him from committing a similar crime, it is not the future you should concentrate upon, but the past. If you can establish a truth using that method, then you will have your point of reference from which everything else will stem."

"So?" Hawkwood said. "In your opinion, *could* he have done this before?"

Gazing back at him, Locke removed his spectacles and the handkerchief from his sleeve and began to clean each lens with slow, circular motions. After several seconds of concentrated thought, he put away the handkerchief, placed the spectacles back on the bridge of his nose, and stared at Hawkwood.

"Oh, yes," he said. "Almost certainly."

6

"That's it?" Jago said, unable to hide his disbelief. "You want to know if any working girls have gone missing? You're bloody joking, right? Know how many there are in this city? Bloody 'undreds – hell, thousands, more like. And you want to track down *one* of them?"

"I don't need to track her down. I know where she is. She's on a slab in a dead house; what's left of her. What I don't know is her name. I'm hoping it's Rose."

"Because of a tattoo? Jesus, that's a bloody long shot."

"You may be right. Most likely you are right, but that doesn't mean I have to send her to Cross Bones to be tipped into another bloody ditch."

Jago frowned. "So, what the hell makes this one so special? Bawds and pimps beat their molls all the time. Kill 'em too, when they're in the mood."

"Not like this," Hawkwood said.

Jago sat back. "That bad?"

"Worse."

Hawkwood described the scene in Quill's dead house.

Jago remained silent throughout the telling. He winced at the mention of the carved wounds. "Jesus," he muttered finally.

"Quill asked me the same question," Hawkwood said.

"What? Oh, you mean, why this one?"

Hawkwood nodded. "I told him it was because one of John

Moore's veterans didn't think it right that someone tossed her into a hole without due ceremony and I didn't want the bloody resurrection men getting to her."

"Sounds good enough to me," Jago said.

"There is another reason," Hawkwood said.

"Which is?"

"The bastards who put her there thought they could get away with it. They're mistaken."

Jago sighed and sat back. He stared into his drink and then looked up. "You want me to ask Connie if she's heard anything."

Hawkwood nodded.

"You do know the old one about needles and haystacks, right?"

"You're all I've got," Hawkwood said.

Jago gave a wry smile. "Now, where've I heard that before? All right, I'll 'ave a word. But I wouldn't get your hopes up. It's likely you'll never know who she was. She'll be just another nameless lass set for a pauper's grave."

"She's somebody's daughter."

"Who you think might be a moll, which means there's a good chance she's either been disowned or discarded."

"Even so," Hawkwood said.

After a second's lapse, Jago acknowledged Hawkwood's response with an understanding nod. "Aye, even so."

Jago lay with his arm around Connie Fletcher's shoulder. Her head rested on his chest, her ash-blonde hair loose about her face.

"Need to ask you something," Jago said.

"You want to go around again?" Connie chuckled throatily as she ran her lips across the still raw wounds in his shoulder. "I'll be gentle."

Jago gasped as her hand began to slide south beneath the bedcover. "Bloody hell, woman, give us a chance. I ain't caught my breath from last time."

Connie removed her hand with an exaggerated sigh and snuggled closer. "All right, what then?"

At the angle they were lying, Jago couldn't see Connie's face, but he sensed she was still smiling. It made him wonder if she was expecting *the* question, the one that tended to end up with a ring and the services of a vicar. He felt a twinge of guilt. He'd been with Connie longer than he'd been with any woman, but marriage? Not that the thought hadn't crossed his mind. Connie's too, he suspected, even though they'd never discussed the possibility. He waited until his pulse had settled down and then said, "There's been a killing. Captain's investigating. He reckons she might have been a workin' girl."

Connie lifted her head. "Why's that?"

"She was young, she weren't dressed in rags and she has – had – a tattoo."

The bedcover slid away as Connie sat up. "That's his definition of a working girl? Someone who's young, dresses decent and has a tattoo? He needs to get out more."

"How many ladies you know have tattoos?" Jago asked.

"Can't say as I know that many ladies," Connie said deftly. Then she frowned. "Hang on. What about my tattoo? What's that make me?"

Jago gazed back at her. "You don't have a tattoo."

Connie raised one eyebrow. "Might have."

"No," Jago said. "I'd have found it. Trust me."

"Just checking," Connie said, patting his chest. "But it proves that not every working girl has one."

Jago pulled his head back to look at her. "You still see yourself as a workin' girl?"

"Well as sure as God made little green apples, I'm no lady."

"You're my lady," Jago said.

Connie smiled. "Good answer, but I *was* a working girl, before I went into management, which doesn't say much for your theory, now, does it?"

"All right, point taken. But like I said, it weren't my theory."

"Which means it's just as likely there are proper ladies out there who *do* have tattoos."

Jago realized he'd been outsmarted. Connie's still-arched

eyebrow and her naked breasts swaying enticingly in front of his nose weren't helping.

"What kind of tattoo?" she asked, after a considered pause.

"A rose." Jago tapped Connie's upper right arm. "On her shoulder. Told him the chances were slim to none, but the captain thinks it could be her name."

Connie went quiet.

"What?" Jago said.

She stared at him, her face suddenly serious. "You're sure it was a rose?"

Jago frowned. "I'm pretty sure the captain knows what a rose looks like. Why? You saying you might've known her?"

"I'm saying if her name *was* Rose, it's more likely it was a coincidence."

Jago sat up. "Sorry, girl, you've lost me."

Connie shook her head. Her eyes held his. "A rose tattoo doesn't have *to mean* it's her name. Chances are it was an owner's mark."

"Come again?"

Connie didn't reply but waited for the penny to drop.

"She was branded," Jago said.

"It's why some people call them stables." Anger flared briefly in Connie's eyes.

"So who owns this one?"

"Those of us in the know call her the Widow."

Jago grimaced. "Cheery. I can see how that'd draw the customers in."

Connie's mouth moved, but if it was meant as a smile, there was no humour in it.

"Well, *she* doesn't call herself that. Her real name's Ellie Pearce. Doesn't like to be called that either, though. These days, she goes by Lady Eleanor Rain."

"Does she now? Well, I suppose it's a tad more swish than Lady Ellie. So, what's *her* story? *She* got a tattoo?"

Connie ignored the quip. "Supposedly started out with her ma. The old girl ran a business over in Half Moon Alley."

"You mean it was a knocking shop. Nothin' like keeping it in the family."

"Well, she might have turned a trick or two in her younger days, but Ma Pearce was more purveyor than prossie."

"What'd she purvey?"

"Perfumes, powders and oils, machines – you name it."

"Machines?" Jago said, startled. "What sort of machines?"

Connie gazed back at him despairingly, dropped her eyes towards his crotch and then rewarded him with a look.

"Ah, right, understood; *that* sort. Bloody glad you and me don't bother; all that fiddling around. Mood's bloody gone by the time you've tied the damned thing on. Talk about a passion killer. Sorry, you were sayin'?"

"Word was that her mother used to pimp Ellie out to help pay the rent when business was slack."

"Wouldn't've thought that kind of business was ever slack," Jago murmured, earning himself another reproving look.

"It happens. Anyway, supposedly, she took to it like a duck to water; went independent and started charging from a room above the Rose Inn over on Chick Lane."

"Nice neighbourhood."

"Nice for her. Made enough she was able to persuade the landlord to rent her a couple more rooms round the back. Started out with three molls, I think it was. That close to Smithfield, they weren't short of customers."

Customers who weren't particular about their surroundings, Jago thought. On market days, the gutters in the adjacent lanes ran red with the blood and offal that seeped out of the nearby slaughterhouses.

"Wasn't long before she'd earned enough to move to better premises. I don't recall where; Holborn, maybe. That's when she branched out. Found herself a rich patron – Sir Nicholas Rain. Bedded and wedded the poor bugger, wore him out; inherited when he died – hence the new name – and used the legacy to expand her business. I heard most of her early clients were swells she'd met through her husband: gentlemen of the nobility and so forth. Never looked back since."

A retort hovered on Jago's lips but was quelled when Connie continued, "Likes to dress her girls in the latest fashions. Her promise is they'll satisfy all desires – and I do mean *all*. Her speciality's organizing tableaux. I heard the Rites of Venus is one. She'll arrange for half a dozen virgins to lose their cherries in front of an audience. When that's over, the spectators are allowed to join in; so long as they pay, of course."

"Of course," Jago said drily.

"Earned herself a fortune, by all accounts; bragged it'd take a working man a hundred years to earn what she's managed to put away for her rainy day."

"She sounds . . . enterprisin'. And all her girls carry the brand?"

Connie nodded. "A rose. That way, anyone trying to muscle in knows they're already spoken for."

"Any idea where she's set up her stall now?"

"Last I heard, she has a fine townhouse up near Portman Square."

"Nice," Jago said. "That way she gets the majors *and* the marquesses."

Portman Square lay to the west, to the north of Oxford Street, within an area containing some of the largest private houses in London. It was also close to Portman Barracks, one of the many London barracks used in rotation by an assortment of cavalry and infantry regiments, among them the Foot Guards who were responsible for protecting the Royal Family.

"Calls it the Salon. Landed on her feet, did our Ellie."

"As opposed to her back, you mean. Don't like her much, do you?"

Connie made a face. "Don't know her well enough to make that judgement. Can't fault her ambition, though; she came up the hard way – yes, you can smile – saw an opportunity and took it. If I was honest, we're probably a lot alike, though neither of us'd care to admit it."

"Reckon you just did," Jago said. "Well, I ain't sure how much that'll help, but I'll pass it on; give the captain the heads-up."

"Yes, well, when you do, you tell him to tread softly. Our Ellie has influential friends."

"Can't say as that'll stop him askin' awkward questions," Jago said doubtfully.

"No," Connie conceded. "I don't suppose it will."

"Want me to go with you?" Jago asked.

"To a knocking shop?"

"Don't think they call it that. Connie tells me it's a salon."

"It's still a knocking shop," Hawkwood said. "Calling it a salon just means it's got carpets on the floor instead of sawdust."

"You want me to tag along or don't you? Guard your back?"

"It's not my back I'll be worried about. No, I appreciate the offer, but I think I'll cope. How's the shoulder, by the way?"

"Hurts when I laugh." Jago grinned.

They were seated at the window table on the first floor of the Hanged Man. Both men had their backs to the newly replaced glass with the table between them and the room.

"In case we 'as to hide behind it," Jago had quipped when they'd sat down.

Hawkwood doubted lightning would strike twice in the same place in the space of a few days, but as it was Jago's home patch he wasn't going to argue with the former sergeant's logic. There was no sign of Jasper, Del or Ned, but Micah was there, seated at the table at the top of the stairs, and Hawkwood had to admit to himself that the young man's quiet presence was surprisingly reassuring.

"Any more Shaughnessys turn up?" he asked.

Jago took a sip from his mug and shook his head. "They have not. I've put the word out, but nothing's come back. With luck, if there were any hangin' round, they've buggered off back to the bogs. Still keepin' my eyes open, though. Can't be too careful and I did suggest that if Del or any of the others wanted to take a leak, they should piss in pairs just in case."

Jago grinned as he topped up Hawkwood's mug from the bottle by his elbow. "Connie said the Widow knows people and I should warn you to watch your step."

"Don't I always?"

Jago snorted. "You expect me to answer that?"

70

Hawkwood smiled thinly.

"Suit yourself,' Jago said. "But if I were you, I wouldn't go talking to any strange women."

"In case you've forgotten, that's the sole purpose of my visit."

Jago winked and took a sip from his glass.

"By the way," Hawkwood said, "in all that excitement, I forgot to ask: did you and Connie ever buy yourselves that carriage?"

"Carriage?" Jago blinked at the sudden change of subject.

"I'll take that as a no, then. What happened? Before I went away, you were thinking of buying a horse and gig so that you and Connie could ride around Hyde Park and mix with the swells."

"Ah, that." Jago stared at him. "Remind me again; how long is it you've been gone?"

"Three months."

"Well, that explains it."

"You mean there was a change of plan?"

"Not certain there ever was a plan, as such; more like a bloody stupid idea." The former sergeant smiled ruefully. "Be honest, can you see me and Connie swannin' round the park in a carriage?"

"Connie, maybe," Hawkwood said. "Not you."

"I'll tell her you said that, she'll be tickled pink." Jago frowned. "What made you think about Connie and carriages?"

Hawkwood did not reply.

"What, you getting maudlin in your old age?" Jago asked. Then his chin lifted. "Ah, don't tell me; you and Maddie had words? Is that it?" Jago nodded to himself as if everything had suddenly been made clear, then tilted his head enquiringly. "What'd she say when you got back?"

"Not a hell of a lot," Hawkwood said.

Maddie was Maddie Teague, landlady of the Blackbird tavern. Three months before, when Hawkwood had been preparing to leave for France with no expectation of an imminent return, Maddie had asked him if she should keep his room. Her green eyes had transfixed him when she'd posed the question. She'd tried to make light of her enquiry, telling him it had been made in jest, but he'd read the concern in her face and her genuine fear for his safety.

Hawkwood had smiled and told her that she should keep the room, but they'd both known there was no guarantee that he'd make it back. Despite that, there had been no whispered endearments, no lingering embrace. Instead, Maddie had stepped close and tapped his chest with her closed fist before resting her palm across his cheek. She had then asked him how long she should wait for news.

"You'll know," Hawkwood had told her.

"Then don't expect me to cry myself to sleep," she'd retorted, but she had not been able to hide the catch in her voice.

It had been a cold and damp morning when the mail coach deposited Hawkwood at the Saracen's Head in Snow Hill. The 270-mile journey from Falmouth had taken four days. If he'd travelled by regular means it would have taken a week. It was the same route by which the news of Nelson's death at Trafalgar had been conveyed to the Admiralty by Lieutenant Lapenotière, commander of the schooner HMS *Pickle*; or so Hawkwood had been informed by the clerk at the Falmouth coaching office. Lapenotière had supposedly made the journey by post-chaise in thirty-eight hours. Having no urgent dispatches to deliver, Hawkwood had been forced to settle for a slower ride. When he alighted from the un-sprung coach for the last time, it had felt as if his back had been stretched by the Inquisition. He wondered if Lapenotière had suffered from the same discomfort.

The Blackbird lay in a quiet mews off Water Lane, a stone's lob from the Inner Temple. It was a short walk from the Saracen's Head and the route had taken him down through the Fleet Market. It had felt strange, making his way past the shops and stalls, because even at that hour of the day they were crowded and after being surrounded by wide open seas and even wider skies during the crossing from America, the hustle and bustle of London's congested streets, while instantly familiar, had come as something of a shock, as had the smells. After the clean air of New York State's lakes and mountains and the bracing bite of the North Atlantic winds, he'd forgotten how much the city reeked. At the same time, it felt as though he'd never been away.

The Blackbird's door had been open, in readiness for the breakfast trade. Maddie's back had been to him. Her auburn hair tied in place with a blue ribbon, she'd been directing the serving girls as they'd flitted between the tables and the kitchen, taking and delivering orders. Hawkwood had waited until Maddie was alone before he'd enquired from behind with a weary voice if there were any rooms to be had. Maddie had turned to answer, whereupon her breath had caught in her throat and her eyes had widened.

The sound of her palm whipping across his left cheek had been almost as loud as a pistol shot. Breakfast diners within range had looked up and gaped; more than a few had grinned.

Hawkwood hadn't moved as the burning sensation spread across his face.

Maddie Teague had stared up at him, her eyes blazing. Then, as quickly as it had flared, the anger left her and her face had softened.

"You could have written," she said.

"On the bright side," Jago said, chuckling. "She could've been carryin' a bowl of hot broth or a carvin' knife."

"Lucky for me," Hawkwood said.

"You made up, though, right? She didn't stay mad?"

"No," Hawkwood conceded. "She didn't."

"There you go then." There was a pause before Jago added, "She asked if I'd heard from you."

Hawkwood stared at him. "She never mentioned that."

"Sent me a message. I called round; told her I hadn't heard but I'd make enquiries."

"That's when you went to see Magistrate Read."

"It was. He told me that, as far as he knew, you were still alive and that if anything did happen, he'd get word to me."

"And you'd pass the word to Maddie."

Jago nodded.

"She *was* angry," Hawkwood said.

"Women are funny like that," Jago replied sagely. "I told her not to worry; that no news was good news. Can't say she was convinced. Think she was all right for the first month. After that . . ." Jago shrugged and then brightened. "I did put in a bid. Told her if anythin' were to 'appen, and if she had trouble makin' ends meet, I wanted first refusal on your Baker."

"That was gallant. How did she take it?"

"Not well. Told me I'd have to join the bloody queue." Jago's face turned serious. "You do know that, if you hadn't turned up, she'd have waited. There's no one else. There's plenty who'd like to step up but, until she heard otherwise, it'd be you she'd be holdin' out for."

"I told her she'd know if anything had happened," Hawkwood said.

"Reckon we both would," Jago said sombrely, and then he grinned once more. "So I'd still be in the queue for your bloody rifle. I'd raise a glass, too, though, for old time's sake. You can count on that."

"I'm touched," Hawkwood said.

"Aye, well, you'd do the same for me, right?"

"Depends," Hawkwood said.

"On what?"

"On whether you had anything worth leaving."

"Jesus, that's harsh."

"The rifle would have been yours anyway," Hawkwood said. "I'd already left provision."

"Now I'm touched," Jago said. "Mind you, the times I've watched your back, it's the least you could do. And so's you know, if I had bought a horse and carriage, I'd have left you them in my will."

"You would, too, just to be bloody awkward."

Jago grinned. "And then I'd come back to see the look on your face."

Emptying his glass, he placed it on the table and looked up. "So, when you plannin' on visiting the Widow?"

"Soon as I finish my drink."

Jago raised a sceptical eyebrow. "Dutch courage?"

Taking a last swallow, Hawkwood pushed his chair back and got to his feet. "You ever hear of a *black* widow?"

"Don't ring any bells. She a coloured girl?"

"No. It's a type of spider."

"A spider?" Jago said doubtfully.

"After she's mated, she eats the male."

Jago's mouth opened and closed. Dropping his gaze, the former sergeant stared down into his own glass as if something might be concealed within it before lowering it slowly to the table.

He looked up. "Any of them around here?"

Hawkwood smiled grimly. "Could be I'm about to find out."

7

Outwardly, there was nothing to distinguish the house from its neighbours. Not that Hawkwood had been expecting any sort of sign above the door. There might have been only a mile or so separating them but the square was a world away from the stews of Covent Garden and the alleys of Haymarket, where, for a pint of grog and a few pennies, you could negotiate a quick fumble in a doorway with a pox-ridden hag who was as likely to rob a man blind as to roger him senseless. Pennies bought you nothing here. The Salon provided for a far more affluent clientele, which meant there was no requirement for it to advertise. Its word-of-mouth reputation was enough, as was the locale.

Bounded on all quarters by three- and four-storeyed town-houses, the centre of the square had been laid out in the style of a formal garden, patterned with winding pathways, ornamental shrubbery and several tall plane trees, all protected by a palisade of wrought-iron railings that looked newly painted. In the far corner, on the square's north side, could be seen the boundary wall of an imposing brick mansion set back from the street, more evidence that the further west you lived, the more affluent you were likely to be.

Traffic was light. A couple of carriages clattered past, harnesses clinking, followed by a trio of riders dressed in smart dragoon uniforms, while a handful of pedestrians picked their way carefully around the carpet of horse droppings that smeared the road. The smell of fresh dung lingered on the damp afternoon air.

Watching them trying to negotiate passage on to cleaner ground, Hawkwood wondered idly how many of the square's residents were aware of the goings on inside this particular house. Most of them, he suspected. And how many of them had visited the premises? More than might be imagined, he was prepared to wager.

Approaching the black-painted front door, a quick glance at the windows above him revealed the drapes on the upper floors to be fully drawn. It was one indication that he'd come to the right address. In lower-ranked brothels, working girls used the windows to display their wares, leaving little to the imagination in the process. In contrast, the houses at the upper end of the scale masked their entertainments by shielding the view from the street.

Hawkwood pulled on the bell handle and waited. He sensed he was being perused for he'd seen the spyhole in the door. Debating whether or not to wipe his boots against the backs of his breeches, he thought, to hell with it. He'd had the breeches cleaned after his graveyard jaunt and he was damned if he was going to dirty them again that quickly. If whoever was studying him through the woodwork chose not to open the door because of his less than pristine appearance, he could always hammer on it with his tipstaff and yell, "I demand admittance in the name of the law!" It wouldn't be pretty but it would be a very effective means of gaining entry, because the occupants wouldn't want that sort of commotion on their doorstep. It would lower the tone of the neighbourhood.

He was reaching for his tipstaff when his summons was answered.

The manservant, a thickset, competent-looking individual in matching grey jacket and waistcoat, looked Hawkwood up and down, paying close attention to his greatcoat and his boots. When he glanced over Hawkwood's shoulder towards the street, Hawkwood wondered if he was searching for the carriage that had dropped him off.

"I walked," Hawkwood said, "all the way from Bow Street. I'm here to see the lady of the house, and don't bother asking if I have an appointment."

Because I've had enough of that.

At the mention of Bow Street, the manservant's gaze flickered. The raised eyebrow that had been there when he'd opened the door was replaced by a new wariness.

Hawkwood sighed and took the tipstaff from his coat. "That would be sooner, rather than later."

The manservant's jaw flexed. "Name?" he enquired, stepping aside to allow Hawkwood entry.

Hawkwood resisted the urge to wipe the supercilious expression from the manservant's face, gave his name and fixed the man with a look. "Yours?"

The manservant hesitated and then squared his shoulders. "Flagg." Adding, somewhat reluctantly, "Thomas."

Through what sounded like teeth being gritted, the manservant instructed Hawkwood to wait. Then, turning, he strode across the hall to a closed door, knocked and entered the room beyond, leaving Hawkwood to mull over a noticeable bulge in the back of the manservant's jacket. A small cudgel stuck handily in the waistband, Hawkwood guessed; definitely not a pistol, which would have been harder to conceal.

Ellie Pearce – or Lady Eleanor, as she was choosing to call herself these days – clearly took the matter of personal security very seriously. Hardly surprising; most establishments of this sort – regardless of their status – employed protection in one form or another, some more covertly than others. Even girls working the street tended to have a pimp hovering nearby, though their presence had more to do with ensuring the safety of their investment than guaranteeing the girls' welfare.

The manservant's absence provided an opportunity to take in the interior of the house, which was as tasteful as the exterior had suggested it might be.

Given the greyness of the day, the lobby should have been cast in a sepulchral gloom, but by the strategic use of candles set in mirrored alcoves, the entrance hall was cast in a warm and welcoming glow. It was a far cry from the cheaper East End houses, which were apt to equal Smithfield on market day for both noise and activity. The main cause for the rowdiness was alcohol. In the rougher parts of the city, the only businesses that outnumbered the brothels were the gin shops.

Such was the ambience created here that a casual entrant could well have missed the more intimate items of décor that suggested the Salon might be something other than a comfortable family residence. These were in the form of porcelain statuettes set in niches around the walls depicting nude male and female figures entwined in a variety of sexual acts. The theme continued up the main staircase, which rose in a graceful sweep towards the first-floor landing, with each tread accompanied by a rising gallery of pencil-drawn images that were so graphic they made the cavorting figurines on the ground floor look positively chaste.

Somewhere above him, a door opened and closed softly, while from the ground floor, behind a door adjacent to the one through which the manservant had disappeared, there came the sound of a pianoforte, accompanied by a short and equally melodic burst of female laughter.

As if the laughter had been a signal, the door across the hallway opened and the manservant reappeared. He looked no happier than he had before as he caught Hawkwood's eye, signalling that despite his own reservations and the state of the visitor's wardrobe, the man from Bow Street had been granted an audience.

"Not your day, is it, Thomas?" Hawkwood murmured as he pushed past and entered the room. He didn't wait for a reaction but felt the manservant's eyes burning into the back of his neck as the door closed behind him.

By their ages, the two women could have been taken for mother and daughter, though it was the older one who was closest to the description given by Connie Fletcher. Connie had intimated that she and the Salon's proprietress were around the same age. Connie, Hawkwood knew, was still on the good side of forty, though only by a year or two. What struck Hawkwood, as the former Ellie Pearce turned to greet his entrance, was that it wouldn't have mattered whether she'd been a park-walker touting her wares behind the wall in the Privy Gardens or a costermonger's wife; like Connie, she would still have turned heads. The thought occurred that maybe he should have cleaned his boots, after all.

It was her eyes as much as her profile and her smooth, near-porcelain skin that drew the attention. Deep indigo, framed by prominent cheekbones and what looked to be shoulder-length black hair drawn up and secured at the nape of her neck by a silver clasp, they regarded Hawkwood in frank appraisal, suggesting she was not best pleased by having her afternoon interrupted at the behest of an unknown and, more germanely, uninvited public servant.

In contrast, her younger companion, who was also slender but with blonde ringlets and clearly less reserve, greeted Hawkwood's entrance with an openly suggestive grin.

"Officer . . . Hawkwood, was it? You must forgive Thomas his manners. He tends to be over protective when it comes to gentlemen visitors he does not know. Even now, I suspect he is listening without, ready to spring to my aid."

There was not the slightest trace of Half Moon Alley in her voice. The refined, almost seductive tones could have belonged to any London society hostess.

"Thank you. I'll bear that in mind."

Surprised by Hawkwood's dry riposte, Eleanor Rain frowned, while the younger woman clapped her hands and beamed as if she had just been gifted with a new puppy. "Oh, I like the look of this one. Can we keep him?"

The older woman held Hawkwood's gaze for several seconds before turning and addressing her more forward companion. "Thank you, Charlotte. You may leave us."

Pouting prettily but without protest, the young woman made for the door, taking time to mime Hawkwood a kiss as she wafted past, while allowing her thigh to brush the back of his left hand and the faint scent of jasmine to linger enticingly in her wake.

Eleanor Rain waited for the door to close before moving to a low, loose-cushioned sofa against which rested a small table, upon which was a tray bearing a China-blue tea service. Taking her seat, she brushed an imaginary speck of lint from her sleeve and regarded Hawkwood with cool detachment.

"How curious; I'm trying to recall the last time a representative of the constabulary came to call, but I declare it's quite slipped my mind. Though, of course, members of the judiciary are always dropping by."

The emphasis placed on the word "members" had been deliberate. It was her way of telling him that she regarded his visit as no more than a distraction and that, as a person of little consequence who could not possibly understand innuendo, his presence would be tolerated only for as long as it took him to state his business.

Hawkwood nodded. "After a hard day on the bench, no doubt."

In the ensuing pause, the ticking from the clock on the mantelpiece sounded unnaturally loud.

Until that moment, Hawkwood had been having difficulty equating the woman seated before him with the Ellie Pearce who'd earned her living servicing a parade of men in the back room of a Smithfield public house, but as her expression changed in the face of his rejoinder he saw caution in her eyes and a growing realization that it was not just her own appearance that might be proving deceptive.

Her swift recovery also told him that this was a woman who was unashamedly aware of the effect her looks had on the opposite sex. If she'd been in the trade for as long as Connie had hinted, the half-smile she now offered in acknowledgement of his response would be as much a part of her repertoire as the way she held herself and her penetrating and provocative gaze.

Similarly, the dress she wore, while appearing simple in cut, served to add to her allure. Cream, with an ivory sheen and inset with fine blue stripes that matched the colour of her eyes, the high waist and hint of décolletage artfully accentuated her shape, with the clear intention of making life a little more interesting for aficionados of the female form.

Her choice of jewellery was as understated as her attire. A blue gemstone the size of a wren's egg hung from a silver chain about her neck, the jewel resting above the gentle swell of her breasts. She wore a ring set with a smaller, similar-coloured stone on the third finger of her right hand, while her left wrist was encircled by a delicate bracelet, also made of silver to match the clasp in her hair and the fine linkage at her throat.

Leaning forward, she reached for the teapot, the motion deepening the shadow at her neckline, as she had known it would.

Hawkwood recognized it as part of a strategy designed to remind her visitor of his true place. Seated, she was Lady Eleanor Rain, granting him an audience. Standing, he remained the underling, the minion who, even though he was an officer of the law, meant there was not the slightest chance he would be invited to take tea. Tea was expensive – the caddy would be hidden away under lock and key – and the idea that she would consider sharing such a valuable commodity with someone she saw as being beneath her station was unthinkable.

He watched as, with precise, almost sensual deliberation, she proceeded to pour herself a cup, using a strainer to catch the leaves. When the cup was three-quarters full, she laid the strainer to one side. Adding neither milk nor sugar, she lifted both cup and saucer from the tray and cradled them in her lap.

Raising the cup to her lips, she took a small sip. Returning it to the saucer with exaggerated finesse, she straightened and regarded him expectantly. "Perhaps you should explain why you are here?"

Hawkwood, tiring of the game, decided to dispense with the niceties.

"I'm here to enquire if any of your girls are missing."

It was not what she'd been expecting. Taken aback by the bluntness of Hawkwood's response, she stared up at him. "Missing? I'm afraid I don't understand."

"A body's been found."

"A body?"

"A young woman."

"I see. Well, that *is* distressing, but what makes you think she might be associated with my salon?"

"She had a rose tattoo on her upper arm. I'm told you're familiar with such a mark."

She stared at him without speaking.

Hawkwood matched her gaze. "Or have I been misinformed?"

He watched the indecision steal across her face, quickly replaced by a more guarded look, which did not make her any less attractive. Two more seconds passed. Then, lifting a hand from the saucer, she made a dismissive gesture. "An affectation; nothing more. A mark of quality, if you will."

"Like Mr Twining's tea?"

She blanched. Then, collecting herself once more, she looked up. "Do you have a description of this unfortunate young woman?"

"Petite, brown hair, blue eyes and young, as I said. We believe she was in her early twenties."

Even as he uttered the words, Hawkwood knew the description was a poor one as it probably covered half the molls in London; a fact mirrored by Eleanor Rain's less than engaged expression.

"And how did she die?"

"Painfully. Beaten and throttled, then tied in a sack."

No point in mentioning the mutilation. It was always best to hold something back.

For the first time a look of genuine shock distorted her features. "Murdered," she said softly.

"I doubt it was suicide."

She coloured. "No, of course not. Forgive me, it's . . ."

Returning the cup and saucer to the tray and placing her hands together on her lap, in a more composed voice, she said, "My apologies. It is difficult to gather one's thoughts after being told of such a thing." She drew herself up. "I can assure you, however, that *all* my ladies are accounted for."

83

Hawkwood nodded. "I'm relieved to hear it. Though ladies do come and go, do they not?"

She frowned, as if the idea had not occurred to her. "They do, but surely I cannot be expected to account for the whereabouts of those who might have chosen to leave my employ."

"That's true. So has anyone flown the nest recently?"

"They have not."

The answer came sharply but then she took another breath and in a considered tone said, "May one enquire when the killing took place?"

"We believe death occurred a day ago; perhaps two."

"Where?"

"That we don't yet know. I can tell you where she was found: in a grave, in St George the Martyr's burying ground."

"A grave?" she said, puzzled. "Then how . . .?"

"An open grave."

Hawkwood watched her as the image ran through her mind. "And she has lain there unseen until now?"

"Yes."

"All that time? How terrible."

"Murder usually is," Hawkwood said.

Her chin lifted. Then, fixing him with a conciliatory look, she said, "And it is your task to discover who was responsible?"

"It is."

She nodded. "Could the perpetrator strike again?"

"It's possible, yes."

"So until you find him, we are all of us at risk."

"I can't say you won't be. We don't yet know his motive."

"You're saying she could have been killed for who she was, rather than for what you think she was?"

"Yes."

"And a rose is not an uncommon adornment. She could just as easily be a washerwoman as a whore."

"She could."

Her eyes clouded. In that instant Hawkwood caught his second glimpse of the woman behind the mask; a woman who, by force of will, had managed to haul herself out of the gutter and into

84

the privileged ranks of society, all the while knowing and resenting the fact that there were elements of her previous life still buried deep within her that she would never be able to erase.

There was fear there, too, he suspected; fear that, one day, someone would confront her and remind her of her former existence. It was the most vulnerable chink in her armour and she was wondering if this was the moment that weakness was about to be exploited. The sudden flare in her eyes was a warning sign that she would defend her reputation to the hilt if she felt it was about to be challenged.

"Which is why we need to confirm her identity," Hawkwood said, and watched as the fire died away.

"Because, whatever their reasoning, the sooner you find the person who killed her, the safer we all will be?"

"Yes."

"Then I am sorry I've kept you from your task and that your journey here has been wasted."

"Not at all. All enquiries are useful."

Acknowledging Hawkwood's response with a small – possibly appreciative – nod, she said, "I will, of course, enquire of my ladies if they have heard of or know of anything that could assist your investigation."

"That would be most helpful. Thank you."

"It is the least I can do." She paused again and said, "And if I should come into possession of information which might be relevant, how may I notify you?"

"Through Bow Street Magistrate's Court."

"Yes, of course."

As if in need of some activity to fill the subsequent pause in the conversation, she retrieved her cup and took an exploratory sip. Finding the brew had grown cold, she wrinkled her nose and returned both cup and saucer to the tray, leaving a faint smear of pink lip salve along the cup's rim.

Hawkwood judged this the opportune moment to take his leave, but as he turned to go she said suddenly, "When Thomas announced you were from the Public Office, I confess, you are not what I was expecting. I apologize if my manner was less than courteous. You are a Principal Officer . . . what they call a Runner, yes?"

Hawkwood wondered where this was going. "We prefer the former, but yes."

She permitted herself a smile. "Duly noted. It has been my experience that most Public Office employees look incapable of breaking into a brisk walk, let alone a run, whereas you look, if I may say so, rather more . . . capable. You have the air of a military man. Would I be right in thinking you have fought in the service of the king?"

"I was in the army."

"I thought as much. I made a small wager with myself when I saw the scars on your face and the cut of your coat. It is military-issue, is it not?"

"It is."

"You look surprised. Did you think I was uninformed about such matters? If I were to name every colonel who sought sanctuary within these walls, we would be here until Easter. I believe I could also name not only every regiment in the British Army, but every fourth-rater in his majesty's navy, given the number of admirals that have raised their flags in my establishment. Not to mention magistrates, ambassadors, assorted aristocrats, clergymen and all but two of Lord Liverpool's cabinet. You were an officer, yes?"

Hawkwood didn't get a chance to respond.

The smile remained in place. "In this profession, if you learn one thing, it is how to read men. Your attire betrays you. Your outer wear may have seen better days, but your boots are of good quality, as are your jacket and your waistcoat, from what I can see of them. It is also in the way you carry yourself."

The blue eyes narrowed. "You would not have moved from colonel to constable – my apologies, to Principal Officer. That would be too far a step down, I think. Too old for a lieutenant, so you were either a captain or a major."

Tilting her head, she went on: "You look like a man who is used to command and yet you have little respect for authority. I suspect you came up through the ranks and proved yourself in some engagement, therefore I choose the former. You were a captain. Am I right?"

"And there was I, thinking I hadn't made a good impression," Hawkwood said.

The frown returned. "Yes, well, in that you are not wrong. Your manners could certainly use improvement. An officer you may have been, but you display the attitude of a ruffian. Has anyone ever told you that?"

"Once or twice."

"Or perhaps it is a deliberate strategy, like the employment of sarcasm," she countered tartly.

"It comes in useful when I don't have a pistol to hand."

Unexpectedly, the corner of her mouth dimpled once more and her gaze moved towards the clock on the mantelpiece. Turning back, she said, "Yes, well, unfortunately, much as I've enjoyed our conversation, I see time is against us. I have an evening's entertainment to arrange, so you must forgive me." She gazed at him beguilingly. "Unless there is anything else you wish to ask?"

"Not at this time. I may need to call on you again at some date."

She inclined her head. "Of course."

Hawkwood was about to turn for the door, when she said quietly, "I think, perhaps, I should like that. Despite your questionable manner and the reason for your visit with all this talk of graveyards and murder, you have enlivened what would otherwise have been an exceedingly dull afternoon."

Her eyes held his. "I have the distinct feeling that there is more to you, *Captain* Hawkwood, than meets the eye. I suspect that, were I to scratch the surface, I would unearth all manner of interesting truths. Why is that, do you suppose?"

"I have no idea," Hawkwood said, "though, curiously, I was thinking exactly the same thing about you."

She continued to regard him coolly for several seconds. "Then, perhaps, if your investigation allows, you might consider visiting in a more . . . private capacity?"

"On my salary? I doubt it."

"Then you do yourself a disservice. Attendance is not solely dependent on the depth of one's purse. If you were to attend, it would be at my invitation."

She let the inference hang in the air between them.

"I wouldn't want to lower the tone," Hawkwood said.

She smiled, more warmly. "Oh, I think you'll find we cater for most persuasions. Who knows? You might even see something you like. And as I mentioned earlier, you would be in excellent company. Our evening soirées are extremely popular."

"I'm sure they are."

Raising her hand, she caressed the jewel at her throat. "Well, then, *will* we see you again?"

"Perhaps."

"Perhaps? That sounds like a man contemplating retreat. I do hope we haven't frightened you away."

"I'd prefer to call it a strategic withdrawal."

She bit back a smile. "In order to advance again at a more opportune moment?"

Before he could reply, she rose sinuously. "If that is your intention, I should probably summon reinforcements. Before I do, though, let me give you this."

From the white marble mantelpiece she took a small silver box. Opening it, she removed what looked like a deck of playing cards. Selecting a card, she held it out. "Should you decide to call."

There was no script. One side of the card was plain and coloured black. When Hawkwood turned it over he saw that the face side was embossed with the image of a red rose on a white background.

She picked up a small hand-bell from the table. At the first ring, the door opened. Flagg stood there, poised and looking not a little disconcerted to find that Hawkwood was still standing and in one piece.

"Madam?"

"Thomas, if you would be so kind as to show the officer out. We have concluded our business. Oh, and treat him kindly, otherwise we might not see him again. And that, I think, would be rather a pity."

Ignoring the manservant's baleful look, she inclined her head. "Until next time."

Hawkwood slid the card into his waistcoat pocket, by which time she was already turning away. As dismissals went, it was hard to fault.

"Ever wear a uniform, Thomas?" Hawkwood asked, as the manservant walked him through the lobby to the front door.

The reply was a borderline grunt. "East Norfolk, First Battalion."

Hawkwood nodded. "Thought as much; seems there's a lot of it about."

The manservant frowned but did not respond. He remained silent as he let Hawkwood out.

A light drizzle had begun to fall. As the door closed behind him, Hawkwood turned up his collar and walked away into the rain.

Wondering what Eleanor Rain had been hiding.

8

"This one's new," Maddie murmured softly, running her fingers along the line of puckered flesh. "Or is it because you have so many now, I'm losing count?"

The furrow followed the curve of Hawkwood's left bicep, as if a spindly grub had burrowed beneath the skin. A musket ball had grazed him as he was leading a Mohawk raiding party against an American advance column which was attempting to seize a British-controlled blockhouse on the Lacolle River, five miles north of the Canadian border. It had been a foolhardy enterprise from the outset, though the mission had been deemed a success because it had delayed the column long enough to allow British forces to launch a counter-attack. Victory, however, had come at a heavy price. All but three of Hawkwood's war band had died and the survivors – Hawkwood, Major Douglas Lawrence and the Mohawk war chief Tewanias – had all received wounds.

Almost two months had passed since the engagement. The injuries – including the cut on his forehead and the bayonet graze on his thigh – had healed well, a process aided by native poultices and the attention of the surgeon on board the Royal Navy frigate that had transported Hawkwood from Quebec to Falmouth. Other than fresh scar tissue and the odd twinge from the damaged arm muscle, everything was back in working order, save for when Maddie went exploring and memories were reawakened.

"And this one?" She frowned and touched the uneven ridge at the edge of his hairline.

"My fault, I should have moved quicker. Not getting any younger."

"Few of us are, but you're not old."

"Old enough."

"And soldiering for what, twenty years?"

"So?"

"So, that long, I'd be surprised if you didn't have scars. It means you were a good soldier, always in the thick of it."

"Who was slow to duck."

"Could have been worse," Maddie said lightly, resting her hand on his thigh.

"How so?"

"There are no wounds on your arse."

The words took a second to sink in. Bemused, Hawkwood stared at her.

Maddie grinned. "Proves you weren't a coward and that no one shot you while you were running away."

"Or that they were bad shots."

"Maybe you're quicker on your feet than you thought you were."

"So, not that old after all."

"There you go."

"That's it? No wounds on my arse so I must be doing something right? I should have that on my gravestone."

"So long as you leave Nathaniel your rifle," Maddie said.

"He mentioned that, did he?"

"Once or twice."

Maddie chuckled and then her face grew serious. "He was concerned about you. Not that he'd admit it, mind. Said that, without him, you were bound to get into all sorts of scrapes."

"Scrapes? He said that?"

"He might have said 'bleedin' scrapes'."

"He worries too much," Hawkwood said. "That's his trouble."

"You were gone three months. He didn't know if he'd see you again. Neither did I," she added a second later.

The faint catch in Maddie's voice caused Hawkwood to look at her. When he did so, she turned her head away. "Think you can disappear for that long and then just waltz back in as though nothing had happened?"

When no immediate reply was forthcoming, she turned back. "What?"

Hawkwood tried not to smile. "Nathaniel said the same thing. If I didn't know any better, I'd say the two of you were in league."

"Well, pardon us for caring," Maddie countered hotly, raising herself on to one elbow, making no attempt to cover herself.

"I'm here now, aren't I?" Hawkwood said in protest.

"But for how long?"

"Well, they can't march me off to war any more. I'm done with soldiering."

As he spoke, Hawkwood's eyes moved to the campaign chest at the foot of the bed. It contained items from his old uniform along with the accoutrements acquired during his years in the field, including his sword and the Baker rifle, wrapped in canvas, laid diagonally across the top.

Maddie moved in his arms. "You know fine well what I mean. You might not wear a tunic, but you're still fighting the king's enemies. That's how you ended up with these." Maddie jabbed a finger at a ribbon of scar tissue. "And don't say you don't enjoy it."

"Getting shot?"

"The danger."

"You make it sound as if I seek it out."

"No?"

"No, usually, it creeps up on you unexpectedly."

Forming a fist, Maddie pouted and aimed a playful blow at his chest. "Now you're mocking me."

"A little, but it's the only life I know. I wouldn't be much use doing anything else. You use what you have."

"And you're good at what you do."

"So far."

"So I should content myself with that?" Maddie said.

"That's not something I can answer."

The response was met with a raised eyebrow.

"You're your own woman, Maddie Teague; always have been. It'd take a brave man to tell you how you should think. Braver than me, that's for sure."

"You're only saying that because you're bare-arsed naked," Maddie said. "You're at my mercy."

"There is that."

Maddie went quiet, then said, "I think you're telling me that there's no knowing what might happen in the future and that we should make the most of the time we do have."

"I believe I am," Hawkwood said.

Maddie smiled. "In that case," she murmured as she lowered herself on to him, "it'd be a shame to waste it."

Hawkwood sipped coffee and watched as the Blackbird came to life.

A couple of lanes away from the Inner Temple, over the years the tavern had become a favoured haunt for members of the bar. All but two of the booths were occupied. Tobacco smoke and the hum of conversation filled the room, interspersed with the rattle of plates as the staff took orders and cleared tables. Watching the diners always reminded Hawkwood of a flock of starlings descending upon a lawn: a lot of chatter upon arrival, gradually replaced by a low, genial hubbub as soon as the food appeared.

"Top you up?"

Lily, one of Maddie's waiting girls, hovered, coffee pot in hand.

Hawkwood held out his cup.

The Public Office didn't open until ten o'clock. A few minutes more at breakfast wouldn't make any difference and it gave him another chance to mull over the progress he'd made with the murder investigation, which, as far as he could determine, amounted to not a hell of a lot. With no names to go on, he was wondering what to do next when a shadow fell across his arm.

"Give us a chance, Lily. I haven't drained the last one yet."

"Sorry, Captain, it's not that. There's someone outside, says they've a message for you." The serving girl jutted her chin to a point over Hawkwood's shoulder. He turned and looked to where a small, stick-thin figure in a coat several sizes too large was sheltering in the doorway.

"I think we're safe," Hawkwood said, and watched as Lily nodded to the figure by the door who, having been given permission to enter, approached Hawkwood's table, drawing more than a few curious stares along the way. Only as the figure drew closer were the features of a young girl finally revealed. Even so, it took a couple of seconds for identification to seep in, as it had been a while since Hawkwood had last seen her.

"Hello, Jen. Got something for me?"

The girl looked around nervously and then nodded as though she couldn't wait to be gone. "Message from Nathaniel; sez you and him should meet."

"He give a time?"

The girl sniffed, then said, "'E said you was to pull yer finger out."

"Did he? Well, that's clear enough."

Hawkwood was about to ask where Jago wanted to meet when a disapproving grunt sounded from the adjacent booth, where two dark-dressed advocates were hunched over their breakfast table. The grunt was followed by a murmured aside that was clearly meant to be heard by those occupying tables in the immediate vicinity.

"Best guard your pocket watch, Arthur; seems the Widow Teague's letting anyone in these days."

Conversation dropped away. Several diners paused in their meal and looked up. They soon bowed their heads again when Hawkwood started to rise from his seat. He was stayed by a hand alighting firmly on his shoulder.

"Finish your breakfast," Maddie instructed. Turning to the girl, who appeared not to have heard the comment, she nodded at the bench opposite where Hawkwood was simmering. "You, sit."

It was a tone Hawkwood had heard before. Lowering himself

back down, he threw the girl a warning glance. "Best do as she says."

Hesitantly, the girl sat and Hawkwood watched as Maddie moved in for the kill.

The advocate who'd spoken, a thin-faced, sallow-complexioned individual, was on the point of slicing into his bacon when he found Maddie looking down upon him.

"A word, gentlemen," Maddie said.

"Of course, Mrs Teague." The advocate smiled patronizingly, his knife and fork raised. "What can we do for you, dear lady?"

"Leave," Maddie said.

The advocate blinked. "I'm sorry?"

"That was the word. It was a simple request," Maddie said. "Please leave."

The advocate threw a startled glance towards his companion, a dumpier, florid-faced man, who looked equally nonplussed. "Why on earth—"

"Because you've insulted one of my customers."

"What? I can assure you, madam, I did no such thing. Which customer? Name them."

The man gaped in astonishment as Maddie stood aside and indicated Jen. Seated at Hawkwood's table and still swathed in her coat, the girl was staring about her like a slightly dazed rabbit.

"Good God, you mean the urchin?"

"In my tavern, she's a customer. So you two will do me the courtesy of vacating the premises. There'll be no charge for the victuals."

"You can't do that!" the advocate protested.

Maddie placed her hands on her hips. "My tavern, gentlemen; my rules."

The advocate bristled. "But this is outrageous!" He looked to his companion. "Arthur?"

Arthur wasn't listening. Painfully aware that there appeared to be no support forthcoming from any of the other diners, he was looking nervously at Hawkwood, who had not moved and who was sitting perfectly still, staring at him over the rim of a coffee mug.

Arthur dabbed his lips with his napkin. "We should go, Mortimer. If you recall, we do have that brief to prepare."

"Brief? What brief?" The advocate stared at his companion in confusion, then turned to see what had ensnared Arthur's attention. When he saw Hawkwood gazing calmly back at him, he paled.

"Ah, yes." He swallowed nervously. "I'd completely forgotten. We wouldn't want to be late, now, would we? No, indeed." The advocate put down his cutlery and scrabbled for his gloves; to his consternation, they had slipped beneath his seat and on to the floor. Emerging slightly crumpled from his exertions in retrieving them, he reached for his hat and coat, which were hanging from a hook on the wall of the booth.

Maddie stood to one side as the two men gained their feet. With a final nervous glance in Hawkwood's direction, they hastened towards the door. Maddie watched them go. As the door closed behind them and the surrounding conversation began to increase in volume, she picked up the first advocate's abandoned breakfast. Purloining a clean knife, fork and spoon from a nearby tray, she carried the plate to Hawkwood's table and placed it down before an astonished Jen.

"Eat up while it's still hot. And you," she said to Hawkwood, "can wipe that look off your face."

Before Hawkwood had a chance to reply, she turned, collected the second uneaten breakfast and stalked off to the kitchen.

Hawkwood watched her go before turning to the girl. "You heard her. You've seen what she's like when she's riled."

The girl looked dumbly at the offering as if expecting the food to disappear at any second. When that didn't happen, she needed no second bidding. Ignoring the fork, she made a grab for the knife and spoon.

Hawkwood wondered when she'd last eaten. Children who lived on the street were forced to fend for themselves. Most led a near-feral existence, living in packs because that was the safest option. The pack offered protection against predators. But, like all packs, there was a strict hierarchy. The pack leaders took the pick of the spoils, leaving the lower-ranked members to fight over the scraps. The weakest – the runts of the litter – rarely survived.

Hawkwood wasn't sure of Jen's standing within her pack. He knew her courier work for Jago offered her a degree of protection, but it wasn't what could be termed a full-time career. Most days she'd be reliant on her wits, with no guarantee of a roof over her head or food in her belly. He suspected there would have been times when Jen had been forced to sell herself in order to survive, so a stranger offering sustenance might be greeted with suspicion. Hawkwood, however, was not a stranger. That was why Jago used her as a messenger whenever he wanted to arrange a rendezvous; he knew the child felt safe in Hawkwood's company. When he invited her to eat, she needed no second bidding.

"Take your time," Hawkwood told her, knowing he'd be ignored. "There's no rush."

He watched as the eggs, bacon and devilled kidneys disappeared. At no point did she unbutton her coat or even look up. All her concentration was on the contents of the plate in front of her. When she finished off the last morsel of kidney, having barely paused to take a breath, Hawkwood passed her a hunk of bread from his own serving and watched, fascinated, as she wiped it around her plate with the artistry of a portrait painter practising her brushstrokes, mopping up the egg yolk and the last of the bacon grease with slow relish. When the plate had been scraped clean, she licked her fingers and wiped her mouth with her sleeve.

"Better?" Hawkwood asked.

He was rewarded with a brusque nod. It was likely to be the only thanks he would receive, but where Jen was concerned, that was as good as a reward.

"I trust everything was to the lady's satisfaction?"

Maddie, a cloth over one arm and a pot of hot chocolate in her other hand, eyed the empty plate with approval and cocked an eye at Hawkwood's dining companion.

Jen gazed up at her, then turned to Hawkwood for guidance. When Hawkwood fixed her with another warning look, the girl offered a tight-lipped inclination of the head.

"I'll take that as a 'yes'," Maddie said, though there was humour not rancour in her tone. To Hawkwood, she said, "Is there any more excitement on the way, or was that it?"

"Reckon that's our cue, Jen," Hawkwood said.

They were halfway to the door when Hawkwood heard Maddie call softly from behind them. "Haven't we forgotten something?"

Hawkwood looked over his shoulder to find Maddie, hip cocked, holding out her hand with an I-am-not-to-be trifled-with expression on her face.

Sighing, Hawkwood looked down at the girl. "Whatever it is, hand it over."

Sheepishly, the girl reached into the pocket of her coat, took out the used knife and spoon and dropped them into Maddie's open palm.

Maddie fixed Hawkwood with a stern gaze. Jen looked up at Hawkwood and grinned.

"Out," Hawkwood said.

Leaving Maddie staring after them, Hawkwood and the girl exited on to the street, at which point it dawned on Hawkwood that he hadn't asked where Jago wanted to meet.

"Connie's," Jen said brightly.

"Connie's? You sure?"

"That's what he said. Told me to tell you . . ."

"To get my finger out, yes I remember."

Hawkwood reached into his pocket for a coin.

Why Connie's? he wondered. Handing the coin to Jen, he watched as she scurried off without a backward glance, coat-tails flapping. It wasn't until she reached the corner that she stopped suddenly and glanced back. To Hawkwood's surprise, she grinned and raised her hand. Offering a wave, Hawkwood thought, until he saw the napkin and salt cellar she was brandishing, at which point she turned tail, ducked into an alleyway and disappeared from sight.

Hawkwood shook his head in wonderment, conscious that he and Maddie had been played like two fish on the same hook. Reminding himself to have words with Jago about his choice of messenger, he headed off towards the appointed rendezvous.

It occurred to him as he walked that the meeting venue might be some sort of omen. Either way, it was a classic example of happenstance: it had been years since he'd seen the inside of a bloody knocking shop, and now here he was, visiting two of them in as many days.

But wasn't that always the way?

"Looks like the bitch *was* lying," Jago growled. He turned to the young woman seated at Connie Fletcher's side. "Tell the cap'n what you told Connie."

They were in Connie Fletcher's drawing room. Connie's establishment lay just off Cavendish Square and, like Eleanor Rain, she maintained her own ground-floor apartment; the rest of the house, including the upper floors, being reserved for entertaining.

The young woman had been introduced to Hawkwood as Theresa. Before she could answer, Connie laid a protective hand on her arm. "Reason we're here is that last night there was a masquerade at Thorne House."

"Thorne House?" Hawkwood said, trying not to let his ignorance show.

"London home of Sir Atticus Thorne. Made his money through trade; exports wool and tin, imports spices, carpets and silks. He's a friend of Lord Camden, among others."

"That's Camden as in the old Secretary of State for War," Jago cut in. "An' don't look at me like that. I know some things."

"Good for you," Hawkwood said. "So?"

"So," Connie said patiently, "it was your friend Lady Eleanor who oversaw the festivities."

"I have an evening's entertainment to arrange."

"Thought that'd perk you up," Jago said, and winked.

Hawkwood stole a quick glance towards the girl, but before he had a chance to speak, Connie said quickly, "No, Theresa wasn't part of that; none of my girls were, although these sorts of events, it's not just the one house that's asked to provide diversions. If they want the best, they'll use the Widow or me or Aubrey's or Porter's over in Soho.

"Didn't happen this time, though. Theresa went as a companion.

Even if I'm not asked to provide the entertainment, chances are some of my girls will attend anyway. Evenings like these, there are always gentlemen who prefer to go with company already on their arm. If one of my regulars wants to invite his favourite girl along, I'm happy to oblige – so long as she doesn't object."

It was obvious why men would want Theresa on their arm. Her olive complexion and thick dark hair hinted at a Mediterranean heritage; Italian, or Spanish, Hawkwood guessed, for he'd seen women with the same striking features during his time in the Peninsula. The name Theresa suggested the same, as did the spark in her dark expressive eyes, which alerted any prospective beau that beneath the sultry exterior there probably lurked a passion that could turn from tender to incendiary at the snap of a finger.

He realized his study of her had not gone unnoticed. She was gazing at him with a half-smile on her face which made him wonder if he'd made the mistake of voicing his thoughts out loud. There was a smile on Connie's face, too, he saw. Jago was shaking his head; whether in despair or wonder, it wasn't easy to tell.

"So, what did you want to tell me?" Hawkwood asked, avoiding Jago's eye.

Given her looks, Hawkwood had been expecting Theresa to have an accent, and in that he wasn't disappointed, though to his surprise it turned out to be more Camberwell than Cordoba. It transpired that she had attended the revels as the companion of the son of Lord Scarsbury, a distant cousin to George Canning. Hawkwood racked his brain for that name and recalled that Canning had once held the post of Secretary of State for Foreign Affairs.

"An' you wonder why the likes of thee and me never get an invite," Jago muttered, then turned apologetically to Theresa. "Sorry, you were sayin'?"

The girl cast a nervous glance at Connie, who told her, "It's all right, go on."

Theresa faced Hawkwood. "It was when Harry – my gentleman – went to the privy; we'd been enjoying ourselves with his friend

Sir Edward Carfax and Eddie's belle for the evening. Eddie went off with Harry and she and I got to talking. She's one of Lady Eleanor's girls, Annie. I know her on account of we've met at other masquerades around town. It helps if there's a friendly face about, especially if you don't know the swell who's giving the party." She threw a quick glance at Connie as if worried she might be revealing too much about Connie's business practices.

"Don't worry," Connie smiled, "you can trust him."

Accepting Connie's reassurance, Theresa continued: "Anyway, Annie was saying there's one of Lady Eleanor's girls who hasn't been seen for a while. Normally, she wouldn't have worried, but there was an officer from Bow Street who paid a call on Lady Eleanor, wanting to know if she were missing anyone because a body had been found."

Hawkwood felt a faint flutter in his chest. "Did she mention the name of the girl – the one who's missing?"

"They call her Lucinda, but it's really Lucy. Lady Eleanor likes her ladies to have grand names."

Jago let go a snort.

"Did your friend say when Lucy went missing?" Hawkwood asked.

"Been four days, she said."

"And there's been no word from her?"

"She says not."

Hawkwood looked to Connie. "Would that be unusual?"

Connie made a face. "Depends; it's not unusual for a gentleman to take a girl to the country for the weekend."

"So it could be that Lady Eleanor arranged for the girl to spend the time away and she wasn't expecting an imminent return, in which case she wouldn't consider her to be missing."

But Theresa shook her head. "That's not how it was. Annie said that Lucy expected to be back the next day."

"So, Madam did speak false," Jago said.

"Maybe; or maybe Lucinda's gentleman friend wanted to enjoy her company a while longer and arranged for her to stay on. I should talk to your friend," Hawkwood said, addressing Theresa. "Annie, was it?"

Which didn't sound that sophisticated, Hawkwood thought. "She wouldn't have a working name, too, by any chance?"

Theresa nodded. "Annette."

Hawkwood thought about Eleanor Rain's promise that she would ask her girls if they'd heard anything. From Theresa's evidence, it didn't sound as though that had happened, so someone else must have spread the message. It was unlikely to have been Flagg, which left the impish Charlotte, who must have hung around outside the door, listening in. She had then passed the word to Annette.

"Annie said she asked Lady Eleanor about Lucy and was told not to worry," Theresa cut in. "She was told Lucy would be gone a little while longer."

"Could be true," Jago said. He sat back. "So, you going to have another word with Madam?"

"I'd be better off talking with this Annie: someone who's concerned Lucy hasn't returned to the fold. If I go for the Widow and she did lie the first time, what's to stop her doing it again?"

"Right, but if you go marching round there asking to speak with Annie, or Annette, or whatever her name is, Madam'll suspect something's up."

"I should still talk to the girl."

It was doubtful that Charlotte had confessed to Eleanor Rain that she'd been eavesdropping, Hawkwood decided. So there was no reason to suppose Rain knew that Annie's concern had reached outside ears, which could be enough to give him the edge he was looking for . . . maybe.

"And how you plannin' on doing that?" Jago asked. "From what Connie says, Madam tends to keep her ladies on a pretty tight rein."

Hawkwood turned to the girl for confirmation that his deduction was correct. "Has Annie spoken to anyone else about this?"

Theresa frowned. "I don't know. She didn't say she had."

"Could be she's scared of makin' waves," Jago said. "What are you thinking?"

"That we keep this to ourselves. That includes you, Theresa.

Don't tell anyone that you've spoken with me – not even Annie, if you see her. All right?"

Theresa nodded.

"Good. Then I'll go and pay her a call."

"Whoa!" Jago cut in. "Weren't you listening? You don't think it'll look a shade odd, you turning up all official and asking to speak to her?"

"Who said it'll be official?"

"Well, if you ain't going in an official capacity, then how the hell . . ." Jago's eyes widened. "Oh, tell me you ain't serious!"

Hawkwood smiled.

"Then you're either earnin' a bloody sight more than I thought you were," Jago said, his eyes narrowing, "or else you're going to try and get it on expenses – an' that I'd like to see. Either way, you've still got to get through the front door. How are you going to do that?"

"That's the easy part," Hawkwood said, taking the card etched with the rose from his waistcoat pocket. "I've been invited."

9

"This house of pleasure," James Read said doubtfully, turning away from the window. "That's your only lead?"

Hawkwood nodded. "So far, yes."

"So you believe the Rain woman *is* hiding something?"

"I've no reason to doubt Connie Fletcher's girl, as I can't see what she has to gain by making the story up. If her account of her friend's concern is accurate, then yes, our Lady Eleanor knows more than she has let on. I think that's a discrepancy worth investigating."

"So you intend to pay the house another visit."

"I do."

The Chief Magistrate pursed his lips. "When?"

Tonight, all being well."

"And you'll question the girl, not her . . . employer?"

"The Rain woman's built up a thick shell for herself over the years. The girl will be the easier one to crack. If I do get information that gives me an advantage, I may be able to play one off against the other. Of the two, Lady Eleanor has more to lose, but I'll need to be certain of my ground before I accuse her of anything. I'd prefer to keep my powder dry in that regard."

Read nodded. "Very well, use your judgement."

The Chief Magistrate looked Hawkwood up and down.

"Sir?" Hawkwood said.

"The house is off Portman Square, you say?"

"That's right."

Read pursed his lips. "And it's a popular haunt for the gentry."

"So they tell me."

"Men of good character and influence."

"I wouldn't go that far," Hawkwood said, "seeing as a fair number appear to be politicians. Why?"

Read drew in his cheeks. "It has been my experience that visitors to such establishments do expect a degree of discretion."

"Experience?" Hawkwood tried to keep his expression neutral.

The Chief Magistrate sighed. "Strange as it may appear to you, and contrary to popular belief, I did not spend my formative years in a monastery."

"No, sir; very relieved to hear it, sir."

The Chief Magistrate threw Hawkwood a peppery look. "The point I was about to make was that you should confine yourself to the appointed task. It is the girl you are going to question and not those on the guest list."

"Yes, sir."

Unless they get in my way.

"So, I do not want to hear that a Bow Street representative – *my* representative – has created mayhem in a house of entertainment frequented by persons in high office which could cause unnecessary embarrassment to those persons or, more significantly, *this* office and my authority. Is that clear?"

"As crystal, sir."

Read picked up his pen. "Good. Then we understand each other."

"Yes, sir, though I'd be obliged if you could define 'unnecessary'."

The corner of Read's mouth twitched. He looked up but did not speak, though his expression spoke volumes.

"There is one other thing," Hawkwood said.

"And that is?"

Hawkwood took a breath. "I may have to pay for information."

Read looked at him. As the realization of what Hawkwood might be hinting sank in, the magistrate's eyes widened.

"That is, if I'm to allay suspicion," Hawkwood finished.

"You mean you will be required to pay the girl for her services."

"If I'm with her for any length of time, yes. That happens, we'll need to make it look as if I'm having a good time, which means Lady Eleanor will expect recompense."

Read pinched the bridge of his nose and sighed. "Perish the thought you would be enjoying yourself."

"I could always try asking for a police discount," Hawkwood said and watched as Read's head came up.

"You seem to be devoting an uncommon amount of time and labour investigating this woman's death," Read said sharply. "Why is that?"

"We're all she's got."

Read frowned.

Hawkwood said, "It's because every now and then, someone – some murderous piece of filth – does something so immensely cruel to another human being that you know you have to do something about it. You cannot step aside."

"And this is such an occasion?"

"Yes. Maybe if she'd just been beaten or knifed – though God knows, that would have been bad enough – I'd feel less . . . compelled. But she wasn't just beaten or knifed; someone took a great deal of pleasure in carving her up. This wasn't some random killing. This wasn't some drunken sot taking it out on his wife, or some jilted bully-boy flexing his muscles. This was something else, something . . . hell, I don't know . . . specific. When I spoke with Apothecary Locke, he told me it's probable – no, not probable, *certain* – that whoever did this has done it before. That means it's more than likely he'll do it again, if someone doesn't try to stop him."

"And that someone is you?"

"No. That someone is us, and being officers of the law gives us the means to do that." Hawkwood fixed the Chief Magistrate with a challenging look. "Doesn't it? That is why we're here, yes?"

Several seconds ticked by before the Chief Magistrate picked up his pen. "See Mr Twigg on your way out. Tell him you are authorized to draw such funds as you deem fit . . . within reason."

Hawkwood nodded and turned about.

Read watched him go and waited until the door closed before putting his pen back down again, only too aware that in not defining "unnecessary" he had, to all intents and purposes, awarded Hawkwood carte blanche. Not always a wise move, as history had shown. Massaging his forehead, Read wondered if his previous instruction not to risk embarrassing the Public Office had just been made redundant.

And yet, despite his reservations, Read trusted Hawkwood's instincts. If Hawkwood suspected that the Rain woman was holding something back, Read was prepared to let the hound off the leash; for a short while, at any rate.

Not that it would have been easy to restrain him, anyway.

Read turned towards the window, where rain was pattering softly against the glass. The investigation of any crime, be it robbery, arson, blackmail or murder, or even a minor infraction, was not unlike shaking an apple tree. Fruit fell to the ground. Some would be ripe and some would be rotten. To men like James Read, it was the rotten fruit that held the most promise; if he had to sift through the good apples to find the maggot at the core of a single bad one, it was worth the effort.

Though, that did often depend on the size of the maggot.

It had been the change of attitude that intrigued Hawkwood the most. While not instantaneous, the transformation from high-minded hostess into cooperative, not to say almost flirtatious, courtesan had seemed a tad contrived, as had been the sudden interest in his background. When something looked a little too convenient to be true, it meant it probably was.

Ellie Pearce hadn't evolved into Lady Eleanor through alchemy or by dabbling in the black arts, even though Hawkwood was willing to concede that the woman would have been forced to sell her soul metaphorically at some point in her colourful past. However she'd achieved her position, it hadn't been through her beauty alone. She may well have used her appearance and carnal skills to get to where she was, but she'd employed her wits, too, which made the transition from condescension to conciliation all the more interesting. Unless, of course, she'd been completely bewitched by his charm and rugged good looks, but Hawkwood didn't think that was likely.

So when he alighted from the carriage that evening it occurred to him that returning to the Salon could be compared to entering enemy territory.

There was more traffic on the street than there had been on his previous visit, which was unsurprising. London after dark was a haven for every breed of criminal; most notoriously, footpads. Thus it was safer to ride than it was to walk. Plus, it was still drizzling and with the amount of mud and manure on the road, any pedestrians brave enough to venture out would have to guard themselves against the muck thrown up by passing vehicles. It had made sense, therefore, to travel in relative comfort and arrive at his destination dry and in some semblance of order, instead of damp and irritable and accompanied by the faint but distinctive smell of horse shit.

"You want me to come back later?" Caleb asked. "Though, if it's only for a minute, I can wait."

Hawkwood looked up to see his driver grinning down at him from beneath the rim of his hat.

"You can be replaced," Hawkwood said. "It wouldn't take much."

"Nah." Caleb shook his head. "Who'd you get who'd be willin' to work these hours?" He winked. "I'll be parked up yonder. Need any help, give me a call."

None of the other drivers would have had the nerve to pass comment, but Caleb had been ferrying Bow Street personnel around the city for as long as Hawkwood had been a Principal Officer. He often acted as a personal emissary for Chief Magistrate Read, and Hawkwood couldn't recall an hour when Caleb had not been available to run errands. He had long suspected that Read paid the man out of his own salary in order to have him on permanent station.

Hawkwood had been driven by Caleb numerous times and had come to trust the driver implicitly. He'd known nothing of the man's background when he'd joined the Public Office but had subsequently learned that Caleb was the son of a West Country farmer and once been a driver for the army's Royal Wagon Train, transporting supplies as well as the wounded to hospital and the dead to grave sites. A ricochet from a musket ball had seen him invalided out of the service and carriage driver for hire had been the obvious choice of career for a man who'd lived around horses all his life. Caleb's army service had also served him well, for he'd learned the importance of the chain of command and of remaining loyal to his employer – in this case, James Read – and, more importantly, he had an understanding of when to look the other way in matters regarding police business.

When Hawkwood had revealed his destination prior to boarding the carriage, he'd expected a raised eyebrow. Caleb – clearly familiar with the address – had not let him down.

"Would that be for business or pleasure, Officer? Only there's different rates for them on their own time – Magistrate Read's orders."

Caleb's face had been a picture of innocence.

He'd also had the last word when Hawkwood had told him it was strictly business, for his immediate and grinning response had been, "Aye, well, they all say that, don't they?"

At which point Hawkwood had decided it was probably best to retire gracefully, sit back and accept the ride.

As Caleb guided the carriage to his chosen parking spot further up the street, Hawkwood checked he had the invitation card to hand. He'd already seen that he wasn't the Salon's only visitor. A carriage had drawn in ahead of Caleb to disgorge two well-dressed men, whose steps to the front door had quickened noticeably as their driver pulled away.

Under the maxim that there was safety in numbers – and to see what special procedure, if any, might be required upon entry – Hawkwood timed his approach to the door to coincide with the arrival of the other dropped-off passengers. Twin oil lamps positioned beneath the portico illuminated the entrance. Hanging back just enough for his fellow guests to precede him and thus take the prominent position in the eyeline of anyone who might be peering through the spyhole, he awaited his moment and followed them through the door.

Hawkwood had half-expected Flagg to be there to greet and inspect the calibre of the clientele. Instead, a much older, smartly liveried footman, complete with powdered wig, cast a cursory glance at the card and offered to take his coat. Handing over the garment, Hawkwood followed the lead of the other guests, who clearly knew the geography of the house, judging by the way they made unerringly for the door from behind which had come the sounds of music and laughter that Hawkwood had heard on his previous visit.

The décor beyond was similar to that of Eleanor Rain's private apartment next door, and Connie Fletcher's drawing room. The furnishings were comfortable and elegant, their pale colours offset by the contrasting darker hues around the walls, which were papered, Hawkwood noted, not painted. Brussels weave carpets, rich drapes, gilded mirrors and several modest landscape paintings added to the luxurious feel, which was further enhanced by the light cast from the central chandelier and candles positioned around the room. The pianoforte stood poised in one corner. In the opposite corner, consigned to a bell-shaped cage, a white-crested cockatiel was quietly preening its feathers. A fire glowed in the hearth.

There were five men and eight women present. All the women were, without exception, young and very attractive. The men were noticeably older. Three wore uniform, which identified two of them as an army major and a lieutenant, while the third wore the blue coat of a naval officer. The pair who'd preceded Hawkwood were clearly known, for they were welcomed good-naturedly by the men already ensconced and with practised smiles by the women, two of whom rose to take the newcomers' arms. Hawkwood was glad he'd changed out of his street clothes and had taken transport. This wasn't the setting where muddy boots would have been appreciated.

"I did wonder if we would see you again," Eleanor Rain said softly from behind him, as conversation resumed.

He turned.

The cream and ivory day wear had been replaced by a midnight-blue evening dress. The raven hair was drawn up on to her crown and interlaced with a string of white beads. The blue stone no longer adorned her neck. In its place was a single strand of pearls, matched by earrings and by a bracelet at her wrist. She still wore the blue stone ring. White satin slippers, decorated around the instep with a silver fringe and white French kid gloves completed her wardrobe. Her gloved right hand held a folded fan.

She smiled and laid her left hand upon his arm. "Come, let me introduce you."

"To the gentlemen or the ladies?"

She laughed softly, causing some of the men to pause in their conversations and glance round. Most smiled, save for couple – one of whom was the naval officer – who didn't look too happy, possibly at the thought that a newcomer might be monop-olizing their hostess's attention. Hawkwood recalled James Read's warning to mind his manners.

"Which would you prefer?"

The smile continued to hover. Hawkwood thought about Caleb's enquiry and smiled. "Well, I *am* here for pleasure, not business."

"I am pleased to hear it. Nevertheless, I shall introduce you to our guests first, for it would be considered bad manners were I not to do so."

Which made sense, Hawkwood conceded inwardly. To appear aloof would likely attract more interest than if he were to raise further objection.

She leaned closer. "Perhaps you would prefer to use your army rank?"

Hawkwood wondered for whose benefit she was asking. Was it his, to spare him from having to identify himself as a police functionary, or was it her own; to avoid the risk of her clientele thinking the Salon's standards were slipping, were it to become known that its doors were now open to the lower rather than the upper echelons of – to use Eleanor Rain's own words – the constabulary? It was on the tip of his tongue to dismiss her suggestion but, then, as if from a distance, he heard himself say, "As you wish."

"Then you will outrank at least one person here," she responded quietly.

The army officers were Fraser and Peterson; major and lieutenant respectively, both with the 1st Regiment of Foot, which, presumably, meant they were billeted at one of the nearby London barracks. Convenient for them, Hawkwood thought.

"And this is Yvette and Marianne," Eleanor Rain said, presenting in turn the young women who'd been talking with the two officers before Hawkwood's arrival.

Their dresses elegant, their complexions flawless, the pair smiled prettily and, it appeared, with genuine good nature. It was a far cry from the way business was conducted in the cheaper brothels, where the louder the clothes the more debauched the women and where lascivious behaviour was the custom whenever a prospective customer came to call. In the expensive houses, the whores were expected to dress like high-born ladies and comport themselves accordingly, at least until the terms of the transaction had been agreed.

He wondered what Yvette and Marianne's birth names might be; Kitty and Mary, probably, if tradition was anything to go by. From what Theresa had let slip and from the introductions that had been made so far, the Salon's proprietress did appear to have a penchant for aristocratic-sounding pseudonyms. But, then, if Eleanor Rain knew anything about running a high-end bordello it was that if you wanted to attract a better class of clientele you employed the best-looking, best-mannered girls, and if that meant you also had to adopt a few minor embellishments to draw the bees to the honey pot, then so be it.

The naval officer, a ruddy-faced man with fresh-shaven jowls, a broad chest and bowed legs, was introduced as Captain Blissett, on temporary attachment to the Admiralty after serving in the West Indies. He grunted disinterestedly as Hawkwood was introduced, offering a brief nod before turning away to resume his conversation with his companion for the evening – a lissom beauty named Cassandra by Eleanor Rain – and one of the civilians, whose face looked vaguely familiar, but whose name was not.

It was only when one of the other guests asked if there was any news from the House that Hawkwood realized it might have been at the Commons that he'd sighted him – a Runner was required to be on duty whenever Parliament was sitting. Hawkwood doubted the recognition was mutual as the observation had been from afar and every politician he'd ever met had been far too enamoured with his own importance to have noticed anyone standing more than three feet from his shoulder.

The same was true of the individuals to whom he'd just been introduced, none of whose names had resonated. While Hawkwood – out of habit as a police officer – had memorized their identities, he suspected that if these same men – with the possible exception of the major and the lieutenant – were asked to repeat his name and his resurrected rank more than five minutes after their first encounter, not one of them would remember. They might all smile at one another and guffaw and exchange slices of gossip, but that wasn't the reason they were there.

"So, *Captain*," Eleanor Rain said, interrupting his thoughts, "would you care to meet the rest of the ladies?"

"Be a shame not to, seeing as I've come all this way."

"And on such a foul night," she countered.

"Though . . ." Hawkwood said and left the pause hanging.

"Yes?" she regarded him expectantly.

"It's just that I was given a name and I was wondering if the lady was available."

"Really?" Surprise flitted across her features "And who might that be?"

"Annette?"

Something moved in the indigo eyes. Hawkwood wasn't sure what; surprise, possibly doubt. Or perhaps it was regret. It was hard to tell.

"Annette? Why yes indeed; a delightful companion and highly thought of by our more . . . discerning visitors."

"I was told she can be very accommodating."

"As can all my ladies," she responded coolly, with a hint of reproof.

There had definitely been a shift of mood. The change was subtle and unlikely to have been noticed by anyone unless they'd been standing close or engaged in the conversation, but it was there, nonetheless.

"I'm sure," Hawkwood said tactfully.

Her chin lifted. "Might I ask the name of the person from whom you received the endorsement?"

Hawkwood allowed just the right amount of hesitation to show on his face and then said, "Sir Edward Carfax."

"Eddie?" The smile was back. "That would explain it. Eddie is one of Annette's staunchest devotees. You know him well?"

Christ, Hawkwood thought. Bad enough I barely remembered the bugger's name, without I have to dig myself further into a bloody hole.

"Not that well. I had occasion to perform a service for him a short while ago."

"How intriguing . . . and how generous of him; I'm surprised he'd want to share Annette with anyone."

Hawkwood dropped his voice. "Well, the service I rendered did require a certain amount of discretion, so I like to think it was Sir Edward's way of showing particular gratitude. Though, if you were to ask him about it, it's certain he'd deny all knowledge, seeing as it did involve a rather delicate family matter. I can say no more."

"Then I will spare you further enquiry." Tapping Hawkwood's arm gently with her fan, she whispered conspiratorially, "I shall leave that to Annette. It so happens she *is* with us this evening and her card, I believe, is free."

"Then it would be a shame to waste the opportunity," Hawkwood said.

So long as Eddie doesn't bloody turn up.

"Indeed it would. Shall we?"

She offered her arm again and led him across the room towards where two unattached young women were about to seat themselves

114

at the sofa next to the pianoforte, one clothed in green, the other in cream and gold.

"You've met Charlotte, of course," Eleanor Rain said, indicating the girl in the green dress.

"I remember," Hawkwood said, as Charlotte, ringlets bouncing, performed a mock half-curtsy, her smile as mischievous as it had been the first time.

"Charlotte," Eleanor Rain interjected smoothly, "I note Doctor Rawlings' glass is in need of refreshment. If you would be so kind as to attend to him, I would be most grateful."

Hawkwood stood aside to let Charlotte pass. Laying a hand on his arm to steady herself, her fingers applied gentle pressure as she moved away.

The separation having been neatly executed, Eleanor Rain drew the second young woman forward. "Captain Hawkwood, may I present the lovely Annette?"

"You may indeed," Hawkwood said, with what he hoped was the right amount of gallantry. "Charmed."

It was a good job Jago wasn't there. All this courtliness, the former sergeant would've been hard-pushed to keep a straight face.

To Annette, Eleanor Rain said, "This is the captain's first visit, so you are to take special care of him. He's just informed me the two of you share a personal acquaintance, so I'm sure you'll have lots to talk about."

Her gaze flitted towards the door, which had opened to admit two new arrivals, proving, Hawkwood thought as Eleanor Rain went to greet them, that timing was everything. If he'd turned up ten minutes later, Annette might have been otherwise occupied.

Sitting down, she patted the seat next to her. "Please, Captain. We're all friends here. Join me."

Hawkwood sat. It would have been rude not to.

Allowing her body to press against his arm, she leant in and placed her lips close to his ear. Her breath smelled faintly of cinnamon. "So tell me; who *is* this mysterious acquaintance? Do tell."

Hawkwood made a play of glancing around for eavesdroppers

before lowering his voice. "Sir Edward Carfax told me if ever I had occasion to visit the Salon I was to be sure to ask for Annette. He said she was the most beautiful girl he had ever met and that she would take very good care of me."

She pressed her hand against her throat in what was clearly a practised gesture. "Really? Eddie said that?"

"He did. He was most complimentary. Now I'm here, I can see why."

Her eyes danced. "Such flattery! How could I ever live up to such high expectation?"

Hawkwood smiled. "The very same question I put to Eddie."

"You did? And what did he say?"

"He said he was sure you'd find a way."

She grinned. "Then I must make sure I'm on my very best behaviour. Or perhaps . . ." Her voice dropped seductively.

"Perhaps . . .?" Hawkwood said dutifully.

"Perhaps you would prefer my bad behaviour."

"Well, that does sound more intriguing."

She trailed a finger along his arm. "Eddie has no complaints."

"No," Hawkwood said. "I don't suppose he does."

"So?" she countered.

"Well, if it's good enough for Eddie."

"Oh, it is," she murmured softly. "He's told me so; quite often."

"Well, then," Hawkwood said. "What do you propose?"

Her hand moved from his arm to his knee. "That we find somewhere a little more . . . private?"

"I do abhor crowds," Hawkwood said, thinking that if Jago ever heard him utter the word "abhor" he'd never live it down.

"Then I know exactly the place." Standing, she took his hand. "Would you care to see it?"

Eleanor Rain obviously didn't have the monopoly on innuendo. Attempting to keep up with every play on words was going to be an uphill struggle. No easy task, because Annette, like the other young women in the room, had the sort of arresting looks that would have made a bishop weep.

Where Charlotte was slender and blue-eyed, with an impish

grin, Annette was taller with a fuller figure and, save for her auburn hair, which seemed to glow like copper in the light from the fire, she could have passed for a youthful Eleanor Rain. Hawkwood wondered about her age. Despite her undeniable charms, she still couldn't be much more than nineteen or twenty. Save for the boots he was wearing, he'd owned footwear that was considerably older. Could that have been the reason for Eleanor Rain's change of demeanour? Had she expected Hawkwood to flirt with her and had her pride been dented, seeing him choose this younger version of her own self?

That view was strengthened when, as he accompanied Annette from the room, he caught sight of Eleanor Rain watching him over the shoulders of her other guests. Her expression was indecipherable save for one aspect. The smile seemed to have disappeared.

10

Bastards, Hawkwood thought; the reason for Jago and Connie Fletcher's exchange of grins as he'd left them having suddenly been made clear. Though it had taken a couple of seconds for him to realize exactly what it was he'd walked into.

The first object to catch his eye had looked innocent enough, standing over in the corner; a cross between a stepladder and an artist's easel. It was only as the door closed softly behind him and he took in the rest of the trappings that his brain was able to absorb the full import of what he was seeing: this was no painter's studio and the room had been conceived not for the application of paint, but of pain.

The clues lay in the rest of the furniture and paraphernalia dotted around the walls. Some of the items displayed wouldn't have looked out of place in a medieval dungeon.

It went a long way to explain the faint look of surprise – and disappointment? – on Eleanor Rain's face. It also told Hawkwood all he needed to know about Sir Edward-bloody-Carfax. This wasn't a boudoir; it had all the requisites of a torture chamber. The "Lovely Annette" was a punishment moll.

Most of the objects on view were recognizable: the canes and switches, the leather thongs, the whips – including a dozen different sizes of cat-o'-nine-tails, some with needles worked into them – and several vases filled with what looked like birch twigs. With water at the bottom, Hawkwood presumed, to keep them green and supple. His back muscles squirmed at the thought.

Other articles were more extreme: strips of leather studded with nails, along with rods and knotted sticks which reminded Hawkwood of the Iroquois war clubs he'd wielded as a boy. One corner table was festooned with sprigs of holly. Another supported what appeared to be a bundle of coach traces, and another, a selection of scourges.

"Like what you see, Captain?"

"Well, it's different," Hawkwood said. "Personally, I'd prefer to curl up with a good book."

She smiled invitingly. "Oh, I think I can dissuade you from that notion." She pointed to the ladder contraption. "That's Eddie's favourite. We call it the *chevalet*. It's all the rage in Paris."

Not when I was there, it wasn't.

But it told him he hadn't been that far out with his initial conjecture; *chevalet* being French for "easel".

The apex of the A-shaped frame stood a little over six feet off the floor. The slanted sides were about three feet wide with one side solid, save for three strategically placed openings. The top opening was at head height and oval shaped. The other two openings were rectangular and sited one above the other, approximately a quarter and halfway up the side respectively. When he saw the switches hanging from hooks set into the side of the frame, Hawkwood realized what the openings were for. They were positioned so that the "victim" could stand close to the board and place his face through the top opening. The other two cut-outs were to accommodate the knees and genitals. A chair occupied the space beneath the frame, facing the openings.

"We don't have to use the cane. We can start off with the twigs." She nodded obligingly towards the conveniently positioned chair. "If you want, I can ask my friend Helena to join us. She'll do the chastising while I take the seat. You can decide if I keep my dress on or if I let you see my bits." She smiled. "Eddie likes to see my bits."

"It's certainly a generous offer but that won't be necessary."

119

I'm going to bloody kill Jago.

"No?" She smiled invitingly, moved in front of him, and placed her hands on his chest. "So it's just you and me, then. Good; much more fun, having you all to myself." Her right hand dropped to his crotch.

"No," Hawkwood said, disentangling himself. "I meant *none* of it is necessary."

A frown crossed her face. But then her features softened. "Oh," she said gently. "Your first time? That's all right, Captain. No need to be shy. We don't have to rush. We can start off slow; try a few things and you can tell me what you like."

Hawkwood shook his head. "Dammit, I'm not here to play, girl. I'm a friend of Theresa."

Which wasn't strictly true but it was close enough.

"Theresa?" she repeated, confused.

"She told me you were worried about your friend, Lucy."

She let out a sharp gasp. Hawkwood stepped back and raised his hands, palms outwards. "It's all right. You've nothing to fear. I'm from Bow Street. I only came to talk."

Her face lost more colour. "Police?"

"Yes."

"Does Lady El—" She glanced quickly towards the door.

"No. She thinks this is a social visit. She doesn't know about you and Theresa, or that Theresa's spoken to me. You and she *are* friends, yes?"

She nodded, still wary.

"Good, then why don't we take a seat?" Hawkwood indicated the bed. Discounting the side tables, it was the least aggressive item of furniture in the room, aside from the restraints affixed to the posts at its head and foot.

She hesitated. Then, without speaking, she sat down, hands in her lap; dominance having given way to submission.

"You told Theresa that Lucy was missing," Hawkwood said.

She took a breath and nodded. "It's been four days."

"That's when you saw her last?"

Another nod.

"And still no word?"

120

"No."

"You spoke with Lady Eleanor."

"She told me not to worry my head. Said Lucy would be back before I knew it and that she was with a gentleman friend in the country."

"Do you know which gentleman friend?"

"Her ladyship's the one who takes care of business. All I know is what Lucy told me; that she thought it was someone who'd taken a shine to her after seeing her at an entertainment over Marylebone way; she wasn't sure, but she thought he might be a foreign gentleman." Her expression faltered. "You're the one who came to see Lady Eleanor. You told her a body had been found."

"I did."

"Is it her? Is it Lucy?"

"That's what I'm trying to find out. If it is, can you think of anyone who'd want to harm her?"

"You mean like one of her gentlemen callers?"

"Or someone she might have had an argument with."

She shook her head. "No, no one. Lucy's really sweet . . . always has a kind word for everyone . . . except when she's working." Her eyes flickered towards the easel.

Hawkwood said, "She's a punishment moll, too?" He realized he was using the present tense as well.

She nodded and smiled, almost shyly, at Hawkwood's expression. "Never think it to look at her, mind. I'm tall and I've got these – she looked down at her breasts – so it doesn't take much for me to play the part. Lucy is Charlotte's size; you'd think butter wouldn't melt. That's why the gentlemen love her. She comes over all coy – until she's behind closed doors, then she can be as stern as you like. Sometimes we'll entertain together, like me and Helena would've done, if you'd said yes. I'll sit on the chair over there and play with their bits while Lucy smacks them across the bum with a paddle. That always gets them going. And all the time Lucy'll be winking at me over their shoulder and trying not to laugh.

"You know what it's like; outside of here, those who don't

know a girl's a moll will ask her what she does, she'll always say the same: that she's an actress. That's what Lucy calls herself even when she's not asked the question. She'll say, 'Annie, we're as good as any of them on the stage at Drury Lane, and don't you forget it.'"

She emitted a small sigh. "Anyone'd think we wander round in our birthday clothes swishing whips all day long. We do it for as long as a gentleman wants us to; ladies, too, sometimes. That's when we're Lucinda and Annette. The rest of the time we're plain Lucy and Annie."

Hawkwood wondered how Eleanor Rain described the services the girls provided. No doubt she used some refined definition in the same way she'd elevated Annie to Annette and Lucy to Lucinda. It would add to the house's reputation for exclusivity.

Not that it was unusual for a house to employ girls who were willing to administer pain if clients were prepared to stump up the fee. Indeed, there were some notable brothels which dealt in nothing but flagellation, like the White House over on Soho Square. Hawkwood had heard that the practice had become increasingly popular among the gentry. Quite why, he couldn't begin to fathom. Neither had he the slightest inclination to seek out the reason. Why anyone would choose to pay some half-dressed moll to whip holly branches across their naked arse was beyond him.

"How long have you been with Lady Eleanor?"

"Two years, nearly."

"And Lucy?"

"She came after me; about a year ago, I think it was."

They must have been recruited young, Hawkwood thought. Though, a lot of men liked that. More than a few establishments advertised pre-pubescent girls as a speciality, referring to them as "nymphs". Clients would pay a premium to be the first to deflower them; not that the loss of virginity posed a hindrance to their earning potential. The really young-looking ones could be advertised again and again. With the aid of a tiny balloon of sheep's gut filled with pig's blood, discreetly concealed in a hand and punctured with the sharpened edge of a ring at the right moment to simulate bleeding, the deception could be repeated over and over, each time with a different customer.

"Why were you worried it might be Lucy?" Hawkwood asked.

She frowned, as if confused by the question. "Because I've been expecting her back."

"Because you thought she'd only be gone a day?"

Annette nodded.

"You believed Lady Eleanor when she told you why Lucy hadn't returned?"

Another wrinkling of the brow. "Why wouldn't I?"

Hawkwood feigned a nonchalant shrug. "No reason; just wondering. She treats you well?"

"No complaints. Better than my last place, that's for certain."

"Which was where?"

"Mrs Samuels over on Brydges Street. Know it?"

Hawkwood shook his head. "Can't say as I do."

"Serviced Mordechais, mostly. Wasn't so bad. Not too many funny habits and they're cleaner than most, on account of . . . well, you know . . . they've had the cut."

"How did you end up here?"

"I was at the theatre – Covent Garden – with a gentleman. Lady Eleanor was there at the same time and saw me and we got to talking. Knew straight off what my business was; told me I could make more if I joined her family."

"Family?"

"That's what she calls us."

It was a variation on a common theme. Procurers and madams always had an eye out for susceptible girls. The favoured haunts were the inns serving as termini for the cross-country coach companies, along with fairs and markets where waggoners brought their out-of-town wares to be sold. Any virginal-looking country waif who arrived on her own was fair game. Accommodation in a house would be offered gratis until the girl decided if she liked the city. Respectable work would then be offered. The threats and the violence used to ensnare them would follow soon after. By her own admission, Annie had been one of the fortunate recruits.

123

Already in the life, she'd viewed employment in the Salon as a promotion.

"What about Lucy's real family? Know anything about where she came from?"

Annette shook her head. "From out of town, that's all I know. Somewhere north, I think it was. She told me she was an orphan. There was an older brother, but he died, too; fighting for the king."

"Did she have a last name?"

"We don't bother with last names. There's no need for them here. I never learned hers."

"How many of you are there?" Hawkwood asked.

"Here? There's twelve."

"Including Lucy?"

"Yes."

"All of you live here?"

"We do. The place is bigger than it looks on account of her ladyship owns next door as well. We can move between the two without using the street."

"That's convenient."

"It's so fine ladies can have their own entrance." She grinned. "If you know what I mean."

More innuendo; it was everywhere, though Hawkwood assumed the ladies Annette was referring to were female clientele and not the girls that Eleanor Rain employed.

"And do you all have tattoos?"

"You mean our rose?"

As Hawkwood looked on, she lowered the shoulder of her dress to reveal the pale upper curve of her right breast and the small flower high up on her arm.

"There's an Eytie artist over near Oxford Market who does the work; he's quick. It doesn't take long."

"You don't mind?"

She shrugged. "Never saw the harm. I'd have had the king's face tattooed across my front if it meant I didn't have to bare my arse down some alleyway."

It was interesting how her accent and vocabulary had become less genteel since they'd entered the room and she had grown

124

more comfortable in his presence. You could take the girl out of the streets but you couldn't ever take the streets out of the girl, Hawkwood thought, which made him think back to his conversation with Eleanor Rain, in whom a vestige of Ellie Pearce still resided. The Widow may have gained control over her vowels, but there had been no hiding the steel core at the heart of the silken exterior.

"Charlotte said that the body you found had a rose on her arm. Is that right?" She looked at him.

Hawkwood nodded. "Yes."

She swallowed.

"It doesn't mean it's Lucy," Hawkwood said.

She drew herself up and looked across the room, her gaze fixed, as if on the opposite wall or at some spot beyond it. In a subdued voice, she said, "But you think it is."

Hawkwood decided to evade the question. "Do you remember what she was wearing?"

She turned. "I never saw her leave. I was here with a gentleman at the time. If I was to guess, I'd say it was her yellow-and-blue striped dress. She'd bought new boots to go with it, so maybe those as well. She likes shopping, does Lucy. Sometimes we shop together. Shoes and boots are her favourite. She's always telling me Grieves in Bond Street has the best boots. She likes to look nice and Lady Eleanor insists on it. I was with her when she tried the boots on. I liked them, too, so I bought a pair as well; blue velvet. They were really pretty, she—"

She paused. Hawkwood knew that his effort to maintain a neutral expression had failed.

"It is her, isn't it?" she said bleakly, turning away again.

Hawkwood conceded defeat. "I think it's likely, yes."

He watched as she closed her eyes and took a long, deep breath, her breasts rising against her bodice. Lungs full, she exhaled slowly, letting her body relax. It took two more inhalations before she said, "I had a feeling."

"It's not definite," Hawkwood said. "Lots of girls have tattoos."

She shook her head. "It's not the tattoo. It's when I mentioned the boots. I saw the look on your face."

"I'm sorry," Hawkwood said.

Without speaking, she nodded, her jaw set firm. Expecting tears, Hawkwood was surprised when none were forthcoming. He waited.

"Thank you," she said eventually.

"For what?"

"For not being a bastard. There's plenty of law officers who wouldn't care that she had friends or people who missed her. They'd be saying it was her own fault and what could she expect, being nothing but a moll."

"Then they'd be wrong," Hawkwood said. "Wouldn't they?"

She was silent for several seconds and then she nodded. "Yes, they bloody would." She lifted her chin and added in a none-too-convincing voice. "And it might not be her."

"And it might not be her," Hawkwood agreed.

"She could walk back through the front door tomorrow."

"Yes, she could."

"So, until we know for sure."

She could identify the body, Hawkwood thought, and then had a vision of her in Quill's mortuary, looking down at the corpse of a murdered girl with skin like candle wax and letters engraved across her belly and Quill standing like the grim reaper in the background, bloody scalpel in hand.

He heard her say, quietly, "You don't look like a police officer." A smile played around the corners of her mouth as she laid a hand on his arm. "Better looking than most, too. Y'know, we could still . . ."

"I don't think that's a good idea, do you?"

"Maybe not, but it'd take our minds off Lucy. Take my mind off her, at any rate. Make us feel better."

"But only for a while," Hawkwood said.

She regarded him shrewdly, her head tilted. Then she gave a nod and lifted her hand away. "You're spoken for, aren't you?"

He thought about Maddie and that morning's conversation between the sheets.

"Yes."

"Wife?"

"No."

He watched as the possibilities ran through her mind, leading to a speculative glance. "She wouldn't have to know."

"I'd know."

"I'll do things she won't."

"Is that right?"

"You could give the *chevalet* a go."

Hawkwood smiled. "I don't think so."

"You might enjoy it."

"I doubt it."

"Won't know until you've tried."

"Nevertheless."

"Some men like it. Prinny does; Brummell, too. Mum's the word, but I had both of them in here a couple of weeks back. Not at the same time, mind," she added in a theatrical aside.

"No," Hawkwood agreed soberly. "I imagine not."

"Or we can stay where we are." She patted the bed.

"It's tempting," Hawkwood said. "It really is, but it's still no."

She sighed. "Don't know what you're missing."

"Maybe that's just as well."

She smiled then, but it was a smile tinged with resignation. "All right, but whoever your lady is, you can tell her from me that if she ever feels like sharing, you know where to find me."

"I'm not sure that'd be wise, either," Hawkwood said.

"Pity. It'd be interesting to see the look on her face."

You're not wrong there.

"There's one thing I would ask, though," Hawkwood said.

"Oh, yes?" A flirtatious glint came back into her eyes. "And that would be?"

"It might be best not to mention our conversation to Lady Eleanor."

"Why's that?"

"Because we don't know for sure it is Lucy who's been found, and I've other enquiries to make and Lady Eleanor might think you've been talking behind her back."

"Which I have."

"Which you have."

She considered that and then said, "All right, but there's still time on the clock. You leave too early and she'll think I haven't pleased you."

"You don't give up, do you?"

She allowed another grin to form. "Can't blame a girl for trying."

"No, you can't," Hawkwood agreed. "Does Lucy have her own room?"

The grin disappeared at the change of topic. "We all do, though we do use them sometimes, when we're entertaining gentlemen . . . and ladies . . . who don't want the whip. Hers is across from mine, up on the next landing."

"Can you show me? I'd like to see it."

"Why is that?"

"I might find something."

"Like what?"

"I don't know."

She frowned. "What if Lady Eleanor . . .?"

"I won't tell her if you don't," Hawkwood said and watched as the significance of that statement took hold.

Her eyes narrowed. "Don't you trust her?"

"If I ask her permission to see Lucy's room, she'll know we've talked. If it's just along the passage, then . . ."

He watched as the hesitation stole across her face, but then, with a quick decisive nod, she rose to her feet. "We'd best be quick. Don't know who's likely to be about."

Outside, the corridor was empty and the house seemed strangely quiet until a low moan sounded from one of the nearby rooms, followed immediately by a dull thump and a whimper that could have been caused by the application of either intense pain or exquisite pleasure. Then the grunting began in earnest. As the noises intensified, Hawkwood heard Annette click her tongue in annoyance, which struck him as an incongruous reaction given that she must have heard and even initiated sounds that were far more expressive than the

128

ululation that followed them as she led him towards the stairs. As the sounds faded, they arrived on the next floor and she drew him towards a closed door. "This one's Lucy's."

The room wasn't locked, which made Hawkwood suspect that it was used when Lucy was absent. The lady of the house wouldn't want a perfectly good bed to stand idle if it could be utilized to its full potential – not unlike the girls she employed.

As they closed the door behind them he was relieved to note there were no whips or scourges or leather straps or sharpened implements or spiked foliage of any description. It was merely a bedroom, with a large brass bed as the focal point. The bed was covered by a thick comforter. The decoration was determinedly feminine in character, rendered in soft colours – mostly yellows – as opposed to the room below where deep reds and black had been the predominant hues. There was a wardrobe, a dresser and chair, a two-seater chaise and a mahogany swivel mirror. A door in the corner led into a small windowless room – in reality no more than an alcove – which contained a commode and a side table upon which stood a porcelain bowl and jug, both empty.

Annette sat on the bed and watched as Hawkwood worked his way around the room, noting how economically he moved, how he treated everything with care, placing each item back where he found it. She'd spoken the truth when she'd told him he was different to other law officers she'd met, almost all of them in the course of her profession, either through being harassed when she'd worked the streets or being pawed by them when they'd presented themselves as paying customers.

Lady Eleanor had introduced him as *Captain* Hawkwood and Annette wondered why. Judging by his appearance, most notice-ably the scars on his face, she assumed the rank had something to do with him being at one time in either the army or the navy. Most naval officers had a slightly stooped posture through having to adjust to a world below deck where it was often impossible to stand upright. This one, she was sure, had never stooped a day in his life. He carried himself tall, like an army officer would. She wondered how he'd come by the scars and if there were any more hidden from view. Probably, she supposed; a good many, most likely. It would be an interesting pastime seeking them out.

There was some grey in his hair and that made her wonder about his age. Certainly not young; in fact, quite possibly old enough to be her father. The blue-grey eyes, she guessed, had seen more than their fair share of trouble, but there had been a humorous glint there when she'd tried to entice him. He had no wife. He'd let that slip. Whoever the woman was, Annie suspected she had character. A man like this wouldn't settle for a homebody. He might have settled for a whore once. If only I'd been ten years older or he'd been ten years younger, she thought. If that had been the case, she might have stood a chance. What was it they said about ships passing in the night?

"What are you looking for," she asked.

"A clue," Hawkwood said.

"Like what?"

"I'm hoping I'll know it when I see it. You can help. See if you can find the dress and those boots she bought."

Better to give her something to do, Hawkwood thought, than have her sit there and watch me searching through drawers.

The top of the dresser yielded a selection of combs and brushes, along with an assortment of scent bottles and jars containing what Hawkwood presumed were salves and lotions to compliment the female complexion. There was also a small, brass-cased clock positioned to face the bed. The drawers held hosiery, gloves and handkerchiefs and other female fripperies. One of the upper drawers held a collection of silken bags tied with ribbons. Cundums, probably made for the house by a local salvator. Nestling alongside the bags was a small opaque bottle which rattled when shook, suggesting some sort of aphrodisiac nostrum. A suspicion confirmed by the label, which read in coppery script: *Doctor Brown's Efficacious Pillules*.

He slid the drawer shut. "Find anything?"

"They're gone," she said.

He turned. She was staring at the inside of the wardrobe. He knew she was referring to the dress and the boots.

"You're sure?"

She turned to him. "That's a clue, isn't it? Her clothes not being here?"

He had found nothing of significance during his own search of the dresser and the rest of the room. Prevarication at this stage seemed pointless. "I'd say so, yes."

Her shoulders slumped. "Even when we came in, I was hoping it wasn't true."

Hawkwood was about to tell her how sorry he was when he remembered he'd already told her that. Knowing the sentiment became devalued every time he uttered the words, he kept silent.

She nodded absently, as if he had spoken, and stared at the bed. "After we'd seen our last gentlemen, we'd often visit each other's rooms to talk about our day."

Reaching out, she ran her hand over the comforter. "We'd cuddle and swap stories about the swells we'd been with and what they wanted us to do. You'd think we'd have heard it all, but there was always something new. Made us laugh, the things we've seen, things we've done."

In a more subdued voice, she said, "Or Lucy would show me her bruises."

Hawkwood felt a chill run down his back. "Bruises?"

"Sometimes she'd allow her gentlemen to scold her. There'd always be one or two who'd get a bit rough; either tie the knots a bit tight or smack her harder than she was expecting."

Hawkwood thought of the devices he'd seen in the room down below. "You said 'sometimes'. How often is 'sometimes'?"

"Not that often. Depends what kind of mood she was in. She used to say it was all part of the act. Usually, it was when she'd seen a dress or a coat she liked . . . or shoes. She'd work out how much spending money she'd need and then she'd charge her callers a bit extra and they'd use the switches on her; the *chevalet*, too, sometimes. You can adjust the position of the openings, so if it's a lady, you can have it so their tits poke through. Don't look like that, Captain. It's not my cup of tea, but it takes all sorts."

Hawkwood thought about the marks on the body. Were they the result of a scolding game that had got out of hand? Had the girl initiated the punishment on herself only to fall victim to an over-zealous client?

The look on Hawkwood's face seemed to jolt Annette out of her reminiscences. She looked towards the clock and then the door. "I don't like being here without her. Can we go?"

Hawkwood nodded. "There's something we should take care of first, though."

She shot him a knowing glance. "I was wondering when you'd get around to it. I thought you might want to do a runner." She smiled shyly at the play on words. "No offence."

"None taken."

Payment for services, he knew, would vary from house to house. At the lower end of the market – for in essence, that's what it was: a market – the proprietress was usually paid up front. Moving up the ladder, it wasn't unusual for some places to have their own counting-house. While on the very top tier, a few of the high-class bordellos would allow clients to open an account. Hawkwood was astute enough to know that Eleanor Rain's invitation would not have included complimentary use of the facilities. Money would still be expected to change hands.

"The gentleman pays me, dependent on the service I provide, and Lady Eleanor deducts what's needed for my keep, in case you were wondering."

"Better break it to me gently, then."

He assumed she knew the difference between "needed" and "wanted" and that she was prepared to disregard the nuance in order to maintain the roof over her head.

The amount, when stated, made him wince inwardly. James Read, he thought, would have a fit.

"And I'm doing you a favour." She moved towards him. "That's my beginner's rate."

Hawkwood prepared to repel boarders again, but the expression on her face stopped him, as did her next words: "But I'll give you a better price. We both know it's Lucy who's been found; there's no denying it now. So you promise me you'll do your best to find the sod who killed her and I'll ask only for what I'd pass on to Lady Eleanor. That way, she'll think we've done the business; she won't know all we've done is talked. How does that sound?"

Hawkwood smiled. "Like you're the one with the head for commerce."

She shrugged. "I've had good teachers."

"She's still likely to ask you about our time together," Hawkwood said. "You might have to lie a little."

Her mouth formed a thin line. "I'm a whore. You think I don't know how to do that?"

The net fee, while it lessened the possibility of the Chief Magistrate suffering a total seizure, was nevertheless liable to send Ezra Twigg's brain into a spin when it came to transcribing the sum into Bow Street's expense ledger. There'd be no receipt, for one thing. Hawkwood decided he'd cross that bridge when he came to it as he removed from his pocket the notes he'd drawn on James Read's instructions. Handing them over, he watched as she counted them out formally before folding them into a small draw-string purse she took from a pocket in her dress. It could have been worse, he supposed. She could have thrust the notes down the front of her bodice.

They let themselves out of the room. Thankfully, the sounds of congress were no longer audible; due, Hawkwood presumed, to either exhaustion or consummation or, conceivably, the expiration of one or both of the participants. Of all three scenarios, the latter hypothesis seemed the most unlikely, though it wasn't an unheard of occurrence. And, Hawkwood was willing to concede, there were undoubtedly worse ways of going to your maker.

A second later he was wondering if Flagg was thinking the same thing.

11

Hearing the girl suck in her breath at Flagg's unexpected appearance on the landing below them, it occurred to Hawkwood that the man could move remarkably softly when he put his mind to it. Why was there never a creaking floorboard when you needed one?

Slipping a proprietorial arm around Annette's waist, Hawkwood adopted what he hoped was a lewd grin, "Thomas! Fancy meeting you here! On patrol, eh? Good man!"

Light from the wall-mounted candles played across the unsmiling face. Hawkwood winked and drew the girl closer. As the manservant made his way up and past them, Hawkwood sensed there were still eyes boring into his shoulder blades and looked back over his shoulder.

"You might want to have a word with one of the servants while you're at it. A man could wander these bloody corridors for days looking for an empty chamber pot. If it hadn't been for this enchanting young lady pointing me in the right direction, there could have been a very nasty accident."

Turning back to the girl, he let his voice carry. "Right, let's see where that old fellow put my coat, shall we?"

"I don't think he likes you," Annette whispered a couple of paces later as Hawkwood released her.

"I'm not sure he likes anyone," Hawkwood said.

"He's only doing his job."

"Stalking the corridors?"

"Looking out for us."

"A house like this," Hawkwood said, "I wouldn't think you'd have that much trouble."

"We don't. Thomas makes sure of that."

"So, what does he do when he's not wandering about the house and answering the bell?"

"You'd have to ask Lady Eleanor. I know that when we make house calls we feel safer when he's with us."

"House calls?"

"Like when we go to the gentleman's place instead of them coming here? There's extra to pay, of course."

"I know what a house call is. But what's Thomas's role? Are you saying he chaperones you?"

"Only if a coach hasn't been sent and we have to take a public carriage and we don't know the driver. Lady Eleanor doesn't like us travelling alone. She prefers us to be escorted."

"When Lucy went to meet with her gentleman friend," Hawkwood said, "was she collected or delivered?"

"I don't know. Is that important?"

"It might be," Hawkwood said.

The murmur of voices arose suddenly from the lobby. Rising shadows flickered across the wall, following the curve of the stairs. Someone was ascending. It was the naval officer, Blissett, and his lithesome companion, Cassandra. She was leading the captain by the hand. He appeared to be having difficulty with the incline. His forehead was shiny and the blood vessels around his nose looked more pronounced than before, indicating an over-indulgence with the port. He gave no sign of recognition as he creaked past and there was a fixed smile on Cassandra's face. A series of wheezing sighs accompanied their progress, which had Hawkwood wondering whether the man was going to expire before they reached the first floor. Despite her polite smile, the look in Cassandra's eyes suggested she wouldn't have minded, were that to happen.

As Hawkwood and Annette reached the ground floor, the footman appeared. Hawkwood was on the point of requesting his coat when he realized the servant was ignoring them and, instead, was heading for the front door, summoned, presumably, by the bell having rung somewhere in the bowels. Not so quiet were the sounds of conversation filtering from beyond the door to the reception room. No tinkling from the pianoforte this time, though. Hawkwood thought he heard a faint squawk, which he assumed had been uttered by the bird in the cage and not one of the room's human occupants.

The footman opened the front door and stepped back to allow a tall figure to enter, coat speckled with rain, which shone as the droplets were caught by the candlelight. Closing the door, the footman inclined his head in subservient greeting and waited patiently as the visitor handed over his coat and hat, to reveal a pale face and thinning hair. Only as the footman turned away did the visitor become aware of Hawkwood and Annette's presence. There followed a formal nod of acknowledgement which, as Hawkwood watched, developed into a frown which then suddenly expanded into a look of startled recognition.

It was a small world, Hawkwood thought as the visitor spun on his heel and made for the reception room door, which the footman had moved towards and was holding open with his free hand.

It had been over a year since Hawkwood had crossed paths with the Right Honourable Richard Ryder. Ryder had been Secretary for the Home Department at the time. Hawkwood had taken an instant dislike to the man's condescending manner and complete lack of understanding of what it meant to be at the sharp end of police work. Ryder had tendered his resignation from the office of State in the wake of the Perceval assassination. The Prime Minister had been a close friend and Ryder's decision to stand down had come as no surprise to those within the establishment, as well as a fair number without, who, in their dealings with the man, had considered him to be a liability of the highest order. Snide rumours abounded that, because of their friendship, Perceval had been carrying Ryder for so long he'd ended up with severe curvature of the spine and that his death – shot by an aggrieved Liverpudlian in the lobby of the House of Commons – had probably come as a blessed release.

Disappearing into obscurity on the back benches, Ryder continued to function as a Member of Parliament for one of the West Country's shared constituencies. It was hinted that he'd been suffering ill health for a while. He was also supposed to be a devout evangelical. Not that devout, obviously, Hawkwood thought, as he watched Ryder disappear from view and the door close behind him.

The footman returned bearing Hawkwood's coat as the door to the reception room re-opened.

"Taking your leave without saying farewell?" Eleanor Rain said. "I do hope not."

Ryder hadn't wasted any time, Hawkwood mused. The bastard had probably passed some pithy comment about letting the riff-raff in.

"The thought never crossed my mind."

She approached and ran her hand along Annette's forearm in a gesture that was both sensual and maternal as she held Hawkwood's gaze. "So, you have enjoyed your visit?"

"It was most invigorating."

"I am delighted to hear it." Smiling at him, as if they shared a secret, she turned to Annette. "It would seem you have a new admirer, my dear."

Making a half-curtsy, Annette met Hawkwood's eye from beneath her lashes and held out her hand. "The pleasure was all mine, Captain."

The enticing tones were back, Hawkwood noticed as he lifted the proffered hand to his lips in what he hoped was an appropriate gesture for a satisfied customer.

"Now, if you will excuse me?" she said, and stepped away.

Hawkwood watched her turn towards the reception room.

Please don't tell me she's going with bloody Ryder.

She did not look back. Hawkwood tried not to feel as though he'd just been jilted in favour of another, more affluent, suitor.

"Will we be seeing you again?" Eleanor Rain asked as she walked him towards the door, where the footman was hovering.

"It's early days," Hawkwood said.

"You are still wondering whether to retreat or advance?"

"I'm marshalling my forces."

"A wise precaution when it involves virgin territory. Or so I've been told."

"Indeed."

Her eyes held his. "And what of your investigation? I neglected to enquire before, but are you any closer to solving your murder?"

Hawkwood thought then about what he'd said to Annette and knew that the precautions they'd discussed had been unrealistic and that there was little choice in what he had to do. Best strike while the iron was hot, he decided. The girl would have to take her chances. Suppressing a twinge of guilt, he nodded, "As a matter of fact, we are."

"*We?*"

"Bow Street."

"But you're still the one leading the investigation."

"I am."

"And you say progress has been made?"

"It has."

"May one ask . . .?"

"One may." Hawkwood dropped his voice. "But I'll be doing the asking and you might prefer somewhere a little more private."

She frowned at the tone and then stiffened. Glancing quickly at the waiting footman, she said, "Thank you, Malcolm; our guest will be staying a while longer."

The footman inclined his head, by which time she was already making her way, straight-backed, across the hall to her private drawing room. She did not look to see if Hawkwood was following.

The door closed. She turned to confront him. "Well?"

"Tell me about Lucy," Hawkwood said.

"Lucy?" Her eyes showed momentary confusion.

"Lucinda, then."

The colour faded from her cheeks.

Hawkwood said, "Why the lie?"

"Lie?"

Hawkwood sighed. "I can't help feeling this conversation will move a great deal quicker if you answer my questions rather than responding with your own. I'll ask you again – why the lie when I enquired if any of your girls were missing?"

Her chin snapped up. "I did not lie. I told you that all my ladies were accounted for. If you're telling me the dead woman is Lucinda, she was not in my employ at the time you made your enquiry. Therefore, she was not one of my girls."

Hawkwood regarded her dispassionately. "A small distinction; I also enquired if any of your girls had recently flown the nest. Your reply, as I recall, was 'no'."

"That is also true. She did not *fly* the nest. I dispensed with her services."

"That's convenient. When was that, exactly?"

"When I discovered she was not complying with the terms of her contract."

"Her contract?"

"It came to my notice that Lucinda had been arranging assignations with gentlemen in a private capacity; gentlemen she met while attending soirées that I arranged on behalf of the Salon. That was not part of our agreement. In securing inappropriate appointments for herself with the Salon's clients, she was taking employment away from my other ladies."

"Not to mention jeopardizing your commission," Hawkwood said, and watched as her spine stiffened once more.

"She betrayed my trust. I place great faith in loyalty. I took her in, fed her and clothed her and taught her how to act like a lady, and this was how she repaid me. Had it not been for me, she would still be on the streets."

"Had it not been for you," Hawkwood said, "she might not have ended up dead in a ditch."

She flinched.

"You didn't tell the other girls about Lucy's dismissal?" Hawkwood said.

"I did not; though it was not my intention to deceive. I planned to inform them in due course. There are a number of important engagements to organize. I did not want to disrupt the harmony within the house."

"Harmony?" Hawkwood said.

"I have important clients, influential clients; drawn from the highest ranks of society. They expect to be entertained in a manner befitting their status. If the girls are distracted, they are not giving full attention to their work. Distractions mean unhappy clients. I have a reputation to maintain. I have . . . obligations. As a consequence, because of her indiscretions, I was forced to let her go. And while I am deeply saddened by her untimely death, the Salon is a business, not a charity. I have mouths to feed."

And men to service, Hawkwood thought, marvelling that the proprietress of a whorehouse had the gall to accuse one of her employees – correction, a former employee: a moll – of committing an indiscretion.

"And I suppose you have no idea where she went when you threw her out, or who she might have met with."

Her jaw flexed defiantly. "I neither know, nor, if I'm honest, do I care. If that sounds harsh, then so be it, but the girl chose her own path. Wrongly, as it happens. No doubt she had thoughts of finding herself a rich patron who would provide for her every need. A lesson learned the hard way, I fear. So sad, but then, I'm sure this is not the first time you have been called to the murder of a working girl with ideas above her station."

Says the woman who started life in a knocking shop above a public house.

"So you severed your ties, when, exactly?"

"Four days ago."

"When you told everyone she was with a gentleman client."

"As I explained: had I divulged the true circumstances of her departure, it would have disrupted the smooth running of the house. I must say, I object to this line of questioning. I find your tone most offensive." She drew herself up. "As I told you, I have . . . obligations."

"Yes." Hawkwood fixed her with a look. "So you said. I also recall our discussion about scratching surfaces and discovering all manner of interesting truths. Is there anything else you want to tell me? If I find you've been concealing information, my offensive manner is going to be the least of your problems."

Her eyes blazed but her voice was cold. "I think it's time you left."

Hawkwood nodded. "I'm on my way. Don't bother to ring for Malcolm. I'll see myself out."

Despite his parting words to Eleanor Rain, the footman was there to open the door. Hawkwood wondered if she'd rung a silent bell while his back was turned, or maybe it was Malcolm's lot to watch the lobby from some unseen vantage point, awaiting his opportunity to emerge from hiding like a mouse from a hole so that he could oversee departures. He did not speak as he saw Hawkwood on to the street. He merely waited until Hawkwood's heels had crossed the threshold before closing the door with a decisive click.

It was still drizzling. Hawkwood turned up his collar and looked for the carriage. It was parked along the road, although Caleb had turned it around and must have been keeping an eye out for his passenger for the vehicle began to move as soon as Hawkwood set off towards it. Bringing the horse to a halt, Caleb gazed down over the stem of his unlit pipe. Even in the dark, something must have shown on Hawkwood's face for this time no banter was offered. All he said, as he removed the pipe from his mouth, was, "Where to?"

"The Blackbird," Hawkwood told him.

Caleb nodded and flicked the reins. The carriage set off. Hawkwood slumped back in his seat and wondered what the evening's activity had achieved.

Other than confirming the dead girl's identity, he decided, not a hell of a lot.

Though he was sure he'd recognize a bloody *chevalet* if he ever saw one again.

Flagg closed the door behind him. Eleanor Rain turned away from the fire. "He knows."

"Knows what?"

"That it was Lucy."

Flagg shrugged. "No surprise. Your brand on her arm, it's obvious they'd come calling. But you threw her out, remember? So not one of yours any more; not your responsibility."

"I don't think he was convinced."

"He has nothing; a bit of muslin in a grave. You think Bow Street's going to waste time over a dead moll?"

"*He* might."

Flagg frowned. "What makes you say that?"

"There's something about him. He's different."

Flagg snorted. "Says who? You didn't see him coming out of the girl's room. The look on his face, he's the same as everyone else." Flagg shook his head. "Thinks with his cock."

"And I think you're wrong."

"And I think you're forgetting your place," Flagg said.

Her eyes flashed. "This is *my* house."

She did not see the blow coming. Flagg's open palm cracked across her unprotected cheek. She let go a cry, more out of shock than pain, though within a second, her flesh where the slap had caught her felt as if it was on fire. She held her hand to her face and stared at the manservant in disbelief.

"It stopped being your house the day the creditors came knocking," Flagg growled. "Now on, you're naught but an employee, like the rest of your brood. Your duty's to smile nicely and take the house's cut. Remember who's financing this. It wouldn't do to cross them. A word from me and you'll be out on your bloody ear. And don't think your rich friends'll step in. You honestly believe they'll flock around, knowing you're skint? All that'll happen is that there'll be a new abbess in charge; Charlotte probably. She's a bright girl. Willing, too; knows which side her bread's buttered. Meantime, you'll be back on the streets, spreading your legs and seeing to the butcher boys and the slaughtermen. It'll be like you never left."

"You bastard!" she hissed.

"And proud of it. Made me the man I am today."

She glared at him. Her breasts rose and fell.

Flagg gazed at her without pity. "You finished?"

A tear glistened at the corner of her eye. When she did not reply, Flagg nodded. "Good."

They remained staring at each other for several seconds, then, finding her voice, she said, "What are we going to do?"

"*We?*" Flagg gave a thin-lipped smile. "You make sure you keep your head down – you used to be good at that, I'm told – and keep your whores in line. He'll have got the information about Lucy from Annette. I'll leave you to deal with her."

"While you do what?"

"While I make sure this bloody mess is cleared up and Bow Street's off our backs."

"How?"

"I'm thinking about it."

"And Officer Hawkwood?"

"Him?" Flagg sneered. "He's nothing."

"You asked me to consult our records," Twigg said.

The clerk was seated at his desk, gnome-like – bespectacled and partly hunched – with ink guards fitted over the end of his sleeves to protect his cuffs from stains. The shoulders of his coat were frosted with dandruff. A tatty grey wig hung from a hook on a wooden stand behind him.

"I did," Hawkwood said.

"I believe I may have found something."

Hawkwood felt his pulse quicken. "Tell me."

It was morning. They were alone in the clerk's ante-room. James Read was not yet at his desk on the other side of the door. The Chief Magistrate's weekly meeting at the Home Department was scheduled for that day and it was customary for Read to attend the meeting from home before arriving at Bow Street to resume his duties. Downstairs, the Public Office had only just opened, so for the moment the Bow Street personnel had the place to themselves and all was relatively quiet. Once the court was in session, however, it would be a different matter. By then, every man and his dog would be clogging the halls and stairways, denying all charges and trying to get their pleas heard by anyone who was prepared to listen but mostly by those who weren't.

Twigg laid down his pen. "You wanted to know if there were any unsolved murders that might be considered similar in nature to the killing of the young woman discovered in St George the Martyr's burying ground."

Hawkwood nodded. "And . . .?"

The clerk reached out a hand towards a thin sheaf of papers bound in a black ribbon and drew it towards him. "I have a report here, though the case is not recent."

"Define 'not recent'."

"Two years ago; April. The body of a young woman – a Liza Briggs, by name – was discovered in an alleyway off Cross Lane."

Hawkwood tried to recall his geography. "Seven Dials?"

Twigg nodded. "The alley runs along the back of the brewery towards a patch of waste ground. There are a number of public houses in the area."

Hawkwood gazed down at the file. Twigg had either recalled the case from memory or else he'd trawled through the records himself. No mean feat, though, knowing Twigg as he did, either scenario was possible. He wasn't familiar with the clerk's filing system or, when it came down to it, where old documents were stored. He presumed they were kept somewhere in the building, either in a cellar or a dusty attic, but other than that he had no clue. What he did know, from past experience, was that whichever records system Twigg was using, if the clerk was unable to lay his hands on a file pertaining to a specific case or individual then the file had probably never existed in the first place.

"You've read it?" Hawkwood asked.

Twigg passed the documents over. "I have, and I have made a note of the pertinent details."

Hawkwood shuffled the pages. "Which are?"

Twigg, he knew, would summarize faster than he could read.

The clerk pursed his lips. "Meagre. The victim was a known frequenter of theatre salons."

"She was a moll," Hawkwood said, turning to the first page of the report.

Outside of brothels, theatres were second only to the street as the main market place for the bulk of the capital's working girls. No venue was considered sacrosanct, with the quality of the women determined by whichever social class dominated the audience at the time. Proceedings often took on the character of a parade which, on a good night, due to the number of girls present, could draw more onlookers than anything taking place on stage. The more astute practitioners used the opportunity to hand out business cards to prospective clients, with the smarter set favouring the Italian Opera House and the Theatre Royal, while the third circle at Drury Lane was the popular choice for the less discerning. The promenades were known as "Mutton Walks".

"The cause of death was—"

"Strangulation," Hawkwood said, his eyes having finally alighted on the relevant passage.

Twigg nodded. "The corpse also bore wounds suggestive of an attack with an edged weapon; a knife, most probably. No blade was found, or much blood, hence the belief she was killed elsewhere – probably by a vexed customer – and moved. The record also states that her hands and ankles were tied."

Making her easier to transport, Hawkwood thought. He turned the page. "Does it say where the knife wounds were inflicted?"

"There were a number of incisions around her bell—, abdomen." The clerk corrected himself hurriedly.

"Incisions? That sounds . . . clinical. Anything unusual about them?" Hawkwood scanned the cramped paragraphs. Nothing jumped out at him.

"Unusual?" The clerk's forehead crinkled. "The record does not suggest so."

Hawkwood chewed on the inside of his cheek. "It says there were two suspects."

Twigg looked down at the pad in front of him. "A tanner called Christie and a pot-man called . . ." Twigg squinted through his spectacles . . . "Bannock. Both men had strong alibis, neither of which could be broken."

Hawkwood sighed. "So the case was dropped."

"The investigation led nowhere. No reliable witnesses came

145

forward and the killing was not deemed of sufficient worth to justify continued use of resources."

"Because she was a moll and no one gives a damn about a moll," Hawkwood said.

Twigg did not respond. There was no need. James Read had summed it up when he'd given Hawkwood permission to pursue enquiries into the St George's killing, but with a time limit attached. As Read had stressed, the Public Office's coffers were not bottomless. It was a simple matter of priority. It was always a matter of priority.

"Who was the investigating officer? Maybe I can pick his brains."

Twigg removed his spectacles.

"Ezra?" Hawkwood said, struck by the expression on the clerk's face. Lowering his gaze and turning to the page bearing the signature of the appointed investigator, his heart sank when he saw the name, at the same second that Twigg said dolefully, "It was Officer Warlock."

Hawkwood stared down at the inky scrawl. As he did so, his gaze moved to the date beneath it. Twigg had mentioned it earlier, but now the relevance of it struck him forcibly. He looked up and saw that the clerk had had the same thought.

Hawkwood said heavily, "The Woodburn case: *that* was the priority?"

Twigg replaced his spectacles. "Yes."

Cruel bloody world, Hawkwood thought.

Josiah Woodburn was a clockmaker who'd left his workshop early one evening and failed to make it home. Due to his standing in the community and, more importantly, his list of influential clients, a Principal Officer – Henry Warlock – had been tasked to investigate the disappearance. Or, more accurately, he'd been reassigned. At the time, Hawkwood had been involved with the murder of a Royal Navy courier, shot during a coach robbery on the Kent Road. The two investigations had become unexpectedly entwined when Warlock's body had washed up on a mudbank beneath Blackfriars Bridge, leading Hawkwood on to a tortuous trail culminating in a failed attempt to assassinate

146

the Prince Regent and the death of the American, William Lee, in a fight in a drowned submersible below the murky waters of the River Thames.

Against which, the killing of a whore would have counted as being of very little consequence in the general scheme of things.

"They stopped looking," Hawkwood said. "Her killer got away."

Twigg nodded.

Hawkwood gazed dispiritedly at the papers in his hand before laying them down on the desk and asked himself what he'd expected to find. The name of a suspect who didn't have an alibi would have been nice.

Then he heard Twigg say, "There is also . . ."

Hawkwood turned.

In a lowered voice, Twigg said, "As you will note, the file I gave you was specific to Bow Street. In case you were interested in the metropolis as a whole, I took the liberty of conferring with my fellow clerks employed among the other offices."

Hawkwood presumed Twigg was referring to the other Public Offices and not the rooms lining the Bow Street corridors. He also wondered what the little clerk meant by "conferring". Recalling his conversation with James Read about the tradition of non-compliance employed by the various Public Offices spread across the capital, he suspected that Twigg, ever the schemer despite his innocuous appearance, had either referred the other clerks to the directive issued by the Home Department – that there should be more cooperation between the districts – or else he'd pulled in some favours. Hawkwood suspected the latter.

In his years as clerk to a succession of Chief Magistrates, Twigg had built up a formidable network of informants. Publicly, the magistrates might have wielded the ultimate power within their boroughs, having an assortment of constables and Principal Officers at their beck and call, but as in the army where the sergeants were the driving force, when it came to the running of the judiciary and, by association, the policing of the city, it was the clerks who were the cogs in the machine. Without men

147

like Ezra Twigg, the entire edifice would grind to a halt within a matter of days, if not hours.

"And?" Hawkwood said.

Wordlessly, the clerk turned in his chair and reached into the alcove beneath his desk. As he withdrew the ribbon-wrapped bundles Hawkwood felt his heart thud.

Twigg said, "I regret my duties here have not yet afforded me the opportunity to familiarize myself with *these* cases. However, I am informed by the relevant persons that the crimes bear similarities to the one you are investigating."

"How many?" Hawkwood asked in a dry voice.

"Three," Twigg said.

12

What became immediately apparent when Hawkwood had sorted the crimes into date order was that none of them were current investigations. The discovery made him wonder by what means the files had been retrieved. It said a lot for the administrative skills – not to mention the gift of recall – applied by Twigg's associates that the information had been excavated so efficiently.

His second thought was that the crimes laid out before him were unlikely to be connected to each other or to the St George's murder because of the time span involved; certainly not the earliest case, which dated back more than three years. It was out of curiosity rather than expectation, therefore, that he drew that file towards him.

But when he took in the details he felt the small hairs rise on the back of his neck.

The case had fallen under the jurisdiction of the Shoreditch Public Office when the naked corpse of a woman had been discovered draped across a stone slab in the burial ground reserved for the St Luke's poor up on Old Street.

The body had been identified as that of Marie Lavasse, a nurse on the staff of the French Hospital, located a couple of hundred yards away on the opposite side of the road. Hawkwood knew of the hospital, though he'd never had cause to visit. La Providence had been built more than a century before by French immigrants on the site of the old City Pest House and had begun

life by dispensing alms to the then growing Huguenot community. Supported by donations and with new buildings added on
over the years, it had turned into a hospital catering for all types
of patients, from the frail and the elderly to the chronically ill
and the mentally distracted.

Gradually, though, it had fallen into decline. No longer set
within rural greenery, and with its founders' successors having
become fully absorbed into society, it had lost its place in the
world. It was hard not to compare its impending fate with that
of Bedlam, which had also been crumbling into the ground for
decades.

The information on Marie Lavasse wasn't exactly comprehensive. What was known about her was that she had worked
at the hospital for a little over a year, having been previously
employed as a seamstress and before that as a maid with one
of the émigré families which, in the wake of the Revolution, had
fled France for England. There was nothing in the record to say
why she'd left her former employment. Though as to how she
had met her brutal end, there was plenty of evidence, notably
the broken cheekbones, the fracture in the back of her skull and
the rope marks around her wrists. The necropsy had also revealed
several deep incisions in the lower torso.

"Killed unlawfully by person or persons unknown" had been
the Coroner's verdict, delivered after only two days' worth of
investigation when, without so much as a pause to gather
momentum, the world had chosen to move on. His skin still
prickling, Hawkwood laid the file to one side.

The next case – picked up by the Whitechapel Office – had
surfaced six months later, quite literally, when a woman's body
had been dragged from the Tower moat next to the path leading
down to the Iron Gate stairs. Due to its condition, it was
determined that the corpse had been submerged for at least
three days, probably after being trapped by a sunken obstacle
or caught in a fissure in the ancient stonework. Identity had
not been established, due to the indentations in the skull caused,
the examining surgeon had surmised, by some form of blunt
instrument and from the effects of the immersion. The cause

of the wounds to the victim's stomach had proved equally difficult to decipher. The surgeon – a former army medic – had recalled a similar sight on the battlefield after birds had been at the bodies of dead soldiers. They were, he had informed the Coroner, very much like peck wounds. Perhaps the Tower's ravens had seized an opportunity to satisfy their appetites? They were large birds who fed on carrion. It wasn't beyond the realms of possibility.

And pigs might sprout wings, Hawkwood thought as he laid the file on top of the other two.

He stretched out his legs. He was seated at a small desk in the corner of Twigg's office, which wasn't the most comfortable of locations. Hearing a sigh behind him, he turned, wondering if he'd vented his contempt for the surgeon's findings out loud and found himself confronted by Twigg's bespectacled gaze.

The clerk frowned, his pen poised. "Do you require assistance?"

"A touch of cramp," Hawkwood told him. "That's all."

The clerk bobbed his head and went back to whatever it was he'd been doing while Hawkwood wondered how anyone could sit for so long in the same position without his knees locking.

The next body had turned up twelve months after the Seven Dials murder. Its discovery, by the side of the Serpentine River in Hyde Park had meant it was the Great Marlborough Street Public Office that had taken up the baton. The corpse had been that of one Lally Cox, a twenty-two-year-old working girl who'd sold her services from a single room above a gin shop on Vigo Lane. No relatives had come forward to claim the body, which, as a consequence, had been buried in a poor hole in a corner of the St James's burying ground. Located behind the houses overlooking Carnaby Market, it was the closest graveyard to the Public Office and the Queen's Arms, where the inquest had been held. The wounds matched those on the other corpses.

Hawkwood sat back.

Five killings in a period of a little over three years; all of them similar in method, though not all of the women had been working girls. There was nothing in the reports to suggest that the ones that had been had had a connection to the Salon. Could it be the same killer?

Murder was hardly an uncommon occurrence, despite what the authorities would have the populace believe. It would be surprising if the same means hadn't been employed by someone else at some time. It wasn't as if death by strangulation and stabbing was exclusive. London was an extremely violent city.

There had been a treatise written – Hawkwood couldn't recall by whom – the contents of which had been quoted to him by Chief Magistrate Read not long after his arrival at Bow Street. It had emphasized the challenges with which the city's law enforcement officers were faced.

London's inhabitants numbered around a million souls; more than a tenth of whom, the writer of the treatise proposed, were engaged in some form of criminal enterprise. The number of bodies recruited to try and stem the rising tide of crime was so pitiful by comparison it was a wonder any arrests were made. It was the law of averages: too many criminals versus too few police officials, and that didn't just mean Runners but also constables, watchmen, the River Police and the horse patrols.

The treatise had included a list of known criminal activities and an approximation of the number of persons involved in each one. The most serious crimes ranged from burglary, highway robbery and river piracy to embezzlement, receiving, pilfering and forgery. A bewilderingly large number of lesser but still morally reprehensible practices was also transcribed, some of which were puzzling in the extreme. Among those accused were cheats and low gamblers, spendthrifts, beggars, Gypsies, dissolute publicans and even strolling minstrels. It was a comprehensive tally.

Murderers were not included.

By their very nature, the majority of unlawful deaths took place within the criminal fraternity and, as had been proved by the encounter in the Hanged Man, the underworld and those living in its shadow had their own way of meting out retribution away from the prying eyes of officialdom. It was more than likely the true murder rate would never be known, partly due to the murky areas of the city in which such crimes tended to occur, but also because the authorities, adhering to the old maxim, out of sight, out of mind, preferred it that way.

According to official statistics, the number of murders per annum was low. Hawkwood had heard it said that only solved killings were recorded; had unsolved murders been part of the equation, the capital's streets would likely have been rendered empty, the general public being too fearful to set foot beyond their own doorsteps. Presumably the government felt it was performing a service in sparing the populace unnecessary alarm.

"Ezra?" Hawkwood said, as a thought occurred.

Twigg raised his head.

"When you spoke to the other clerks, did you tell them you'd made the same request to *all* the Public Offices?"

The clerk pursed his lips. "I did not apprise them of that fact, no."

"Because?"

"It is *our* investigation, is it not?"

"So much for the Home Department's directive," Hawkwood said.

"Directive?" Twigg responded, in a tone that wouldn't have fooled anyone.

"That there should be closer cooperation between Offices."

Twigg dabbed at an imaginary ink stain on his cuff. Without looking up, he said quietly, "I've always considered it to be more a recommendation than a directive."

Hawkwood swallowed the retort that had been about to break forth. Instead, he said, "You mean, if anyone's going to take the glory for solving these crimes, it should be us?"

The question was met with a look that suggested any verbal response would have been superfluous.

"Well, I admire your faith, Ezra, I surely do. But *five* murders? We don't even know if they *are* connected. It could be a coincidence."

"But you don't think so," Twigg said, tilting his head, "do you?"

"Once is misfortune, twice is coincidence, three times means enemy action."

Twigg blinked.

"Another old army saying. It seems appropriate."

Twigg regarded him intently. "Tracking down the offender will do no harm to our reputation."

"No," Hawkwood said. "I don't suppose it will."

He watched as the little clerk dipped his quill in the inkwell and drew his pad towards him. Twigg's reason for not confiding in his fellow clerks had prompted an interesting train of thought.

Bow Street hardly needed its reputation enhancing. As the first established Public Office, it was already widely regarded by the press and the public as the guiding light in the fight against crime, a fact not much appreciated by the other Offices. In their collective mind, Bow Street, because it had been the first, had always considered itself superior; a cut above the rest – and that rankled.

It must have grated, therefore, Magistrate Turton going to James Read, cap in hand, asking for assistance. But the fact that he'd approached Bow Street and not Shoreditch or Great Marlborough Street, whose boundaries also bordered those of Hatton Garden, indicated that he had chosen expertise over prejudice.

It also didn't help that Bow Street had become the acknowledged conduit between the ranks of law enforcement and the Home Department, not to mention other branches of government. Hawkwood's attachment to the Alien Office the previous autumn was proof of that. Turton and his peers would probably have had something to say, had they been made aware of *that* secret liaison. In their world, the arrangement would have smacked of partisanship, and that wasn't conducive to inter-Office cooperation either.

"And is Magistrate Read aware that we've been in communication with Shoreditch and the rest?" Hawkwood asked.

This time, the clerk nodded. "He is. I advised him of our interest when he commented on my absences. Under the circumstances, I thought it would be inappropriate to delegate a junior clerk to pursue enquiries. I therefore made my applications in person."

154

Absorbing that, Hawkwood said, "So to your knowledge, no other Office is aware that these murders may be linked?"

"That is correct. Each office believes they are the only one to whom I made my enquiry."

"And it wasn't your place to enlighten them otherwise?"

"It was not," Twigg said, managing to look mildly affronted by the suggestion.

Old habits, Hawkwood thought. "Do we know if any of the previous investigators considered that their killer might have struck before?"

"That possibility may well have occurred to them," Twigg pointed out, "but as these records show, there has been no more than one such murder in each district – that we know of. If the crime was not repeated within the area covered by each Office, it's likely there would be no thought of approaching the other Offices for either information or assistance."

"Because they guard their own," Hawkwood said. "As we do, which would seem to be a good reason for the Home Department's concern."

"It was Apothecary Locke's contribution that led us to make *our* enquiries," Twigg said.

"You mean the other offices didn't have a tame mad-doctor to hand."

"Would you have thought to consult Doctor Locke if Colonel Hyde had not existed?"

"Probably not," Hawkwood conceded. "Though, it was your initiative that brought the connections to light. None of this would have become visible if you had restricted yourself to checking Bow Street's files alone. You did well, Ezra."

"I am but a humble public servant. My duty is to serve."

"Humble, my arse," Hawkwood said.

Twigg inclined his head in mock acknowledgement of an undisputed fact.

"Question is," Hawkwood said, "now that we have it, what do we do with the information?"

Twigg's head lifted. "If you don't mind me saying so, I believe that's rather more your department than mine."

A silence followed.

"There goes our reputation," Hawkwood muttered quietly.

"Murder, you say?"

Henry Addington, Secretary of State for the Home Department, stood with his back to the window. Over his shoulder, the view could have been of any one of London's many squares. Except it wasn't; this one lay at the heart of government.

The first-floor office overlooked the closed end of Downing Street. On a dull day, the surrounding buildings had a tendency to block the light and so the square was often cast in shadow. The shabby condition of the stonework did little to help illuminate the scene and as this was another grey day with a small patch of leaden sky visible above the rooftops, the atmosphere in the room was one of gloomy functionality, even though there was a fire burning brightly in the grate.

James Read nodded. "My office has taken over the investigation at Magistrate Turton's request."

Addington looked down at the papers in his hand. "According to your report, he has a temporary shortage of staff due to . . . illness?"

"He is down two Principal Officers."

"Out of six? Not a helpful ratio. It's fortunate Bow Street had the manpower to assist."

"Temporarily; I've assigned my best officer to the case."

"And do you anticipate a speedy resolution?"

Read hesitated.

"Chief Magistrate?" Addington prompted.

"There are aspects of the crime which are . . . unusual."

"Explain."

Read did so. The Home Secretary moved over to the fire. A tall, bony man, his movements were not unlike that of a heron stepping across a lily pond. Grateful for the warmth, for he had an abiding hatred of the cold, the Chief Magistrate was content to follow.

"It's been proved the dead woman *was* associated with this . . . Salon?" Addington said.

"Yes."

"Otherwise, you would not be bringing the case to my attention. Had she been a two-penny whore plying her trade along the Haymarket, I would likely have remained ignorant."

Addington paused then went on: "As it happens, I am not unfamiliar with the name of the proprietress – not that she and I have ever met," he added hastily. "However, her late husband and I did share a number of mutual . . . acquaintances. Indeed, there was talk of his taking up a constituency for us, until the lady's history came to light. Perhaps it was fortunate he passed away when he did, before any embarrassment was caused by his candidature being rejected; for the sake of propriety, you understand."

Propriety? Read wondered. Or the Party?

"Her establishment has accrued something of a reputation, I'm told." The Home Secretary fixed Read with a penetrating gaze. "Among the well-to-do."

"So I believe," Read said, though a small voice told him that Addington probably knew fine well about the Salon's reputation and hadn't needed his statement confirmed.

The Home Secretary's prominent forehead and mild, intelligent eyes gave the impression his was an academic rather than a political brain. Appearances, in this instance, were misleading; Addington had been a Member of Parliament for nigh on thirty years, rising to the very top of the tree by eventually serving as Prime Minister in the wake of Pitt's resignation. Having initiated the negotiations that culminated in the Peace of Amiens, he'd then fallen from grace following the re-declaration of war against France a year later. His star had continued to wane to the point where he'd been forced to suffer the ignominy of being replaced by the very man he'd succeeded, a newly invigorated William Pitt. The following year, as compensation, he'd been created Viscount Sidmouth, and when Lord Liverpool took over from the assassinated Perceval, Addington had returned to government as Secretary of State for the Home Department.

Read had often wondered whether the man felt resentment

157

or regret when, in walking to his current fiefdom, he was forced to pass the door to his former office. Did Liverpool wave to him from the window to rub salt into the wound? Presumably, the viscountcy had helped ease the hurt.

"So." The Home Secretary cleared his throat. "In light of the connection to the Rain establishment, and given its clientele, has your officer reported any information likely to be, ah, detrimental to those in high office?"

"He has not," Read said.

So far.

"You've advised him to tread lightly?"

"I have."

"And has he been mindful of that advice?"

"I can assure you, he knows how to conduct a confidential investigation."

Which didn't really answer the question, Read knew, but it was the only response the man standing before him was going to get. Judging by his expression, the Home Secretary wasn't entirely convinced.

Nevertheless Addington nodded. "Very well; then we must trust in your man doing his job and that the unfortunate woman's murderer is delivered to the court without delay. It is our sworn duty to keep the streets safe. The people expect it and we must not – we *shall* not – fail them."

"No, Home Secretary," Read agreed, sounding more solicitous than he'd intended. Addington was a man who tended towards pomposity, a characteristic Read found wearing, particularly in politicians.

Addington nodded again. "Very good. However, we must not let the distraction of what is more than likely to have been the result of a domestic squabble or a transaction gone wrong to deflect us from our prime responsibility."

"*Prime* responsibility?" Read enquired cautiously.

"These are dangerous times, Read. We must not lose sight of the fact that the enemy is pushing at the gates. Bonaparte will be anxious to flex his muscles after his Russian defeat. Vigilance must still be our watchword. While crime and the murder of our citizens is of paramount concern – as it should be – as a nation we must look to our greater priority in these times of conflict. The security of the State has to take precedence."

"Of course, Home Secretary," Read replied dutifully, wondering where on earth this was leading. But before he had a chance to respond, Addington said, "Now, is there any other business that demands my attention?"

Still nonplussed and keenly aware that he was being ushered out, Read gathered his papers. "No, Home Secretary. Not at this time."

"Very good. Then I'll not detain you."

As if that wasn't a further hint that their appointment was over, using a bell to summon his clerk, Addington walked Read to the door. "A pleasure as always, Chief Magistrate," he said as they paused upon the threshold.

Read inclined his head. "Home Secretary."

Having seen off his guest, Addington returned to the fire. He looked up as a door in the far corner of the room opened. The man who entered offered no greeting and gave no sign of deference. Shorter than the Home Secretary by several inches, his patrician features were accentuated by a condescending gaze. Greying hair, cut short in the Roman style, served to emphasize the darkness of his well-cut jacket and breeches.

"Saxby," Addington said.

"Well?" the new arrival enquired brusquely and without preamble. "Should we be concerned?"

Addington gestured to one of the two empty chairs that faced the hearth. As the visitor took his seat, Addington said, "How much did you hear?"

"Some of it; perhaps you should summarize. I thought you did well, by the way, acting unaware."

Addington ignored the comment and remained standing. "He tells me he's put his best man on to it. He's instructed him to use discretion."

"I'm not sure that's much of a guarantee, given what I've heard of the fellow."

Addington stared at him.

His visitor offered a wintry smile. "Friend Ryder does have his uses."

Addington's eyes widened momentarily. "And how does *he* know him?"

The visitor settled into his seat. "Had cause to meet him a year or so back, while occupying your chair. I'm not entirely sure what the circumstances were, but Ryder made it plain he didn't take to the fellow. Found him exceptionally boorish – his words, not mine."

"Do we have a name?"

"Hawkwood."

"Besides that, anything . . . useful?"

"He was a soldier, apparently."

"Oh, yes?"

"With the Rifles; an officer, not a ranker."

"He's not without *some* intelligence, then," Addington murmured cuttingly.

"Interesting you should say that. Word is he served Wellington as an Exploring Officer in the Peninsula."

Addington's eyebrows rose.

"So it would be best if he didn't explore this too closely," his visitor added pointedly before frowning at the Home Secretary's expression. "What?"

"Initial reconnaissance has already been made. There was a request from Bow Street to the other Offices asking for information on unsolved murders with similarities to Read's killing."

"That's unfortunate. And you know this how?"

"I'm the Home Secretary."

Saxby forced a smile of acknowledgement, then said, "Read didn't mention that he'd put out feelers?"

"He did not."

"Which is of concern in itself."

"Indeed."

Both men looked thoughtful. Saxby was the first to speak. "We need to nip this in the bud, as quickly as possible."

Addington paused and then said, "From Ryder's assessment of this officer, does he think he can be . . . manipulated?"

"I didn't ask the question, but I suspect not. There was another word Ryder had for him: recalcitrant."

"Recalcitrant?"

"Not easily dissuaded."

"I know what it means," Addington said testily.

His visitor wafted an apologetic hand and threw Addington a speculative glance. "Which leaves Read. Perhaps *he* can be persuaded to have words."

Addington made a face. "We do that and we run the risk of drawing more attention to the situation. That would not be helpful."

"So, what? We wait? We don't want this getting out of hand."

"I agree; it's unfortunate. The woman's death should have been Hatton Garden's investigation but they're short-handed, which is why Read's office took over the case. I doubt Magistrate Turton would have been so assiduous."

Saxby frowned. "It must mean that Read's resources have become over-stretched, too, surely? Which could work to our advantage . . ." When Addington did not reply, he continued: "She was only a whore, after all. No one's going to miss her. Plus, they'll be looking for a swift result. If they don't get it, the chances are Bow Street will file it away with all their other unsolved crimes. Life will move on."

"And if Read's man unearths something?" Addington responded. "Is that possible?"

"Anything's possible. Perhaps you *should* speak to Read again; press him to close the case down."

"He would demand a reason. And were I to provide it, I'm not sure he would understand."

"That's the trouble, isn't it? Read's not one of us."

Addington shook his head. "Never was; never will be. We realized that when he refused the knighthood. Too late, by then, though."

"Well, we could hardly force it upon him."

"No, but it means we can't offer it as an inducement either. A pity; under normal circumstances, that would have been the way to go."

As if brushing away a speck of dust, Saxby ran a hand across the arm of his chair, his movements languid and precise. "Well, if we can't dissuade them, perhaps we can . . . divert them."

Addington looked at him. "How?"

"Find the culprit before they do."

The Home Secretary's eyes widened. "You're not serious?"

"I'm perfectly serious. Though, I of course meant *a* culprit, not . . . well . . ."

It was a second or two before Addington said, "And how do you propose to do that?"

"I've already given the matter some thought."

Addington stared at him.

"There's a fellow I know . . ."

Addington frowned. "A *fellow*?"

"We've made use of his services before."

"We?"

"The Committee."

"And in what capacity did you make use of him – or shouldn't I ask?"

"Probably best if you don't."

"I assume he's discreet."

"Extremely; he's also very efficient."

Addington considered this, then said, "It won't come back to this office?"

"It hasn't before. There's no reason to suppose it will this time."

"And it will stop Read's investigation in its tracks?"

"I believe so, if we act swiftly."

Addington stared into the fire. His visitor waited patiently. Finally, Addington looked up. "You'll see to it?"

"Of course."

There was a pause.

"Then make it so," Addington said.

13

South of the river, in the cellar of the Broken Lamb, the crowd was growing restless.

There were more than one hundred and fifty spectators packed into the underground arena, which had been created by combining the cellars of the pub and the house next door. Entry was reached by way of a wooden staircase that led from a trapdoor behind the counter on the ground floor. A thick cloud of tobacco fumes hugged the underside of the ceiling and the place was rank with the stench of flat beer, blood, faeces and piss. Illumination was provided by whale-oil lamps set in niches around the walls and by candle stubs attached to the rim and spokes of a large wagon wheel suspended above the pit. The pit itself was enclosed by a circular wooden barrier. Rough bench-seating, arranged in circular tiers, rose from the side of the barrier to just below the smoke-blackened roof.

The pit-men were removing the last of the debris from the previous fight. It had been a frenetic affair and torn remains were scattered in a bloody swathe across the floor, so it was taking a while to clean up. As miscellaneous body parts were tossed and shovelled into metal pails, bets were already being laid on the outcome of the next contest. The excitement gener-ated by the previous spectacle added to the frenzied atmosphere in the room, making it hard to hear some of the wagers being placed.

It had been, by everyone's estimation, an astonishing perform-
ance. The record up until then had been one hundred kills within
a period of eight minutes, made by a Norfolk Terrier called Josh.
The last dog – a brindle crossbreed named Peg – had eclipsed
that number completely, dispatching one hundred and ten rats
in six minutes and twenty-seven seconds, by which time the
hound's face was a mask of gore and the pit floor was ankle-
deep in corpses, many of which were still twitching. As the
victorious, blood-splattered animal was led from the arena to
the baying of the crowd, a fresh layer of sawdust was put down
and the excitement began to build once more. A murmur ran
through the seats as an eight-foot chain was brought out and
secured to a ring set in the arena's centre post.

The dog's name was Caesar. A bull-and-terrier, it was a
fearsome-looking animal. Stockily built; broad across the head
and chest, its black-and-white pelt was criss-crossed with scars,
old and new. Held by the scruff and led into the pit by its owner,
a barrel-chested man with arms covered in tattoos, the dog
sniffed the air, nose vibrating as it picked up the scent of blood
from the previous bout. At a word, the dog sat and allowed its
master to stand behind it and raise its forelegs in the air so as
to display its potency for all to admire. The crowd roared its
approval. Lowering the animal back down, the owner led it over
to the edge of the pit where they waited for their rival to be
introduced, an event greeted by a collective gasp of astonishment
and then laughter.

The contender approached the centre post on all fours and
remained placid while the leather band around its waist was
attached to the chain. There were more than a few in the gallery
who had probably taken it for another hound, for it was about
the same size as the dog, with a similar compact build. Only
when they spotted the bald aubergine patch on its rump and
the colour of its muzzle, which was equally striking, did they
realize their mistake: this was not a mongrel but a monkey.

A red stripe ran from the base of the mandrill's eye sockets
and down the length of its nose to the tip of its flared pink
nostrils. The stripe was framed on either side by a bright blue

patch of scalloped skin. There were red patches of fur above its eyes while the rest of its body was olive green, save for the area directly beneath its chin, from which sprouted a yellow mane-like beard.

Unconcerned by the fuss its entrance had aroused, the monkey swivelled its head from side to side, blinking engagingly as it surveyed the pit and its surrounds. Struggling against its master's hold, the dog growled deep in its throat, its eyes fixed on the strange animal that was now squatting on its haunches and scratching lethargically at its underbelly.

Two men seated together on the second tier – one heavy-set with a scalp as bald as an egg, the other slighter with thick black curly hair – regarded the build-up with amused interest.

The bald man, whose name was Israel Mudd, jerked his chin at the dog. "Bet you wish yours were that big."

His companion nodded towards the monkey. "An' I'll bet you wish you had hair like that. You already got the nose."

"Sod you," the bald man growled.

The dark-haired man, who went by the name of Jackson Ridger, grimaced. "Wish they'd get a bloody move on. My arse is about ready to nod off. What sort of monkey you reckon that is?"

"Mandarin," the bald man said confidently. "Saw one in a market when I was in Portugal. Fella kept it on a lead. Used to do tricks; smoke a pipe, too, I was told, though I never saw it meself."

Ridger stared at the monkey. "They say there's a few of them about. Tars bring 'em home on board ship. That's how this'n got here, supposedly. Ugly bugger, ain't he?"

"Well you're no bloody Byron," Mudd said, throwing a glance at his companion's locks. "Though you do have the ringlets."

Ridger grinned and passed Mudd a silver flask. The flask had been stolen from the body of a French dragoon and Ridger liked to keep it topped up with Spanish brandy.

Mudd took a swallow and passed the flask back. "What odds you get?"

"Ten to one."

"On the dog?" Mudd showed his surprise.

Ridger shrugged and grinned. "Monkey."

Mudd returned the grin.

They watched as the ringmaster called for the crowd's attention while he introduced the contestants. The dog, which was a cellar favourite with more than a dozen fights under its collar, was greeted with loud cheers. The monkey, who was now staring at the hound with a tense look on its face, as if it had just recognized the seriousness of its predicament, received a mixture of cheers and whistles and no small amount of rollicking, some of which was good-natured, some of which was not. The monkey's name, which proved to be Mister Jakes, drew fresh laughter, and even more when, without missing a beat, the mandrill defecated into its right paw and hurled the results at his opponent. The offending projectile missed its target by several feet, but the action caused the ringmaster to step back hurriedly and glower at the mandrill's handler as if he'd performed the act himself.

"Explains the name," Ridger murmured. "I *was* wondering."

Recovering, the ringmaster held up a hand to calm the room and proceeded to explain the contest's sole wager, which was that Caesar would dispatch the monkey in under six minutes. As a concession, based on the dog's fighting history and the inevitability of the outcome and to therefore give the monkey a sporting chance, it had been agreed that the beast should be given a stick to defend itself.

At a nod from the ringmaster, the mandrill's handler took a foot-long rod from his jacket and placed it in the monkey's hand. The mandrill regarded the stick with mild interest, put its head back and yawned.

"Jesus," Mudd said reverentially, for the mandrill's upper incisors had to be close to three inches long; while the lower pair, although slightly shorter, looked every bit as impressive. "Reckon this just got interestin'." Switching his gaze, he saw that the dog – whose attention was focused solely on the primate – was braced against its owner's grip, quivering like a coiled spring.

The ringmaster nodded to the monkey's handler, who stepped away. The ringmaster followed. As the two men vacated the ring, the ringmaster nodded to the tattooed man to release the dog. Freed from restraint, it attacked.

Leaping vertically three feet off the pit floor, the mandrill's evasive manoeuvre took dog and spectators completely by surprise, as did its chattering shriek when, on the way back down, it rapped the stick sharply across the dog's muzzle. Landing nimbly and grunting angrily, the mandrill scampered across the sawdust, the chain unravelling behind it. It was only when the chain ran out with a sharp jerk that the animal was forced to turn, by which time the dog, recovering from its shock, had swerved and was homing in again, saliva spraying from its mouth.

The mandrill sprang to one side, teeth bared. Once again the dog missed, but it was close. Its jaws snapped shut a hair's breadth from the mandrill's left hind leg, its momentum carrying it past, paws scrabbling, exposing its flank.

It was enough of an opening. With a screech, the mandrill launched itself across its opponent's hind quarters. Yelping madly, the dog twisted and made a lunge for the mandrill's throat. As mongrel and monkey bit and tore their way across the floor, entangled in the chain and stirring up shit, sawdust and blood, the spectators shot from their seats.

Howls and growls split the air as each animal scrabbled for a dominant hold. Even though it was hampered by the linkage, because it was the more agile of the two and could grip with its hands and not just its teeth, the mandrill had the advantage. It would not be shaken off.

Locked in a ferocious embrace of grunts and yelps, thrashing limbs and fur, the two enraged beasts slammed against the centre post, drawing more yells of encouragement from the spectators. Their grips loosened by the impact, the animals separated, but only for a few seconds. The dog darted in again.

But it went in too low and the mandrill saw its chance. With a bark that would have drawn a comparison with any hound, it launched itself into the air, pirouetting as it did so, to land squarely on to the dog's back. In a move almost too fast to follow, it then lunged forward, seized the dog's right ear, pulled its head to one side and sank its teeth into the exposed neck.

And bit down.

A novice to the ring might have thought the mandrill was trying to employ the same tactic as the crossbreed, Peg, who'd laid waste the rats by seizing them by the throat and shaking them, breaking their spinal cords. Given Caesar's bulk and musculature, that would have been an impossible objective. What the mandrill had gone for was the windpipe. Instead, it had hit the carotid.

At first, the dog appeared unresponsive to the injury, but then, as blood began to pump from the wound in its neck, it staggered. Spurred on by the dog's struggles, the mandrill bit down harder. The crowd – Mudd and Ridger included – was still on its feet. The noise in the cellar was deafening.

After what seemed an age, the dog collapsed. Still the monkey did not relinquish its grip. The floor grew red with blood, too much for the sawdust to soak up. As the dog's legs thrashed, its owner pushed his way into the ring. Fearing an ambush, the mandrill finally released its hold and backed away, chittering angrily to itself.

It had taken less than three minutes.

With a wild cry, the dog's owner swept up the rod that had been abandoned during the skirmish and raised it above his head. The mandrill's eyes grew wide in shock and before its owner could intervene it leapt at the new attacker, jaws agape.

At which point, the chain parted.

Whether the clasp had not been secured correctly or the links had been weakened in the fight, it was impossible to say, but in the confines of the underground arena the effect was spectacular: instant pandemonium.

Caught wrong-footed, the dog owner's attempted strike missed by a mile. The mandrill's reactions were far quicker and much more instinctive. Using the tattooed man's shoulder as a springboard, it threw itself towards the ring's wooden barrier, its weight knocking the man off his feet as it did so. As the seats emptied and the crowd scattered, the mandrill landed atop the barrier, found its balance and made a swift second leap, this time into the seating gallery.

Mudd and Ridger remained rooted; islands of calm in a sea of confusion. A small, bespectacled man with a look of terror on his face tried to push past. Turning a hip, Mudd thrust him away, causing him to fall into the path of other frightened patrons, who went sprawling. Letting go a curse, Mudd looked for the nearest exit. As he did so, a hunched, demonic shape appeared at the corner of his vision and he heard Ridger say, "Christ!"

Mudd turned. Unencumbered by the short length of chain still attached to its waistband, the mandrill was perched on the first set of seats less than two yards away. There were bloodstains around its mouth. For a split second, man and beast regarded each other warily. As the mandrill emitted a series of hoarse grunts, Mudd reached inside his coat.

By the time the mandrill pushed off, Mudd had drawn and cocked the pistol. The mandrill was in mid spring when he fired. The cellar reverberated with the sound of the shot. The ball struck the mandrill in its left eye, blowing its brains through the back of its head. As the carcass fell away Mudd lowered his weapon.

"Shit," Ridger said. Holding his own pistol in his hand, he stared down at the bundle of fur at their feet and nudged the body with the toe of his boot. The mandrill's chest rose and fell weakly. *Not so fearsome now, are we?*

"Heads up," Mudd said.

Ridger looked to where the mandrill's handler, a large, red-haired man who, having pursued his charge out of the pit, was clambering towards them, eyes bulging. He'd regained the mandrill's stick en route and was brandishing it like a club.

"You or me?" Ridger said calmly.

"You." Mudd held up the discharged pistol. "I'm out."

Ridger sighed.

The mandrill's handler arrived, breathing hard. He stared aghast at the corpse. His grip on the rod tightened. When he looked up his face showed a mixture of rage and disbelief.

"You murdering bastard!" He started forward, only to stop dead when Ridger, his expression unchanged, placed the muzzle of the pistol between his eyes.

Ridger pulled back the hammer. "Ask yourself, cully: who do you think's more likely to end up on top of Mister Jakes? You or me?"

"Easy," Mudd murmured. "Witnesses."

The sound of the shot had halted people in their tracks. Those that had reached the stairway were looking back to see what had happened. Some of the more curious were edging forward.

"Up to you," Ridger said calmly. "But don't take too long."

The mandrill's handler let the rod fall.

Ridger smiled. "There you go. I'd've hated for us to end on a bad note, seeing as Jakesy here just won me ten guineas. Now, why don't you take him away and give him a good send-off and we'll say no more about it?"

The pistol muzzle moved back an inch. It took another second for the red-haired man to let out his breath and nod acceptance.

"Good lad," Ridger said. He lowered the gun and his eyes swept the cellar. "All right, nothing to see here, gentlemen. What say those of us who've had the luck go an' collect our winnings? And in case you're forgetting, there's an ale house up top. Reckon we *all* owe ourselves a wet after this, eh?"

As the red-haired man crouched by the mandrill's body, stroking its fur, Ridger slid the pistol back into the holster beneath his coat. Together, the two men made their way down to where the banker was paying out. The dead dog had been hauled out of the pit and left in a sack by the privy for the night-soil men to cart away. Ridger doubted there'd be a wake held for the mandrill. It would likely end up on the barge with the hound. Not that much of a send-off, he mused, as they headed for the stairs.

Seated at a table at the back of the room, the two men cradled their drinks. The hubbub around them was all about the fight and its unexpected outcome. Every so often someone would glance in their direction, only to turn away quickly to avoid being noticed.

"An' we thought it was just another day," Mudd said. "Goes to show, eh?"

They touched mugs. Ridger looked over the rim of his and said softly, "Reckon there might be more to come."

Mudd followed his gaze to where a rake-thin man was approaching through the tables and the tobacco smoke. A grey wig covered his scalp and he was walking with a distinct limp, favouring his left leg, which appeared to have no discernible movement from the knee downwards. He increased his pace as he neared Mudd and Ridger's table, as if worried they might depart before he got to them.

"You ever seen him when he ain't hurryin'?" Mudd asked.

Ridger shook his head. "Can't say as I have, now you mention it."

"Man on a mission," Mudd said. "Quick march, double time an' move your arse!"

"Sounds familiar," Ridger said. "Difficult with that leg, mind." He looked up as the object of their amusement arrived at the table. "Well, now, Private Kite, we were just talking about you. What's got you all of a bother?" Ridger looked at Mudd and winked. "No don't tell me, let me guess."

"Captain wants to see you." The reply came before Ridger had a chance to expand on his witticism.

"Course he does," Mudd said. "Why else would you be inter-rupting our drinkin' time?" He grinned at Ridger.

"Said to tell you that means right away," Kite said, stepping back as the smile dropped from Mudd's face and Ridger's hand tightened around the base of his mug.

"Did he?" Mudd said. "That case, we'd best drink up. Wouldn't want to be charged with malingerin', now, would we?" He threw Ridger a meaningful look. Draining their mugs, they got to their feet.

"You were right," Mudd muttered as they followed Kite towards the door. "Looks like a job."

Ridger did not speak.

"By the way," Mudd continued, "almost forgot to ask: Mister Jakes's old man – he 'adn't stood down, *would* you 'ave shot 'im?"

Ridger turned. For the first time his eyes were cold. "What do you think?"

"I think they'd've been pickin' his brains off the floor with a spoon, along with his monkey's."

171

"There you go, then," Ridger said.

Mudd grinned and laid an arm across his colleague's shoulder.

"That's my boy, Jack," he chuckled throatily.

"Turn," Eleanor Rain said. "Slowly."

As Charlotte made a circle, Eleanor Rain nodded approval. "Very good. You chose well. The ivory suits you. Now, make a curtsy."

Charlotte did so, the movement revealing the hint of shadow between her breasts.

"And rise."

Charlotte straightened. With the candlelight behind her, the dress's delicate fabric did little to conceal the sylphlike form beneath.

"Exquisite," Eleanor Rain said as she ran her fingers gently across the curve of Charlotte's left breast, tracing her décolletage. "You will have Sir Hugh eating out of your hand."

"Not just my hand," Charlotte said, and grinned.

Eleanor Rain smiled seductively. "Indeed not, and I expect you to provide every encouragement. Sir Hugh is not without influence and a reference from him to his associates extolling our virtues would prove most fruitful, for all of us. Now, then, you have everything?"

Charlotte nodded.

"Cundums?"

Charlotte lifted her right wrist to display the purse suspended from it. Fashioned in ivory-coloured silk, it matched the dress perfectly.

"Excellent. House rules include house calls, and as they are a gift of the house, I'm sure there will be no objections. After all, we don't want any unfortunate accidents, do we?"

"No, Lady Eleanor," Charlotte said dutifully.

"Never forget you represent the finest salon in London. I expect you to be on your best behaviour at all times; unless, of course, his lordship requests otherwise; in which case you can be as wicked as you like."

Leaning forward, she kissed Charlotte on the cheek and took

her arm. "Now, Sir Hugh has advised me, sadly, that his coachman is out of commission due to an unfortunate accident in the Strand. I have, therefore, arranged a public carriage to deliver you to his address. Thomas will accompany you. You have your coat? It's a chilly evening. We wouldn't want you to arrive covered in goose bumps. His lordship might think you were nervous and that wouldn't do at all. You are to beguile him, my dear. Goose bumps are not beguiling, unless you are twelve years old and it's your first time."

Flagg and the manservant, Malcolm, were waiting in the lobby.

"Carriage is here, madam," Malcolm said.

Eleanor Rain watched with a critical eye as Malcolm helped Charlotte on with her coat. Adjusting the string of beads threaded through Charlotte's hair, she smiled. "There, all set. Enjoy yourself, my dear. I'm sure Sir Hugh will."

She watched as Charlotte and her chaperon entered the carriage before turning away. As the door closed, she turned to the manservant. "I shall be in my apartment. Alert me when the first guest arrives. I'm expecting Chancellor Vansittart. He prefers to be greeted personally and, as his title suggests, he's a man who likes to get his money's worth."

"You're not saying much," Charlotte said. "Cat got your tongue?"

They'd been driving for some five or six minutes. The steady clop of the horses' hooves formed a rhythmic accompaniment to the rattle of the carriage wheels.

"Lot on my mind," Flagg said.

She threw him a teasing look. "Like what?"

"Nothing that concerns you."

"No? And there was I thinking you quite fancied me." Charlotte grinned impishly.

"Sorry to disappoint."

"Oh, it's no disappointment. Relief, truth be told."

"And why's that?"

"You're not my type."

"Too old?"

"Too skint."

Before Flagg could reply, Charlotte grinned. "Been poor. Don't want to go there again."

"And you have a plan, I take it?" Flagg said scornfully.

"I'm going to do the same as Lady Eleanor: find myself a rich milord, so when I tire him out I'll inherit all his money and live like a duchess."

"You want to be careful what you wish for, girl."

Charlotte frowned. "Why'd you say that?"

"Grass ain't always greener on the other side."

"And you'd know that, how?"

Flagg shrugged. "Seen enough of the real world to know what it's like."

"So how come you aren't living in a big house with servants?" Charlotte asked jokingly.

"I *am* living in a big house with servants," Flagg said.

"Well, yes," Charlotte said. "As one of the bloody servants."

"Least I earn my living upright," Flagg shot back.

"That may be so," Charlotte said, unperturbed, "but look at my prospects compared to yours. What chance have *you* got of finding rich pickings? Least I've got these to help me along." As she spoke, Charlotte pointed to the rise of her breasts beneath her coat. "What have you got?"

"This," Flagg said, tapping the side of his head. "Brains."

"You think brains'll beat a nice pair of tits, you're dreaming," Charlotte snorted derisively. "You taking me to visit a knight of the realm's proof of that. And for why? 'Cause he's paying a lot of money to fiddle with my tits. While you do what: stay in the carriage and twiddle your thumbs? Who's the clever one here? You or me?"

The girl had a point, Flagg thought. She could earn more on her back in a week than he could earn in a year; five years probably, and that was after she'd paid her cut to the house. He was trying to think of an appropriate response when he realized the carriage had come to a halt.

"Here we go," Charlotte said, checking her purse and patting her hair. "Bottoms up."

As was customary, Flagg went to step out and help Charlotte

down from the carriage, only to find he'd been pre-empted when the door swung back.

"Well, now," Israel Mudd said breezily, rising into view. "Ain't this cosy?"

"Nothing personal," Ridger said, sounding as if he actually meant it.

Mudd nodded. "He's right, Tommy. You know that, old son. It's strictly business."

"Orders," Ridger said, shrugging apologetically. "What can you do?"

"Who are they, Thomas?" Charlotte stared at the two men, her right hand drawn protectively across her chest.

"Don't tell me you never mentioned us?" Mudd said, feigning surprise. He eyed Flagg and shook his head admonishingly. "Shame on you." He turned to Charlotte. "We're old comrades, darlin'. Fought together in Portugal. Did a lot together, in fact. Ain't that right, Tommy?"

Flagg did not reply. He was thinking feverishly. Uppermost on his mind was the realization that he should have paid more attention to the view beyond the carriage window. If Charlotte, the little cow, hadn't been so intent on goading him, he might have deduced that something wasn't quite right. He wasn't sure what, exactly, as there wouldn't have been that much to see, given it was dark and street lighting was non-existent in all but a few select locations. House lights wouldn't have been much use either. And Flagg hadn't given the driver the address. Lady Eleanor had taken care of that. Sod it.

Flagg had tried to take a bearing when he and Charlotte had been escorted from the carriage, but in the darkness there'd been no convenient reference points to latch on to. He knew they'd set off north along Baker Street, but they'd made several turns en route and after that, details of the journey were vague.

Flagg's best estimate was that they were somewhere north of Portland Place. The building they were in wasn't any help. The outside, from what Flagg had been able to see of it, had looked quite grand if somewhat anonymous. The same couldn't be said of the windowless interior, which had been accessed by steps leading down. There were lots of cobwebs and the floor was covered with rat and mouse droppings and a few items of furniture in the form of the chair he was sitting on and some wooden benches and a cloth-covered table at the far end of the room, which made Flagg wonder if it had once been part of a school. Whatever the place had been, it looked as if it had been abandoned for quite a while. He tried to remember if there had been a name above the entrance, but it was hard to concentrate with Mudd standing over him, pistol in hand.

"*Whose* orders?" Flagg said.

"Captain's," Mudd said. "Told us to tell you he was sorry, by the way."

"What's he talking about?" Charlotte asked. "Who's the captain? What orders?"

She was still on her feet, looking about her nervously. Flagg ignored her. He looked at Ridger. "And who gave *him* the say-so?"

It was Mudd who answered, looking contrite. "Can't help you there. All we know is someone passed him the nod and the captain's passed it on to us. Line of command. You know how it works."

Candles had been lit around the room and the light was playing across Mudd's bald pate, making it gleam. It was also creating shadows across the wall. Mudd wasn't a small man and the shadow he was casting made him look even bigger, like some kind of ogre. Ridger was standing off to the side. His silhouette was taller and more angular.

"Was it Rain?" Flagg said, as an unpleasant thought struck him.

Mudd frowned at the name and shrugged. "Like I said, Jack and me weren't privy. Anyways, don't matter now, does it?"

"I saved your bleeding life when the *Ariadne* went down," Flagg spat, "in case you've forgotten. Hadn't been for me, you'd be rotting in a Frog prison."

"Ain't forgotten," Mudd said, "and don't think I'm not grateful, which is why this don't come easy. It's hard. Right, Jack?"

"Hard," Ridger agreed, nodding.

"Thomas?" Charlotte said. When Flagg didn't reply, she turned

176

to Mudd and drew herself up. "Don't know what your game is, but if you *are* Thomas's pals, you'll know we ain't worth stealing from, 'less'n you think Lady Eleanor's going to pay a ransom. That's the case, you'll have a long bloody wait. Or are you hoping Sir Hugh'll shell out?"

Mudd turned to her before turning back to Flagg and grinning. "She's a caution, ain't she?"

"There is no Sir Hugh," Flagg said, in a moment of startling clarity. "You stupid cow; there never was."

"Shut her up," Mudd said.

As Charlotte's eyes widened in confusion, Ridger's fist thudded against the side of her face and she went down without a sound into the dust and the droppings.

Mudd turned to Flagg, who wisely – or unwisely – hadn't moved.

Flagg stared at Charlotte's prone body and then up at Mudd. "You're making a mistake, lads. You *know* me! There's got to be another way! Christ's sake, I had it planned! Take a girl off the street, do her in and find someone to pin it on. Streets are crawling with soaks and men looking for work."

"You mean, persuade one of 'em you've a job needs doin', do the business and leave signs making it look as though they did it?"

Flagg nodded.

"It's a sound plan, right enough," Mudd said admiringly. "Jack, what do you reckon?"

"It'd work," Ridger said.

"There you go then," Flagg said quickly. "You've got the carriage. Won't be difficult persuading some moll to climb aboard. Same with a culley; 'specially if he's the worse for wear." He looked down at Charlotte's prone form. "She's Rain's top earner, for God's sake. Any other moll'd do."

He had harboured thoughts about Annie. Despite her denials, there was little doubt she'd been the one who'd given the Runner Lucy's name, but punishing her that extremely would have been too close to home and therefore unwise. It would have been guaranteed to increase Bow Street's interest in the Salon, not lessen it. The plan had been to distance the house from all suspicion.

Appearing to mull the proposal over, Mudd nodded thoughtfully. He looked towards Ridger. "Great minds, eh?"

Ridger said nothing.

Mudd looked down at the crumpled form at his feet and then up at Flagg. "Charlotte, right?"

Flagg nodded.

"Ah, well y'see, Tommy, Captain didn't want just any moll. He was . . ." Mudd looked to Ridger for help.

"Specific," Ridger said.

"That's the word," Mudd said. "Specific. Means it has to be her." He fixed Flagg with a pointed gaze. "Same as it has to be you."

A coldness surged through Flagg's gut which had nothing to do with the temperature in the room. He looked past Ridger's shoulder, searching for an escape route. They'd seated him because that way he'd be easier to control. He still had his cudgel stuck in his belt. It was digging into his spine but it might as well have been back in the bloody carriage for all the good it was going to do.

"I've got money," Flagg said quickly. "Been putting it aside."

It wasn't enough to keep Charlotte in lip balm, but with these two it was worth a try.

"Always nice to have something for a rainy day," Mudd agreed. "My old man used to tell me that. Useless git."

"Look the other way," Flagg said, "and it's yours."

Mudd's eyes took on a speculative glint. "You mean that?"

Flagg nodded. He didn't dare speak for fear of the tremor there would be in his voice. Mudd and Ridger were the sort of men who could smell fear and Flagg didn't want to give them an opening, or the satisfaction.

"Don't know what to say," Mudd said.

A flicker of hope rose fleetingly in Flagg's breast, but it sank like a stone a second later when Mudd shook his head and said, almost sadly, "Only, no can do. Be more than my life's worth, and I'm not just sayin' that, am I, Jack?"

178

"He's not just saying that," Ridger agreed and before Flagg could protest further, Mudd rammed the pistol against Flagg's right temple and fired.

The report echoed off the walls. Flagg's head jerked back with the impact of the ball, and blood and brain matter burst from the top of his skull. As his corpse slumped, haloed with powder smoke, Mudd gave a sad shake of his head. "He was right, y'know. He did save my life. Hadn't been for him, it would have been one of them Frog prison cells for certain."

"Valenciennes," Ridger said wearily. "I know. I was there, remember?"

Mudd nodded absently. A groan came from his feet and he looked down to where Charlotte was beginning to stir.

"Best get on with it," Ridger said, following his gaze. "You or me?"

"Your turn," Mudd said.

As Ridger nodded and drew the knife from his belt, Mudd knelt down and placed the spent pistol on the floor close to Flagg's downward-reaching right hand. He looked up. "You got the note?"

Ridger reached into his pocket and withdrew a folded piece of paper.

"Off you go, then," Mudd said. "Least this time we don't have to dump 'em in a pit. Bloody near did my back in, lifting the other one over that bleedin' wall."

Charlotte's eyes opened.

The first thing she saw was Flagg's dead body, leaking into the floorboards. She had no time to react before Ridger grabbed the back of her coat collar and pulled her towards the table at the end of the room. As he did so, the beads in her hair came loose and cascaded on to the floor like tossed shotgun pellets.

Only then did she start to scream.

14

Winter, Hawkwood reflected, was the time you'd have thought there'd be less flies around, until a dead body turned up and then the little bastards were everywhere. In this case, with two bodies on offer, the damned things were spoilt for choice.

A few were exploring the exit and entry wounds in Flagg's skull. Hawkwood wafted them away as he bent over the corpse. Some were reluctant to depart and stayed where they were, clustered around the edges of each cavity while others crawled between strands of hair as though looking for a place to hide.

No doubt about the cause. The evidence was as plain as day. Hawkwood picked the pistol from the floor. An anonymous but effective weapon; the same could be said for the knife, which looked as if it was about to fall from Flagg's half-open left hand; the blood congealed along the blade and around the hilt and on Flagg's palm and fingers. Blood had also settled around the shoulder of Flagg's jacket, while some had pooled and dried around the inside of the collar. To judge by the close-contact powder burn around the entry wound, death would probably have been instantaneous.

A grim way to welcome the morning.

Though the day had started pleasantly enough. He'd been at breakfast, chatting to Maddie, when word had arrived in the form of a Bow Street constable who'd been dispatched by Ezra Twigg on Magistrate Read's orders.

"*Another* messenger?" Maddie said warningly, as she eyed the constable's approach. "I find any of my napkins missing and there'll be the devil to pay."

Baulking at the sight of the Blackbird's landlady, hand on hip and eyebrow aslant, the constable threw Hawkwood a questioning glance.

"Don't look at me," Hawkwood said as he beckoned the constable forward. "I only lodge here."

Behind him, Hawkwood heard Maddie mutter something inaudible beneath her breath as she shook her head and turned away, leaving the constable to complete his errand and pass on the instruction that Hawkwood was to report to Bow Street directly.

"We have two bodies," James Read told him when he arrived. "They require your attention."

"*We?*" Hawkwood enquired cautiously.

"By virtue of proxy; they were discovered off Paddington Street, on the Somers Town border."

It took a second for the significance of the address to sink in.

"That's the Garden's domain."

"So it is," Read said.

"They're still short-staffed?"

"You know," Read said blandly, "I do believe they are."

Straightening from his examination of Flagg's corpse, Hawkwood looked to where Quill was leaning over the second body.

"I'll say one thing," Quill said over his shoulder as Hawkwood approached, "with you, it's never boring."

"Got you out of your damned cellar," Hawkwood said.

"True," Quill agreed, "though I'd hardly call this a change of scenery."

"You complained the last time," Hawkwood said. "You asked why you couldn't have examined the body where it was."

"So this time you provide me with a brace of them? I'm touched."

"Consider them tokens of my esteem."

"More like a bloody liberty," Quill muttered. Taking a rag

from behind his apron strings, he wiped his hands. "You recognize her, you say?"

"Yes."

"Working girl?"

Hawkwood nodded.

The surgeon indicated the rose high up on the corpse's right arm. "Were they related?"

"Same family."

Quill stared at him.

"Not in the way you think," Hawkwood said.

Quill let that one go, perhaps sensing that Hawkwood wasn't in the mood to expand.

"Well?" Hawkwood said. "Do I have to ask?"

Quill pursed his lips. "I'd say not; asphyxiated, severe fracturing of the facial bones, lacerations across the lower torso. See for yourself."

The surgeon stepped back.

The bodice of the dress and the thin cotton chemise beneath it had been torn and pulled down to the waist, making the tattoo visible, while the hem had been raised to reveal silk stockings tied above the knee and pale thighs splayed above. The body bore little resemblance to the vibrant young woman Hawkwood remembered.

The scratches were there, scabbed with blood:

⟨ A R I T A ⟩

Reaching forward, Hawkwood drew the chemise back over the corpse's breasts. "Violated?"

"The way her clothing's in disarray would suggest it, but there's no sign of bruising or forced entry, so I'd say no." He turned. "She *was* a moll; maybe she offered it up in exchange for her life."

"Didn't work, did it?" Hawkwood said.

Quill jerked his chin at the body in the chair. "Looks like you have your man, though. Did you know him, too?"

Hawkwood nodded. "Name's Flagg."

"Who was he?"

Hawkwood explained.

Quill frowned and then made a face. "Can't have been easy, surrounded by all that flesh; knowing all those callers were enjoying something he couldn't afford. So much for not shitting on your own doorstep. He must have known you were closing in and decided on one last play before ending it." The surgeon looked about him. "Wonder why he chose this place; wherever the hell we are."

"Hopkins thinks it could have been a chapel."

"Hopkins?"

Hawkwood jerked his chin to take in the other end of the room and the constable guarding the entrance.

"Ah," Quill said, "thought he looked familiar."

"His father's a vicar. He says the benches could be pews and this was probably the altar."

"Does he?" Quill glanced down at the stringy remnants of what might once have been a lace-trimmed linen cloth, upon which the body was lying and which concealed the oblong structure beneath it. "I'll be damned. I hadn't realized. Mind you, doesn't look like any chapel I've been in." He stared up at the walls and the mass of cobwebs suspended from them.

"Me neither," Hawkwood said.

"Don't tell me the lad's father held services here."

"No, though it's possible he knew the priests who did."

"Priests?" Quill's chin lifted. "Papists?"

"French émigrés, on the run from the Terror."

Surprise showed on the surgeon's face. "That's going back a while."

"Before my time," Hawkwood said. "Hopkins says he remembers his father telling him that when the émigrés arrived a lot of them were clergy with nowhere to worship."

"No Papist chapels?"

"Only the ones attached to embassies. They petitioned King George and he gave permission for them to put up their own, so long as they didn't include bells or steeples."

"*Hopkins* told you all this?" Quill said.

183

"The font of all knowledge in religious matters," Hawkwood intoned solemnly.

Quill stifled a groan.

"Started off by converting derelict buildings and cellars, apparently. It seems there were quite a number dotted about the city: Soho, Tottenham, Cripplegate – wherever the Frogs settled. There's one that's still intact over on Little George Street, so he tells me: the Chapel of the Annunciation."

"Did this one have a name?"

"He doesn't know."

"Not entirely omnipotent, then," Quill said wryly.

"No, but he's keen. He assisted me with the Hyde case. He'll go far, if he plays his cards right. I'm told he wants to be a Runner."

"God save us," Quill said. "Bad enough with just the one; not sure I could manage two of you."

"You'll miss me when I'm gone."

"The sad thing is, you're probably right," Quill agreed morbidly. Turning, he approached the chair and the body slumped bloodily upon it. Casting a dispassionate eye over the entry hole and the fist-sized exit wound, he let out a grunt. "Well, I doubt he'll have felt much, which is more than can be said for his poor bloody victims. Quicker than the rope, that's for sure, which is a damned shame. You said he was a soldier, yes?"

Hawkwood nodded.

The surgeon pursed his lips. "Probably accounts for his means of self-dispatch. Accepted his guilt, was overcome with remorse; didn't want to go through the indignity of a trial; decided this was the honourable way out."

"I'd question the word 'honourable'," Hawkwood said. "Any thoughts as to when they died?"

Quill made a face. "Well, judging from the degree of rigor and the clotting around your man's skull, it's been more than a few hours. Midnight or thereabouts; possibly an hour or two earlier. Who found them?"

"A watchman."

"I'll wager that made his night. Do we know the circumstances?"

"Does that make a difference?"

"Not especially, just curious."

"Let's say it's open to debate."

"Really?" Quill said. "This, I've got to hear."

"It's only that the man was worse for wear when he made his report, white as a sheet and reeking of rotgut. Plus, he's seventy if he's a day, so he wasn't very coherent. Either he was looking for a place to sleep off the booze or enjoy another snifter and found more than he bargained for or else he stumbled across the bodies while doing his rounds, took the grog to get over the shock and passed out. Then came to, found it wasn't a bad dream after all and decided to cover his arse by sounding the alarm. Whatever the case, we've got another young woman, beaten and stabbed. Hopkins thought it might be connected to our earlier find and delegated himself to pass the word."

"And here we are," Quill said.

Hawkwood nodded. "And here we are."

"Hell of a thing," Quill said, running a hand across his bald scalp.

"Indeed," Hawkwood said.

Quill's hand stilled. "You don't sound that convinced."

"I'm not."

"Because?"

"I'm not sure." Hawkwood stared down at Flagg's body. "Too convenient, maybe?"

Taking the knife from the bloody fingers, he examined the blade. "This *is* the weapon, yes?"

Quill held out his hand. Hawkwood passed the knife over and followed the surgeon as he returned to the altar. As he did so, he felt something crunch beneath his foot. He looked down. Several small white beads were scattered across the floor. They looked like calcified rabbit droppings.

At the altar, Quill turned down the chemise and placed the blade against one of the incisions. "I see no reason to suppose otherwise." Before Hawkwood could comment, Quill shifted the point of the blade and scored it through a patch of unmarked skin. As the flesh parted, Quill raised the blade away. "I'd say that answers your question. In my considered opinion, based on my experience as a Coroner's surgeon, this *was* the knife used."

When Hawkwood did not reply, Quill said, "Are you familiar with the principle of Occam's razor?"

Rearranging the chemise so that the body was again covered, Hawkwood stared down at the bruised face and the blonde hair and the remains of the pearl string that had been braided through it. "No, but I'll wager you're about to enlighten me."

"He was a friar, a learned man – scholar, theologian, philosopher – of the Franciscan order, I believe. It was his contention that when faced with a problem, the explanation that required the fewest assumptions was most likely the correct one. There's a Latin term for it."

"I thought there might be."

"*Lex parsimoniae*: the law of parsimony. In other words . . ."

"The evidence speaks for itself. We have two bodies and two weapons. Flagg killed the girl and turned the gun on himself to avoid the noose."

"Yes."

"That simple?"

"Don't blame me, blame Occam."

"Pity he's not here; otherwise he and I might be having a serious discussion."

"You'd have to dig him up. He's been dead four hundred years."

"In that case, I'll let him rest in peace. I've had my fill of raising the dead this week."

Quill handed back the knife.

"Wise choice," he said amiably.

"*Too* convenient?" Read, with his back to the fire, looked sceptical. "How so?"

"Well, for a start, how many foot soldiers do *you* suppose are versed in Latin?"

Looking affronted at being challenged by a subordinate, Read said huffily, "I do not have the slightest idea."

"Me neither. Most of the ones I've served with could barely write their own bloody name."

"But it is not outside the realms of possibility," Read said calmly. "You had Surgeon Quill with you?"

"Yes."

"And what was his verdict, based on the evidence?"

"Murder followed by suicide."

"Well, then."

"I know," Hawkwood said. "Occam's bloody razor."

Read's right eyebrow formed a questioning arc.

"He was a monk. He . . ." Hawkwood began, only to be silenced by the Chief Magistrate's raised finger and weary expression.

"Thank you, but I am not *un*familiar with the theory."

Lowering his coat-tails, the magistrate retreated behind his desk. "On this occasion, despite your reservations, I'm inclined to side with Surgeon Quill: the obvious solution *is* the most tangible. You have your killer. The mystery is solved."

"I'm not sure anything was solved; more like handed to us on a platter."

The magistrate spread his palms. "Either way, the case is closed." Bringing his hands together, Read leaned back. "Would that every investigation was brought to such a tidy conclusion."

Too tidy, Hawkwood thought, though he wasn't sure why. It was just a feeling, like an indistinct shape glimpsed at the edge of a fog before the mist closed in around it.

"Which means," Read said, "that *this* Office's investigations can now take priority." Adding pointedly: "I'm sure I can find a fresh case worthy of your . . . talents."

"There is something I should do first," Hawkwood said, adding tactfully, "with your permission."

Read's head came up. "And what would that be?"

"Offer my condolences."

The magistrate frowned, instantly suspicious. "To whom?"

"The grieving widow."

* * *

Clothed informally in a white morning dress, her dark hair held in place by an opal blue bandeau, Eleanor Rain laid down her cup and, in a measured movement, dabbed a napkin to her lips.

"Did I not make myself clear? You are no longer welcome here."

"This isn't a social visit," Hawkwood said, aware of the manservant, Malcolm, hovering apologetically in the background by the drawing room's open door.

She laid the napkin down. "It could not have waited?" She threw the man-servant an accusatory look. "It's barely morning."

"Ah, now," Hawkwood said, "there's the rub. With homicide, there's rarely a convenient moment."

She'd been on the point of reaching for her cup. Her hand paused. "Homicide?"

"The killing of one human being by another; it's from the Latin."

That was for Quill.

She flushed. A nerve pulsed along the underside of her jaw. "There has been another?"

"Tell me about Thomas Flagg," Hawkwood said.

Startled by the deflection, she frowned. "Thomas? I don't follow . . ." When Hawkwood made no move to respond, she stared at him, before remembering there was a third party in the room. She turned. "Thank you, Malcolm. That will be all."

The door closed. She regarded Hawkwood for several seconds. "You were saying?"

"Flagg. How long did he work for you?"

Her chin rose. "*Did?*"

"How long?"

She frowned. "I believe it is almost four years, or thereabouts. May I ask why—"

"What do you know about him?"

A fresh flicker of irritation crossed her face. "He was a soldier, a sergeant. He served in the Peninsula; Ireland, too, I understand. Why are you asking?"

"And how did he enter your employment?"

"There was a vacant position. He was recommended. I—"

"By whom?" Hawkwood wasn't entirely sure why he was asking that question.

"It was Thomas's predecessor who arranged his appointment. I merely gave my approval. I seem to recall the suggestion came from one of our gentlemen who'd experienced military service and who was distressed by the number of former soldiers forced to resort to begging on the streets. My thought was he knew Thomas and believed him to be of sound character and wanted to repay his years of service to his regiment and his country. We took him on as a factotum. When Francis – my former man – left my employ, it was only natural that Thomas succeeded him. Now, I insist you tell me—"

"Flagg's dead."

The room went quiet. She stared at him.

"He killed Charlotte and then he shot himself."

"Charlotte . . .? What— No!"

"Their bodies were discovered earlier this morning."

She shook her head dully. "There must be – there has to be – some mistake."

"No mistake. I identified them myself. Did Flagg own a pistol?"

"What? A pistol? I have no idea. It's possible. Something he acquired from his soldiering, perhaps? Was that how he . . .? And Charlotte? How?"

"Beaten and stabbed."

The words took a moment to sink in. Then: "The same as Lucinda," she said hollowly. "He killed them *both*?"

"The Coroner's surgeon will testify to that effect, yes."

Eleanor Rain fell silent, hands clasped in her lap. After several seconds she drew herself up, fixed Hawkwood with a steady gaze, and said calmly, "It is over then?"

Hawkwood said nothing.

She continued looking up at him. "What am I to tell the others? Poor Charlotte; all the girls loved her. And how am I going to explain the monster was here all the time, under our own roof?"

"Were he and Charlotte close?"

189

"Close?" She frowned at the word. "You mean . . .? No! Of course not! Why would you think that?"

"Trying to get a measure of the man, that's all."

She stared at him and then looked doubtful. "I suppose it is possible they formed an attachment without my knowledge. Though why then would Thomas kill her? Unless he discovered that Charlotte knew he had killed Lucy and realized he had to silence her. Who knows what goes through a murderer's mind when he knows there is no way out?"

Her face took on a thoughtful expression. "He told me once that he would never forget the things he had seen as a soldier. You were one . . . before. Is it possible that a man's mind can become so affected by the horrors of war that he commits horrors of his own, killing defenceless women?"

Hawkwood thought back to his conversations with Apothecary Locke, recalling how Locke had once told him that even retaining the memory of a single catastrophic event could alter a man's behaviour. "With some men it would be inevitable."

"So much that he could be overcome by the depravity of his crime and end his own life?"

"War affects men in different ways, so I'd say yes, it is possible. I'm told he chaperoned the girls when they made house calls."

She frowned again at the shift of emphasis. "On occasion, yes."

"Were he and Charlotte making a call last night?"

On the verge of replying, Eleanor Rain hesitated and then, as if struck by a sudden realization, she said, "Forgive me, but I fail to see how that is relevant. Your investigation is over, is it not? You have your culprit."

"I'm considering every option," Hawkwood said evenly.

"What does that mean?"

"It means I'm considering every option."

Something moved behind her eyes, as if a shutter had snapped shut.

"In that case, then so must I. You have your killer. He is dead. As far as this establishment is concerned, I see no legitimate reason for continuing this conversation. The matter is closed."

Pursing her lips, she added: "My clients expect privacy and

discretion, and I intend to honour that pledge." Her eyes glinted a warning. "I would remind you that I am not without influence in certain quarters. It would be a great pity were you to jeopardize your career over an irrelevance."

"An *irrelevance*? Two of your girls murdered?"

"And *you* have informed me the individual who killed them is dead. There is an end to it. I have reputations and livelihoods to protect, while you have your career to consider. I'm thinking it would not benefit your situation were I to spread the word that a certain Bow Street officer has developed an unhealthy interest in the personal business of those who would govern us and keep us safe. I would also remind you that two members of my family have been cruelly slain by a person they thought was their protector. It is a time for mourning, not an excuse to engage in needless persecution of the innocent. This interrogation is over. Good day to you, sir."

She rose swiftly and reached for the bell, half turning as she did so, allowing Hawkwood sight of the blemish on her right cheek, the attempt to conceal it beneath a layer of blush having been unsuccessful.

He was debating whether to comment upon it when the door opened.

"The officer is leaving, Malcolm. Please be so good as to show him out."

Hawkwood turned. "No need, I'm on my way." On the threshold, he paused. "Oh, I almost forgot; my congratulations on your promotion."

"Promotion?" the manservant said, puzzled.

"Damn it," Hawkwood said. "Now I've spoilt the surprise. Ah, well, never mind. I'm sure her ladyship will explain everything."

Before either could respond, he closed the door behind him. He was halfway across the lobby when a voice called softly from behind his shoulder: "Changed your mind about the *chevalet* then?"

He looked towards the stairs.

"You're an early riser, Captain," Annette said.

"Occupational habit," Hawkwood said.

She was dressed in morning attire, similar to Eleanor Rain,

save for the lack of a bandeau. Instead, her hair was drawn back and contained in a loose twist. The seductive smile was in place, the play on words as brazen as it had been at their first introduction and yet Hawkwood sensed there was something amiss. The smile did not extend to her eyes and, in fact, looked oddly forced, like a child who, having been coached to be on her best behaviour, was wary of putting a foot wrong now that an unexpected visitor had turned up.

She cast an eye towards the door from which Hawkwood had exited as if expecting it to open at any second. When it didn't, her gaze swung back. "Have you found him?"

She meant Lucy's killer.

Hawkwood paused. "We believe so."

She left the stairs and crossed to him quickly. "Who?"

He was on the point of referring her to her employer, but the intense look in her eyes brought back the memory of the other evening and his betrayal of her confidence. She had to be aware of that and yet she was still talking to him. He wondered why.

"It was Flagg."

She gasped and dug her fingers into his arm. "*Thomas* killed her?"

Them, Hawkwood almost said. Instead, he nodded.

Her eyes misted, her fingers loosened their grip. "I swear, when the bastard hangs, I'll be there. Front bloody row."

"Too late for that."

"What do you mean?"

"He saved them the job."

She stared at him. "He topped himself?"

"Blew his brains out."

Absorbing the information, she nodded and said forcefully, "Then I wish I'd been there to see *that*."

No, Hawkwood thought, you wouldn't; not if you'd seen the results.

She was still holding on to his arm, Hawkwood realized. He laid his hand on hers to lift it away. When she winced he looked down. Her sleeve had ridden up, exposing her wrist and the purple blotches that had until then been concealed beneath the muslin. She went to pull the hand away, only to succumb to his hold as Hawkwood held on and gently raised the sleeve further. She remained silent as he lifted the other sleeve. The same degree of bruising was visible on both arms.

Hawkwood felt the anger rise. "Who did this?"

"It's nothing. My last gentleman got a bit carried away, that's all."

"Carfax?" Hawkwood said.

"Eddie?" She looked horrified at the suggestion. "No, Eddie wouldn't hurt a fly." Taking her hand back, she glanced again towards the drawing room door. Warily, Hawkwood thought, and then he remembered.

It's not my cup of tea, but it takes all sorts.

"Was this punishment . . ." Hawkwood asked softly, ". . . for talking to me? Is that what this is? Was this on her ladyship's orders?"

He wondered about the mark on Eleanor Rain's cheek. If Rain was responsible for the bruising, had there been a moment of retaliation?

"I told you; it's nothing." She adjusted her sleeve. "I should be getting dressed."

A memory of their conversation came to him.

"You might have to lie a little."

"I'm a whore. You think I don't know how to do that?"

Not on this evidence, Hawkwood thought, as the door to the drawing room opened.

She turned away quickly.

"Annette?" Eleanor Rain said sharply.

The girl's face adopted a false brightness. "I was just bidding the captain a good morning."

"And now that you have done so, you may return to your room." Turning to Hawkwood, Eleanor Rain's eyes darkened. "You should leave."

Offering Hawkwood a quick look of regret, the girl turned to go.

"Not yet," Hawkwood said.

She paused, unsure.

"Your room," Eleanor Rain commanded again.

Annette threw Hawkwood a look of mute appeal.

"*Now*," Eleanor Rain said.

"No," Hawkwood said. "I don't think so." He turned to the girl. "Unless that's what you want?"

Annette stared at him. She looked, Hawkwood thought, like a trapped deer. "If it's not," he heard himself say, "then come with me."

Eleanor Rain drew in her breath. When she spoke, there was flint in her voice. "Upstairs, Annette."

Hawkwood turned to the girl. "Your choice, Annie."

"You'll be out on the street," Eleanor Rain said. "Don't listen to him."

"No," Hawkwood said. "She won't." He looked at the girl. "I can promise you that."

"You came with nothing, you leave with nothing," Eleanor Rain said. "You walk out of that door and your only possession will be the dress on your back."

"If you've a valise," Hawkwood said. "I'll wait for you."

Eleanor Rain went to take a pace forward.

"One more step," Hawkwood said, "and I'll arrest you for intimidating and assaulting a witness."

The blue eyes glittered. "A witness to *what*?"

"I'll think of something." Hawkwood turned to the girl. "Go now; get your things; if not for me, then for Lucy."

When she failed to move he thought he'd lost her, but then, favouring Hawkwood with a knowing grin, and gathering up her dress, she ran towards the stairs.

"Annette!" Eleanor Rain went to step forward again, only to be blocked by Hawkwood's raised hand.

Over her shoulder, Malcolm was looking on, indecision written across his face.

"What?" Eleanor Rain spat. "You think you're doing the girl a favour? She'll be back on the street in hours, and in that time there'll be fifty queuing outside, looking to take her place."

"Quite possibly," Hawkwood said. "Though I'm wondering

194

what recruitment's going to be like when word gets out two of your girls were murder victims."

Eleanor Rain let go a mirthless laugh. "You think that will make a difference? Take a look around. No moll is going to turn down an offer to work in a place like this. I take some whore off the street, dress her in silks and teach her how to walk and talk, she'll think she's in heaven. And all she has to do is open her legs. That stupid girl'll never have it this easy again – as she's about to find out."

"Her choice, though, not yours."

Before she could reply, Annette appeared on the stairs, dressed in a coat and carrying a small bag. Her left hand held a pair of blue velvet-sided boots.

Eleanor Rain's reaction was a vibrant hiss. "You ungrateful little bitch."

"Temper," Annette said. Head held high, she walked past Hawkwood and waited by the door.

With a wary glance towards his mistress, the manservant hurried across the lobby.

"You'll regret this," Eleanor Rain said, incensed by Annette's parting shot. "Both of you."

Malcolm opened the door and stood aside.

Hawkwood let the girl lead the way. There was a moment of hesitation as she approached the threshold, and then she was gone. Hawkwood followed. He looked back as the door started to swing shut. Beside him, he heard the girl let out a sigh. At which point, as the door closed, what looked like a small smile of regret crossed the manservant's lips.

"She'll make his life a misery," Annette said sadly. She stood there: a slight figure, her worldly belongings in her hands. Looking up and down the street, her gaze was forlorn. "So, now what? You going to take me home?"

"No."

Her expression changed. She fixed Hawkwood with a wary look. "You're not going to try and save me, are you? Had a vicar promise to do that after I spanked his bum with a bunch of holly twigs."

"Not that either," Hawkwood said.

"In that case, I give up. Where *are* we going?"

Hawkwood smiled.

"I thought I'd introduce you to a friend of mine."

15

"And what makes you think," Connie said sternly, "that I can afford to take in waifs and strays just because *you* feel sorry for them?"

"Took *me* in," Jago said, turning from the window. "Didn't have a problem with that."

"That's because you're old and on your last legs. You *need* looking after."

Jago threw Hawkwood a crooked grin. "And they say romance is dead."

"I'm sorry," Hawkwood said, "but I couldn't think of anywhere else."

"Oh, well, that's all right, then," Connie said, and shook her head wearily. "You men."

"If you do take her in," Hawkwood added cautiously, "she won't need coaching."

"I ain't going to ask how you know that," Jago said.

Connie looked at Hawkwood askance. "I know Runners do the odd job on the side, but I always thought that was protection work, not procuring."

"Nice one," Jago said, still grinning.

"And you can wipe the smirk off your face," Connie said.

"Me?" Jago protested. "What the hell did I do?"

"Guilty by association," Connie said.

"If you must know," Hawkwood said, "it didn't feel right,

leaving her there. She wouldn't admit it but I'm damned sure those bruises are Rain's doing. She'd have known it was Annie who told me about Lucy."

"And you didn't think they'd take it out on her after you'd left?" Connie said, incredulous. "Shame on you."

"Captain was only doing his job," Jago cut in, earning himself another accusing look.

"No, Connie's right," Hawkwood said. "It *is* my fault."

"Well, hallelujah," Connie retorted. "A man with a conscience."

Before either Hawkwood or Jago could respond, in a softer tone she said, "You think it was Rain who hit her?"

"Well, the bitch has a temper. I saw some of it in action. But with Lucy dead, I think it's more likely she rented Annie off to some of Lucy's more forceful gentlemen callers. Annie told me that Lucy didn't mind being chastised because it earned her extra money. From what I understand, Lucy was Rain's number one punishment moll, so she'd have needed someone to fill in. There's a girl called Helena, but I'm guessing Rain chose Annie out of spite. I doubt it was voluntary. When we talked, Annie told me she didn't take punishment herself; she only gave it out."

"You believed her?"

"I did, yes."

"I took a look," Connie said. "She's got the marks on her backside as well."

"Lucky it wasn't the face," Jago growled.

Connie shook her head. "It's never the face; bad for business. No one'll go with a girl with a split lip and a black eye."

"Where is she now?" Hawkwood asked.

"Theresa's keeping her company. By the way, you know the girl has a soft spot for you, don't you? Though Lord knows why, considering what you did."

"That ain't good," Jago said. "She knows you're taken, right?"

Hawkwood nodded. "She knows."

He looked at Connie, who looked back at him. "If it had been anyone else asking . . ." Connie said.

"So she can stay?"

Connie sighed resignedly. "If she wants to. As you say, she's a bright girl and Theresa vouches for her and she'll be safe here. She won't have to do anything she's uncomfortable with. Don't know what we'll do about that bloody tattoo, though."

"She could get another one done over the top," Jago said. "A daisy or something."

Connie threw Hawkwood an exasperated glance. "You see what I have to put up with? It's a wonder we let him out on his own." She rose to her feet, smoothing her dress. "Anyway, I'll go tell her the good news."

"Connie?" Hawkwood said.

Connie turned.

"Thank you."

Connie smiled. "That's what friends are for."

The two men watched her leave the room.

"So," Jago said, leaning forward. "You got the bastard."

"Looks like it," Hawkwood said.

"Bleedin' Tommy Flagg; who'd've thought? And the beggar was under her ladyship's nose all the time. That had to hurt. How'd she take it?"

"Not well; though not that badly, either, considering. She seemed more aggrieved about Annie walking out than she was knowing Flagg killed two of her girls."

"Tells you everything you need to know about the bitch, then, right? Then again, she did take Tommy in; I suppose that's a mark in her favour."

"How well did you know him?"

Jago shrugged. "Like I said when you mentioned him after your first visit: word gets round. You pick up snippets, and I did see him out and about. You know what it's like: old soldiers tend to 'ave regular haunts. Can't say as I'd've stood him a wet, mind."

"Why's that?" Hawkwood asked.

The former sergeant released a look that was part awkward smile, part grimace.

"What?" Hawkwood pressed.

"Not sure we had a lot in common. One of those snippets I

mentioned? Didn't tell you before, but I did hear tell he wasn't exactly one for the ladies." Jago threw Hawkwood a pointed look. "If you know what I mean. Only a rumour, mind; nothin' in the way of proof, and it ain't as though he'd shout about it. Can't recall how I 'eard, so there might not be anything in it." He paused, then added speculatively, "Could account for why her ladyship employed him, though."

"You mean, there was no chance of him wanting to sample the merchandise?"

"Like I said, only a rumour."

Hawkwood absorbed the information and put it to one side in his mind. "He told me he'd served with the East Norfolk."

Jago nodded. "The Fighting Ninth. Hard bastards."

"Weren't we all," Hawkwood said.

Jago gave a wry grin. "You can say that again. So maybe the rumours are just rumours. Mind you, from what I heard, he was lucky he made it that far. He was on the *Ariadne*."

For a second Hawkwood thought Jago was referring to the warship in which he'd arrived from America but then he recalled there had been an earlier vessel of the same name; a transport ship.

"The run-aground?"

"That's the one."

Hawkwood remembered reading the accounts. The event had stuck in the public's mind because it had happened the month after Trafalgar and although the news hadn't eclipsed the sorrow that Nelson's death had caused, it had been, nevertheless, another unforeseen naval catastrophe. Three transport vessels, deployed to move troops from garrison duty in Ireland to Germany in expectation of joining the allied armies on the continent, had been caught in a gale. Two ships had been driven into the Downs while the third, the *Ariadne*, had been wrecked off the coast of Calais. Nearly three hundred men had been taken prisoner.

"Tommy Flagg was one of the ones that got away," Jago continued. 'Tommy and some of 'is mates managed to avoid the Frog patrols. Made their way to Gravelines and fell in with some Kent free traders who brought them back home. It's what got him his corporal's stripes. For using his initiative, would you believe? Earned his sergeant's stripes a couple of years later, when the Ninth stormed the hill at Roliça. He received his wound at Vimeiro."

"He was wounded?"

Jago nodded. "Heard tell it was a bayonet thrust, cut through one of the sinews." Jago held up a fist to demonstrate. "Bolloxed up his trigger hand. He . . ."

His voice trailed off when he saw the expression on Hawkwood's face. "What?"

"*Which* hand?" Hawkwood said.

Jago realized his own was still raised. "Dunno. No wait, I remember; the times I saw him, he was always holding a glass in his left mitt, so it must've been his right one that got cut; meant he couldn't hold a musk— ah shit." Understanding flashed across the former sergeant's grizzled features. He looked up as Hawkwood rose to his feet. "Where you off to, or shouldn't I ask?"

"To get my coat."

"Right, and . . .?"

"A second opinion."

"Christ," Quill said wearily as Hawkwood entered the dead room. "Don't tell me there's been another one?"

Hawkwood shook his head. "No, though the day's still young. For now, I'll settle for what we have already. Where is he?"

"He? You mean our friend from the cellar?" Quill frowned and jerked his thumb towards a table at the back of the room. "Something wrong? You have that look."

"Have you examined the body since it was brought here?"

"I thought I'd save it for later," Quill said drily, "when I had a moment. Why?"

"Mind taking another look now?"

"I ask again, why?"

Hawkwood looked around, picked up one of the lighted candles and headed for the table. Quill, wiping his hands with a rag, had little option but to follow. "All right, don't bloody tell me."

"This one?" Hawkwood asked, indicating a body covered by one of Quill's filthy sheets.

Quill nodded. "Unless he got up and walked."

Hawkwood pulled the sheet back. "His right hand. Tell me what you see. Anything noticeable about it?"

Quill let go a theatrical sigh, tucked the rag into his apron strings and stepped forward. Hawkwood held the light close as Quill lifted the hand and turned it over in his own.

"Well?"

"Don't rush me," Quill said. Then his eyes narrowed. "Ah, I see what you're getting at. Tell me, you ever heard of a fellow called Galen?"

The name sounded vaguely familiar. Hawkwood didn't know why. He was about to ask if he was another Franciscan friar, when Quill said, "He was a Greek physician; plied his craft at the gladiator school in Pergamum, treating the wounds of men who fought in the great arenas."

"So he's been dead a while, too," Hawkwood said.

Ignoring the jibe, Quill said, "He warned that any attempt to suture a tendon would result in severe pain, convulsions and in, some cases, death. A gross misconception, of course, but it wasn't until a thousand years later that Avicenna recommended that repair *was* possible after such a laceration."

"Another Greek?" Hawkwood ventured, wondering why he was even asking.

"Persian. And it took another six hundred years before the Italians took *him* seriously."

Hawkwood's head was starting to spin. Then Quill said wearily, "So much for progress."

Turning the hand so that it was caught in the candle glow, he indicted two lines of ragged suture marks in the dead skin. "See how the thumb and forefinger are out of alignment? The tendons have been severed, here and here. Sword cut, would be my guess. You said he was a soldier. I'd say we're looking at a battlefield injury, poorly mended and done in a rush. I've seen better stitching on a foresail. I doubt he could aim his cock to piss with this hand, never mind fire a gun. You were right to have doubts."

"I never noticed before," Hawkwood said.

"No reason why you should," Quill said, lowering the hand down on to the table. "It's not immediately obvious, unless you're looking. What made you think of it?"

"Something a friend told me."

Quill nodded and let go a sigh. "Which puts you in a quandary, doesn't it? It means he didn't shoot himself. If he had done so, it would have been left hand, left temple. Whoever killed the girl is still out there."

"And someone," Hawkwood said darkly, "doesn't want us to know that."

"You're certain?" James Read said.

"As I can be. Quill is, too, and that's good enough for me. We've been duped. Or, rather, someone thinks we have."

"Who?"

Hawkwood shrugged. "If I knew that . . ."

"And for what purpose?"

"Apart from concealing the killer's true identity? I don't know that either."

Read sighed and placed his hands flat on his desk. "Not as tidily concluded as we supposed, then." He looked towards the window, where a light rain was pattering against the glass. "Damnation."

It wasn't often that Hawkwood heard the magistrate use a profanity, even a mild one. "I'll speak with the nightwatchman."

Read's attention swung back. "I thought you'd spoken to him already."

"Hopkins took his statement. He relayed the details to me. I wasn't thorough enough. I have no excuse. I was persuaded by the evidence at the scene."

"You said you had your doubts."

"I did. I should have listened to them, damn it."

Hawkwood knew he'd broken one of the first rules of any investigation. Never assume anything.

"You'll talk to him, you say?"

"He's the nearest thing we have to a witness. Hopefully, he'll have sobered up by now. He might remember something."

Read looked sceptical but nodded in agreement. "Very well, I'll await your report."

He watched as Hawkwood left the room and then sat back.

It looked as though Hawkwood's suspicions had been proved correct, but where that left them, Read did not know. He did know the Home Secretary would be expecting a progress report. In fact, a summons to present himself to Downing Street had arrived less than an hour ago. It was unusual to have meetings so close together, so the omens were not good. What had started off as a fair-to-middling morning was descending, Read suspected, into one that was likely best forgotten. That prompted the uncomfortable thought: would it not be better to accept the initial – albeit apparently constructed – evidence and let sleeping dogs lie? In his heart he knew the answer was no. His own conscience would not permit it and neither would Hawkwood's. Decision made, he called for his clerk. "Please tell Caleb to bring the carriage round."

Twigg scurried off. Read turned back to the window. The sky was the colour of slate.

It matched his mood perfectly.

The nightwatchman's name was Walter Cribb. Standing over him, Hawkwood, not for the first time, pondered the wisdom of trusting the night-time protection of the city to a motley crew of mostly elderly, arthritic men armed only with a staff, a rattle and a lantern. It wasn't as if they could hold all three objects at the same time. By the time they'd sorted themselves into any semblance of order, any miscreant they'd chosen to pursue was likely to be five streets away, enjoying a wet in the sanctuary of a convenient grog shop.

They were in the watch house. Clad in a scruffy greatcoat, leather helmet askew, Cribb was slumped on a wooden bench in the corner of the room, snoring gently. A portly man with a drinker's complexion and breath, his coat added to his bulk. His staff was propped against the wall; his lantern and rattle were on the bench beside him.

Watchmen patrolled their beats between the hours of eight in the evening and seven in the morning. The watches were divided into two shifts so Cribb, who, presumably, had been on the second shift, wasn't the only man sleeping off the night's travails, though how much actual patrolling had gone on, given the advanced ages of the men gathered around the room, was anyone's guess. Watchmen did not enjoy a good reputation; Londoners considered them lazy or infirm or both – in effect, just plain useless. Any villain worthy of the name knew that you only had to grease their palms and the majority of watchmen would happily look the other way at the opportune moment.

In an attempt to improve the situation, night patrols, consisting of part-time, plain-clothed constables, had been introduced, but the calibre of the men employed still left a lot to be desired. Many weren't much better than the watchmen they were intended to replace and some parishes lacked the resources to recruit sufficient numbers. As a result, the city was full of black spots where criminals could ply their trade with impunity, not least the Hatton Garden Liberty, which had one of the lowest number of watch patrols in the capital.

Hawkwood had commandeered Constable Hopkins to accompany him. The constable went to tug on the watchman's arm.

Hawkwood reached for the rattle. "Allow me."

Hopkins stepped aside.

Composed of a simple cog and spring mechanism, the implement wasn't that big; perhaps nine inches in length, with a handle similar to that of a Runner's baton, but the noise it produced made up for its lack of size, especially when placed close to the ear. Cribb jerked awake like a startled badger, while around the room other watchmen came to in varying degrees of responsiveness, ranging from half-comatose to instant panic. To those who'd been the most rudely roused, the din had probably sounded as loud as musket fire. When they saw that the reveille did not apply to them, they immediately drifted back into their slumbers.

"Morning, Walter," Hawkwood said jovially as the watchman blinked in rheumy confusion.

"Eh?" The syllable emerged from the old man's mouth in a

tobacco-induced croak. Sitting up, he used the heel of his hand to wipe the sleep from his eyes then stared about him.

"Looks like it's conscious," Hawkwood said. "Let's see if it talks."

"Heard that," Cribb said grumpily. "Same as I heard that bleedin' row. What's all the excitement? I finished me rounds."

"We know, Walter," Hopkins said. "That's what we want to talk to you about."

"That's *Mister Cribb* to you, boy." Cribb threw Hawkwood a suspicious glance. "Who's this?"

"He's *Officer* Hawkwood to you, and he has questions about the bodies you found."

"You and me spoke already," Cribb said, still addressing the constable. "Why don't *you* tell him, or weren't you listenin'?"

"I want to hear it from *you*," Hawkwood said, "*Mister* Cribb."

While it might have been on the tip of the watchman's tongue to give a young constable the edge of his tongue, the expression on Hawkwood's face must have told Cribb not to try the same tactic twice. "Tell us how you found them," Hawkwood said.

The watchman stared into Hawkwood's eyes, moved his gaze back to the constable then shifted uneasily in his seat. "Heard the yellin', didn't I?"

"Yelling?"

"It were that fella. Came out of that alleyway like 'is breeches were on fire."

Hopkins frowned. "What fellow? You didn't mention this before."

"Forgot," Cribb said blithely, before hawking up a mouthful of phlegm and spitting it into a nearby fire bucket. "Didn't have no time to think before."

"So who was he?" Hawkwood demanded.

The watchman looked blank. "How the 'ell would I know? All I *do* know is he was in a tearin' hurry. Grabs my arm, tells me there's been a murder, points at the entrance to this big house and limps off before I could stop him."

"He was *limping*?" Hawkwood said, wondering if Hopkins

would step in if he made a lunge for the watchman's throat. "Was he hurt?"

"Dunno. Maybe. Didn't seem to slow him down none. It *were* dark, mind."

"You didn't see his face?"

"Like I said, it were dark, and he was wearing a hat," Cribb added defensively.

"And all this slipped your mind until now?" Hopkins said disbelievingly.

"God's teeth!" Hawkwood swore. "What time was this?"

Cribb looked as if he was about to say something and then a shifty look crept over his face. "Not rightly sure."

As if his amnesia was of no consequence, the watchman shrugged, reached into his pocket and pulled out a small metal flask. He was on the point of removing the stopper when Hawkwood yanked the flask out of his hand.

"'Ere!" Cribb went to grab it back, only to find himself held down by Hawkwood's free hand on his chest.

Ignoring the reek of booze which still lingered on the watchman's breath, Hawkwood leaned in close. "Listen to me, you drunken sot. I don't think you're being entirely straight, so I'm giving you one more chance. I want you to think very carefully about what you were doing and what you saw and heard before and after you found the bodies. Lie to me and I swear to God your spit won't be the only thing that ends up in that pail. I'll cut your balls off and they'll go in there, too. Do we understand each other?"

The watchman stared at him. "You can't—"

"I said, *do we understand each other?*" Hawkwood increased the pressure on the watchman's chest.

Cribb flinched and looked about him, suddenly aware that the room wasn't as full as it had been and that the watchmen who remained were unlikely to leap to his defence. At the far end, the eyes of the watch house's night officer were cast downwards, the paperwork on the desk in front of him having suddenly attained critical importance. Cribb swallowed nervously and stole a glance at Hopkins; it was clear there would be no support there either. Staring longingly at the flask in Hawkwood's hand, he finally gave up and nodded weakly.

"Say it," Hawkwood said.

The response came as another dry croak. "I understand."

"Good. So?"

It didn't take long for Hawkwood to learn from the watchman's grudging confession that the discovery of the bodies bore a very close resemblance to the scenarios he'd outlined to Surgeon Quill.

It had been an hour into his shift – having spent the time until then in his shelter, fortified by grog to ward off the chill – that Cribb had finally decided to venture forth. Two streets into his patrol, he heard the sound of uneven footsteps hurrying towards him.

He'd called out "who goes there?" but there had been no answer, save for the appearance of a stumbling figure who'd almost knocked him over in the darkness. Jabbing a finger towards a nearby doorway and babbling "Murder! Murder!" the figure had disappeared lopsidedly into the gloom, leaving a startled Cribb to recover his wits as best he could.

It occurred to Hawkwood, as the watchman recounted his tale, that it had taken no small amount of gumption to enter the building and investigate. As it had been with Sexton Stubbs and the body in the grave, it would have been easier for Cribb to ignore the alarm and return to his shelter, leaving someone else to sound the alert. That he hadn't done so made Hawkwood reappraise his opinion of the old man, though he suspected it had been the alcohol, or possibly morbid curiosity that had given Cribb false courage. No doubt he was beginning to regret it now. Handing back the flask, he waited as Cribb took a swallow.

"Anything else you remember? Was there anyone else about?"

"Didn't see no one. Mind you, it were—"

"Dark," Hawkwood murmured. "Yes, so you said."

"Thought I 'eard a carriage, though." The admission emerged as a thin, asthmatic wheeze.

Hopkins' head came round. "Carriage?"

"Could've been wrong. I was fair shaken up. But I thought I 'eard hooves and wheels heading away. Didn't see nothing, though, on account of—"

"It was dark?" Hopkins suggested wearily.

The old man nodded.

"Then what?" Hawkwood pressed.

The watchman seemed to shrink down into his coat. His gaze drifted away and he shifted in his seat.

"Tell us," Hawkwood said, though he could guess what was coming.

"You went back to your shelter, didn't you?" Hopkins said.

Cribb's face crumpled. Falteringly, he confirmed the constable's suspicions. Horrified by what he'd seen, he'd returned to his lean-to and tried, with the aid of the grog bottle, to erase the murder scene from his memory. Eventually, he'd drifted into a drunken sleep. Upon waking, the memory, rather than subsiding, had come flooding back, whereupon, driven by both remorse and a dormant and newly awakened sense of duty, he'd made his way back to the watch house to report what he'd seen.

The watchman took another swig from his flask and shuddered. His eyes were moist. "Never saw anything like it; don't want to again, neither."

The slumped shoulders told Hawkwood it was unlikely any more information would be forthcoming. Reluctantly, he rose to his feet. "All right, old man. Go home, get some proper sleep."

In answer, Cribb looked about him and hunkered further down into his coat. "Reckon I'll stay here, if it's all the same to you. It's warmer'n my place. Besides, can't say as I want to be on my own yet awhile, if you want the truth. Not after all that's occurred."

As he spoke, the watchman's eyes clouded. Without a word, he raised the flask and tilted it towards his mouth. There didn't seem to be anything else left to say.

"What do you think?" Hopkins asked cautiously as he followed Hawkwood outside.

Hawkwood thought about what they'd been told. "I think

whoever staged the scene had to make sure the bodies were found sooner rather than later and that whoever did it chose their spot well. I think they probably knew the place was lightly patrolled and that Cribb liked to spend the night in his box with his flask, so they waited until he surfaced and then intercepted him, pointing him in the right direction while he was still sober enough to sound the alarm."

"The limping man? You think *he* might have been the real killer?"

"I think it's possible."

The constable frowned. "Forgive me, Captain, but it all sounds a bit . . ."

"Fanciful?"

The constable hesitated. "I was going to say . . . convenient."

"It does, doesn't it?" Hawkwood agreed. "But if you can think of an alternative, sing out."

Hopkins couldn't think of an alternative, which annoyed him. Hawkwood had been treating him almost as a trusted confidant, sharing with him the information that the murder scene might have been staged, and the young constable was anxious to prove that the Runner's faith in him was justified. It irked him, therefore, when he found himself with no option but to shake his head and say helplessly, "So where does that leave us?"

He was unprepared for the response.

"Damned if I know," Hawkwood said quietly.

16

"You have news," Addington said.

It was a statement, not a question; a fact not lost on James Read as he entered the Downing Street office.

"Home Secretary," he responded guardedly, glancing towards the fire and the suave-looking man seated in the chair beside it.

"You know Sir Edmund Saxby?" Addington said smoothly, as his secretary drew the door shut.

Read didn't and so offered a formal nod.

"Chief Magistrate." Saxby made no attempt to rise.

"Sir Edmund and I had a prior appointment," Addington said, "and he will be sitting in. He *is* privy to the workings of this office, so you may speak freely. You come bearing glad tidings, I understand. Your murder is solved."

Read switched his attention from the man by the fire. "Forgive me, Home Secretary, but might I ask how you came by that information?"

Addington looked down his long nose. "I *am* the Home Secretary."

Read thought he saw a half-smile appear on Saxby's face, while managing to keep his own expression impartial. A mistake, he realized, because Addington then frowned and said, "I sense a certain . . . reluctance. Is there something you're not telling us?"

Read considered his words. "There has been a . . . development."

Instantly the atmosphere in the room changed. It became distinctly chilly.

"*Development?*" The word emerged as a sibilant hiss. "Meaning what?"

"That our initial optimism may have been premature."

Addington fixed Read with a stare almost as cold as the falling temperature. "I was given to understand the murderer was found dead alongside the body of his last victim, having taken his own life to avoid capture. You're now telling me you are unconvinced?"

"I'm saying there are aspects of the case that may need re-examination."

"And you are basing that on what?"

"The evidence is still being assessed."

"By whom? Your *best officer?*"

"*And* the Coroner's appointed surgeon," Read said, and watched as the skin went taut along the Home Secretary's jawline.

"All this for a moll?" Saxby said from behind. "It does seem a trifle excessive."

Ignoring Addington, Read turned. "*Two* molls."

And a former soldier, if the murder scene was manufactured.

Saxby's eyes darkened. Then, abruptly, he inclined his head in acknowledgement and offered Read a condescending smile. "I stand corrected; two molls."

"You have something on your mind, Sir Edmund?" Addington said. "You have the floor."

Saxby hesitated. "Forgive me, Home Secretary; it's just that, as a not-inconsiderable contributor to the Exchequer, it does strike me that any investigation into the deaths of two whores would seem to be a rather unnecessary drain on the public purse. Surely, there must be other cases more deserving of the expenditure? 'Tis but a thought," he added, as if the comment had been of little consequence, even though he knew it hadn't.

Read sensed that an unspoken message had been passed. But to what end? Certainly the comment about the public purse appeared to have struck a chord, judging by the less than enamoured expression on the Home Secretary's face.

212

It had been Pitt, Addington's predecessor as Prime Minister, who'd introduced the tax system less than fifteen years previously, in order to fund Britain's war machine. Addington had abolished the system in the wake of the Amiens peace treaty, only to re-introduce it a year later when hostilities recommenced. Pitt had adopted the system when he returned to office two years after that, with one major amendment: he'd increased the maximum rate from five to ten per cent, a rate that had been maintained ever since.

Addington cleared his throat. "Sir Edmund makes a valid point. How significant is this new evidence?"

"At the present time? Circumstantial."

Addington's eyebrows rose. "Forgive me, but I'm not sure the Treasury can afford the luxury of funding further investigation based on circumstantial evidence when the prima facie evidence would appear to be staring you in the face. Do you have any other suspects?"

"Not as yet, Home Secretary."

"I see, so what you do have is your prime – your *only* – suspect, who was found *with* the body, an edged weapon in one hand, a pistol in the other, and what would appear to be a self-inflicted gunshot wound to the temple. And that's without the mutilations on the woman's body being an apparent match for those that were inflicted on the earlier victim. I'm wondering what could be clearer. It seems to me, Read, that you have all the evidence you require. Should that not suffice?"

"Suffice?" Read said. "Surely it is the truth that should suffice; truth that has yet to be determined."

"Perhaps you are in pursuit of a truth that is not there," Addington said.

Saxby shifted in his seat. Then Read said, "Are you proposing I close down the investigation, Home Secretary?"

Saxby's head came up. "Two whores and a bawdy house bully-boy – hardly pillars of society. Give it a week and I doubt any of them will be missed."

Read turned. "*That* is your reason for abandoning the enquiry? Because of their social standing, the victims' deaths are of no consequence?"

Even as he spoke, Read was uncomfortably aware that Saxby had come very close to echoing the words he had himself employed when assigning Hawkwood to the case. When he'd briefed Hawkwood he had stressed the need for a swift conclusion based on a lack of resources, both human and financial. Addington's associate had put forward virtually the same argument. Facing Saxby, it occurred to Read that, of the three victims, there was only one whose surname he knew: Flagg. The women were, and had been, known by their first names alone. In that one moment he wondered if Saxby was right. Here today, forgotten tomorrow.

But, then, if that was the reality, why did it feel so . . . unjust?

Addington placed his hands behind his back. "I should tell you that I have considered the matter carefully and on this occasion I'm of a mind to agree with Sir Edmund. I see no valid reason for prolonging this particular enquiry. If something looks like a mule, walks like a mule and brays like a mule, you have to at least consider the possibility that you have a mule on your hands."

Occam's razor, Read thought.

Addington hadn't finished. "As Chief Magistrate, you of course have autonomy over the deployment of your personnel. However, your budgetary restraints are governed by *this* office. Must I remind you of our previous conversation? There are far more pressing matters deserving of your attention *and* the Treasury's funding. In this case, I believe justice and the Treasury would be best served by submitting to the evidence already collated."

"Even though the real murderer may still be out there?"

Addington's eyes narrowed. "You do not know that for certain."

"No," Read conceded. "Nevertheless, we suspect—"

"You may suspect," Addington interjected sharply, "but I repeat: you do not *know*. Do you?"

Turning his back abruptly, Addington gazed towards the window. "Terminate the investigation, Read. Bow Street has better things to do. My decision."

Read felt the anger rise.

Addington, perhaps sensing it, turned. "You wish to respond?"

214

Read glanced towards the man in the chair and found that Saxby was regarding him closely with what might have been a thin smile of satisfaction on his jowelled face.

There's an agenda here, Read thought. What am I missing?

He kept his tone even. "Merely to request that my objection be noted, Home Secretary; for the record."

Addington's reply was brusque. "So noted."

"Well?" Saxby rose from his chair and moved to where Addington was standing by the window, looking down into the square below. "Will he comply?"

They watched as James Read climbed into one of the waiting carriages. They continued watching as the vehicle pulled away and disappeared round the edge of the building, heading towards the exit on to Whitehall.

Addington turned away from the glass. "Oh, I believe so, yes."

"Let us hope that *is* the case," Saxby said. He threw the Home Secretary a speculative sideways glance. "Perhaps we should have taken him into our confidence."

Addington shook his head. "A step too far, I think. Regrettably, our Chief Magistrate tends to view things as either black or white. You and I, on the other hand . . ." He let the sentence hang.

"Deal in shades of a more . . . greyish hue?" Saxby finished.

Addington remained silent.

"He has an exceptional record from his time on the bench," Saxby murmured.

"And his administration of the Bow Street Office has been extremely efficient. Yes, I'm aware. However, I'm not sure he would appreciate the nuances associated with this particular . . . situation."

"Despite the circumstances?"

"Despite those. Between you and me, I'd rather not place him in a position where he was forced to give us his decision. We might not like the answer."

"You'll keep an eye on him, though?" Saxby said.

"Of course, though it probably wouldn't be necessary had he

been satisfied and your man not been so careless, as would appear to have been the case."

"He won't have performed the task himself. He uses . . . intermediaries."

"Who appear to have been extremely lax in the . . ." Addington paused. "I was about to say the execution of their task. That is, if Read's suspicions have indeed been alerted."

"Yes, well, fortunately, our Chief Magistrate's suspicions – whatever they might have been – will remain exactly that: suspicions. There's no proof of culpability now that the investigation's been laid to rest."

"Nevertheless, it might be worth pointing out the lapse when next you speak with your associate."

"I'll make a point of it," Saxby said, "which brings us to our . . . friend. I use the term loosely."

"I understand he is suitably contrite," Addington said.

"As he was the last time . . ." Saxby took a breath, ". . . and the time before that. Cleaning up after his sordid dalliances has become rather a chore. Though I suppose we should be thankful they have been infrequent and thus not drawn the attention of the masses, and that his indiscretions have been confined to women of the lower orders rather than the upper strata. Had the opposite been the case, I doubt we'd have been able to contain the situation."

"Small mercies?" Addington murmured.

"Indeed. Though some might say it's been a modest investment, considering the possible return. And if all does go to plan we'll soon be rid of him and that will be the end of it."

"He'll have served his purpose, you mean."

Saxby nodded. "Don't get me wrong; if there wasn't so much at stake, I'd be tempted to throw him to the wolves. Our compliance does leave rather a sour taste in the mouth."

An understatement, if ever there was one, Addington thought. "I take it he's still under supervision?"

"He is."

"And the arrangements; how are they are proceeding?"

"Well, so far. A few days should see us ready."

"Good. This is one opportunity we can't afford to let slip by. As I mentioned to Read, our little corporal is on the back foot. His Russian escapade cost him dear in men *and* equipment and Wellington's gained the upper hand in the Peninsula. The Malet coup came within a hair's breadth of succeeding. We'd be fools not to take advantage of the disruption *that* caused."

"*Carpe diem?*"

"Indeed."

After several moments of contemplative silence, Saxby said quietly, "Talking of Malet . . ."

Addington turned. "What about him?"

"Some rather interesting information has come to light concerning Read's man . . ."

Addington frowned.

"Hawkwood," Saxby prompted. "The officer leading the investigation."

"So?"

"It turns out he was involved."

"Involved? I don't follow."

"He was there, in Paris. He was part of it: General Malet's coup attempt."

Addington stared at the other man. "Say that again."

"It appears one of your departments had ideas above its station. The Al—"

"One of *mine?*"

"The Alien Office. Superintendent Brooke persuaded Read to let him borrow Hawkwood for the duration. The plan was to infiltrate a brace of agents into Malet's group with a view to influencing his decision to subvert the empire – while the cat's away, and so forth. Buggers damned near got away with it, too."

Addington's face was still. "You said *a brace.*"

"Did I? Oh, yes, the other fellow was Wellington's man: Colquhoun Grant."

"Grant? I thought the French had him?"

"They did, for a while. He escaped during a prison transfer and ended up in Paris, of all places. It was he who got word to Brooke suggesting Malet might be pliable, but that he required assistance. Brooke sent him Hawkwood. They knew each other from Spain; comrades-in-arms, apparently. Anyway, we know the outcome. Read's man made it out. Grant stayed behind, lurking in the bushes. He's still sending Brooke regular dispatches."

The Home Secretary's eyes narrowed. "I was not told any of this."

Even though you're the Home Secretary? Saxby thought. "No? Well, Brooke likes to keep his cards close to his chest when it suits him. I'm not even sure the Prime Minister was informed. Had the venture succeeded, I've no doubt you'd have been given the word soon enough. Failure does tend to be less well-advertised."

Addington let that truth sink in before responding. "And you're telling me this now? Why?"

"I thought it might be of interest, given he's the fellow Read assigned to the investigation. It's as well Read's heeded your directive, is all I'm saying. The man's obviously brighter than your average police officer. We didn't need him on our backs."

Addington nodded absently. He was busy wondering if Saxby had told the truth about the Prime Minister not having been informed that a department of the British Government was attempting to overthrow Bonaparte's empire via a clandestine liaison with a cadre of renegade French generals. Had Liverpool really been unaware, or had he been in on the plot and chosen to keep his Home Secretary in the dark? That was worrisome in itself.

His thoughts were curtailed when he realized Saxby was still speaking. "My apologies," he said quickly. "I didn't quite catch that."

"I was saying that it gives us a clear run," Saxby said. "No distractions."

"One hopes so. What about transport?"

Saxby nodded. "All arranged: a navy cutter."

"And Jersey has been informed?"

"Governor Don and Auvergne are standing by."

Addington frowned. "Auvergne's due to retire, isn't he?"

"He is. Doesn't mean we can't take advantage of his expertise, though. His knowledge is too useful to have him put out to grass."

"Very well. In the meantime, let's pray that our man can control his urges. We've indulged him long enough."

"In a good cause."

"You believe that?" Addington asked quietly.

"I have to. We all have to, otherwise what has it all been for?"

"The greater good?"

"I sincerely hope so, though I can't say it's been easy, having to put up with his . . . proclivities."

"How were we to know?"

"Or guess at, given his particular calling."

"Quite," Addington said, unable to keep the distaste from his voice.

"Mind you, he's proved his worth so far. We can't deny that. It was through intelligence received from *his* informants that Brooke decided Grant's idea had legs. It was sheer bad luck that brought the plotters low. That's not something you can plan for. The good thing is, despite the generals' failure, we've been given another chance."

"Best not waste it then." Addington moved towards the fire, Saxby at his shoulder.

"Brandy?" Addington nodded to the decanter on a table by the wall. "I need something to warm me. There's a fearsome draught coming through that damned window."

"Most kind. Thank you."

Brandy poured, Addington passed Saxby a glass.

"We should drink to our endeavours," Saxby said, "now that the coast is clear." Adding with a thin smile, "So to speak."

Addington looked into his glass and then lifted it up. "The defence of the realm."

Saxby followed suit.

"Always," he said.

* * *

219

"And you *agreed*?" Hawkwood said, unable to restrain the disbelief in his voice. "Why would you do that?"

James Read looked up from his desk and said patiently, "Because he is the Home Secretary and, in case you've forgotten, we function at the behest of the *Home* Department."

"So, we capitulate?"

James Read sighed. He was on the point of responding when the door opened. Twigg stood there, bearing a sheaf of documents. Read waved him in with relief.

Twigg said, "I have retrieved what I could on Sir Edmund Saxby, sir. I hope it is sufficient."

"Saxby?" Hawkwood said. "Who's Saxby?"

"Mr Twigg is about to shed light on that, I hope." Read nodded to his clerk. "Proceed."

The clerk threw a quick glance at Hawkwood, adjusted his spectacles and consulted the papers in his hand. "Sir Edmund Saxby is a distant cousin to Viscount Althorp, with estates in the West Country, principally Devon. He was educated at Harrow and Trinity College, where he studied to become a barrister-at-law. Five years after being called to the bar he was returned as the second Member of Parliament for the pocket borough of Okehampton. He is a Trustee of the British Museum and served for a brief time as secretary of the Roxburghe Club."

"Roxburghe . . .?" Hawkwood enquired helplessly.

"Book collectors," Read said.

"They call themselves" – the clerk offered the magistrate an apologetic look – "bibliomaniacs."

Read winced as Twigg consulted his notes and continued: "Sir Edmund's main interest would appear to be religious tracts, obtained from monastic libraries dissolved during the Revolution and after Bonaparte secularized the religious houses in southern Germany. Supposedly, both he and Viscount Althorp use local agents to acquire rare books and manuscripts. He is reputed to have built up an extensive private library."

"Fascinating," Read murmured without enthusiasm. "What else?"

"He served as Lieutenant-Colonel to the North Devon Militia."

"And?"

Twigg blinked at the magistrate's clipped tone.

Read eyed his clerk. "I've a mind to know why the Home Secretary has such a high regard for his opinion. I doubt it's because he's well read."

Twigg checked his notes. "He is a former secretary to the Lord of the Treasury . . ."

Read's eyes brightened. "Ah, now we are getting somewhere."

". . . and a senior advisor to the Committee."

"The Police Select Committee?" Read sat back. "Well, that would also explain it, but I was not aware he was—"

"No, sir." It was Twigg's turn to interject.

"No?" Read said, perplexed.

"Forgive me, sir, I was not referring to the Police Committee. I was about to say the Committee for the Relief of French Emigrants."

There was an awkward pause during which the Chief Magistrate stared at his clerk.

Twigg took a breath and said, "It is not public knowledge, but the consensus appears to be that it was Sir Edmund Saxby who took over the running of the Committee upon the retirement of its founder, John Wilmot."

Read frowned. "You're referring to the Emigrant Office."

"That is the current incarnation, yes, sir."

"Emigrant Office?" Hawkwood said as, at the back of his brain, a tiny thought, like a small worm, wriggled hesitantly into life.

Read looked up. "John Wilmot was – is – a philanthropist and a former Member of Parliament – Tiverton, as I recall, and then . . . Coventry?" He glanced at his clerk, who nodded in affirmation. "He came to prominence when he was appointed to head a commission to enquire into the claims of American Loyalists who sought compensation for losses incurred during the American Revolution.

"It was through that endeavour that he became similarly moved by the plight of the émigrés who fled to London in the wake of the Revolution across the Channel. The Committee was set up to provide relief funds, initially for members of the clergy. He drew a lot of wealthy patrons to his banner – the Marquess of Buckingham, the Bishop of London, Wilberforce, among others – all championing the cause. Housing, clothes, bedding and food were the main provisions.

"When public subscription ceased, the Government stepped in and issued a Treasury grant, on the understanding that charity was extended to the laity because their numbers were also increasing. Eventually, it was deemed more beneficial if the exiles tended to their own relief, so the main committee – under Wilmot – was left to deal with policy, while a separate committee composed of émigrés was created to administer the funds, a proportion of which also provides comfort to their countrymen held in English prisons. The arrangement continues to this day, I believe."

Read fell silent, his brow still furrowed, then said. "You have something to add?"

Hawkwood realized that it was he, not Twigg, who was being addressed. "Maybe."

"At this juncture," Read said, "I am open to any and all suggestions."

"It's the place the bodies were found."

"What of it?"

"Constable Hopkins thought it may have been an old émigré chapel."

Read listened without interruption as Hawkwood explained.

"We're missing something, aren't we?" Hawkwood said.

Read threw him a sharp look before turning to his clerk. "Is there anything else on Sir Edmund?"

Twigg scanned the papers. "He is a Privy Counsellor and for a brief period held the office of Special Embassy to Vienna."

"And his current post?" Read prompted.

Twigg chewed his lip. "As far as I have been able to determine, Sir Edmund Saxby holds no official position within the current administration, at least at Cabinet level."

"And unofficially?"

Twigg hesitated and then said, "That is not entirely clear."

"What the hell does that mean?" Hawkwood asked before the Chief Magistrate had a chance to respond, earning himself another reproving glance from Read, who rose to his feet and moved to stand in front of the fire.

The Chief Magistrate chewed the inside of his lip. "The French have an appropriate term for it: éminence grise – one who wields influence from the shadows."

"Sounds like that bastard I met in France – Fouché," Hawkwood said. "So why the interest in Saxby?"

"The Home Secretary deferred to him during our meeting."

"Did he? Well then, I'd say we're definitely missing something, wouldn't you?"

At which point another tiny worm of thought raised its head.

"Damn it," Hawkwood said softly. "Bloody Ryder."

Twigg looked up from his notes.

"Rider?" Read said sharply. "What rider?"

"Not what – who," Hawkwood said. "I'm talking about our former Home Secretary."

"Richard Ryder?" Read frowned.

Hawkwood nodded. "It slipped my mind, but he was there when I visited the Salon. Maybe I've got it wrong, but doesn't *he* have a seat down in the West somewhere?"

"He does. He's the member for . . ." Read's face went still. ". . . Tiverton. As was his older brother, Dudley, and his father, Nathaniel, before him. In fact, it was Nathaniel who was succeeded by John Wilmot, who was in turn succeeded by Dudley."

"Well now, ain't that convenient. When I came up from Falmouth, the coach brought us through Okehampton. I remember there was a signpost: Tiverton, 30 miles. That's no distance. What are the chances that Ryder knows Saxby? Hell, Ryder being Home Secretary, their paths must have crossed at *some* point, surely."

Read sucked in his cheeks. "Which leads us where, exactly?"

"I don't know," Hawkwood admitted. "Frankly, I'm grasping at straws."

James Read bowed his head. A brooding silence followed,

punctuated by the slow ticking from the long-cased clock over in the corner of the room.

"Do you still want to close down the investigation?" Hawkwood asked eventually.

The Chief Magistrate raised his chin. "I think there may well be a few more questions that need answering."

Hawkwood smiled grimly. "I had a feeling there might be."

17

"Dear lord," Connie said, making a play of looking past Hawkwood's shoulder as he was shown into the drawing room. "Don't tell me you've brought another one. I'm running short of beds."

"In a bordello? That'd be a miracle."

Connie fixed him with one of her looks.

"Not that I'd dare to, anyway," Hawkwood amended hastily. "I know my place."

"That'll be the bloody day!" Connie murmured.

Hawkwood held up his palms. "I come in peace."

"That's all right then," Connie said, relenting. "But if you're after Nathaniel, he's out on business."

"Good for him, but it's Annie I'm here to see – if she's available."

"She is." Connie eyed him suspiciously. "And settling in nicely."

"I'd like a word," Hawkwood said.

Conscious of Connie's expression and of the emphasis she'd placed on the last part of her statement, he added in what he hoped was a reassuring voice, "Information; that's all I'm after."

Connie continued to scrutinize him. If confirmation were needed that the decision to bring the girl here had been the right one, it was the look on Connie's face. To the girls under her wing, Connie Fletcher was both employer and protector. Astute businesswoman and mother hen was a fearsome combination, and although he knew that Connie counted him as a

225

friend, Hawkwood couldn't help but release an inner sigh of relief when, finally, she relented and said quietly, "I'll go fetch her."

"Why, Captain Hawkwood," Annette said. Her smile seemed to indicate genuine pleasure as she entered the room, Connie at her shoulder. "How nice to see you again." Laying her hand on his arm, she whispered conspiratorially but loud enough for Connie to hear, "If you've changed your mind about the *chevalet*, I'm afraid there isn't one here. I've checked."

"Probably just as well," Hawkwood said, ignoring Connie's raised eyebrow. "How are you?"

"I'm very well, thank you. Mrs Fletcher has been most kind. She said you wanted to talk to me. Is it about Lucy?"

"Partly," Hawkwood said; which drew puzzled frowns from both women.

Connie turned for the door. "I'll leave you to it. If you want anything, ring the bell."

"No need," Hawkwood said. "It's likely you can help, too."

Connie paused, looked at the girl, eyed Hawkwood again to confirm she hadn't misunderstood and then nodded to the sofa and chairs. "Why don't we sit?"

Hawkwood remained standing while the two women took their seats. They gazed at him expectantly.

Hawkwood addressed the girl. "Annie, when I came to see you at Lady Eleanor's you said that Lucy had told you she was going to see a gentleman she thought might have taken a shine to her at an entertainment. Yes?"

She nodded. "I remember."

"And that he might have been a foreign gentleman."

"That's what she said."

"But she didn't know who, exactly?"

"No."

Hawkwood looked to Connie.

"It happens," Connie said. "A gentleman spots a lady across a room, but if he's with someone else at the time, or otherwise engaged, he makes a note for later. Then, when it's more convenient, he makes an enquiry. Or it could be that Lady Eleanor's running an introduction house as well." She regarded the girl carefully as she spoke.

Introduction houses, Hawkwood knew, were profitable businesses in their own right; well organized and offering what amounted to a bespoke service. Leading establishments provided male as well as female companions and were very exclusive. Through them, men and women – often with a spouse at home – could obtain an introduction to a person of their choice – male or female. Traditionally, it was more difficult for men to gain access, but once inside they could be assured that the women were beautiful and the males handsome and at the height of their profession – fashionable *and* accomplished.

A common practice was for a note to be sent to a gentleman at his club advising that new wares were available for viewing. Arrangement could also be made whereby the chosen "gift" was delivered to a certain address at a certain time, not unlike an upmarket tailor delivering a suit or a milliner a new hat.

"Wasn't my job to ask where they came from, so long as they coughed up the readies." The girl offered Hawkwood a knowing grin as she responded to Connie's implied question. "As I said, Lady Eleanor took care of business. We took care of the other."

"Lucy thought the entertainment might have been held in Marylebone," Hawkwood said. "Any thoughts as to where?"

The girl shook her head. "I don't recall mention of an address."

"How about when? Did she say?"

The girl's brow crinkled. "I don't think she was sure. It would've been recent, I expect, but not anything we'd both attended or she'd have told me, which means it was probably when I was having my monthly visit from Aunt Ruby. That'd make it two weeks ago last Tuesday or Wednesday." She glanced pointedly towards Connie as she spoke. "I know that 'cause I'm pretty regular." She looked towards Hawkwood. "The only one who'd know for certain would be her ladyship, but I can't see her telling you anything; not after you took me away."

"It'd be your word against hers, anyway," Hawkwood said, adding quickly, "Don't take offence. It's just that her answer's likely to be that Lucy was playing her own game and that she fed you a lie to cover the fact she was already arranging appointments for herself, which is why her ladyship threw her out. In other words, Rain will say she doesn't know who Lucy had an appointment with, and that brings us back to where we started. Unless . . ." Hawkwood turned to Connie, "you have any ideas?"

"Me?" Connie said.

"It could have been a soirée you were asked to provide for, or maybe some of your girls were taken there as companions. Two weeks ago at a Marylebone address? That sound familiar?"

"Unless Lucy was lying," Connie pointed out.

"There is that. But given Rain's habit of being economical with the truth, I'm inclined to believe Lucy told Annie exactly what Rain told her: that someone asked for her specially."

"And that she wasn't working for herself."

"And that she wasn't working for herself," Hawkwood agreed. "So if we *can* narrow it down to when and where, maybe we'd be getting somewhere."

Connie frowned and then her chin rose. "Y'know, I do seem to remember there was something . . . Wait, let me take a look." Rising to her feet, Connie moved to a small writing desk in the corner of the room. She removed a leather-bound diary from the top drawer, opened it and ran a practised eye through the pages. A few seconds later, she looked up, her expression thoughtful. "There *was* an entertainment – in Welbeck Street on the fifteenth."

Hawkwood drew a quick map in his mind. "That's close enough. Not far from the Salon, either. What can you tell me about it? Who was the host?"

"Sir Randal Gaunt."

"Who is . . .?"

"Rich," Connie said, with a wry smile. "Filthy rich."

"A regular?"

"So-so; generous, though."

"Landed gentry?"

Connie made a face. "Aren't they all? Made his fortune through the plantation trade. Rumour is, the family lost lands and money in the American Revolution. Still had enough left over to purchase a couple of merchant brigs and a partnership in Drummonds Bank, mind you, so it wasn't all tears."

Hawkwood was not at all surprised by the extent of Connie's knowledge. In her line of work, it paid to know as much about her patrons as possible. Her filing system was unlikely to be as comprehensive as Ezra Twigg's, but Hawkwood was willing to bet that Connie knew more about the background and preferences of London's aristocracy than they did themselves.

No doubt Eleanor Rain would have accumulated similar intelligence on the Salon's clientele. In fact, given the variety of customers who frequented both Connie's establishment and the Salon, and the propensity of men to wax lyrical about their achievements in the company of an experienced moll, it wouldn't have surprised Hawkwood to learn that the girls who worked both premises were better informed on the country's foreign and domestic policies, not to mention naval and military manoeuvres, than the Cabinet, Horse Guards and the Admiralty combined.

"How about names?" Hawkwood asked.

Connie shook her head. "Can't help you there, sorry. I've only Sir Randal's request and the date. I wasn't able to oblige as I'd a soirée over in St James's. Which is maybe just as well," Connie added softly. "Seeing as what happened."

"So he'd likely have asked the Salon to provide entertainment instead," Hawkwood said.

"Or as well as. It'd depend on the size of the guest list. What I do remember is that the lady of the house wasn't going to be present."

"Well, she wouldn't have been," Hawkwood said. "Would she?"

Connie shrugged. "You never know; it doesn't always follow. Once in a while, there'll be a host *and* a hostess, in which case they might require young men for the evening, as well as ladies. I've none on my books, but I know where to go if that's what's required. It was definitely gentlemen only, this time, though." Connie paused. "Another thing I do recall is I was asked if I had any French or French-speaking ladies available."

A small tingle ran along the back of Hawkwood's neck. "Is that unusual?"

"A request for a girl who speaks French? Happens occasionally; depends on who's asking. I've a few continental gentlemen – the Swedish ambassador, for one, though you didn't hear me say it – who prefer ladies who speak their own lingo; makes life easier if there's a misunderstanding or a mishap. Then there's others – military men, mostly – who like foreign girls on account of they find them more exotic. Likewise, there's a few that have a penchant for a coloured lass. There's one East India captain who has a fondness for the Oriental. As I said, there's all different tastes out there. Everything's available, if you know the right person."

"You'd better give me the address," Hawkwood said.

Connie gave it to him. "You're not going to do anything stupid, are you?" she enquired warily.

"I'm not sure," Hawkwood said. "Maybe."

Connie glanced at the girl, shook her head and sighed. "Sometimes, I wonder why I bother."

"He in?" Hawkwood asked.

Ezra Twigg looked up from his desk. "Chief Magistrate Read is away from his office at the present time." Glancing up from his work and down at the floor over the top of his spectacles, he clicked his tongue at the line of muddy boot prints Hawkwood had left in his wake.

"Would you know when he'll be back?"

"I would not." The clerk put his head on one side and fixed Hawkwood with a resigned look. "Perhaps *I* could be of assistance?"

"Sir Randal Gaunt," Hawkwood said. "Does the name mean anything?"

"Possibly," Twigg replied, somewhat guardedly, Hawkwood thought. "Might one be permitted to ask why?"

"One might. I plan to invade his privacy and I wanted to give His Honour fair warning. I also thought it would be useful to find out who I'll be confronting."

"Or who's likely to make a complaint against this office when you annoy them?" the clerk muttered, not entirely under his breath.

"Forewarned is forearmed, Mr Twigg."

"That'll be another old army saying, will it?"

"Why, Ezra," Hawkwood said, "and I thought I was the cynical one."

Twigg sighed, which Hawkwood had come to recognize as not necessarily a negative response. "How soon would you require the information, or shouldn't I ask?"

Hawkwood smiled.

At which Twigg shook his head wearily and laid down his pen.

Connie Fletcher's information was correct: Sir Randal Gaunt did come from land-owning stock, the greater part of the family's fortune having been accrued from plantations in the Carolinas. The main seat was a large estate in rural Wiltshire. As Connie had also intimated, the American Revolution had cost the family their colonial holdings, which they'd been coerced into selling at a substantial loss, not to a private investor but to the new Congress.

A period of consolidation had followed, during which time the foundations for fresh ventures had been laid, with new trading links established in the East Asian markets, ensuring a fresh fortune with which Sir Randal could indulge in whatever new interests caught his fancy, which over the years had encompassed steam boilers, canals, cotton mills, ordnance, a large London townhouse and various entertainments of the more intimate variety.

"Another pillar of society, then," Hawkwood said. "Anything I can use as a lever?"

Twigg did not look up but continued to study the papers he'd brought from the archives.

"Ezra?"

Eventually, the clerk raised his head. "There was a rumour, unsubstantiated."

"I'll bite. What sort of rumour?"

"It concerned the Committee."

"*Saxby's* Committee?"

The clerk nodded. "Though this would have been during John Wilmot's reign."

"You have my attention." Hawkwood waited.

"When John Wilmot resigned from the Committee, his leaving was . . . unexpected. He received no honour, nor, it would appear, any expression of gratitude for his works."

"Sounds odd, considering he was the guiding light."

"Indeed." Twigg laid the paper down and took off his spectacles, wiping the lenses with a handkerchief he took from his sleeve. "What is also most intriguing is that the previous year there was an investigation into the Committee's accounts by the Audit Office."

"Wilmot was implicated?"

Placing his spectacles back on, Twigg shook his head. "He was not. There is neither evidence nor any suggestion that funds were misappropriated in his name. There is merely an entry in the Committee's minutes chronicling his resignation."

"What was the result of the investigation?"

"No further action was taken."

"So there was no impropriety," Hawkwood said. "Everything was above board."

"The records merely state that no further action was taken," the clerk intoned pedantically.

Which didn't address the question, Hawkwood thought. "Is there something you're not telling me?"

"Only that John Wilmot's immediate successors did not stay long in office."

"Until Saxby," Hawkwood said. "We're back to coincidences again. So where does Gaunt fit in? And how come you've a file on the man, anyway?"

"One never knows when certain information will prove advantageous," Twigg said primly.

Hawkwood held the clerk's eye. "Did anyone ever tell you that you have a very devious mind?"

"Oh, indeed; several persons, which is why I have files on them, too."

Hawkwood tried to think of a suitable response. None was immediately forthcoming. He assumed Twigg was joking, but it wasn't always easy to tell. "All right, so, Gaunt . . .?"

"There was talk behind closed doors when Sir Randal Gaunt's claim for compensation for the loss of his American estates was met with a favourable response."

"Is there any reason it shouldn't have been?"

"The land was not confiscated. It was sold. Sir Randal received recompense."

"Well, yes, but far less than the land was worth. Wouldn't that entitle him to something?"

"Possibly, were he an *American* Loyalist. However, Sir Randal Gaunt is not an American. He is English."

"So he was not strictly entitled," Hawkwood said.

"He was not, and that was the Commissioners' first finding. This was also based on the fact that the overall amount being distributed in compensation was becoming harder for the Treasury to bear. The decision, however, was overturned on appeal."

"The American Revolution was a long time ago. This must have been a while before John Wilmot's resignation?"

"Yes, but claims are still being considered even now. On this occasion, Sir Randal Gaunt's claim appears to have been denied and appealed *before* John Wilmot's resignation and awarded *after* he left."

"When Saxby was in charge."

"Correct again."

"So maybe," Hawkwood said, "Wilmot resigned because he wasn't happy with the way things were going. Maybe he'd discovered other irregularities and didn't want to be tainted."

"By all accounts, he *is* a man of principle."

"And the Audit Office found nothing."

"It did not."

"But we do end up with a possible link between Saxby and Gaunt."

"It would appear so."

"The plot thickens," Hawkwood murmured.

"*Is* there a plot?" Twigg asked over the top of his spectacles.

"Based on the number of coincidences, I'd venture to say there's a fair chance. Though what it might entail, I have no idea."

"Then perhaps Sir Randal Gaunt can shed some light," Twigg said.

"I doubt he'll shed it voluntarily."

The clerk muttered something inaudible beneath his breath.

"Sorry, Ezra, I didn't quite catch that."

The clerk blinked. "I said that's never hampered you on previous occasions."

"Yes, well, I wouldn't get your hopes up," Hawkwood said. "There's a first time for everything."

18

As James Read followed the waiter through White's elegant first-floor coffee room, he saw that Henry Brooke was at his usual table. As if sensing the magistrate's approach, Brooke turned from the long window and its view over St James's Street and rose languidly from his seat. "Magistrate Read! How long has it been? How are you?"

They shook hands and Read smiled politely, knowing full well that Brooke would know exactly how long it had been since their last meeting, down to the minute. "I'm well, thank you. I was hoping I might find you here."

"And now you have." Brooke matched the magistrate's smile and indicated the seat opposite him. "Have you eaten? May I order you something?"

"Just coffee, thank you," Read said.

Brooke nodded to the waiter, who inclined his head in response and turned away smartly. Both men sat down.

"So?" Brooke said, the smile still in place. "How goes the fight for law and order? You'll be up to full strength now that your man is home safe."

The smile may have been there, but Read knew the statement was Brooke's less than subtle reminder that he had eyes and ears everywhere and thus was fully aware Hawkwood had returned to London, which, in itself, was revealing. It told Read that his visit to White's might not be a complete waste of time.

He offered a non-committal smile in return. "A perennial struggle, but we stand resolute."

Leaning away from the table, Read allowed the returning waiter to set down the coffee cup and dispense the beverage from an accompanying silver pot.

"And for you, sir?" The waiter addressed Brooke, who nodded and watched as his cup was refilled.

Swapping Brooke's cooled pot for the fresh one, the waiter retreated. Brooke reached for the cream jug. "And how *is* Officer Hawkwood?"

"As recalcitrant as ever."

Read saw a light flicker in the other man's eyes. Through acknowledgement or continued amusement, it was hard to determine. It was a description with which both of them were familiar. Brooke had used it to summarize his opinion of Hawkwood when confirming to James Read that his officer's secondment to the Alien Office had been agreed.

"But mercifully unscathed, one trusts?"

"There are a few new scars visible. As to what might lay beneath the surface, who is to say?"

Picking up his spoon, Brooke stirred his coffee. "It was a valiant effort. His Majesty's Government is most grateful for your man's assistance."

"I wasn't aware His Majesty's Government was in full possession of the facts," Read said carefully.

"Those that needed to know knew. Those that did not need to know . . . well . . ." Laying down his spoon, Brooke smiled cosily. "Either way, it was a close-run thing."

"He was lucky to get away with his life," Read said.

"As they all were," Brooke said. "Though I did hear your man took something of a round-about route home."

Read helped himself to cream. "I have yet to hear the full story."

"As have I," Brooke said primly, "at least from his lips. Fortunately, Major Grant sent me a full report of their Parisian adventure, so I have no need of further interview, but you might like to inform your man that I would have appreciated some form of communication." Brooke's gaze remained pointed and fixed.

"I'll speak with him," Read said.

The man's superior manner was beginning to grate. Brooke's world was one in which James Read had never sat comfortably. Not that Read was averse to taking advantage of his position and his association with those who operated in what might have been termed diplomatic circles; it was that he had little time for the often Machiavellian relish with which party loyalties were negotiated and intricate games played among the political hierarchy. Brooke, with his expensive tailoring, distinguished features and urbane manner, was a prime example. Beneath the well-upholstered façade, Read knew there lurked, if not a grand inquisitor, then a ruthless manipulator – a chess-player – who would think nothing of sacrificing his correspondents – his pawns – in order to protect king and country.

"Well, it's good to know he *is* back within your ranks." Brooke took a sip from his drink, set it back down and patted his lips with his napkin. "So, to what do I owe this unexpected pleasure?"

"Sir Edmund Saxby," Read said.

"What of him?"

So you know the name, Read noticed.

"I was wondering what his current role might be."

"His *role*?" Brooke said.

"I had occasion to be introduced to him during my last consultation with the Home Secretary. I was unaware of his status, yet he appears to wield no small amount of influence. I thought, as Superintendent of the Alien Office, which comes under the direct jurisdiction of the Home Department, you might enlighten me."

Brooke's eyebrows rose. "I'm not entirely sure that's within my remit."

"Really?" Read said. "And I thought you had a finger in every pie."

Brooke's lips twitched good-humouredly. "Oh, I wouldn't say that. Well, not *every* pie."

Read waited.

"I take it there's a reason behind your enquiry," Brooke continued smoothly.

"There is." Read moved his saucer to one side. "Correct me if I'm wrong, but your office was originally established in order to implement the requirements of the Alien Act; that is, the inspection and registration of aliens, and to address the security concerns arising from the influx of French émigrés. Is that not so?"

Brooke took his time brushing errant crumbs from the table-cloth on to the floor. "Those *were* its tasks in the beginning. However, our responsibilities have broadened somewhat since its inception, as you well know. These days, most of our trade tends to be plied further afield. Officer Hawkwood can attest to that."

"But you've not renounced all aspects of your domestic mission."

"Not quite all," Brooke responded silkily. "There are still areas that interest us."

"Which, presumably, necessitates working closely with the Emigrant Office," Read said, without missing a beat.

Brooke's face stilled. "When necessary."

"Which is Sir Edmund Saxby's bailiwick," Read said, "or so I've been told. Is that not correct?"

As if scouting the room for eavesdroppers, Brooke lifted his eyes and looked beyond Read's shoulder. It took several seconds before his gaze swung back. It was clear that the affability that had been there when Brooke had invited Read to sit was dissipating fast. "Forgive me, but one wonders why you pose the question when it appears you already know the answer."

Read reached for his coffee cup. "I did not *know*. I merely suspected. My one regret is that it has taken this long for my suspicions to be confirmed. Now that they have been, perhaps we could dispense with this needless jousting?"

Brooke's eyes narrowed. Then, offering another patronizing curve of the lip, he tilted his head in acquiescence. "As you wish; I take it there is a specific purpose to this line of enquiry?"

"Saxby," Read said, noting the frown the lack of a title

elicited. "I'm wondering why the Home Secretary, when receiving an updated report on a Bow Street murder case, sought to include him in the discussion that followed, which resulted to my being directed to abandon the investigation."

"*Sir Edmund* ordered you to close the case?" Brooke said, sounding surprised.

"Not directly, no, but I was left with the distinct impression that he and the Home Secretary had conferred beforehand *and* reached a mutual decision, which was then relayed to me. My question is, since when does the Home Secretary consult with the head of the Emigrant Office over a murder enquiry? To my knowledge, the man holds no ministerial post within the Home Department. He is a functionary: a civil servant holding an ancillary position."

"As are we all," Brooke countered with a half-smile.

Read did not return the gesture. "Indeed, but that does not give *me* the prerogative to involve myself in the activities of the Alien Office, any more than it gives *you* a mandate to participate in the administration of Bow Street's operations."

In the far corner of the room, from behind the door leading to the kitchens, there came the sudden clatter of a saucepan falling to the floor. Disturbed by the abrasive sound, several diners looked around. Read and Brooke were among the few who did not.

"There *is* something I'm not being told, isn't there?" Read said.

Brooke pursed his lips. "If there were, what makes you think *I* would be privy to such information?"

"I rather think you've answered your own question," Read said wryly. "Don't you? And I thought we'd agreed to forego the tilting."

Brooke's chin lifted. A calculating look took over his face, as if somewhere, in the dark recesses of his brain, small cogs were turning.

Read leaned forward. "Allow me to speak plainly. I have at least two – possibly three – current, unsolved yet connected murder cases on my hands. There could well be more. I would appreciate knowing why I have been told to consign them to the midden at what appears to be the behest of an individual of whom I was unaware until a short time ago. The Home Secretary was not forthcoming, so I approach you, for no reason other than I lent you my most trusted officer, whom you were quite prepared to send into the heart of Bonaparte's empire on an almost impossible mission with no thought as to his well-being. What I am asking for is some information in return. I do not consider that an unreasonable request."

"*Quid pro quo?*"

"Seeing as you put it in those terms, then yes."

Brooke regarded Read levelly for what seemed like several minutes but which could only have been seconds. Eventually, he gave a resigned sigh and nodded. "Very well. I cannot tell you all of it but I will tell you what I can; in the strictest confidence, you understand?"

Read realized that Brooke was waiting for his verbal assent. "Of course."

Brooke gathered his thoughts, glancing around the room again as he did so. Then, leaning across the table, he said quietly, "There is an enterprise afoot, clandestine in nature, which has been in preparation for some time. If successful, it'll see our little corporal either dead or deposed. We'd prefer the former, but if needs must we'll settle for the latter. The upshot is, we are on the eve of putting the plan into action, to take advantage of the confusion on the continent and the disillusionment that's spreading through the Empire following the man's Russian defeat and the generals' attempt to unseat him back in October. Malet's group might have failed, but by God they set the cat among the pigeons. They proved the bugger's vulnerable on home soil."

As if suddenly aware that he might have spoken with more enthusiasm than was considered seemly, Brooke allowed his tone to mellow. "Didn't stop him executing the ringleaders and weeding out a lot of malcontents, of course, but the thing with weeds is, if you don't destroy the roots you never get rid of them entirely. They continue to spread."

Leaning further in, he said, "And we've been cultivating them, using our correspondents and our links with the Bourbon rebels. We've been providing them with funding *and* weapons, helping them ferment unrest in the places that matter: Paris, Lyons, Toulouse, Bordeaux, Orleans . . .

"There are other locations, which I won't go into here, but I can tell you, a groundswell's been building for quite a while among those who would see Bonaparte deposed; Royalists for the most part, of course, but you add in the growing ranks of disaffected senior officers and the clergy, given the power *they* yield, and the numbers in opposition become ever more impressive. And they're about to come together."

"Come together?"

"A joint insurrection. Everything's in place. All that's left is to give the word."

As Brooke straightened, Read stared at him. "Forgive me, but what has this to do with my being instructed to halt a murder investigation?"

Looking more than a little nonplussed by Read's lack of deference to the information he had divulged, and to the revelation that the emperor's days might be numbered, Brooke took his time in answering. When he did, he spoke with measured deliberation. "It would be viewed as most inconvenient were you to continue your investigation at this time."

"Because?"

The other man paused as if thinking over his words and then said, "Let us say that certain allegiances would be compromised."

"Meaning?" Read pressed.

A spark of irritation flared in the other man's eyes.

"Meaning the interest of the nation comes first. Trust me when I say this: if you were to jeopardize this undertaking in any way, you and your officers would be subject to the severest reprimand. I cannot emphasize that strongly enough."

Read sat back. "You've known about Bow Street's investigation all along, haven't you?"

Brooke paused before answering, then said, "We've been keeping vigil, yes."

"Through Saxby?" Read felt a surge of anger.

241

"Not entirely." Brooke's jaw flexed. "Though, our paths do intersect from time to time."

"I see. So exactly how much influence *does* the man exert?"

Brooke kept his voice pitched low. "The insurrection cannot proceed without the authorization of the Royalist government in exile – Artois and Louis Stanislas. Sir Edmund's role, as head of the Emigration Office, gives him access to both the princes' inner circles based here in England *and* the Home Department. In effect he has become to domestic security what the Alien Office is to foreign surveillance. We are opposite sides of the same coin, if you will."

Read nodded. "A most convenient arrangement. However, I'm still having trouble understanding his interest in *my* murder investigation."

Brooke did not respond immediately, which was when all became stunningly clear.

"He's protecting someone," Read said, ". . . someone important to the enterprise. That's the reason, isn't it?"

Brooke dusted another minute speck of food from the tablecloth with the edge of his right hand. "You might think that, I could not possibly comment."

"Three people are dead," Read said. "Perhaps you'd care to comment on *that*?"

A nerve shimmered beneath Brooke's right cheek. "Only in as much as the deaths are regrettable but of less import when weighed against safeguarding the sovereignty and the security of the nation."

Read was about to respond when Brooke held up his hand. "My duty – my privilege – is to protect this country to the best of my ability. In the fight against tyranny, it is inevitable that there will be losses – great and small. I have no doubt God will be the final judge, but my conscience remains clear. In war, sacrifices have to be made."

"Sacrifices?" Read's attempt to keep his anger in check was not entirely successful. "That is how you regard them? These were not combatants. They were not victims on a battlefield or even in your employ. Irrespective of their profession or their vices, they were members of the public, and as such they are victims of what appears to be officially sanctioned malfeasance and subterfuge."

Brooke stiffened. Anger clouded his face. But gradually his features took on a conciliatory slant. "Perhaps not the best definition under the circumstances, I'll grant you, but I do believe it to be relevant in this instance. I do not have to tell you that we live in an increasingly dangerous world. If we are to make it safe, we cannot permit the deaths of a few inconsequential members of the populace to divert us from that objective. You may think me heartless, but the future of England depends on us remaining steadfast. Our cause *is* just." Leaning forward, Brooke dropped his voice once more. "So hear me, for I speak to you now as a friend. Heed the Home Secretary's directive."

Read gazed back at him. "And if I choose not to?"

A look of shock bordering on disbelief crossed the other man's face. "You cannot be serious? You would consider such a thing?"

"I merely pose the question."

In the blink of an eye, the look of surprise was replaced by a hard mask and an uncompromising growl as Brooke said, "Then let this be my answer. You came to me for information. I have given it as far as it is in my power to do so. It's likely that in a week I may be able to tell you more. Until then, you will let the matter rest. There is nothing for you to pursue. Stand your man down."

"Does that come from *your* lips?" Read asked calmly. "Or are you speaking for the Home Department?"

Before the other man could reply, Read pushed back his seat and rose to his feet. "I thank you for your time, Superintendent. I found our discussion to be most illuminating."

Gripping his napkin in his fist, Brooke hesitated, then rose with him. "As did I."

Brooke's gritted-teeth response confirmed to Read that a line had been well and truly crossed, while a small voice inside his head told him that the traverse had, more than likely, been inevitable. It was the same small voice which, mid-way through their conversation, had informed him there was little doubt that

Brooke had been expecting him to pay a call, if not at White's then at the Alien Office's discreet Crown Street address, where the outcome, Read suspected, would have been the same. Executing a curt nod, he turned from the table. As he made his way through the room he knew Brooke was following his every move. He did not look round.

Back at the table, Brooke watched as the Chief Magistrate made his exit. His face still, he summoned the waiter.

"Paper and pen, and be so good as to advise one of the messengers that I have a communication requiring immediate dispatch."

Watching Sir Randal Gaunt propel himself around his drawing room was, Hawkwood thought, not unlike watching a beetle manoeuvre its way awkwardly across a tabletop, the sound of skittering feet having been replaced by a series of mechanical rattles and squeaks.

Unlike the invalid chairs with which Hawkwood was more familiar, which were guided either by someone pushing or by the occupant gripping the wheel rims and hauling him or herself either forwards or backwards, Gaunt's contraption was driven by two cranks attached to the arms. At the base of each crank shaft were a series of cogs connected to a hub set in each of the chair's side wheels; thus when the crank handles were turned, the wheels rotated. A smaller, independent wheel at the back provided stability.

Hawkwood had been told what to expect by Connie Fletcher.

"It was either a riding accident, an infection of the brain, or divine punishment. His words, not mine. Says if it hadn't been his legs, it would probably've been his eyesight, on account of too much self-indulgence." Connie had executed a wry smile when she'd said it.

"He *can* walk unaided if the mood takes him, and he does use crutches sometimes to get about – up and down stairs and the like – but if it's the one room he's in, he'll use the chair. I've heard it said that he keeps one on each floor. Don't know if that's true, but I've a very reliable source who tells me he likes to use them when entertaining the ladies; helps him gain entry and distributes the weight, apparently."

Connie had allowed a full grin to escape her lips when she'd revealed that gem; observing the dexterity with which Gaunt rode the chair between the gaps in the furniture, Hawkwood was quite prepared to take Connie's word for it.

Wheeled chairs weren't a common sight, at least not on the streets. Those that Hawkwood had come across had always been of the most basic design. In such cases, it was noticeable that male occupants who did not suffer from advancing years were often prone to a broadness across the chest and shoulders, their upper muscles having become over-developed due to the sheer effort of having to generate motion. In stark contrast, the lower limbs tended to be severely withered.

From what Hawkwood could see, Gaunt's upper body was in proportion to the rest of him, with no significant wastage of his lower half. Seated, with his hands gripping the crank handles, his back looked straight and strong, as though he had been strapped in place, while his legs appeared as firm as they would have done had he been standing unaided. Notwithstanding the chair's design, it made Hawkwood wonder if the man was as incapacitated as he would have others believe, and if the rumoured use of the chair in his extra-curricular pursuits wasn't merely a cunning ploy to attract either the curious or the more adventurous females into his bed, or, as was reputed, the seat of his ingenious wheeled carriage.

On the face of it, the intriguing visions those musings conjured up seemed preposterous. Then again, as Hawkwood's visit to Annette's punishment room had revealed, when it came to the pleasures of the flesh, invention appeared to have no boundaries. Given his family background and wealth, Gaunt was unlikely to lack female company, his apparent preference for whores notwithstanding.

It wouldn't hurt that he was also somewhat younger than Hawkwood had expected – hovering around middle rather than old age. His face was strong-featured, and a full head of greying hair swept back off a high forehead accentuated a pair of hooded eyes which, Hawkwood suspected, would either cause women to question their fidelity or an enemy to think twice about advancing. Having placed himself with his back to the window, Gaunt was regarding Hawkwood with the same expression he might have reserved for a turd he'd found adhered to the wheel-chair's foot-rest.

Aided by Connie's character reference and the unwelcoming look on Gaunt's face, it had not taken Hawkwood long to dismiss his supposition that the man seated before him might be someone humbled by his impediment. Hawkwood was reminded of the expression on Eleanor Rain's face when he'd been shown into her presence for the first time, though in this instance, curiosity had been usurped by an aura of lofty disdain. An impression further enhanced when, without preamble, Gaunt fixed Hawkwood with a cold stare and in a clipped tone ordered him to confirm his name and state his business.

Hawkwood did so while holding his temper in check, though he felt his hackles rise when the man in the wheelchair drawled condescendingly, "And why would an entertainment held two weeks ago be of *any* interest to a member of the Constabulary?"

Hawkwood kept his voice civil. "I was hoping you could provide me with a list of the persons in attendance, Sir Randal."

Immediately, Gaunt's eyebrows rose. "Were you, indeed. And for what purpose?"

Hawkwood counted to five under his breath. "I'm conducting a murder enquiry. Aspects of the investigation have led me to your door."

"I trust you're not accusing *me* of committing murder?" Gaunt said sharply.

"I'm not accusing anyone, Sir Randal. I am merely exploring a number of avenues, one of which has brought me here."

Gaunt's eyes narrowed. "On whose authority?"

"Bow Street's." Hawkwood reached inside his coat for the hollowed baton. "Would you care to see my warrant?"

The man in the wheelchair stiffened and in a moment of renewed speculation, Hawkwood wondered if Gaunt employed the chair in an effort to elicit sympathy for his plight. From his current expression, it was clear he was unused to being addressed so bluntly by someone he'd only just met for the first time and whom he clearly considered to be of plebeian descent; another similarity to that first encounter with Eleanor Rain. Hawkwood's mind went back to Connie's comment about the possibility of doing something stupid. Judging by the look on Gaunt's face, that question may already have been answered.

"I've no interest in your damned warrant, sir! Your lack of civility, however, is another matter. You have the nerve to address me in my own house as if I were a common criminal? You may count on my having serious words with your superiors. Bow Street, you say? That's Magistrate Read's territory, is it not?"

"*Chief* Magistrate Read," Hawkwood said, and saw Gaunt's knuckles whiten around the handles of his wheelchair. "I'll be sure to pass on your compliments. Does this mean I'm to be granted access to the names of those attending?"

Gaunt's eyes blazed. "No, sir, it does not!"

"Might I ask why?" Hawkwood was interested to see Gaunt's reaction to being challenged.

"Notwithstanding your damned impertinence, it was a private engagement."

"Well, yes," Hawkwood said evenly, "I imagine it was. However, you do understand that I *am* conducting a murder investigation?"

"Then I suggest you conduct your enquiry elsewhere," Gaunt snapped. "The list of guests is confidential and shall remain so."

Hawkwood nodded as if accepting the explanation, then said, "Very well, if that's your answer. However, I should warn you, Sir Randal, that your refusal to cooperate could be construed as an obstruction to the pursuit of justice. You *do* realize that?"

The angry flush that had coloured Gaunt's cheeks began to spread across the rest of his face. Furiously, he rotated the handles on his chair, which rattled forward at a lick, almost knocking over a small table en route, before stopping abruptly in Hawkwood's shadow. "You dare to *threaten* me? Do you have *any* idea who you're talking to?"

"That," Hawkwood said calmly, "has never been in doubt."

For one heart-stopping moment it looked as though Gaunt was about to try and make a grab for Hawkwood's throat. If, as a consequence, the man toppled over, Hawkwood wondered if he was prepared to haul him back up. In the end, it didn't come to that. Gaunt managed to restrain himself, making do with shooting Hawkwood a look of undiluted malice as he put the chair in reverse, almost dislodging the table for a second time. "Out, damn it! Get out! Now!"

Half rising from his seat, Gaunt reached for the bell pull set against the wall and tugged it hard, nearly over-balancing in the process. Releasing the pull, he sat down heavily as the door opened.

"I want this man out of here! Remove him!"

The manservant hesitated and then puffed out his chest and took a pace forward.

"Don't." Hawkwood stopped him with a warning glance. "You'll only embarrass yourself."

The manservant paused in mid-stride. Hawkwood turned to the man in the chair. "No need to fret, Sir Randal; I'm on my way. But before I go, would you like to know what I found most interesting about our conversation? You would? Well, curiously, it's not what *was* said; it's what wasn't."

Gaunt continued to glare at him.

Hawkwood smiled. "You never once asked me who'd been murdered."

The statement hung in the air between them. A flicker of unease crossed Gaunt's face.

"Now why is that, do you suppose?" Hawkwood said as he made for the door. The footman stepped aside hurriedly. "I don't know about you, but it certainly makes *me* wonder."

Pausing, Hawkwood glanced towards the table Gaunt's chair had almost collided with, and the pair of exquisitely cut wine glasses that sat upon it, one of which held a thimble's worth of tawny liquid in its well and a waxy, faintly pink mark around the rim. He looked up. "You should consult with the lady. Perhaps *she* can tell you where you went wrong."

*   *   *

248

Gaunt turned as the front of the bookcase swung open behind him. Entering the room, Eleanor Rain glanced cautiously towards the door through which Hawkwood had departed. "How did he know?"

As the bookcase panel clicked shut, Gaunt indicated the wine glasses. "The question is: what else does he know? Bow Street's clearly not satisfied with your man Flagg being the culprit."

"*My* man? He was never that. We both know he was *your* watchdog."

Gaunt smiled thinly. "My dear Eleanor, he was fulfilling a duty. It was never personal."

She eyed him coldly. "And yet I always felt it was."

Gaunt gazed up at her, the smile still affixed, and she wondered again if he'd been the cause of her descent from grace. It was a suspicion she had harboured for some time. The rumours that the Portuguese-owned mining company in which she'd invested a considerable amount of her capital was in trouble and the warning that her holding was at stake if she didn't act swiftly had come as twin bolts from the blue. She'd heeded the advice but had sold too late on a sliding market and, as a consequence, had lost heavily, only to see the shares rally less than a week later. Had she stayed the course – or, as Gaunt had opined, not lost her nerve – the value of her investment would have tripled.

The pharaoh tables had seemed the obvious solution to try and recoup her losses, but the cards had not fallen kindly. Loss had followed upon loss and in no time the creditors had started circling. Gaunt had been the one who'd come to her rescue, purchasing her debt in exchange for a controlling interest in the Salon. Ever since then, Eleanor Rain had wondered if that had been Gaunt's plan all along, and whether he had been acting on his own initiative. Somehow, she didn't think so.

Rumour had it that Gaunt had bought when the shares were at their lowest, earning himself another fortune. And now she was beholden to him. But it was either that or, as Flagg had put it so succinctly, a return to Poor Street and all that entailed. Eleanor Rain had known poverty and she had known wealth, and wealth was by far her preferred option. But maintaining her position had come at a price.

Gaunt did not respond to her retort. His thoughts were of Hawkwood and the threat the man posed.

Having instructed the Salon's proprietress to find a suitable victim in deference to her knowledge of working girls, he'd been alarmed by her choice, though her reasoning had been understandable. In designating Charlotte as the prey, he knew she had effectively eliminated the queen-in-waiting and consolidated her own reign.

Gaunt also recalled the moments that had led to Flagg being nominated as the pigeon in the strategy. He'd been enjoying the feel of Eleanor Rain's lips around his cock and the movements of her tongue along his swollen member had been almost too much for Gaunt to bear. She'd been looking up at him, her blue eyes fixed unwaveringly upon his, never taking her gaze from his face as she'd coaxed him towards his exquisite climax, after which she had continued to caress him with her hands while stating her case in a voice as seductive as her touch. At which point Gaunt would willingly have staked his own ailing father across an ant hill in order to prolong the waves of pleasure coursing through his body.

Upon recovering his poise, his first inclination had been to reject the idea outright, due to Flagg's past usefulness. Instead, swayed by Eleanor Rain's endearments and her skilful manipulations, he'd allowed himself to be enticed into the realization that there was, given the equally unsuspecting Charlotte's role in the deception, a perfect symmetry to the plan.

It was an acknowledged fact that most murderers were known to their victims. Pinning the killings on someone close to both Lucy *and* Charlotte, rather than a perpetrator picked up from the streets, therefore made sense. Flagg's association with the Salon and the women employed there made him the ideal candidate.

And yet, despite all the apparent evidence, for reasons not yet determined, Bow Street had not been taken in.

"We were wrong," Gaunt said eventually. "Using Flagg *was* a mistake."

She eyed him, her expression scathing. "The *mistake* was in the employment of fools to take care of him. Had they performed their duty more efficiently, Bow Street would not be knocking at your door. In fact, one wonders how they found *your* door in the first place, for I assure you it was not my doing."

On the verge of remonstrating, Gaunt hesitated. The matter of why the subterfuge had not worked and how Hawkwood had ended up in his drawing room was academic. Nevertheless, he could not help but ruminate. There were, he thought, two likely scenarios. Either Magistrate Read had elected to disobey the Home Secretary's instruction to close the investigation, or he *had* obeyed and his own officer, despite asserting that he was acting under Bow Street's authority, had turned renegade and was thus operating without official sanction. Either way, remedial action was required.

"What does that mean?" Eleanor Rain asked.

Gaunt realized he must have spoken his thoughts aloud. He looked up at her, placing a hand on her arm. "Leave that to others, my dear. If I were you, I'd concentrate on what you do best."

She bit back what would have been a withering reply but did not draw away. Despite the assertion that Flagg's presence had been solely a business arrangement, she knew, irrespective of the latter's demise and Charlotte's removal, that her hold on the Salon remained tenuous and rested entirely on the whim of Gaunt and his associates.

Savvy enough to know that her role was to provide the respectable face to a disreputable profession, she was, nevertheless, determined to protect her crown for as long as she was able, or, as was more likely, as long as she was permitted to do so. If that entailed pandering to Gaunt's occasional lechery, so be it. That was a small price to pay, compared to the indignities she'd endured whoring out of a rented attic. But that didn't mean she couldn't or wouldn't guard against any future attempts to seize the throne, whether they came directly from Gaunt or indirectly from the individuals behind him.

Eleanor Rain was uncertain as to the identity of these men.

Beyond being powerful figures in positions of authority, she could only guess. It was they, she suspected, who'd been behind Gaunt's requirement that she procure a girl whose demise would not cause waves, a working girl, whom no one would miss. It was an order she'd complied with, because to have refused while Gaunt held her marker would have placed her own position in jeopardy. Flagg had been right when he'd told her that she was naught but an employee, but it wasn't Flagg who'd held the cards, it was Gaunt. He held them still, but Gaunt was himself directed in turn.

Flagg had intimated that Charlotte had been chosen as her understudy. By eliminating that threat, she had been defending her own position. As for nominating Flagg as Charlotte's – and, by association, Lucy's – killer; that had been an act of revenge, nothing more, nothing less. When Flagg left his mark on her cheek, she had sworn that the bastard would pay for the insult. And he had.

It had helped that Gaunt considered her his personal consort. His demands were never excessive and rarely involved activities in which she wasn't already well-practised. She indulged him because it was during those intervals that Gaunt was at his most amenable and susceptible, a situation she had exploited to the full, with the result that Charlotte and Thomas Flagg could now rot in whichever holes had been reserved for them.

She could tell that Gaunt had been rattled by Hawkwood's visit and the touch of his hand made her wonder if, despite her actions, her position might not be as secure as she had thought. She moved closer, placing her own hand gently on Gaunt's shoulder. "If he had proof, he would not have come alone."

"That," Gaunt said, as he reached for the bell to summon his manservant, "does not make him any less dangerous."

19

The boys had been baiting the dog for some time, teasing it with sticks and broken barrel staves. The small black-and-white mongrel was secured about the neck with a noose of coarse twine, the other end having been tied to a wooden gatepost. The badges on the shoulders of the boy's ragged jackets identified them as pupils of the St Giles's charity school.

Other children, dressed similarly in tattered hand-me-downs, were milling about the yard, pursuing their own activities, playing hopscotch, tossing a ball back and forth or drawing chalk figures on the surrounding wall. A couple – a boy and a girl – squabbled over possession of a toy soldier while the rest bore witness to the dog's increasing torment, some with grimaces of distaste, others with shrieks of high-pitched laughter.

The dog's mood had changed since the first few minutes of play, when it had viewed the teasing as a fine game, lunging for the sticks, tail wagging excitedly. Gradually, however, with the sticks and staves remaining maddeningly out of reach, the animal had become ever more frustrated. As the sticks began to make contact, the fun had turned to frenzy and then to fear. Now, as it was driven back against the wall, the dog's barks had subsided into low whimpers and finally shrill yelps of pain as the blows rained down in earnest.

From the long window of the building overlooking the school-yard, Saxby watched dispassionately as the animal sank beneath a flurry of vicious strikes, blood seeping from deepening wounds along its heaving flanks. He continued his observation as the children, having grown bored with the entertainment, turned away from the still and crumpled body. Those with sticks trotted off to stage mock swordfights, while the rest drifted away to join in other games. As order was resumed, a male member of the school staff approached the pathetic bundle of matted fur, bent down, undid the twine and, without ceremony, tossed the dog's bloodied corpse over the wall. As if at a given signal, a bell sounded and the children began to wend their way slowly into the school building.

Saxby turned away from the window to find Henry Brooke staring at him.

"You realize what you are saying?" Brooke said.

"I do," Saxby said.

"We're talking about an officer of the law," Brooke said.

"I am fully aware of his status."

"I know the man."

"I'm aware of that, too. You told me: the affair in Paris."

"He's a good officer."

"He's a liability; as is Read."

"Read?" Brooke said, aghast. "Good God, you cannot be serious?"

"Don't worry. Addington is dealing with Read. Read's man, however, is another matter. From what you and Ryder have told me, once he has the bit between his teeth, he's hard to shake off. In your meeting with Read, you confirmed the Home Secretary's order. Bow Street was to close the file. Clearly, as far as this Hawkwood is concerned, the message has not sunk in. He must be tethered before he does any more damage. This mission is far too important to have it sabotaged by an over-enthusiastic constable."

"He's not a constable; he's a Principal Officer, a Runner."

"He's an impediment," Saxby said, "a stone in our shoe."

Brooke continued to stare at him.

"You know I'm right," Saxby said. "This enterprise has been too long in the planning. Bonaparte's teetering on the edge. It

only needs a small push to tip him over. Think of your correspondents, the risks they've taken to bring this to fruition. Not
to mention Artois' network. The last thing we need is this man
breathing down our necks. We lose momentum now and there's
no telling when the chance will come again, if at all."

"Does the Home Secretary have any idea as to what you are
proposing?"

Saxby left the window. "What the Home Secretary does not
know cannot come back to harm him. I was present when he
told Read to drop the investigation. Read's conversation with
you is a clear indication that he is not following instructions.
That makes it a disciplinary matter and, as I said, Addington
can deal with that himself. As to the other, that requires a more
direct approach."

"Read can speak to his man."

"Read should have warned the fellow off already. Had he
done so, the impudent devil would not have called on Gaunt
asking to see the guest list."

"Which Gaunt refused to give him."

"The fact that he knew there *was* a gathering is worrying
enough. He's too close." Saxby fixed Brooke with a calculating
eye. "From what you know of the man, would Gaunt's stance
deter him from making further enquiry?"

Brooke hesitated. Saxby waited.

"I suspect not." Brooke sighed heavily.

Saxby nodded. "So . . ."

Brooke thought back to his conversation with James Read.
The meeting had not ended well. Though, in truth, Brooke had
not been that surprised. He knew there were those in positions
of governmental authority who regarded Read as an outsider, a
magistrate who ploughed his own furrow in the pursuit of justice.
He was known to give his officers a wide degree of latitude,
and that did not sit well with either his fellow magistrates or
the Home Department. But he achieved results and to those who
supported him, that was what counted. On this occasion,
however, Read appeared to have overstepped the mark. Saxby
evidently thought so, and the evidence appeared to support him.

More importantly, Saxby had the ear of the Home Secretary, a man upon whose decision James Read's tenure as Chief Magistrate rested.

"Well?" Saxby pressed, interrupting Brooke's train of thought.

"You're sure there's no other way?" Brooke said.

"Not at this stage," Saxby said. He thought of the dog and the casual way its remains had been tipped over the wall. There one minute, gone the next; out of sight, out of mind. He waited.

Brooke stared back at him, took a breath and then nodded. *For king and for country – and God help us if we fail.*

"Penny for them," Maddie said, as she reached across for Hawkwood's empty plate.

"If that were the case," Hawkwood said, "I'd be a rich man."

Maddie favoured him with an amused look. "I'll bring coffee."

As Maddie headed off through the tables, Hawkwood returned to the *Chronicle*'s front page. As he did so, a shadow fell across his arm. He looked up.

The scar drew immediate attention. A sabre slash, Hawkwood guessed, and a vicious one at that. It looked as though the point of the weapon had penetrated the mouth and ripped sideways, splitting open the lip to create what could have been taken for an extended grin, had not the incision turned up and across the right cheek to where it finally petered out at the edge of the jawline. Considering the severity of the wound, the surgeon had made a good fist of the suturing, but from the looks of it the nerves had suffered irreparable damage. As a result, the right side of the face looked as if it was suffering from the early stages of rigor or, as was more likely, some sort of residual paralysis.

"Would this seat be free?"

Hawkwood was rarely inconvenienced by such requests. He usually had a booth to himself, a privilege accorded to him due to the Blackbird's regulars being disinclined to share their meal with a Runner, as though being a law officer was some sort of contagious disease. Maddie and her girls, attuned to such prejudice, invariably did their best to accommodate other diners among the remaining tables, but on this occasion the Blackbird was filling up and it would have seemed churlish to say no, so he nodded wordlessly, allowing the stranger to take the bench opposite.

"I'm obliged. I hadn't realized the place was so popular."

Hawkwood remained silent and reached for his newspaper, trusting the speaker to take the hint. Maddie, he saw from the corner of his eye, was en route, coffee pot in hand, which was when the stranger said, "Reminds me of a tavern I had the pleasure of frequenting back in Lisbon; the Taberna da Viúva, I believe it was called. Something like that, at any rate. I never did get the hang of the lingo. Do you know it?"

Hawkwood said nothing.

"It is Captain Hawkwood, yes?"

Above the scar, the face was lean, the hair black and swept back from the forehead, the eyes dark and penetrating.

Hawkwood looked up. "Not any more."

The stranger frowned and then nodded as if all had been made clear. "Of course. It's *Officer* Hawkwood now, isn't it? My mistake. I should have been more specific."

The long coat, Hawkwood noted, was of a distinct military cut, not that far removed from his own, while the jacket and breeches worn beneath, from what he could see, looked well-tailored, the bow of the grey cravat tied with just the right amount of flair.

"And you are?"

"My apologies – Vaughn, Captain Dominic Vaughn."

The voice was smooth, aristocratic in tone.

Before Hawkwood could respond, Maddie arrived with the coffee pot. Hawkwood sat back, allowing her to fill the mug by his elbow. As she poured the coffee, she rested her free hand lightly on Hawkwood's shoulder.

Beverage dispensed, she smiled at Vaughn. "And for you, sir? Will you be dining with us?"

"Not at the moment, thank you."

"Coffee, then?"

"You're most kind."

257

Maddie stood the pot on the table. "I'll bring another mug. Change your mind about the food and one of the girls will take your order."

Vaughn watched as Maddie walked away. "Handsome woman." His gaze lingered on Maddie's hips before swinging back.

"Have we met?" Hawkwood asked.

It wasn't a face he recognized. It certainly wasn't one he was liable to forget in a hurry.

"Not formally, though our paths may well have crossed without us being aware."

Hawkwood waited.

"Corunna, possibly." The right side of the captain's face lifted. Hawkwood assumed it was meant to herald a smile but the scar managed to turn it into something more reminiscent of a grimace.

It wasn't beyond the bounds of credibility, Hawkwood thought. Anyone who'd served in the Peninsula had probably passed through the port at one time or another, the city having been the main embarkation point for the retreating British army, as proven by his conversation with Sexton Stubbs.

Maddie returned, promised mug in hand.

"Here we are." Placing the receptacle on the table, she poured the coffee, set the pot down, smiled at Hawkwood and turned away.

Vaughn helped himself to cream, raised the beverage to his lips and took an appreciative sip.

"What can I do for you, Captain?" Hawkwood asked.

Vaughn lowered the cup and dabbed his mouth carefully with a napkin. "Actually, it's more what *I* can do for *you*."

"How so?"

"I have a message."

"From whom?"

It wasn't just the facial disfigurement, Hawkwood decided. Something else about Vaughn was unsettling; his stillness, perhaps, or the sense that while he might have been addressing Hawkwood, he was also surveying the room.

"An interested party."

"Interested in what?"

"I believe the message is self-explanatory."

"And that is?"

"Cease and desist."

"Meaning?" Hawkwood knew he was being deliberately obtuse, but the upper-crust enunciation in Vaughn's voice was beginning to irritate.

"Your enquiry into the death of Flagg and the whore . . ."

"What of it?"

"You would be wise to let it go."

"Now why," Hawkwood countered, "would I want to do that?"

"You'll find there's no future in it." Vaughn took another slow sip of coffee.

"That sounds ominous."

Vaughn said nothing. Instead, he merely returned Hawkwood's steady gaze. Hawkwood allowed a few more seconds to slide by and then said, "And if I don't . . . let it go?"

Vaughn lowered his cup. "I would consider that . . . unfortunate."

"And *that* sounds like a threat."

"Call it a courtesy, to a fellow officer."

They considered one another for several heartbeats. The background hubbub from the Blackbird's dining room continued around them.

"Captain of what?" Hawkwood said.

"You're referring to my regiment?" The ruined lips twitched again as if in response to some private joke. "They called us the Holy Boys. Something of a misnomer, I fear."

"The Ninth," Hawkwood said. "There's a coincidence."

Vaughn's head tilted. There was another attempt at a smile, with the same disconcerting effect. "Not really."

"No." Hawkwood reached for his coffee. "On second thoughts, I don't suppose it is. Captain to courier, though? Sounds like a demotion."

"It isn't. I'm currently employed in a private capacity."

"Bully for you." Hawkwood dropped his eyes to take in

Vaughn's apparel. "There's an improvement in remuneration, I take it?"

"By a considerable margin. Never looked back since."

Hawkwood lifted his gaze. "From now on, you might have to."

Vaughn's right eyebrow rose. "Why, Officer Hawkwood, if I didn't know any better, I'd say *that* sounded like a threat."

"Call it a courtesy. Did *you* kill him?"

"If you're referring to the late Sergeant Flagg, it's my understanding he took his own life."

"Yes, but things aren't always as they appear, are they?"

Vaughn's eyes widened as if he was vaguely surprised by the suggestion. "Oh, I don't know. This occasion, I think you'll find that's exactly what they are."

"Well, I've no doubt your employer would like us to think so. Is it Gaunt?"

The surprised expression disappeared, replaced by a frown of genuine puzzlement. "Is *what* gaunt?"

"Saxby, then," Hawkwood said.

There was a more positive reaction that time. Even so, had he blinked, Hawkwood suspected he might have missed the slight flaring of the nostrils and the crinkling of the crow's feet at the corner of each eye. Small movements, but they were enough.

"Mind if I make a suggestion?" Hawkwood said.

The thin lips formed a pout. "Oh, by all means."

"Your employer has a grievance; he should take it up with Chief Magistrate Read."

"Ah, that furrow has been ploughed, but without success, alas."

"So you've come to me? Working our way down the ranks, are we?"

Vaughn's right hand played with the handle of his mug. "Not exactly; I thought it would be best if you and I talked."

"Man to man?" Hawkwood made no attempt to hide the sarcasm.

Vaughn, though, looked unperturbed. "I was thinking more soldier to soldier."

"I told you, I'm not—"

"Yes, you said. But we know the drill: once a warrior and so forth. How about two former comrades-in-arms choosing to converse in convivial surroundings over a warming beverage? Would that suit you better?"

"Comrades?"

"Humour me," Vaughn said. "It's in a good cause."

"So *you* say."

Vaughn sat back, his face set, and then he nodded. "All right, if that's how you want it. But you *were* a soldier; an officer, no less, and a fine one, too, until that run-in with Delancey." Leaning forward, Vaughn dropped his voice. "Oh yes, I know about that. And between you and me, I'd probably have done the same, had I been in your shoes. I knew his cousin. He was an incompetent arse, too."

Someone's been thorough, Hawkwood thought.

Delancey was the major Hawkwood had killed in a duel in the aftermath of Talavera, the major having demanded satisfaction when Hawkwood accused him of taking a reckless decision on the battlefield; a decision that had seen the needless slaughter of British soldiers. The major had died with Hawkwood's pistol ball embedded in his heart; his second miscalculation of the day.

Vaughn's voice cut into Hawkwood's ruminations. "What I'm trying to say is that it wouldn't matter a damn what we are or were – chosen man, captain or, if you'll forgive me, constable. To those at the rear, the ones who employ us, we're no better than footsloggers in the end. They've no idea what it's like at the front. They ain't the ones who storm the hill and raise the flag. All they do is give the order and we obey. But it don't mean we have to like it. You and me? We know the futility of advancing against a stronger, better-equipped foe. We've been there. That's how come we know that sometimes, just sometimes, it's wiser to concede the ground. Better to live and fight another day than march into oblivion. You get my drift?"

"You know something?" Hawkwood said. "I believe I do."

"Well, then?"

"Question is: what if I don't . . . concede the ground?"

Vaughn sighed. "Then I'm afraid I'll be forced to obey the orders I've been given. Measures will have to be taken. That's the way of things."

"But you won't like doing it."

"I will not." Vaughn gazed into Hawkwood's eyes. "But there's no reason why it should come to that. Soon as I knew it was you, I said to myself, now there's a man who'll be receptive to reason."

Hawkwood smiled. "Receptive? You wouldn't be trying to *bribe* a police officer, would you?"

Vaughn's chin lifted. "Would that work?"

"What do *you* think?"

"I think I'd be wasting my time, so no, I offer no financial inducement. I rely entirely on your better judgement."

"Then you'll have a long wait. That's something I lost a long time ago. You do realize I could place you under arrest, for withholding information and attempting to intimidate an officer of the law."

"Do you *feel* intimidated?"

"What do *you* think?"

Once again, the dark eyes held a trace of amusement. "Well, you could *try* and arrest me, I suppose, though I'd advise against it. Look about you; all these good people, all this sharp cutlery. Can you image the mayhem that would ensue if things got out of hand? Casualties would be inevitable and you wouldn't want that on your conscience. In any case, what's that expression about harming the messenger? Also, you didn't really think I'd venture in here alone, did you?"

Hawkwood didn't bother looking around. The tavern had filled up and what with the walls of the dining booths and the movements of the bustling waiting staff blocking the view on all quarters it would have been a pointless exercise.

"Best to be on your way, then," Hawkwood advised. "You can tell whoever sent you I'm not interested."

Vaughn held Hawkwood's gaze. "You're sure? I can't persuade you to reconsider? A small delay in the execution of your enquiries would suffice."

Hawkwood looked at him.

Vaughn sighed. "I know: what do *I* think." He nodded. "Very well, so be it; a great pity. Though, I'll be honest. I expected nothing less."

Dabbing his mouth with his napkin and rising to his feet, he smoothed his coat and looked down. "A most enjoyable discourse. If you'd be so kind as to pass on my regards to Mrs Teague, I'd be most grateful. Tell her, next time I look forward to sampling the menu. I'm told the beef and oyster pie is quite exceptional. Good day to you, sir."

"Captain," Hawkwood said.

He watched Vaughn stride away.

"Your friend not stopping, then?" Maddie said from behind Hawkwood's shoulder.

Hawkwood turned back. "Not this time. Lost his appetite."

Maddie arched an eyebrow. "I know that look. Something you said?"

"More like something I didn't. He asked me to pass on his regards, by the way."

Maddie stared at Vaughn's retreating back. "Sounds like a real gentleman."

"No," Hawkwood said. "I don't believe he is."

20

"How about *now*?"

Twigg looked up from his desk. There was a subdued expression on the clerk's bespectacled face that Hawkwood had not seen before. "The Chief Magistrate is in his office."

Finally, Hawkwood thought.

He'd already visited Bow Street once following his visit to the Gaunt residence, only to discover that James Read had returned to his office earlier but had then received a message requesting his presence at the Home Department. Hawkwood had taken advantage of the magistrate's continued absence to retrace his steps to the Blackbird for something to eat. He'd told Vaughn that he was no longer a soldier, but traditional habits die hard. After twenty years campaigning, Hawkwood still followed the old military adage: eat when you can because there's no knowing when your next meal will be.

He was about to cross the room when Twigg rose to his feet. "It would be better if I announced you."

Something in the clerk's voice beyond the instruction made Hawkwood pause. "Ezra?"

Twigg made no reply but held up his hand. Mystified, Hawkwood waited as the clerk knocked upon the office door, opened it and spoke into the room.

"Officer Hawkwood requests a meeting, your honour."

There was no audible acknowledgement, but Hawkwood

assumed a visual response had been given for Twigg stepped aside and motioned him forward. The clerk's face remained impassive but then his eyes shifted sideways behind his spectacles, triggering some kind of warning which Hawkwood was unable to decipher, until he moved past Twigg and saw the stranger seated at James Read's desk, who wasted no time once the clerk had closed the door behind him.

"Officer Hawkwood, we've not met. I am Magistrate Conant, *Chief* Magistrate Conant. At the request of the Home Secretary I shall be taking over all Magistrate Read's duties with immediate effect."

Conant was heavier-looking than James Read, both in body and in the shape of his pale face, which was doughy in consistency, heavy browed and surmounted by a bristly thatch of salt-and-pepper hair. His gaze was not welcoming.

Hawkwood stared back at him. "Why? What's happened?"

The other man's chin lifted. "It's perfectly simple. Magistrate Read has relinquished his post."

The words struck Hawkwood like a hammer blow. It was a second before he found his voice. "Relinquished? What the hell does that mean?" The question sprang forth before he could stop himself. He saw the other man's jaw clench.

"It means Chief Magistrate Read tendered his resignation to the Home Secretary earlier this morning."

Hawkwood felt his insides lurch.

"There is to be an official announcement. It will state that, due to failing health, Magistrate Read has regretfully decided he is no longer able to provide the Home Secretary with the support expected of him. The announcement will also state that the Home Secretary has accepted Magistrate Read's resignation, albeit with reluctance, and he thanks him for his years of selfless public service to the police force, the Home Department and the country. While he will be sadly missed, the Home Department understands fully his desire to be with his family at this most difficult time."

Hawkwood listened to the mantra and tried to keep his voice steady. "I wasn't aware the Chief Magistrate was ill. Am I permitted to ask what's wrong with him?"

"I regret I'm not at liberty to divulge that information even if I were privy to it. That is a confidential matter. Suffice it to say, I do know he was held in the highest regard by the personnel here at Bow Street, who I am sure will join me in wishing him well in his retirement."

Twigg's subdued behaviour now made awful sense. Hawkwood's brain reeled but he was given no time to dwell on the matter. The man behind the desk had not finished.

"Now that my role has been established, it's my intention there should be as little disruption as possible during this transition period. To that end, I have been acquainting myself with this office's current investigations."

The magistrate waved a hand to encompass the paperwork on the desk before him. "I note you've recently provided assistance to the Hatton Garden Public Office. A murder enquiry; which, I am reliably informed, resulted in a most satisfactory conclusion. Excellent work."

Hawkwood wondered if he might be losing his mind as the magistrate looked up and said, "I know Magistrate Turton is exceedingly grateful for your assistance, as is the Home Department. In fact, when I received my appointment, the Home Secretary himself made a point of instructing me to thank you for your dedication."

A condescending smile spread across the pale face. "Now that case has been resolved, you must be pleased to be back on your own beat, yes?"

Hawkwood said nothing.

This reeks. This bloody reeks.

"Officer Hawkwood?" Conant prompted.

"My apologies, sir, but it's my belief the Hatton Garden case is *not* resolved. There are aspects that still require investigation."

"Excuse me?" The magistrate's gaze was cold.

"It's my understanding that Magistrate Read is of the same opinion . . . sir."

Conant's chin lifted. "Yes, well, as I have just explained, the current situation dictates that Magistrate Read's opinion is of no further consequence."

"Sir, there are—"

"Enough!" Conant said sharply, holding up a hand. "Perhaps you didn't fully comprehend. As I told you, both Magistrate Turton and the Home Secretary have expressed their satisfaction with the outcome. The Hatton Garden case is, therefore, closed. It is no longer Bow Street's concern. Put bluntly, that means it is no longer your concern. Let that be an end to it. It is time to move on. That, in case you were still of the opposite *opinion*, is a direct order."

The magistrate emitted a judicious sigh. "Your loyalty to Magistrate Read does you great credit, but as far as it pertains to the supervision of this office it is no longer relevant. Do I make myself clear?

Hawkwood took a breath.

Conant fixed him with a flinty gaze. "I believe I asked you a question."

"Yes, sir, you've made yourself perfectly clear."

"Good. So, now that has been settled, there is work to be done. You will receive your new assignment shortly. That is all. You may go. Please ask Mr Twigg to attend me at his convenience."

"You couldn't have given me a hint?" Hawkwood said when he was back in the outer office.

"Would it have made a difference?" The clerk spoke softly, as if wary that their conversation might be overheard on the other side of the closed door.

Following the clerk's lead, Hawkwood kept his voice low. "I'd have been better prepared, damn it. What the hell's going on? I doubt Magistrate Read's had a day's illness in his life. If he did resign, I'm the Emperor of China. He didn't jump, he was bloody pushed. And where did *that* bastard come from?"

"Magistrate Conant is late of Marlborough Street."

"Is he? It's a pity he didn't bloody stay there. Christ! You asked me before if there was a plot. If this doesn't prove it, I don't know what does. Magistrate Read knew it, too. That's why they got rid of him."

"They?" Twigg said dubiously.

"Saxby, Gaunt. Addington, maybe."

"The Home Secretary?" Twigg looked aghast.

"Don't look so shocked, Ezra. We're answerable to the Home Department. Who else has the authority to remove a Chief Magistrate from his post?" Hawkwood nodded towards the inner office door. "You'd better leap to it. Our new lord and master struck me as a man who doesn't like to be kept waiting."

Twigg said nothing, his face sombre. Then, as he turned to go, he took a piece of folded paper from his waistcoat pocket and held it out. "I was instructed to give you this."

Hawkwood took the paper and opened it out. In the seconds it took him to read the contents, Twigg was already knocking on the office door. As he opened it, he looked back at Hawkwood and nodded. Before Hawkwood could respond, he was gone.

Hawkwood took another look at the note.

Conant was wrong. It wasn't over.

Cutting across the top of King's Bench Walk and down through the narrow water-logged alleyway joining Temple Lane to Boverie Street, Hawkwood made his way towards the rear of the Blackbird tavern. The cloying smell of river mud combined with that of damp timber and tar drifting up from the nearby wharves lay heavy on the nostrils and mingled uneasily with the equally throat-clogging stench of sewage and rotting produce awaiting removal by the night-soil barges.

The tavern's back door was propped open. Skirting the privy entrance, Hawkwood passed through the doorway. It was a route he'd used before and so although his appearance was acknowledged by the cooks and a couple of kitchen maids, no one questioned his right of access. Maddie was nowhere to be seen. Pausing to purloin two glasses from a shelf and a bottle of brandy from a tray, with a courtesy nod to the staff, Hawkwood headed towards a door at the end of the passage which gave access to one of the two small dining rooms Maddie reserved for special guests who wished to hold private functions. Hands full with bottle and glasses, Hawkwood tapped on the first door with the toe of his boot.

"You don't look like a man on his last legs," Hawkwood said as the door was opened.

James Read stepped aside and smiled thinly. "Your solicitude is unconvincing."

Hawkwood entered quickly. As Read shut the door behind him, he held up the bottle. "I took the liberty."

Read nodded, gestured to a place at the table and sat down.

Hawkwood took the seat opposite, uncorked the bottle, poured the liquor and passed the magistrate a glass. "I'm assuming your leaving wasn't voluntary."

The statement was rewarded with a dry look.

"If it makes you feel any better, I don't think Mr Twigg's too impressed with your successor."

"Nathaniel Conant is a very able magistrate."

"Another Nathaniel? Well, I know at least one who'll think that's amusing, not that there's much chance of getting them mixed up." Hawkwood raised his glass. "Confusion to the enemy . . . whoever the bastards might be."

They drank. Hawkwood returned his glass to the table. "I nominate Saxby. Would I be correct?"

Read nodded. "He does have a hand in it, but he is not alone."

"Who else is there?"

"Superintendent Brooke has also declared an interest."

"The Alien Office? What the hell have they got to do with it?"

"It seems our investigation posed a risk to the nation's security."

"Brooke told you that?"

"In no uncertain terms."

"I've a feeling I might have been subjected to part of the same lecture," Hawkwood said, "though from a different tack. The security of the nation wasn't mentioned."

"Brooke's spoken to you?" Read said, surprised. "He told me—"

"Not Brooke; a Captain Vaughn."

The magistrate frowned. "I'm not familiar with the name."

"Neither was I until a couple of hours ago. I think he's Hermes to Saxby's Erebus. At least, there was no denial when I accused him of it. He paid me a visit here earlier, tried to warn me off; told me there'd be consequences if I didn't stop asking questions."

"Consequences?"

"Nothing you could put your finger on, but I got the gist. Magistrate Conant was less subtle. He gave me a direct order to cease all investigation. I'm assuming in response to a command from on high. As far as the Home Department's concerned, the case has been put to bed. What with Gaunt's involvement, we appear to have stirred up quite the hornet's nest."

"Gaunt?" Read said, his brow furrowing again.

"Sir Randal Gaunt; his name cropped up in conversation. He's connected to Saxby and to the Rain woman. I've no proof, but I'd say he's in it up to his neck, too. The cockroaches are coming out of the woodwork faster than we can bloody count."

"I believe the expression is *closing ranks*."

Hawkwood smiled grimly. "I'm familiar with the strategy. They'll be trying to cover their own arses as much as anything, though I'd wager their main intention is to protect someone else: Lucy's 'foreign gentleman' would be my guess. Is that why Brooke and Saxby are involved?" Hawkwood registered the look that crossed the magistrate's face. "Damn it, I'm right, aren't I?"

James Read looked out of the window, where rain had begun to spatter against the glass, and then back at Hawkwood. "I think it's time we compared notes, don't you?"

"According to Magistrate Conant, the case is closed."

Read held Hawkwood's gaze. "But we know differently, do we not?"

"He also said your opinion was no longer relevant," Hawkwood added drily.

For the merest second, a look of surprised hurt appeared in the magistrate's eyes and Hawkwood cursed himself, wishing he could take the words back. But then he watched James Read's face change and a new expression appeared, one of such fierce intensity that Hawkwood almost felt his breath catch. It was a look he'd not seen before and he knew he was seeing a side of the man that was in complete contrast to the correct, unruffled individual he'd come to admire over the past three years.

"And what do you say to that, Officer Hawkwood?"

Hawkwood smiled. "I say to hell with Magistrate Conant."

The thin mouth twitched.

"But I'd like to know why," Hawkwood said.

"Why?"

"Why you appear to have gone quietly and yet, here we are, having this conversation, when we were both told to drop the investigation. You lost your standing because of it. So, yes, I'm asking you: why?"

There was no immediate reply. Then, finally, the magistrate sighed. "It was made clear to me that as I no longer had the support of the Home Department my position had become untenable. Doors that were once open would be closed." Read cupped his glass. "I was given the option: resign quietly with my reputation intact, or under protest and suffer the consequences. As I consider the integrity of the office of Chief Magistrate to be far more important than my personal sensitivities, I agreed to the terms. Bow Street's reputation must remain unsullied."

"So they concocted an imaginary affliction? It's going to raise a few eyebrows when you're seen out on the street."

"By which time I will have made a miraculous recovery."

Hawkwood lifted his glass in a mock toast. "For which we will all be eternally grateful, but it still doesn't explain why we're here."

"Would you believe me if I said I cannot abide unfinished business?"

"Not entirely, seeing as there are other unsolved cases pending. Your replacement's looking through them even as we speak. So, is that the real reason, or are you bored with retirement already?"

James Read's chin lifted. There was a new firmness in his expression. "I am here because you were right."

"I was? When?"

"When I asked why you were devoting what I perceived to be an uncommon amount of time and labour investigating the young woman's death."

"I remember," Hawkwood said.

"Do you recall your answer?"

"I do. I said 'we're all she's got.'"

The magistrate looked Hawkwood full in the face, his gaze unblinking.

"*That,* Officer Hawkwood, is *my* answer. I'm here because we *are* all she's got and all she will ever have."

"I'll be damned."

"And you?" Read countered. "Why did you agree to meet with me when my opinion is considered – what was the phrase you used – *no longer relevant?*"

Hawkwood smiled. "Would you believe me if I said *I* can't abide unfinished business either?"

The magistrate allowed himself another small smile in return before sitting back in his seat. "So, how do we proceed?"

Read nodded. "So, your thoughts?"

"Well," Hawkwood drained his glass, "I'm going to have a refill. Then you and I are going to consider those notes you mentioned. How does that sound?"

The contents of the bottle had been lowered by a good four inches when Hawkwood leaned forward across the table. "It's agreed, then. Our killer – a foreign gentleman – was a guest at an entertainment held at Sir Randal Gaunt's townhouse; the evening having been arranged by Rain, who also supplied the women, one of whom was Lucy."

Read nodded.

Hawkwood continued. "At some point subsequent to that event our man made it known that he'd been so taken with Lucy, he wanted to see her again. Rain arranged the meeting, during which the girl was murdered. To cover up the death, her body was taken to the graveyard by persons unknown and dumped in the hope it would stay buried. What they hadn't allowed for was a downpour and a sharp-eyed sexton, which was where we came in and when it started to get tricky.

"Rain tried to distance herself from suspicion by telling me Lucy had left her employ and was working for herself by the time she was killed, which would have worked if I hadn't spoken with Lucy's friend, Annie. It was only when I took Annie away from the Salon and lodged her with Connie Fletcher that Gaunt's role came to light. We can connect Gaunt to Saxby through Wilmot's Committee and the Emigrant Office, which in turn links Saxby to the Home Department, which is where Addington comes in."

Hawkwood sat back. "Which brings us to our friend Brooke. Refresh my memory: when Saxby's name first cropped up, you referred to him as Addington's man in the shadows."

"Your point?"

"My point is that I've only ever had the one encounter with Brooke, but from what I saw of him I'd say the scheming bugger fits that description as well. It's clear Bow Street's had a close connection with the Alien Office over the years so it's likely you're more familiar with his work than I'll ever be. I'm assuming he's more than a spymaster. A man in his position, he'd have to be. Brooke, Saxby and Addington – an unholy bloody Trinity if ever there was one." Taking a sip from his glass, Hawkwood held it to the light. "Forgive the language, but my blood's up. Or it could be the brandy talking. Take your pick."

Read permitted himself another small smile. "Bow Street's links with the Alien Office were forged by my predecessor, Magistrate Ford. Brooke's incumbency is as old as the Office itself. William Wickham was the first named Superintendent, but much of his time was spent abroad so it was Brooke who pulled the strings at home. He became the official head of department when Wickham was appointed Secretary to Ireland."

"So he knows where the bodies are buried," Hawkwood said, adding in response to Read's frown, "It's something I heard Nathaniel Jago say once, which is not to say it isn't true."

Offering no contradiction, the magistrate went on: "Henry Brooke has always had the ear of those that matter. He's close to Grenville – it was he who introduced the Alien Act to the House – as well as Addington *and* Liverpool."

"Is there anyone he *doesn't* know?"

"Unlikely. His link to our current Home Secretary, by the way, dates from when Addington set up the Commons' committee back in '02 to investigate all aspects of foreign and domestic

273

secret service activities. It was he who saw the full potential of the Alien Office as a tool against Bonaparte, especially with regards to fermenting insurrection within France, which we – the British – have been funding by way of the Bourbon rebel networks. A secret account was set up with Drummonds Bank to finance the Office's activities. I—"

"Drummonds?" Hawkwood interjected. "Gaunt holds a partnership in Drummonds Bank."

A glint appeared in Read's eyes. "Does he indeed?"

"Small world," Hawkwood said before adding apologetically, "Sorry, I interrupted. You were about to say?"

"I was about to say that I'm not sure I should be telling you all this. It is highly confidential information."

"I'd say it was a bit late for that now. Besides, it's not as though you're beholden to anyone, is it?"

Read looked at him, his face still. Finally, he nodded. "As I was also about to say, Brooke's responsibilities were further extended when Liverpool appointed him principal liaison between the Home Department and the Bourbon Government in exile."

"Artois?"

"And Louis Stanislas. It was Liverpool – he was Home Secretary at the time – who dispatched Brooke to Yarmouth to meet Louis when he landed in England and to see him settled at Gosfield. They've remained close ever since. Brooke receives much of his intelligence from both Artois' and Louis' correspondents across the Channel. They use the Channel Islands as their centre for operations. Being close to the French mainland, they're the ideal location. That's why most of the émigrés used Jersey as a stepping stone when they fled the Revolution."

Hawkwood sat back. "Damn it, we're up to our hocks with foreign bloody gentlemen. From your conversation with Brooke, did he give any hint of which one it might be?"

"Regrettably, he was not that forthcoming."

Hawkwood stared down at his glass, took a breath and looked up. "At a guess, I'd say we're looking for one of Saxby's high-placed émigrés, wouldn't you?"

"I see no reason to disagree with your reasoning. From what

Superintendent Brooke told me, our quarry is one of either Artois' or Louis' principal agents."

"And if the bastard's responsible for the previous killings listed in the other Public Office's files, it means they've been protecting him for some time, maybe years. It might explain why there was no mention of bodies being carved up in some of the other reports. Could be they were marked but they erased that detail from the records to lessen the chances of someone linking the deaths, as we've done. One of the murder files referred to a Marlborough Street case. That was Magistrate Conant's stomping ground. Makes you wonder if he was subjected to the same pressure you were and decided discretion was the better part of valour. It could explain why they chose him as your replacement; they think he'll be easier to control. And now the case has been closed officially, it looks as though they've won. Maybe Vaughn was right."

"In what regard?"

"That when you're up against a stronger, better-equipped foe, it *is* wiser to concede the ground, even if it does stick in the bloody craw."

"And yet . . ." Read said quietly.

"And yet, what?" Hawkwood looked expectantly at the magistrate.

"And yet, despite your Captain Vaughn's adage, here we both are, desirous to see justice done. What does that tell you?"

"That we're idiots?"

This time Read did not smile. "No. It tells us we are not prepared to let the matter lie."

"You mean I don't like being threatened and you don't like the idea of being considered irrelevant."

"As I recall, your precise words were, 'You cannot step aside.'"

"How much brandy had I consumed?"

"I believe you were quite sober at the time."

Hawkwood smiled. "Storm the hill, raise the flag."

Read looked at him.

Hawkwood gazed back. "Or more likely we're the forlorn bloody hope."

Read said nothing.

"Flagg and Charlotte," Hawkwood said. "We know Flagg didn't kill her. The scene was staged to throw us off the scent. I asked Vaughn if he'd killed them, not that I expected him to admit it – which he didn't – but he didn't deny it either, which tells me he might not have wielded the knife or pulled the trigger, but I'll stake my life he knows who did. He struck me as a man with an over-inflated view of his own importance. His coming to see me was to throw down the gauntlet as much as it was to issue a warning. I accused him of being Saxby's lapdog, but maybe I picked the wrong master. From your knowledge of Brooke, is that something he might have arranged?"

"You're suggesting the head of the Alien Office might have sanctioned murder on British soil?"

"You're telling me that's not within the realms of possibility?"

"Possibility is not proof, and proof is something we do not have, for any of it. What's more, they know it."

"And there's the rub," Hawkwood said.

Read nodded in agreement. "As you say: there's the rub."

"And we're running out of time," Hawkwood said.

Read looked at him.

"Vaughn said if I were to delay my enquiries, the problem would go away."

"Define 'delay'," Read said.

"I can't; not precisely. I got the impression he was talking days rather than weeks, which would explain the strength of his warning and Brooke's sermon to you."

The magistrate pursed his lips.

"What?" Hawkwood said.

"Brooke told me that in a week it was possible he'd be able to tell me more about the enterprise he was involved in."

"Which suggests whatever the plan is, it's well advanced."

"One must presume so."

"So we *are* talking days if we're to nail our man."

"We may already be too late," Read said.

"And even if we do find something, they're likely to get away with it," Hawkwood said.

The violent knock on the door gave Read no chance to respond. Before the magistrate or Hawkwood could give the person on the other side leave to enter, the door was thrust open. The waitress, Lily, stood on the threshold. Her desperate expression drew Hawkwood to his feet.

"It's Maddie," Lily blurted, before he could speak. "Someone took her!"

21

"He said to tell you two days and you'll have her back unharmed."

Her name was Cassie. A member of Maddie's staff, she performed a variety of duties around the tavern, from running errands and cleaning rooms to helping in the kitchen and waiting on tables when the place got busy; an engaging girl, usually seen with a cheerful grin on her face; but not now. Her cheeks were streaked with tears and her voice broke as she recited the message she'd been given.

It had happened so quickly, she told Hawkwood between the sniffles. She and Maddie had been on a shopping trip to Waithmans on Fleet Street, to buy bed linen and napkins. They'd been on their way home when the abduction occurred. Their purchases made and delivery arranged, their return route had taken them into Bride Lane, past the high wall of St Bride's churchyard, where a carriage had driven up suddenly alongside them, causing them to step back from the road and into the shadow of the wall. Without warning, two men had appeared. Knocking Cassie to the ground, they'd thrust a sack over Maddie's head and bundled her into the vehicle. As Cassie tried to stand, one of the men had pushed her back down, telling her to deliver a message to Captain Hawkwood at the Blackbird tavern. Whereupon the carriage had driven off at speed, disappearing around the corner in the direction of New Bridge Street.

The incident was over in seconds. So quickly, in fact, that the few people who'd been in the vicinity were unaware of the event, their vision having been blocked by the halted vehicle. Only as Cassie staggered to her feet had anyone taken notice, but as they'd moved to help she'd pushed them away, retrieved Maddie's purse, which had been dropped in the scuffle, and taken off running.

She winced as Lily dabbed the blood from her arm with a damp cloth, cleaning the graze sustained when she'd tripped in her frantic haste to get back to the tavern. Bursting through the front door, coat torn and muddied, out of breath and barely able to speak, it had taken all Lily's patience to calm her down. When her garbled words had begun to make sense, Lily, with startled staff and customers looking on, had grasped the distraught girl by the wrist and steered her straightaway to the room reserved by James Read and where Hawkwood had been seen to enter.

Hawkwood poured a finger of brandy into his empty glass and placed it between the girl's shaking hands. "Drink this."

Lily, who was kneeling, helped Cassie lift the glass to her lips. Turning, she threw Hawkwood a bleak look.

"The man who gave you the message, Cassie," Hawkwood said. "Can you describe him?"

The girl, having swallowed the liquor, clasped the glass in her lap and looked at Hawkwood in dull comprehension.

"Did he have a scar near his mouth?" Hawkwood pressed.

Cassie continued to stare at Hawkwood in confusion before finally shaking her head.

"No? What *did* he look like?" Hawkwood fought to control his exasperation.

"He had no hair." The girl's voice shook.

"Was he big, small?"

Another frown, then: "Big, heavy looking."

"And the other one?"

Lily rose and placed her arm around the girl's shoulders as fresh tears welled and trickled down her blotched face.

"It's all right, Cassie." Realizing he might have been pushing her too hard, Hawkwood attempted a calmer tone. "I know it was a shock and you're frightened, but no one can touch you here. You're safe. Take your time."

"They were so quick." She stared up at him helplessly. "I didn't get a good look before they knocked me down."

"Anything will help," Hawkwood said.

She fell silent, which made Hawkwood wonder if she'd heard him. Then she said falteringly, "I do remember the other one weren't so big. He did have hair; black it was, and wavy-like"

"That's good. Did *he* have a scar?"

"A scar?"

"On his face." Hawkwood touched his jaw. "Here."

The girl shook her head doubtfully. "I don't think so." Her face crumpled as she gazed upon Maddie's purse, which Lily had placed on the table beside her. "I'm sorry. I couldn't help her."

"You're not to blame, Cassie. There's nothing you could have done."

"He told me not to call the constables but to come straight here, else they'd hurt her." Her features twisted with the memory. "Said if you weren't here I was to tell you what happened soon as you got back."

Quelling the rage burning inside him, Hawkwood turned to James Read, who had also risen to his feet. "Vaughn. It has to be."

Read nodded, his face sombre. "He knows you would have no concern for your own welfare, but for someone else's you would take his threat seriously."

"Oh, I'm taking him very seriously. The bastard has my full attention." Hawkwood turned to the girl. "You need to tell us everything you know, Cassie."

She paused as if about to apologize again and then said, "I think the bald one might have called the other one Jack."

"Jack?" Hawkwood felt a glimmer of hope.

She nodded again, though more firmly than before.

"No other names?"

She shook her head. Lilly took the glass, placed it on the table and cradled the girl's hands in her own.

"What about the carriage, or the driver, maybe?"

"I didn't see the driver's face. I remember there were two horses, black; a matched pair."

"What about a crest on the doors? Anything like that?"

"I don't think so." She began to sob once more.

Hawkwood thought about the carriage heard by the watchman, Cribb. He looked at James Read, who followed him out of the room.

"Two days," Hawkwood said. "We were right. They are putting their plan into action. But we have a name. It's a start."

"Two names," Read said. "You have Vaughn as well." The magistrate lowered his voice. "Do you believe it, that Mrs Teague will be returned if you hold fast?"

"I'm not waiting around to find out."

"You're planning to hunt them down?"

"Oh, I'll do more than hunt them."

"You're taking a huge risk."

"We know they're prepared to kill. It's Maddie. I can't leave it to chance that they won't hurt her."

Read moved closer. "If it were in my power, you would have every Bow Street resource at your disposal. Regrettably, they are no longer mine to command. Magistrate Conant . . ."

Hawkwood shook his head. "At this point, I'd trust Conant as far as I can spit. In any case, I don't need the Shop's help. I have my own resources."

The magistrate's eyes narrowed. "I believe I understand, but if you feel you do need my assistance in any way, do not hesitate to ask."

"I appreciate that, but this has just become personal. I might have to resort to extreme measures. Best if you're not seen to be involved."

Read looked at him, his face softened. "I'd say it was rather late for that, wouldn't you?"

Hawkwood stepped back into the room and drew Lily to him. "If she remembers anything else, make note of it."

Lily nodded. "You're going to look for Maddie?"

"Yes, but I need you and Cassie to keep this to yourselves. I know it will be hard; you're both upset and worried, but I don't want to put Maddie's life in further danger. I mean that. So you tell Cassie that, if anyone asks, Maddie's with me. Meantime, you look after things here, all right? Maddie trusts you. *I* trust you. You know what to do."

Lily stared at him, then drew herself up and nodded, even though Hawkwood could tell that fear dwelt behind her determined gaze.

Hawkwood turned to go and realized Lily had taken hold of his arm.

"You bring her back safe," Lily said.

"I intend to," Hawkwood said.

"I don't care what it takes. I want them. Three men; one well-built with a shaven scalp; the other not so large, with hair, maybe called Jack. They're the ones who took Maddie. The other one's a Captain Dominic Vaughn; supposed to have served with the Ninth as well."

Jago's eyes glittered. "Same as Tommy Flagg."

Hawkwood nodded. "Makes me wonder if the others might have been Holy Boys, too. The way Cassie told it, they knew what they were doing."

"You reckon they might have seen discipline a while back?"

"That'd be my guess, but they made a mistake. They didn't bother to cover their faces. That makes them either cocky or shoddy, and it's given us a chance. It's a long shot, I know, but if they did know Flagg, we also have an edge. You know where Flagg drank. Old soldiers stick together, especially if they served in the same regiment."

"Like us, you mean?" There was no accompanying smile.

"No," Hawkwood said. "They're nothing like us."

Hawkwood had tracked Jago down to the Hanged Man, where he'd found him at the table in the first-floor taproom, going through a small ledger, a mug of dark amber liquid resting by his elbow. One look at Hawkwood's face and the ledger and the drink were swept aside.

Jago held Hawkwood's eye and then looked to his right, towards where Micah – the only other customer in the room

– was seated at the top of the stairs. No words were spoken. Micah laid down his reading matter and walked across.

"I want the word put out." Jago kept his voice low even though there was no one within earshot. The nearest was the landlord, Bram, who was minding his own business over behind the counter. "We're looking for three men." The former sergeant glanced questioningly at Hawkwood.

Hawkwood nodded. "Tell him."

Jago indicated the seat next to Hawkwood. Micah sat and listened. In the times he'd spent in Micah's company Hawkwood had rarely seen Jago's lieutenant express emotion, but this time there was no hiding the stone-cold look that came over his face.

"Flagg drank in the Mitre," Jago said. "Might be an idea to . . ." He paused, struck by a change of expression on his lieutenant's face. "What?"

"Mudd and Ridger," Micah said.

Jago stared at his lieutenant for a full three or four seconds then sat back. "Ah, Christ, I must be getting old."

"You *know* them?" Hawkwood said. His spine prickled.

"I heard it was Mudd who shot Billy Cobb's monkey," Micah said.

"Monkey?" Hawkwood said. "What bloody monkey?"

Jago shook his head. "Not important; a bit of bother over the other side of the river." He turned back to Micah. "That was Mudd?"

Micah nodded. "Ridger was with him. There were some there who thought he might shoot Billy on account of him voicing a protest. Fortunately, Billy saw sense and backed down."

"Wise lad," Jago said. He turned to Hawkwood. "Could be we've struck gold first time out."

"Who are they?"

"*They* are Israel Mudd and Jackson Ridger. Scum for hire; no job too small, and they ain't that particular about the kind of job, nor who does the hiring either. Ain't averse to using their weight when needed; Mudd's usually. He's what you might call the brawn to Ridger's brains, though if you were to ask me, there ain't that much between 'em. They'd likely sell their own mothers for candle fat if they could find someone to render 'em down. Now I think on it, I do recall hearing they were in receipt of the king's shilling a long time back; something about them falling foul of the Provost and bein' brought up on charges, around the time you and me came back home. Supposedly escaped a flogging by desertin' from the ranks. What we must have done to have 'em wash up here, God knows. They stay out of my way an' I stay out of theirs. But they have their uses, so they're what you might call 'tolerated'. Could be they did serve with our Tommy at some point," Jago said speculatively and eyed his lieutenant. "You hear anything about that?"

Micah frowned. "I have no knowledge of Flagg. If they did serve, it would have been with the infantry. If you're asking which regiment, I couldn't tell you."

Jago straightened and looked Hawkwood full in the eye. "Don't know about you, but they just moved to the top of *my* shit list."

Hawkwood turned to Micah. "How about Vaughn? That name ring any bells?"

Micah shook his head apologetically. "Can't help you, Captain; sorry."

Jago sucked in his cheeks. "Probably not surprising, given what you said of the bugger. If he is what he said he is, he'd see the Mitre as bein' beneath 'is station. Two out of three ain't bad, though."

"It's more than I had when I sat down," Hawkwood said. "Taking Maddie in broad daylight – would this Mudd and Ridger be capable of that?"

Jago looked at Micah, who returned his gaze with a look that required no explanation. Jago smiled grimly. "Be right up their street, if they thought it worth their while. They wouldn't worry about anyone gettin' in their way, neither."

Pushing back his chair, Jago stood. Draining his mug, he stowed the ledger in an inside pocket. "Time to pay the Mitre a visit, then; you reckon?"

But he was talking to himself. Hawkwood was already heading for the stairs.

"Whoa, hold up!" Jago said quickly. "I know you're burnin' up inside, but if you reckon I'm heading after those two without insurance, you've another think coming." Turning to his lieutenant, he jerked his chin towards the counter. "Do the honours." To the landlord, Bram, who looked up from the news sheet he'd spread out on the counter top, he said, "Cellar open?"

Bram nodded and Hawkwood watched as Micah lifted the counter flap and disappeared through the curtained doorway that lay behind it.

"Two ticks," Jago said.

The pistols were Binghams; man-stoppers, conveniently small, less than fourteen inches in length – eight of which was the octagonal Damascus barrel – but with a very impressive bore.

"Got spare powder and shot," Jago said, as Micah distributed the weapons, along with a bandolier holster each, adding, as Hawkwood tested the gun's weight, "Help yourself, though if we do have to re-load, we're likely past savin'." As he spoke, Jago removed his jacket and slid his head and shoulder through the harness so that the pistol lay snugly against his left hip, concealed by the jacket's cut when he put the garment back on.

Hawkwood and Micah followed suit. With weapons stowed and spare shot and powder distributed, Jago gave each of them the once-over and nodded his satisfaction.

"*Now* we can go."

Turning to Bram, who had returned to his newspaper, totally unfazed by the sight of three men preparing for war, he threw the landlord a feral grin.

"Don't wait up. We could be a while."

Tucked away in a grimy courtyard at the end of a cobbled passageway halfway along Holborn, in the rain and in the grey afternoon light, the Mitre had all the attraction of a coal merchant's outhouse. Turning into the passage, Hawkwood wondered how anyone managed to find the place in the dead of night. Which was probably the point, he reflected, when the passage finally opened out and the tavern's black-painted frontage and soot-stained mullioned windows were revealed. If it hadn't been for the splintered wooden sign hanging above the door, it was doubtful anyone would have taken the building for licensed premises.

A rag-covered object lay half-in and half-out of a large puddle in the lee of the wall close by the tavern's front door. Only the sound of laboured breathing, interspersed with incoherent groans, gave any indication that the bundle was human and still alive. A broken rum flask lay a foot away from outstretched fingers.

Hawkwood side-stepped the obstruction and was heading for the door when he was stopped by Jago's hand on his arm. "You want blood; I know that, and you ain't in uniform, but you go in there and it'll be like watching rats disappear down a bloody drainpipe. You want to catch a particular rat, you 'ave to use a ferret." Catching his lieutenant's eye, he jerked his chin. "Micah, my son, you're on."

Before Hawkwood could object, Jago drew him towards another passageway, which until then had been concealed within the deeper shadows in the corner of the yard. Hawkwood just had time to look back and see Micah let himself in through the tavern door before he found himself enveloped in almost Stygian darkness.

"Tradesman's entrance," Jago muttered. "'T'ain't far."

The inner passage opened up to reveal yet another rank-smelling yard with more openings leading off it. Their boots squelched uncomfortably with every step they took. As the stink was coming from what was obviously the tavern's privy, Hawkwood could only guess what they were wading through. It was clear that a good number of the Mitre's customers didn't care whether they pissed or shat inside the privy's retaining walls or around the outskirts.

Jago indicated a half-open doorway silhouetted against a dim-lit corridor beyond and pressed himself against the wall. "Right," he murmured as Hawkwood followed suit. "Let's see what shakes loose."

It was around three minutes later when the sounds of

someone hurrying came to them from the other side of the door. As the door flew back and a wiry, dishevelled shape stumbled into the yard, Jago stuck out his boot. Hawkwood caught a quick glimpse of pasty white features, a balding pate and a mouth open in shock as the figure went sprawling.

"Looks like we got one," Jago said.

Hawkwood turned as a second figure emerged from the doorway.

Micah, who was not even breathing hard, looked down without sympathy at the prostrate form being pressed into the ground by the sole of Jago's right boot and a tatty grey wig that had been dislodged in the fall and which lay in the filth along-side Jago's left foot.

"Right," Jago said as he lifted his boot away and hauled the squirming man upright by his collar. "Let's see *who* we've got. God's sake, keep still, you little shit."

Hawkwood looked around but there were no other signs of life. They had the yard to themselves. Jago wasted no time in slamming the man against the wall. "I told you; it ain't no good protesting, so stop wrigglin'." Frowning, he peered into the frightened face. "Name?"

It took a couple of seconds before an answer was forthcoming. "M-Moses."

"That so? They call me Jago. That mean anything?"

It took a further heartbeat for the name to sink in and for the question to be answered with a swift nod.

"Good, then you'll know not to piss me off. I'd like you to tell me why, when my associate here asked if anyone had word of Israel Mudd and Jack Ridger, you took off like a scalded whippet. Weren't thinkin' of warnin' 'em, were you? I'd take that as a personal insult."

Maintaining his hold, but easing the pressure on his victim's scrawny neck, Jago took half a step back.

"Don't know no Mudd nor Bridger!" The words emerged in a strangled yelp.

Immediately, Jago tightened his hold and leaned forward. "*Bridger?* Nice try, son. I'll ask again . . ."

"I don't know 'em! I told you! I was only after the bleedin' privy!"

"You always sprint for the privy, do you?"

"No! An' I weren't sprintin'! Leastways not 'til I saw that'n followin' me. The look on his face, 'course I bloody ran. Anyone would!"

"Well, *you* certainly did; you were flyin'. So you're sayin' you never heard of Israel Mudd and Jack Ridger?"

Emboldened by Jago's more amenably posed query, the luckless Moses attempted to draw himself up to his full height, which wasn't that impressive. It brought his eyeline on a level with Jago's shoulder. "That's right."

"I see." Jago nodded sagely. Releasing his grip but blocking the man's escape route, he folded his arms. "An' yet I could've sworn I saw you drinkin' with the two of them not a week back. Thick as thieves, you looked. You mind explainin'?"

Even in the poor light Hawkwood caught the flash of fear lance across the thin face.

"Weren't me . . ." Moses began.

The rest of the denial was cut short as, lightning fast, the knuckle side of Jago's right hand slammed into Moses' right cheek. Moses' head rocked backwards, striking the brickwork, bringing forth a sharp cry of pain.

Jago leant forward. "You got five seconds, then, unless you come clean, I'm going to have Micah slit your throat. Folks'll be steppin' round you to use the facilities. In fact, I dare say there'll be those who couldn't be bothered to make the effort. Come morning, you'll be covered in piss and shit. Mind you, you'll be dead, so you won't notice."

The man's eyes flicked towards Hawkwood. The movement was instantly rewarded with another back-hander. Jago's voice was a snarl. "Don't look at him. Look at *me*! I'm the one asking the bleedin' questions! Micah, you got your blade?"

Without speaking, Micah reached inside his coat, making sure the butt of his pistol was revealed, and drew out a folded razor. Moses' eyes showed white as Micah flicked the razor open.

"Your choice, son," Jago said cajolingly as a trickle of blood and snot emerged from Moses' right nostril. "I ain't goin' to ask again. An' if you think I give a toss if he opens you up, you'd be wrong. It'll mean no more to me than swattin' a fly. Him neither. So, what's it to be?"

A tear weaved down a bony cheek.

Jago sighed and turned to Micah. "All right, make it quick. Some of us have homes to go to."

Micah stepped forward without expression, the razor poised.

"Wait!" The word emerged as a petrified bleat.

Micah moved snake-quick, spinning Moses round and using his left hand to pull the head back, exposing the neck.

"Somethin' to say there, Moses?" Jago enquired softly.

"I remember! I *do* know them!"

"Say again?" Jago cupped an ear. "Not sure I caught that."

"I know them! I know them!" A streak of yellow snot shot into the air.

Jago nodded to Micah, who released his hold. "Well, *I* know that, lad. What I'm after is their current location."

Moses blinked. "I dunno that! Why would I?"

"Oh, for Christ's sake," Jago snapped in exasperation. "I ain't botherin' to go through all that again. Life's too bleedin' short. Micah . . ."

"Sharp's Alley!" The words tumbled out.

Jago held up a hand. Expressionless, Micah lowered the razor. Jago moved forward and placed his hands around both of the quaking man's cheeks, cupping his face, like a mother might soothe a frightened child. "What about it?"

"They've a crib that backs on to the workhouse!"

Jago frowned. "You talkin' about St Sepulchre's?"

"Mudd's brother runs one of the knacker's yards!"

"He have a name?"

"A-Aaron."

Jago released his grip and Moses let go a soft exhalation.

"I find you've lied to me," Jago growled. "You an' me'll be payin' Tommy Reilly a visit. I hear tell his boys ain't been fed for a week. You with me?"

A desperate nod followed.

Reilly's hogs again. The animals were fast acquiring mythical status, Hawkwood thought. When mere mention of them was able to loosen the most stubborn tongue, it proved, if nothing else, that they had to be the best-known swine in the capital. If their reputation for impartial dining was even halfway accurate, quite possibly the best-fed, too.

"There you go." Jago patted the man's chest consolingly. "Weren't so hard, was it?"

Moses said nothing. Fear looked to have frozen him to the spot.

Jago gave a satisfied nod. "Well, all right, then."

Whether it was the tone in Jago's voice or the words that alerted him, Hawkwood wasn't sure, but he sensed what was about to happen. From the sudden look of shock on his face, Moses realized the same thing, but by then it was too late. Jago's hands were already moving. Cupping Moses' chin with his right hand and the back of his skull in his left, he jerked hard. There was an audible click as the neck snapped.

Releasing the body, Jago wiped his hands on his jacket. "Sup with the Devil, my son, you should have used a longer bloody spoon." He looked at Hawkwood, his eyes hard. "Changed my mind. They took Maddie. That's a threat against you. A threat against you's a threat against me. I'm not havin' that. An' if you're considering chastisement, you know the last thing we needed was him spreadin' the word we were on our way. Plus it means there's one less to worry about."

Hawkwood eyed the body and the wig that by now looked as though someone had stomped on a dead rat. "*Did* you see him drinking with them?"

Jago shrugged dismissively. "He thought I did. That's what counted."

"He could have been lying," Hawkwood pointed out, "about where we might find them."

"If he was lyin', he wouldn't have given us Mudd's brother. Besides, if you'd been him, would *you* have lied?"

"Probably not," Hawkwood conceded.

He turned. Jago regarded him, eyebrow cocked. "Well?"

Hawkwood looked again at the corpse and nodded. "They wanted a war, they've got one."

"Reckon that answers that question, then," Jago said.

22

The parish of St Sepulchre bordered Smithfield Market; a short distance as the crow flew, but the geography of the area necessitated several detours through a labyrinth of lanes and crooked passageways, some no wider than a handcart. Not that an intimate knowledge of the area was required, for the smell alone would have served as a marker. London was a far from fragrant city and her citizens had long become used to her foul odours, but in and around the market and the streets bordering it the stench was beyond description.

The livestock trade had occupied this part of the metropolis for the past ten centuries. Nearly all the routes leading to and from Smithfield had started out as drovers' roads and as it was more economical to drive animals than transport them, local slaughterhouses and their attendant trades – supplied by water from the Fleet River and Faggeswell Brook – had flourished.

Over the intervening years, parts of the river and stretches of the brook had either been diverted or covered over, but the slaughterhouses, tanneries, bladder-dealers, tripe-dressers, soap-makers, catgut workers, knackers and bone-pickers remained. As a result, from the depths of the dingiest alleyways to the highest chimney pots, the reek from the killing yards and the detritus they produced was all pervasive. There were breweries in the locality, too, and the scent from stored hops added an extra piquancy to the miasma.

The entrance to Sharp's Alley was situated on the north side of Chick Lane, less than a stone's throw from the western side of the main market square, and the fetid emanations from the pens lay heavy on the air, scouring the back of the throat.

"Runs north to Cow Cross and Turnmill," Jago murmured, nodding towards the entryway, which was flanked by a pair of squalid half-timbered houses, so run-down that their rotting façades and grimy windows bore an uncanny resemblance to the stern quarters on two derelict men-of-war. "They're shit holes, too."

Given its location and the trades it housed, Hawkwood guessed the alley probably traced part of the Fleet's original course, which, if it wasn't a section that had been bricked over, undoubtedly accounted for some of the other noxious smells he was inhaling. What soon became clear was that not only was it a corridor linking the market to the northern pack roads, it was also the conduit to a hive of winding lanes, squalid courts and interconnecting staircases as extensive as anything at the heart of the St Giles Rookery.

Above their heads, stout timber beams spanned the alley's width like the spars on a main mast, bracing the buildings on either side as prevention against them collapsing into the space below. To add to the nautical illusion, the gaps between the beams were festooned with ratlines, from which items of grubby laundry hung in limp clusters, dampened by the thin rain that continued to fall and which had turned the ground beneath their feet into thick black mulch.

Hemmed in by the dilapidated buildings and the strands of washing suspended above them, all of which blocked a clear view of the sullen sky, it was hard to make out features, but as Hawkwood's eyes grew accustomed to the late afternoon gloom the surroundings gradually took shape.

Dingy shops and crude stalls lined the alley, while signs above a couple of doorways advertised cheap lodgings for travellers. Here and there, metal braziers glowed brightly, casting sparks and creating shadows across the faces of those who were gathered around them, bodies hunched, cap brims pulled low, hands held out towards the flames. Their forms hidden beneath shapeless apparel and their faces cast down, it was hard to differentiate male from female, for the only parts of their features caught by the firelight were the whites of their eyes and that was only if they raised their heads.

It occurred to Hawkwood as they skirted the fires and the loiterers and the piles of rotting refuse and the gutters overflowing with effluent, that this was close to where Eleanor Rain had first lifted her skirts for money. With her looks, she must have turned heads wherever she went. Hawkwood wondered how many customers she'd been obliged to service before making the transition from back-room harlot to woman of substance with access to society and the fine townhouse she now inhabited. Hard to imagine anyone could have made such an impressive leap, let alone a girl who, for a handful of pennies, had launched her career catering for strings of nameless men, the blood not yet congealed beneath their fingernails and their clothes greased with the residue from the bone yards.

At the sound of a creaking axle they stepped aside to give way to a bullock-drawn wagon piled high with cow carcasses. The stench that arose from the cargo as it trundled past was overpowering.

Carcasses weren't the only commodity being traded. Live animals were also in evidence. Scrawny chickens pecked for scratchings in the mud, while hogs rooted for scraps among the piles of rotting food, dodging as they did so the sheep, cattle and horses that were being herded along the lane. Horses were in the majority and all, almost without exception, were in a pitiful condition. Their numbers and their state of health reflected the preponderance of knacker's yards in the vicinity, not to mention the growing trade in horse flesh as a food source. In the seriously deprived areas of the city it was the one meat anyone could afford. As a consequence, with demand for the product rising, horse-theft had become a thriving cottage industry.

Casual enquiry had revealed that Mudd's brother's yard was located not on the main alley but at the end of a side lane that led on to a rough patch of open ground squeezed between a row of broken-down hovels and a crumbling brick structure which Hawkwood took to be part of the boundary wall surrounding St Sepulchre's workhouse. If there had ever been a sign denoting the yard's ownership or tenancy it had long since rotted away, like most of the architecture around it. The gate was propped open, allowing a partial view of the squalid premises beyond.

"You do know she might not be there, right?" Jago said gently from beside Hawkwood's shoulder.

Hawkwood eyed the collection of buildings. "I've nothing else to go on. I don't have a choice."

Jago leaned in close. "*We* don't have a choice. There's no way you're on your own with this. You remember that. Any case, Micah's worth two of anyone's best." Adding laconically and sotto voce, "Hell, we've damn near got the bastards surrounded."

Micah gave no sign that he had heard. Standing off to the side, his eyes were fixed resolutely on their objective.

"Any ideas on how we get in?" Jago murmured.

Hawkwood studied the open gates. "Maybe."

Jago let out a low grunt. "*Maybe?* I was hoping for something a tad more positive. You want to give us a hint?"

Hawkwood looked about him, then back at the yard.

"We'll need a horse."

"Ah, Christ," Jago muttered in disgust. "Wish I'd never bleedin' asked."

Maddie Teague had cried out with shock and struggled wildly when they'd snatched her off the street and had even managed to claw a deep furrow into one of her captor's cheeks with her nail before a strong hand was clapped over her mouth. From then on she had not stood a chance. Her abductors had proved too strong, pushing her to the floor of the carriage with a sharp warning not to struggle or scream or call for help or they would hurt her. Pressure on the small of her back – it felt like someone's knee – had kept her low and she'd had little option but to obey.

Stunned by the speed of the attack and unable to see, she had flinched at every touch but, confined within the narrow space between the seats, there had been nowhere for her to go. Knowing that her captors had her at their mercy, and with visions almost too terrible to contemplate flooding her mind, she had fallen silent, hoping against hope that an opportunity to escape would present itself.

To begin with, from her cramped and helpless position, she'd been unable to gauge the direction in which they were travelling; with the clatter of hooves and wheels being so close to her ear, trying to identify specific ambient sounds had proved an elusive task. She thought they were moving north, for no other reason than the general city noises she could make out remained constant, whereas she had reasoned if they had turned south the route would probably have taken them over Blackfriars Bridge which would, possibly, for the duration of the river crossing, have been a quieter ride.

But then, a few minutes later, from close at hand, she heard the cries of several street vendors, one of whom she thought she recognized; a stall-holder from whom she purchased produce for the Blackbird's kitchen. Almost immediately there came a familiar chiming sound. It came, she knew, from the clock at the top of the turret at the centre of the Fleet Market. They were definitely heading north.

The market cries had faded swiftly after that, however, and following several sharp turns sounds had become merged and less distinct, indicating that the main thoroughfare had been left behind. A short time later they had halted and with another harshly worded instruction not to cause trouble she was transferred from the carriage to what felt like some kind of wooden platform. As the boards beneath her creaked and rocked, she realized she was lying on the bed of a cart. Before she could move she was covered by a layer of sacking. Several heavy objects were then positioned about her to keep the covering in place, their combined weight causing the cart's timbers to groan alarmingly. The accompanying smells almost made her retch.

The cart's tailboard was secured and then they were off again, though for a much shorter duration this time. After what felt like a few hundred yards, the vehicle halted once more. The load and the covering were removed and she was dragged to her feet.

She felt her coat catch on something and tear in the process. Still rendered sightless by the sack over her head, she gasped as her arms were held fast from behind. She felt the rain patter lightly on to her hair and shoulders as she was led across boggy ground into a building and down a slippery, sloping floor which then levelled off, at which point the hood was removed and she was able to take her first look at her surroundings.

It appeared to be a cellar; lantern-lit and perhaps thirty paces square. The only aperture apart from the door was a small, barred, horizontal window set a foot above head height. The walls were of cold grey brick. The floor was part earth and part flagstone, covered with matted straw, scraps of hessian and animal droppings and large patches of what looked like dried blood. The two items of furniture – a straight-backed chair and a wooden trestle cot upon which lay a thin, stained palliasse and an equally filthy plaid blanket – looked completely out of place in this setting. A wooden pail sat in the corner. Maddie had never been in a prison cell but she imagined this was what one looked like, albeit on a larger scale. There were markings on the wall; crude anatomical drawings which left little to the imagination or to the musings of the individual who'd scratched them into the brickwork. They did not look as though they had been carved recently. The room smelled of dirt, dampness, wet straw, piss and shit, mostly shit. She wondered if it was animal or human in origin.

Her coat torn, her hair in disarray and her pulse racing, she stared at her captors. The bald one she remembered. He was the one who'd grabbed her and taken her weight when they'd picked her up. His shaven scalp glistened as he stared back at her. It felt as if he was undressing her with his eyes as he drew a palm across the crown of his head, wiping away the beads of moisture. Her eyes took in the thin crust of dried blood that ran from beneath his left eye and down his cheek and she felt an immediate stab of satisfaction in knowing he'd been the one she'd caught with her nail. As she watched, he ran a grubby finger down the length of the gouge, placed the tip of the finger between his lips and mimed the act of sucking. Then he grinned.

Her skin crawled.

His companion, meanwhile, gazed at her impassively. She wondered which of the two was the more dangerous. The big one was clearly the more brutish. She had felt the strength of his grip, and his stance and expression left her in no doubt as to his character. He was a man who relished using his size to threaten. She had felt the pressure of his palm against her breasts as he'd pushed her down and transferred her between vehicles, and knew the touch had not been accidental but a deliberate attempt to violate her body and to impress upon her the inescapable fact that she was the prisoner and he the captor.

And yet, despite his slighter stature and calm manner, there was something about the other man that was equally intimidating. Perhaps it was his quietness. She recalled that the bald one had referred to him as Jack. Even as she remembered that, she wondered if, in knowing his name, her position had been made even more precarious. Of the pair, he appeared the less aggressive, more contained one and therefore the more thoughtful, but she knew appearances were deceptive. The bald one had relied on his size to intimidate, but the quiet one's unassuming passivity suggested he might be the individual with the greater capacity to do her harm.

She drew her coat close about her. "Who are you? What do you want with me?"

The bald one spoke. "Don't matter who we are, darlin'. That ain't important. As for what we want . . . well, let's just say you'll be our guest for a while." He grinned again, showing yellowing teeth. "As you can see, we've prepared your quarters. It's got all the facilities." He nodded towards the mattress and the bucket. "Ain't quite up to the standard of that tavern you run, mind, but then it ain't as if we get that many visitors – leastways, not unless they got four legs." He chuckled throatily.

At the mention of the Blackbird, Maddie frowned. "Do I know you?"

The bald one smiled again. "Not yet, but you will."

The threat in his voice was implicit. Maddie steeled herself not to show fear. "I don't understand. Why have you brought me here?"

"Leverage."

It was the quiet one who answered. His face showed no change of expression.

Maddie gazed at him with increasing confusion. "What does that mean?"

"Your man," the bald one said, "is what it means."

It took a second for the implication to sink in. Maddie felt her stomach drop. She swung her gaze towards him. "Matthew? What does he have to do with this?"

"Been stickin' 'is nose in where it weren't wanted; askin' awkward questions. He was given a warning – told to stop – an' he refused. It was decided he needed a little extra persuasion."

"Persuasion?" Maddie said.

"That's where you come in, sweet'eart. Soon as he stops asking questions, he gets you back safe an' sound. 'Course, if'n he persists we'll have to see what happens, won't we?"

Maddie stared back at him.

Mudd smiled. "If you're thinkin' of runnin', I wouldn't. There ain't nowhere for you to go. Best thing is, you make yourself comfy for a couple of days while your man does as he's told; which he will." Catching his companion's eye, he winked. "You were mine, there's no way *I'd* risk doin' anything stupid."

Maddie's brain continued to race. She considered them both and decided she had nothing to lose by responding, though with more bite than she had intended. "You think that will deter him?"

The slim one's eye flickered.

"You're sayin' he won't take no notice?" the bald one glowered.

Maddie's eyes flashed defiantly. "I'm telling you the opposite. He *will* take notice. And the first thing he'll do is look for me."

Ridger's chin came up.

"And when finds me – and he will, believe me – he'll deal with you."

Mudd grinned at that. "Well, course he will. He ain't got no choice."

"That's not what she meant," Ridger said softly.

"He's a Bow Street Officer." Maddie paused to let the information sink in. "A Runner."

"Now I'm really scared," Mudd said, and winked again.

"You should be. He was a soldier before that . . ."

Mudd cackled hoarsely. "So were we, darlin', an' there's *two* of us."

". . . with the 95th Rifles," Maddie said.

Mudd blinked. For the first time, he looked uncertain.

"Now *that*," Ridger murmured softly, his eyes narrowing, "we didn't know."

"And you won't be the first men he's hunted down," Maddie finished.

And as long as she clung to that certainty, she told herself, she would get through whatever tribulations were about to befall her.

"Then sod him," Mudd snarled. "*Let* the bastard come. Eh, Jack?"

Ridger said nothing.

"An' if he does," Mudd added, enthused by a gleeful afterthought, "maybe we'll let him watch while you and me become better acquainted. We can deal with him after. How's that sound?"

Sickened by the lustful expression on the bald man's face, Maddie fell silent, reluctant to dignify the taunting with a response.

"Meantime, if you mind your manners, maybe I'll see what I can do in the way of victuals. Wouldn't want you wastin' away, now, would we? Captain wouldn't like that."

"Captain?" Maddie said sharply.

Ridger threw his companion a barbed look. "Enough. Let's go."

Mudd stared at Maddie, a speculative expression on his simian-browed face. Then, grinning again, he said brightly, "Can't say I've ever done a Runner before – could be interestin'. I'll wager they ain't so tough once you face 'em down."

"You'll find out soon enough," Maddie said, adding before she could stop herself, "Don't say I didn't warn you."

Anger lit up the bald man's face. Maddie flushed. The retort had been a mistake.

Don't challenge them. Don't give them an excuse to hurt you.

"I can see," Mudd growled, "that pretty soon you an' me are goin' to have a serious conversation. You think on that, darlin', while you're pissin' in the bucket an' tryin' not to get any of it on your fine coat."

Turning, the two men made for the door. Ridger exited first. Mudd was halfway through when he turned, unable to resist a parting shot: "Don't want you smellin' like a midden when your man turns up, do we?"

Then, with that snide grin fixed upon his face, he was gone.

The sound of the key turning in the lock sounded like a pistol being cocked, and just as final.

As soon as the men's footsteps retreated, Maddie spun, the gorge rising into her throat. She reached the pail in the nick of time. The resultant foul smell rising from it as she vomited filled her nostrils, increasing her nausea. Bent over, one hand braced against the wall, the other holding her stomach, she threw up again, her belly heaving through a sequence of contractions until it felt as if there was nothing left of her insides.

Breathless and perspiring, she straightened herself and undid her coat buttons. Gradually, the heat dissipated, only for chills to take over as the shock moved through her afresh. The nausea came roaring back, so acutely that she thought she might faint. Moving unsteadily to the chair, she sat down and closed her eyes, opening them quickly when she felt the floor begin to tilt. It took several seconds before the dizziness subsided. Sitting up, forcing herself to breathe slowly and evenly, she relived the moment when the carriage had drawn alongside and the door had sprung open, disgorging the two men. There had been no warning, no time to defend herself. There was nothing she could have done.

And what of Cassie? The girl had been pushed to the ground in the attack. Had she been hurt? But then she remembered that her abductors would have needed Cassie to carry their message back to Hawkwood. She tried to picture what his reaction might have been when the message was delivered.

She could not envision him flying into a rage. That wasn't his way. In the time they'd known each other, she couldn't remember a single display of anger. He would, she thought, have received the news calmly, weighing the implications. She recalled his expression when she'd expelled the two lawyers from the Blackbird's dining room. The controlled way he'd got to his feet, preparing to deal with the situation, had been warning enough.

She assumed Hawkwood would enlist Jago's help in tracking her down. It would be the logical thing to do, given the former sergeant's standing in the London underworld. If Hawkwood had Nathaniel by his side then the bald man and his accomplice faced an even greater degree of retaliation than either of them could begin to imagine.

Fortified by that thought, she turned her attention to her confinement.

At least they'd left her the lantern. She went to the door and tried the handle even though she knew it was locked. Placing her ear close to the wood, she listened. There were vague muffled sounds coming from beyond which might have been voices, but they were too faint for her to make out what was being said. She went to move away but then another noise came to her. It began as a groan, as if a door was being dragged open on a rusty hinge, before stretching into a drawn-out ululation which then ceased abruptly.

She backed away from the door, the fine hairs rising along her arms and across the back of her neck, and turned her attention to the window. Picking up the chair, she placed it beneath the opening. Then, lifting her skirt, she climbed on to it and peered through the bars. Aside from a section of iron railing and an anonymous brick structure braced by several wooden trusses, all she could see was a portion of roof and a patch of sky.

Still none the wiser as to her location, she climbed down from the chair. What had the bald one said? If Matthew obeyed instructions, it would be "a couple of days" before she was released? The thought that she would be held in this foul hole for two days filled her with dread.

She looked again towards the window; the stains and dark streaks on the wall beneath it extended down to floor level.

302

There was mould growing from them. She stared at the floor, at the straw and the dung and what she had presumed was dried blood. Then she thought about the sounds she'd heard and how they might be associated with the smells that surrounded her.

Not a rusty door hinge, nor any other sort of inanimate object being moved. The sound had been made by a living thing. If Maddie Teague had to make a guess, it was the sound of a horse that was suffering ill treatment. But the droppings on the floor weren't from any horse. Being the size of dates, they were too small for that; sheep droppings, most likely. She thought of the smells she'd passed through when they'd brought her from the cart to the cellar and the softness of the ground underfoot and what her nose had told her when she'd tried to look through the window. Cautiously, she lifted her right foot and stared at the sole of her boot and the shit adhering to it. Animal shit.

Blood and dung. She heard the whinnying sound again, then; louder and even more pathetic this time before it was cut off as suddenly as it had been before. She thought of the direction the carriage had travelled and the elapsed time between her being snatched to the moment the hood had been lifted from her head.

She looked about her. It was common, she knew, for sheep to be contained in cellars. Add to that the sound of horses in pain and the aromas both inside and outside. Animals weren't being kept here, she realized, they were being culled.

She raised her eyes to the stains on the wall, caused not by water dripping from a leaky roof but by water rising up from beneath the floor, or from a breach in the bank of a swollen river due to heavy rain or some obstacle trapped downstream and spilling through the open window. Though above head-height when viewed from within the cellar, the aperture would be set at ground level outside.

Smithfield, she thought, or somewhere very near, which suggested the water-course was probably the Fleet or one of its tributaries. Which meant, if her suspicions were correct, she was being held less than a mile from the Blackbird.

Not that the knowledge brought her any comfort; it felt more like a thousand miles, and might as well have been, unless help was forthcoming.

She eyed the mattress and blanket with revulsion. I'll die before I sleep on that, she thought, though she knew that, come nightfall, if she was still being held, other than the chair the mattress would be the one thing separating her from the filth on the floor. She was relieved that she had her coat and was grateful for its warmth. She wondered what had happened to her purse. Hopefully, Cassie had picked it up.

Cassie's testimony would be all Hawkwood had to go on. She was a bright girl, but how much would she have been able to tell him? Would it be enough to set him on the trail? Another uncomfortable thought struck her. Was she relying too much on Hawkwood's ability to track the carriage and the men who'd taken her?

Assailed by this sudden wave of doubt, Maddie struggled to shake off the fear building inside her. If Matthew could not be relied upon to save her, her only hope would be to defend herself. Desperately she scanned the cellar for a makeshift weapon. Aside from the chair and the pail, there was only the lantern.

Heart sinking, she pushed a strand of hair from her face. Her hand stilled. Reaching behind her head, she pulled out the comb that had been holding her chignon in place. Fashioned in silver, with four-inch twin tines and a head in the shape of a flower, it had been a birthday gift from her late husband – a captain with the East India Company, lost when his ship foundered on a reef off the Andaman Islands. The comb had once belonged to a Balinese princess, or so he'd told her. Maddie slid the comb up into the lining inside her left coat sleeve.

But would it be enough?

"Jesus!" Jago said, in something approaching awe. "What the hell is *that*?"

Micah was leading the horse by a rope halter, though to call the poor beast a horse was stretching the definition to breaking point, such was its emaciated state. Its hide was as taut as a drum skin, the ribs clearly visible, each one outlined in perfect anatomical detail, as if every bone in its body had been picked clean of flesh. How the animal managed to remain upright, Hawkwood couldn't begin to guess. Sinew appeared to be the one thing keeping it together. Nothing could disguise the pitiful look in the half-closed eyes or the sores on its body, the knots in the tail and the filth that coated its hooves and haunches.

"Quick sale," Micah said as he passed Jago the grog bottle he was holding in his other hand. "Two bob."

"That its name or what you paid? In which case, you was robbed." Jago looked at Hawkwood. "This do you?"

"So long as we can get it to Mudd's yard in one piece."

"Best get a move on then. Poor thing don't look too steady on its pins." Jago stared at the animal, his expression doubtful. "Bloody breaks your heart. Bastard owner who let it get to this should be strung up."

It was on the tip of Hawkwood's tongue to remind Jago that less than half a dozen streets away, he'd snapped a man's neck with no thought as to the heartlessness or the illegality of the deed, and yet here he was voicing contempt for the person who'd worked a dumb animal to the brink of expiration. He wondered if Jago was aware of the irony.

Jago uncorked the bottle and took a swig, rinsing out his mouth with the contents before spitting them on to the ground. "You think this'll work?"

Hawkwood studied the yard entrance. "We'll know soon enough."

23

Head drooping, eyes dull and red-rimmed, stringy mucus clogging her nostrils, the mare allowed herself to be led without protest. Only as Jago walked her through the open gate and into the yard did she offer a reaction, as if suddenly aware of the fate that awaited her. Ears pricked, eyes rolling white in their sockets, she whickered softly and strained against the rope halter. But there was no strength left in the wasted muscles. Exhausted by the effort, her head slumped once more, thin flanks heaving. It was the smell of death, Jago knew, that had caused the mare to shy; that and the blood. The cobblestones were awash with it.

Jago had seen plenty of dead and injured horses on the battlefield, more than he cared to remember. He'd seen mounts writhing in agony, limbs missing, entrails protruding from bellies ripped open by cannon shot. He'd heard them screaming, legs thrashing, and he'd seen crows and buzzards pecking at their eyes while they lay on the ground, the life force draining out of them. He'd seen them whipped, slashed by sabre, pierced by lances and put out of their misery by a pistol shot to the brain to spare them a lingering death, and he'd seen their corpses butchered for meat when field rations ran low. But he could not recall seeing a picture of such utter wretchedness as the one that confronted him now.

It wasn't so much the blood that drew the eye, however, as

the bones and body parts. Skulls, vertebrae and ribcages littered the ground, many of them, like the hides hanging from hooks along the wall, with strips of raw meat still attached. Over by a stable block, a row of large barrels filled to the brim with gore and offal stood next to a pile of severed heads and hooves, while in another corner, two equine corpses lay on their sides awaiting render. The rain and the blood had turned the ground into slush around them.

"Help you, culley?" a gravelled voice enquired.

Letting the grog bottle trail from his hand and allowing his shoulders to slump, Jago took a breath, assumed a hangdog expression and turned. "Got a nag for sale. You interested?"

The man was almost twice Jago's size; wide-shouldered, with a broad belly that hung over his breeches like molten tallow. The flesh bulging from his collar was as swollen as a goitre. Rolled-up shirtsleeves revealed forearms the size of hams. A blue woollen cap covered his sweating crown while about his waist he wore an apron streaked with mud and matter, the origins of which Jago didn't care to speculate upon. A butcher's steel and a leather sheath containing two long knives hung from his belt. His right hand held a poleaxe, the head of which was matted with congealed blood and what looked like fragments of brain tissue. He regarded the mare through a pair of small, suspicious eyes without enthusiasm. "Give you a bob."

Jago shot the man a look of outraged disgust. "One bob? Jesus! She's worth at least four!"

The fat man spat into the mud. "Not round here, she ain't."

"What about three?" Jago adopted a wheedling tone. "Pity's sake, I got young 'uns to feed."

The fat man eyed the bottle dangling from Jago's left hand. "You weren't listenin'. I said it's one, it's one. Take it or leave it."

"An 'alf-bull, then? Come on, that's only another tanner."

"That it is, but it's still a bob."

Jago let his eyes drift sideways, allowing him a recce of the yard, before closing them and reopening them as if despairing of his options.

"I ain't got all night," the fat man growled impatiently.

Jago eyed the poleaxe, let go a resigned sigh and nodded. "All right, one. Jesus."

The fat man slid a podgy hand beneath his apron and fumbled in the pocket of his breeches.

Jago let go of the halter, took the proffered coins and made a face as he looked down at the two sixpences in his hand. "I should've bloody listened. He said you were a fly bastard."

"Who's that, then?" the fat man responded, though his expression suggested he wasn't the least bit interested in the reply.

Jago's head came up. "Your bleedin' brother, that's who. Mind you, he'd had a few. He could've just been spoutin' off."

The fat man's eyes narrowed.

Jago pocketed the change. "We've shared a few wets down the Mitre. Told me if I wanted to sell, I should come see you 'stead of that bastard Atcheler. Not sure it was such a good idea, seein' as this is all I got. You *are* Aaron, right?"

The fat man looked at him. "An' you are?"

"Nate."

The fat man looked unimpressed.

"He around?" Jago asked.

"Who?"

"Jesus! Your brother – who'd you think I meant? Between you an' me, I've a mind to give him what for, 'cept I owe him for a job he set me up with. Told 'im I'd give him his cut when I saw him next. Ain't much, just a coupla shillin', but it'll stand him a few rounds. Though, if it's anyone's shout, it's that bugger Ridger's. Now there's a man as tight as a duck's arse."

At the mention of Ridger's name, the fat man's eyes flickered.

"What?" Jago said.

The fat man shook his head as if Jago's mention of the name was irrelevant.

"So?" Jago pressed. "He 'ere, or what? Only I ran into Moses earlier. He said I should try you first."

"Moses?" the fat man said.

"Useless sod, looks like a stringy piece of gristle? Wears his old man's wig? Leastways, it looks like his old man's."

The fat man gave a non-committal grunt. Jago held his gaze

for a couple of seconds and then shrugged. "Aye, well, I've a message from the captain, so if your man and Jack *are* here, they should sing out."

"Captain?"

Jago straightened. As he did so, he undid the button on his jacket one-handed, allowing the garment to fall open, revealing the pistol at his hip. "Name of Vaughn, and he ain't known for 'is patience."

Nothing on the man's face indicated the name meant anything. Over the mare's withers, Jago saw two figures emerge from one of the stable's doors. Similarly dressed to the fat man but not as large, they were still of sufficient stature to draw the gaze. Neither of them was Israel Mudd or Jack Ridger. They looked more like reinforcements, a notion enhanced by the nature of the tools they were carrying. One held a large meat hook, the other a broad-bladed butcher's knife. The implements gleamed as they were caught by a spill of lantern light from a nearby stable door. Jago let his gaze travel over them before moving back to the fat man. "It weren't a trick question. They about or not?"

"Trouble, Aaron?" the man with the hook called. Bare-headed, his hair lay in lank strands across his scalp. The front of his clothing and his forearms were dark-stained. Some of the stains carried a faint sheen, suggesting they were fresh. There were dark spots on his chin and forehead, too, which also looked wet.

As if alerted by the question, the fat man fixed Jago with a look of renewed suspicion. "Ain't sure. Could be."

The two men approached. As they did so, the mare uttered a harrowing whinny and dropped to her knees. She remained vertical for several seconds but then, letting out a low exhalation, her head flopped and she collapsed on to her side in the mud, her flanks unmoving.

"I know you," the knife man said as he drew closer, unperturbed by the mare's subsidence. Bearded, with a pugilist's stance, he stared hard, looking suddenly puzzled. "You're Jago."

The fat man frowned at the name and then his eyes widened. His grip on the poleaxe tightened.

Jago's sharp whistle broke the spell.

For a big man, Aaron Mudd moved quicker than expected, swinging the poleaxe up as if it were no heavier than a twig to block the strike as Jago curved the grog bottle towards his skull. The bottle struck the poleaxe halfway down its handle, shattering upon impact, showering glass and grog across the mare's prostrate body. As the other two slaughtermen raised their weapons, Jago heard a grunt and jerked his head back just in time. He felt the wind from the poleaxe blade as it scythed past his ear.

By which time, Hawkwood and Micah, summoned by Jago's signal, were in the yard, pistols cocked.

"Drop it," Jago snapped. Stepping away, he drew his own pistol as Aaron Mudd, recovering from his first attempt to land a blow, raised the poleaxe once more. Drawing back the pistol's hammer, Jago sighted on the fat man's chest. "Now."

The two slaughtermen had come to a halt, frozen in place by the guns levelled at them.

"Hook and knife on the ground," Hawkwood said.

The two men did as they were bid, tossing the weapons on to the cobbles.

"On your knees. Hand behind your heads."

"You can't—" the one who'd been holding the knife protested.

"I can and *you* will," Hawkwood said as Micah took a pace towards them.

The men sank down.

"Ain't tellin' you twice," Jago said to the fat man.

The poleaxe dropped.

"Move away," Jago instructed.

The fat man took a pace backwards, his eyes fixed on the pistol bore. Jago addressed Hawkwood over his shoulder. "Your shout. These two ain't going anywhere."

Hawkwood turned away from the kneeling men and faced Aaron Mudd. "I'm looking for Israel Mudd and Jack Ridger."

The fat man stared at Hawkwood without speaking.

Hawkwood picked up the poleaxe. At almost three feet in length, its weight was comparable to that of a Baker rifle. If the fat man was surprised by the ease with which Hawkwood hefted the tool, he didn't show it.

Hawkwood holstered his pistol. "Israel Mudd, Jack Ridger. Where are they?"

The fat man sneered. "Kiss my arse, culley."

Hawkwood swung the poleaxe.

While Aaron Mudd's strength and familiarity with the tool had enabled him to deflect Jago's attack with some deftness, his size and weight did not allow him the same degree of agility when it came to avoiding Hawkwood's strike.

Designed to stun livestock with a single piercing blow to the front of the skull, a poleaxe was a fearsome implement. The hammer end of the head slammed against Aaron Mudd's right kneecap, splintering bone and tearing through ligaments, cartilage and muscle. The screech that burst from the fat man's mouth as he collapsed writhing on the ground rebounded around the walls of the yard. His companions stared at Hawkwood, their mouths slack with disbelief.

Jago and Micah did not move. Their hands remained steady.

"Either of you have information on the matter," Jago told them, "now'd be the time to speak up."

Rooted in place, neither man uttered a sound.

Hawkwood rooted the poleaxe's handle in the mud and squatted down next to the fat man, his right hand resting on the steel head. "Let's try again. Israel Mudd, Jack Ridger."

The fat man's hands pawed impotently at the shattered joint, as if hoping to put the shards of bone back together. His eyes were clamped in pain. Tears had created pale tracks in the grime-coated cheeks. A thin mewling sound began to issue from between his lips, as if air was being released from a slowly deflating bladder.

"All right, then." Poleaxe in hand, Hawkwood rose to his feet.

And Micah said suddenly, "To your right!"

Hawkwood turned in time to see a stocky form duck out of sight behind the corner of the stable wall. Had it been his imagination or had the movement been accompanied by a sliver of light glancing off a bald pate?

Jago swore. Swiftly, he passed Micah his firearm. "They move, kill 'em."

As Micah took the gun, Jago swept up the discarded knife and followed Hawkwood, who'd dropped the poleaxe in favour of his own pistol and was heading across the yard at a slithering run.

When Maddie Teague heard the scream, her blood ran cold. She knew it hadn't come from any four-legged animal. It was too primal for that and so when the key turned in the lock she rose quickly from the chair. The door swung back. Her kidnappers stood framed in the opening.

Israel Mudd thrust his way past Ridger and into the cellar. "Come 'ere."

Maddie backed away hurriedly, forgetting, in her haste, that the chair was behind her. Swept aside by the hem of her coat, it toppled, unbalancing her in the process. By the time she'd recovered her footing, Mudd had her by the wrist. "Not so fast, darlin'."

Maddie's first instinct upon being seized was to claw for her assailant's face with her free hand. Batting her arm away with ease, Mudd hauled her towards the door.

"Better head for the bridge." Ridger, pistol in hand, indicated a passageway to their left.

Mudd swore as Maddie fought his grasp. "Hold still, bitch!"

She did not see the blow coming until the last second. The world tipped on its axis as the back of Mudd's closed fist struck the side of her jaw. Then her arm was twisted behind her back. The bald man's breath was heavy in her ear. "Try that again and I'll snap you like a twig. Now, move."

By the time Hawkwood reached the corner of the stable block, the figure had vanished.

"Shite," Jago muttered.

"You saw him?"

Jago nodded.

"Mudd?"

"Only got a glimpse, but if it weren't him, it was his twin brother. An' he ain't got a twin, just that sack of shit you put down."

"Not Ridger?"

Jago shook his head. "Don't mean he's not around. If one of them's here, the other one ain't far behind."

Behind the stable, another smaller yard was revealed. As before, the cobblestones were strewn with animal remains and coated with blood and dung. A flat-bed cart was parked in one corner next to a row of familiar overflowing wooden tubs.

"Christ," Jago muttered. Nose wrinkling, he peered through the drizzle. "Now, where?"

"There," Hawkwood said, nodding towards the opposite side of the yard where a low archway beckoned.

Jago tapped him on the shoulder. Hawkwood pushed himself off and would have sprawled headlong when his boot slid on a trail of viscera had it not been for Jago's steadying hand beneath his arm. By the time they got to the arch, there was no sign of movement.

Jago muttered another curse. "Christ, place is a like a bloody maze."

Hawkwood did not reply as he plunged into the narrow passageway that led off into the gloom.

Knife in hand, Jago followed.

Mudd had one hand round Maddie Teague's mouth and the other about her waist, trapping her right arm. She had tried to extricate herself but the man's grip was so strong it was like pulling a hawser apart. The ripe smell coming off him would have felled an ox; with his hand clamped over her mouth it was all she could do to breathe.

She had no idea why the two of them had panicked. The scream she'd heard had clearly been perceived as a threat, but as to the nature of the threat, her abductors had given her no indication. Was it Matthew? Had he discovered her location already? Her spirits had been lifted by that possibility, but quickly stifled when she realized that the men who'd taken her were not, despite their earlier boast, prepared to make a stand. Then she remembered that the requirement had been for them to hold her for at least two days. If they were running, it must mean that their intention was to stick to the original plan, which meant finding an alternative place of detention, somewhere there was less chance of her being discovered.

And she could still hear the bald one's voice in her ear.

"*. . . pretty soon you an' me are goin' to have a serious conversation.*"

Her throat constricted at the thought. Conversation, she knew, would be the last thing on his mind.

There had been no opportunity to call for help, despite the bald one eventually removing his hand from her mouth. The promise of physical harm had been a sufficient deterrent. She knew he meant it. The man had already proved that he was prepared to use violence to muzzle her. She did not want to give him an excuse to escalate the degree of hurt he was capable of inflicting. An opportunity to escape might still present itself and she didn't dare risk jeopardizing her chances of getting away. If she were hobbled, that opportunity would be lost.

Their transit through the slum had not gone unnoticed; several times, she'd been aware of silhouettes at windows and shadows in unlit doorways, but no one had issued a challenge or attempted to intervene. It was a stark warning that, despite her earlier estimation, she had no real knowledge of where she was. Were she to call for help, it was unlikely any would be forthcoming. Within these hidden corners of the city, people tended to their own business. They were too afraid of reprisals. The neighbourhood's stray dog population was less reticent. A collection of raucous barks followed them as they made their way through the rat-run.

The bald one was forcing the pace while the dark-haired one brought up the rear, covering their retreat. They obviously knew where they were going. Mention of "the bridge" and the ease and haste with which they were negotiating the alleyways indicated they were on familiar ground, whereas any sense of direction Maddie might have had when they'd left the cellar had soon disappeared. They might as well have placed a sack over her head for all the use her eyes were in identifying their location.

When they finally emerged from the warren, she tried again to take stock and to calculate how far they'd come; probably not that great a distance, had a straight line been drawn from the cellar to their current location. While it felt as if they'd been moving for some time it had probably been four or five minutes at the most. The twists and turns had added to her feeling of disorientation.

The bald one was breathing heavier than before, she noticed, though his grip on her wrist had hardly slackened. He addressed his companion. "You think we lost 'em?"

Ridger looked back the way they'd come, wondering how the hell they'd been tracked down so quickly. "Maybe. Either way, we keep moving."

He thought about Mudd's description of the three men who'd attacked the yard. It wasn't that big a stretch to suppose that one of them – possibly the individual who'd poleaxed Aaron – had been the Runner. The fact that he hadn't come alone meant that retreat had been their only option. So much for Captain Vaughn's bloody ultimatum.

Ridger supposed they could have left the woman behind, but he and Israel had been given a job to do and, as had been explained to the unfortunate Tommy Flagg, orders were orders, especially when they'd been given to you by your commanding officer. Hold the line, was the directive, and hold the line they would. So they were running, taking the woman with them. He peered forward, past Mudd's shoulder.

It wasn't so much a bridge as a sagging walkway composed of worn timber slats supported by a precarious cat's cradle of ropes and joists strung across a twenty-foot-wide, effluent-filled ditch, the surface of which had all the colour and consistency of treacle.

Staring at the structure, Maddie felt a shiver run up her spine. There was something undeniably menacing about the view over the other side of the ditch, which was still and eerily silent. She had the sense that if they were to cross the catwalk she would be swallowed up, making it impossible for Hawkwood to find her.

Mudd led the way. Close by, another dog began to bark lustily. The clamour was met by a torrent of abuse, which in turn was

315

followed by a shrill yip of pain as punishment was administered. Mudd turned towards the racket, causing Maddie to stumble into him. As her boots lost their grip on the soggy ground, she fell to her knees. Releasing her arm for the first time, Mudd transferred his hold to the back of her neck, heaving her up. As he did so, her boot caught on her trailing coat hem and she slid once more.

Mudd let go an angry snarl. "Christ's sake, you clumsy cow!"

This time she managed to push herself up and on to her feet. For a moment she thought Mudd was going to shake her as he might have done a disobedient child, but instead he put his hand in the small of her back, as if to guide her to the front of him. It gave her the opportunity to reach into her left sleeve. Mudd was looking to his side when she straightened, and with all her strength drove the tines of the hair comb towards his right eyeball.

Because he'd sensed movement and had been turning towards the strike, the prongs missed his eye socket and instead skewered his cheek up to the comb's hilt, missing teeth and gums by a fraction and piercing the soft palate at the back of his mouth like a twin-bladed rapier.

Mudd roared like a wounded bull.

When they reached the first fork in the alleyway, Hawkwood and Jago halted.

"Shit," Jago said.

Squatting, Hawkwood held the lantern low and quartered the ground. "They went right."

"Good to see you ain't lost your touch," Jago murmured. "Just like the old days, 'cept this time we're after felons, not Frogs."

"We're lucky. The rain's softened the surface; it's made them easier to track."

"Can you tell how many?"

"Three: one heavy-footed, the other two lighter. One of them has a smaller heel; could be a woman's shoe print."

"Maddie's with them?"

Hawkwood did not reply.

If I'm wrong, all this is in vain.

He stood as a fresh outbreak of barks broke out ahead of them, closer than before. Then came the angry threat to cut the animal's throat if it didn't pipe down, followed by a high-pitched squeal.

Jago stared off in the direction of the ruckus. "That way!"

"Know where we are?" Hawkwood asked.

"Not a bleedin' clue."

Five seconds later, they heard the bellow of pain.

"Run," Hawkwood said.

When Mudd let rip, Ridger spun to find his companion howling profanities into the sky and pawing furiously at his face as if he'd been stung. Ridger looked for the woman. She was on the point of turning away. Letting go a curse, with remarkable speed he thumbed back the pistol hammer and aimed at Maddie's fleeing form.

Hawkwood fired on the run. The flash from both weapons came simultaneously, as did the reports. He saw the shooter falter and take a sideways stagger and then keel over.

Mudd, finally wrenching the comb from his cheek, pivoted at the sound of the shots, in time to see Ridger go down. Tossing the comb aside and ignoring the pain, Mudd dragged the pistol from his belt. Beyond Ridger's sprawled body two men were coming towards him. Mudd recognized them as the ones from the yard. One of them, the tall one in the coat, was the scum who'd done for Aaron. Mudd's eyes dropped to the pistol in the man's hand. He'd downed Jack, too. Seeing Ridger fall was like a bomb exploding inside Mudd's chest.

The scream burst from him as he hauled back the pistol hammer. "Bastard!"

He felt the impact the second he fired. It didn't seem like a particularly heavy blow, but for some unaccountable reason it was enough to knock the wind from him and distract his aim. It wasn't until the pistol barrel drooped and he took a pace forward that the pain hit him. Startled, he stared down at the knife jutting from his belly. He hadn't even seen the sod throw it. The pistol slipped from his fingers and he groped for the hilt with both hands. The blade had not penetrated fully and half the steel was still showing. Gripping the haft, he tried to prise the weapon free. Fire scoured through his insides. His hands were still wrapped around the hilt when he fell to his knees and then to the ground and lay still.

Hawkwood felt the relief surge through him as Mudd went down and Maddie appeared from the darkness, her coat filthy, her hair wet, loose and bedraggled. He ran to her.

Maddie smiled tiredly. Reaching out a hand she laid her palm against his cheek. "I knew you'd come."

Hawkwood placed his hand over hers, holding it against his face.

"Good to see you, lass," Jago said. "You gave us quite a turn."

"Nathaniel," Maddie said.

Jago smiled. "Come on, let's get you home."

About to concur, Hawkwood sensed movement. He looked beyond Israel Mudd's body to where the one he'd shot was attempting to crawl away, dragging his wounded leg behind him.

Seeing Hawkwood's expression harden, Jago followed his gaze and swore beneath his breath.

Hawkwood let go of Maddie's hand and threw Jago a look. "Wait here."

Jago took Maddie's arm, nodded and said softly, "You do what you have to do."

Ridger's hands were clamped to his thigh. Blood was seeping through his thin fingers. Face drawn, hair plastered to his scalp, he looked up. "You'll be the Runner, then?" What might have passed for a rueful smile flitted across the lean features. "She said you'd come."

Hawkwood said, "Where's Vaughn?"

Ridger blinked. His eyes seemed to drift out of focus. When he spoke, the pain was evident in his voice. "He ain't here."

"I can see that. Where is he?"

Ridger looked across to where Israel Mudd lay curled around the knife handle. A look of sadness tinged with regret moved across his face. He turned his head back. "Told you; he's gone. You're too late."

"Gone where?"

Ridger grunted as a shiver moved through him. He shook his head as if to clear it.

Wordlessly, Hawkwood turned and walked to Israel Mudd's body. Placing his boot on the dead man's chest and ignoring the sound of cracking ribs, he pulled the knife from the corpse and walked back to where Ridger lay. Jago, he saw, had moved to block Maddie's view. "Gone where?"

Ridger eyed the blood-smeared blade. His face was damp from the rain. He sighed resignedly. "Coast. There's a ship waitin'."

"Which coast?"

"Don't know that. He doesn't tell us everything."

"Did he tell you why he needs a ship?"

"To transport the Frenchie."

"Frenchie?" Hawkwood felt a cold wind run along the back of his neck.

"Don't know his name; only that the captain was in charge of delivering him on board." The man on the ground winced again and drew in a sharp breath. "Jesus, my leg; I think the bloody bone's broke."

"Was it you who killed Flagg and the girl?" Hawkwood asked.

A painful smile crossed Ridger's face. "Captain's orders."

"Vaughn?"

Ridger nodded.

"And the carving into the girl's flesh?"

"We were given a note, told the letters had to be cut that way."

"Did he tell you to kidnap Mrs Teague as well?"

Squatting, Hawkwood laid the bloody knife blade against Ridger's wounded thigh and repeated the question.

Ridger flinched and nodded again, weakly. "Said that way you'd know he was serious."

"When did he leave?"

"Can't say. He'd've had to round up his escort. But it would have been a while ago. Too long a time for you to catch him up, even if you knew where he was bound."

"Escort?" Hawkwood said.

"Men he can call on. Like Israel and me."

"Men from the Ninth."

Ridger frowned at the extent of Hawkwood's knowledge and then nodded. "Some of them."

Hawkwood rose. Ridger stared up at him. "You planning on leaving me like this, then?"

"No," Hawkwood said and, with a single stroke, drove the butcher's blade down and across Ridger's throat.

As he did so, he heard Jago call urgently, "Cap'n!"

Hawkwood turned quickly to see that Maddie had fallen into Jago's arms. Casting the knife aside, he ran forward. When he reached them, he saw that Maddie's eyes were closed. Jago, who'd been cradling Maddie's limp body, drew his hand from her waist and stared down at his palm. It was black. "Ah, Christ," he said desperately.

Hawkwood realized he was seeing blood.

24

"Wait here," the manservant instructed.

Hawkwood looked down at himself. Streaked with mud, blood and shit, his coat, breeches and boots looked as though they'd come through an epic battle. The manservant's reticence at admitting him was understandable.

"Officer Hawkwood?"

The manservant beckoned from a doorway. As he did so, James Read hurried from the room behind, consternation on his face; an expression which intensified ten-fold when he took in the state of Hawkwood's attire. "Mrs Teague?" he enquired immediately. "You have word?"

Then he read the look in Hawkwood's eyes.

He turned quickly to his manservant. "That will be all, Duncan, but stay close. I will ring if I need you." To Hawkwood he said, "This way."

Read guided Hawkwood through the open door into his library, where a small, bewigged and bespectacled figure rose to his feet.

Hawkwood turned to the magistrate. Read waved away the unspoken question and ushered him towards the fire's warmth. "All will be explained, and Mr Twigg has my full confidence. Now, tell me."

Hawkwood fought to remain calm and keep his voice measured as he relived the events that had led him to the magistrate's door. Even though the arrival and appearance of his visitor had prepared James Read to expect the worst, the latter's usually stern features gave way as he listened to Hawkwood's account of how he'd carried Maddie's limp body back through the maze of alleyways to the slaughterhouse yard and then, with Jago leading the way and Micah protecting their backs, out of the slum and on to St Bartholomew's Hospital.

Located on the south-eastern side of Smithfield Market, the hospital was less than a quarter of a mile from Mudd's yard. Brandishing his warrant, Hawkwood had browbeaten the startled and soon-cowed medical staff into taking Maddie into their care, telling them to await instructions.

"How bad is it?" James Read asked.

The ball from Ridger's pistol had struck Maddie on her right side, as Hawkwood had discovered when, feverishly, he had torn open her coat, searching for the source of the blood loss. In the fading light it had been impossible to determine the extent of the damage so, relying on battlefield knowledge, the only recourse had been to pack Jago's rolled kerchief against the wound and to use his own neckcloth as a bandage to keep the makeshift pressure pad in place. The one glimmer of hope was the faint beat Hawkwood had detected when he'd felt Maddie's throat for a pulse.

"The surgeon said the ball cut across her ribs. If it had taken her an inch to the left and penetrated, she'd be dead. The blood made it look worse than it was and from what they can tell it was the shock of it that caused her to collapse. They're sure there's no material in the wound and they say she's strong so there's every chance she'll recover, but they'll watch her for signs of further injury and infection. She was sleeping when I left her."

Seeing Hawkwood's fists clench, James Read did not reply. Instead, he went directly to the door and summoned his manservant. "Duncan, you are to go immediately to the office of Doctor Marcus Gillray in Harley Street. Please convey my compliments and tell him that I would deem it a great personal favour if he could proceed with all possible dispatch to St Bartholomew's

Hospital; there to determine the welfare of Mrs Madeleine Teague, recently delivered to the hospital by a member of the Bow Street Constabulary. He is to use my name to impress upon the staff that Mrs Teague is to be placed in a private room and treated with the utmost care and attention. Do you have all that?"

The manservant nodded. "Sir."

"Good man. Leave now. Do not tarry."

The servant left. Read turned back. "My physician; he served under Guthrie in the Peninsula and knows how to treat gunshot wounds. He is also beyond reproach. He will see Mrs Teague is taken care of. My dear fellow, I am so dreadfully sorry."

Hawkwood nodded dully. Turning to the fire, he stared down into the flames. "It's my fault she—"

"No," Read interjected sharply. "Do not berate yourself. It was not you who pulled the trigger."

"It might as well have been. If I hadn't gone after them . . ."

The magistrate moved in closer. His voice softened. "You do not know that. Given the information we had, there was no knowing what their intentions were. They had already killed. There was no guarantee that they would have released Mrs Teague unharmed. You did what you thought was right. Console yourself with the knowledge that thanks to you and your swift action, she is alive and in the best possible place."

When Hawkwood did not reply, Read enquired hesitantly, "The men who took her; did they say who . . .?"

Hawkwood closed and opened his eyes and then raised his head and took a deep breath before answering. "Vaughn gave the order. They killed Flagg and the girl, too."

Read waited.

"The bastard wasn't with them."

Exchanging a glance with his former clerk, the magistrate said quietly, "That may be because he is on his way to Portsmouth."

As the words penetrated, Hawkwood turned.

The magistrate met his gaze. "You are not my first visitor. Superintendent Brooke was here. He called to make amends after our last encounter; to express his regret that our parting had not been on the best of terms and to say how dismayed he was to hear of my resignation."

A grim smile flitted across Read's face in response to Hawkwood's frozen expression. "Indeed, the same thought occurred to me. But there was more. In light of all that has occurred since that last meeting, he felt I was owed further explanation. I can only assume his conscience got the better of him."

There was a pause, eventually broken when Hawkwood said, "So who is he?"

"He?"

"The Frog; the one we've been after: Vaughn's charge."

"You know about that?" Read said, noting the shift of tone in Hawkwood's voice; a new intensity that had not been there before. Concern and self-recrimination, Read sensed, was turning into a cold, calculating anger.

"One of Maddie's abductors; a death-bed confession. He told me Vaughn was heading for the coast with our man, though he didn't know where. He also said they'd been kept in the dark as far as the bastard's identity was concerned."

Lips pursed, Read nodded. "Yes, well, our suspicions were correct. He is indeed a representative of the Bourbon princes."

"I take it he has a name?"

"He does." The magistrate hesitated and then said, "Pierre-Vincent-Jeannot de la Basse. He is also known by his title: the Abbé Jeannot."

The room went very quiet once more. The sound of the flames spitting and crackling in the hearth seemed unnecessarily intrusive.

"He's a goddamned *priest*?"

A nerve flexed along the magistrate's cheek. "He's more than that. He's one of Artois' most trusted correspondents. He is also, Brooke informed me, a senior member of the Chevaliers." Read paused. "I believe you are familiar with their aims?"

The magistrate waited.

"*They're* behind this?" Hawkwood straightened.

"I see you remember," Read said.

Hawkwood moved away from the fire. "Damned right! They're

bloody fanatics; a secret union of Aristos and Frog clergy who don't like the way Bonaparte's running the Empire. They aim to rescue the Pope from Fontainebleau and put the Bourbons back on the throne. Grant told me about them when I was in Paris. Our government's been funding them for years. I met one of them: the Abbé Lafon. He was General Malet's personal confessor, until things turned nasty. Then he took off for the hills as fast as his feet could carry him."

"Yes, well, I think it's safe to assume that *Monsieur* Artois sets greater store in Abbé Jeannot's loyalty."

"He'd bloody well have to. So where did *this* one come from?"

James Read turned to his former clerk. "Mr Twigg . . .?"

Hawkwood looked at the clerk, who'd been sitting motionless until then.

Sitting up, Twigg removed the handkerchief from his pocket. Taking off his spectacles, he began to polish each lens in turn.

"Abbé Jeannot is a native of Brittany; a graduate of the seminary in Rennes and a member of the Order of Saint Vincent de Paul. The original de Paul was a priest famed for dedicating himself to serving the poor and the needy. From the information gathered, it would appear that the Abbé followed in Father de Paul's footsteps, though it seems he was viewed less favourably than his Order's namesake, at least by the Revolutionary authorities. The Assembly imprisoned him in '92 for holding open-air masses and refusing to swear allegiance to the Constitution."

Lenses cleaned, the clerk looped the spectacles carefully back over each ear. "As a result of his stance, the Abbé was one of several hundred priests deported from France. He was among the first of the émigré clergy to land in Jersey, where he resumed his good works, devoting his time to the needs of his countrymen. He was prominent in the founding of a relief committee similar to that of Wilmot's in London: the Comité de Secours."

"Interestingly," Read interjected, "the individual responsible for distributing the *Comité's* funds was Philippe d'Auvergne."

"Why is that of interest?" Hawkwood asked. The name wasn't familiar.

"Because at the time of Jeannot's arrival on Jersey, Captain – now Vice Admiral of the Blue – Auvergne was not only the senior naval officer on station – the commander of the Royal Navy's Channel Island flotilla – he was also Pitt's main spymaster in the region; Jersey's answer to Henry Brooke, if you will. Auvergne is less active than he was, or so I'm told, but his organization is still operating. It goes under the name La Correspondence. Its main task is to maintain relations with the Bourbon loyalists in Northern France; essentially, it's there to provide succour and support for Artois' royalist friends. The island's long been the base for Artois' clandestine activities. It's where intelligence is gathered and where his forces are trained." The magistrate looked towards his clerk. "But I digress. Mr Twigg . . ."

The clerk blinked. "Yes, sir. As I was saying; the good works undertaken by the Abbé included the building of a chapel and a school for orphaned children . . ."

Pausing, Twigg stole a glance towards the magistrate, as if seeking guidance.

"What?" Hawkwood demanded.

Twigg pursed his lips. "Abbé Jeannot and his fellow emigrés named themselves after an ancient order of monks who ran a hospital for the sick and the poor back in the time of the Medicis: Les Frères de la Charité; the Brothers . . ."

"I know what it means, God damn it! When did he come here?"

Unfazed by Hawkwood's outburst, the clerk said calmly, "In '97. There were worries about a French invasion and it was decided to move those clergy who were living in English coastal areas further inland. The Abbé came to London, where he was provided with accommodation in Fitzroy Square."

"Would that have been courtesy of Wilmot's Committee, by any chance?" Hawkwood enquired caustically.

"It would."

"There's the link to Saxby," Hawkwood said, looking towards James Read for confirmation before turning back to Twigg. "Go on."

The clerk cleared his throat. "While there, he went on to found several more schools, for girls as well as boys, following the example of the ones in Jersey. He also organized religious instruction for émigré children and even set up a seminary for those who wished to take Holy Orders."

"Sounds like he was angling for sainthood himself," Hawkwood said, unable to keep the contempt from his voice.

The clerk ignored the gibe. "His diligence did not go unrecognized. When the Comte d'Artois arrived in London he became one of the Abbé's strongest supporters. There is a record of him providing funds as a donation towards the maintenance of the Abbé's institutions."

"Saw something in the man and stored the knowledge away for further reference, no doubt," Read said.

Twigg kept his expression neutral. "The Abbé returned to France after Amiens, when Bonaparte reopened the churches and issued his decree of amnesty."

Read turned to Hawkwood once more. "Did Major Grant tell you anything about the Chevaliers' origins?"

"I know they're the bastard children of an earlier organization; other than that, not much."

"That would be the Congrégation?"

Hawkwood nodded. "They started out doing missionary work but turned rebellious when Bonaparte decided to make himself emperor. The Abbé was one of them?"

"It's believed he was inducted into its ranks not long after his return to France. Pope Pius is known to have granted an audience to members when he travelled to Paris for Bonaparte's coronation and to have authorized the creation of affiliated congrégations throughout France. It's more than likely Jeannot was one of the emissaries sent to spread the word. It ties in with when we believe he became a spy for Artois. He'd have been ideally placed to gather intelligence."

"How come he ended up back here?" Hawkwood asked.

"According to Brooke, and as Grant may have told you, Bonaparte had his suspicions about the Congrégation's influence from the outset. He became convinced it was in league with the

327

rebels – which it was, of course. In the end, he banned it completely, which meant in order to continue, the members were forced to meet in secret. The Chevaliers de la Foi – the Knights of the Faith – were born out of that necessity."

"The Abbé Lafon was a Chevalier courier," Hawkwood cut in, remembering. "What are the odds the bastards knew each other?"

Read waited and then said, "It's quite possible. Intriguingly, the date of the Chevaliers' inception does coincide closely with Jeannot's arrival back in England in '09. He'd have been a close confidant of the princes-in-exile by then."

"Which would give him access to their social circle," Hawkwood said.

"Indeed, and that would include not only the princes' London court, but their circle of patrons, too, many of whom hold high office in our own government and who, as we know, do like their entertainments. It stands to reason that émigrés moving among the higher echelons would appear on the guest lists of such events."

"Explains how the bastard got himself in through the door. So much for the vows of celibacy."

"Perhaps he considers them to be not so much vows as recommendations," Read responded archly.

Electing not to notice the clerk's head lifting, Read went on, "Given his past membership of the Congrégation and his rank as a senior Chevalier, it's thought he might even be one of The Nine."

"The Nine?" Hawkwood said. "Who the hell are they?"

"Forgive me. It's what they call the Chevaliers' senior councillors. They wield the most power because they have links to the princes – Artois is rumoured to be the Grand Master. There are ranks below them: the Sénéchaux, who direct the armed missions, and the Bannières. They're the ones who control the individual groups distributed throughout the French departments. They're independent of one another but guided by a single doctrine. The Bannières are themselves made up of tiers: Partners, Squires, Knights, Knight Hospitallers and Knight of

Faith. You can tell by the appellations that they take their adherence to the chivalric code very seriously."

The magistrate paused, then said, "You may be interested to learn that during the ceremony to select a new knight, the initiate is presented with a ring as a symbol of his office. The inside of the ring carries a single-word inscription: *Caritas*."

Letting the information sink in, Read cleared his throat. "It's plain, therefore, that the man has considerable influence not only within the Church but also among the rebel factions, so from the princes' point of view he's ideally suited for the role of ambassador. Brooke informed me that the current activity has been the precursor to a conclave to which the most senior Sénéchaux have been summoned."

"In Jersey?" Hawkwood said, taking a guess.

"No, that is merely the Abbé's transit point and where he will receive his final travel instructions. The meeting place is on the French mainland: a Benedictine Abbey on the outskirts of Argentan that managed to survive the purges. The gathering's a call to arms. The Abbé will convey to the Sénéchaux the date upon which the insurrection is to be launched. The intention is to create a coordinated wave of fear and confusion throughout the country."

The magistrate's expression grew more serious.

"Bonaparte's Grand Army has been severely depleted by his Russian fiasco. There are reports of more than three hundred thousand dead. His eastern front has all but collapsed. It's more than likely, therefore, that Prussia will re-enter the war, at which point Bonaparte will face a massive dilemma. He'll be fighting on too many battle fronts, which means he'll be unable to withdraw men from one to bolster another. He's run out of reserves at home; his recruitment for his winter campaign saw to that, so the last thing he needs is an armed civil uprising in his own country. If that happens, he'll be forced to deploy troops from the closest point to the areas of unrest."

"Spain," Hawkwood said.

Read nodded. "By weakening his Iberian front, he strengthens ours, which will allow Wellington – assisted by our Spanish allies

– to push northwards at greater speed. Joseph and Jourdan will be forced to retreat. If we break the French in Spain, we'll have a clear run to the Pyrenees and the border."

"Invasion," Hawkwood said softly, as a glimmer of understanding began to dawn.

"Precisely. Success hinges on the Sénéchaux reporting back to the Bannières who will carry the word to their regions. If the message the Abbé conveys is coherent and powerful enough, it will move beyond the Chevaliers' sphere and into the countryside, and then the people will follow. You saw that with the Malet affair. Admittedly, that was just Paris, where the plot, once it was discovered, was easily contained. But imagine a spontaneous, nationwide uprising, in Flanders, Artois, Auvergne, Aquitaine, the Vendée or Provence. Bonaparte would be forced to draft troops in to cope. He'd have no other choice."

Read paused then said, "Without going into specific detail, Brooke told me that since his return, in between continuing his philanthropic works here, Jeannot has travelled between London and the continent on frequent occasions, passing information back and forth, paving the way."

"Do we know when?" Hawkwood asked.

"When?" Read said, puzzled. "Ah, you're wondering if his times here coincide with the killings unearthed by yourself and Mr Twigg?"

Read looked at Twigg, who nodded and said, "It has not been easy to verify information, but from the little we do know, there does appear to be a correlation." The clerk paused, then said, "One of his self-appointed tasks when he first came back was to establish a hospital for female émigrés."

Hawkwood looked at the clerk. "Any record of him visiting La Providence?"

Twigg shook his head. "Not specifically, but, given his history, it would be logical to assume he did so as part of his pastoral duties. The women's hospital would have employed ladies from the émigré community as nursing staff. Preference would be given to those with experience."

"You're thinking of the Lavasse girl," Read said.

Hawkwood nodded. "We should check further back; see if there were any unexplained killings when he first arrived and before he returned to France after the peace."

Read's brow furrowed. "I'm not sure that's necessary. I'd say Whitehall's protection of him and Brooke's intervention is evidence enough, wouldn't you?"

Hawkwood thought about that and nodded grudgingly. "But it makes you wonder if his Chevalier friends know about his little hobby and what their attitude would be if they were to discover their Messiah likes to cut up women in his spare time. It'd be most inconvenient, discovering their favoured messenger has a blood lust. I can't see the Church wanting that information to get out."

"Set against their hope that the man's word could help bring about Bonaparte's defeat, I suspect they would be more than willing to ignore his transgressions."

"You think I give a *shit* about Bonaparte?"

Although he'd been expecting an eruption, at hearing the sudden vehemence in Hawkwood's response the magistrate stared back at him in shock. "What are you saying?"

"I'm saying this isn't about defeating Bonaparte or setting some Frog prince back on his throne. Far as I'm concerned, it never was. This is about catching a killer who's been protected by our own government. Addington, Saxby, Brooke – they're all complicit. They might not have done the killing, but they all have blood on their hands – including Maddie Teague's. They think, because of their position, they've got away with it. And if we do nothing, they bloody well have!"

In speaking Maddie's name aloud, it had been impossible for Hawkwood to tamp down on his anger. He'd been controlling it up to that moment.

"You're implying that the protection of the State is not important?" Read ventured cautiously, wary of the renewed fury in Hawkwood's gaze. "There are many who'd regard that as treason."

"The protection of the State can go to hell! The same with Addington and his cronies. And if I can send Vaughn and his damned priest to hell, too, then I'll have done my job! Our job! You told me that if I needed your help, all I had to do was ask. I'm asking now."

Read's eyes narrowed. "For what purpose?"

"What the hell do you think?"

The magistrate's chin rose. "You intend to give chase?"

"I do. The talking's over. It's time we did something."

"Vaughn and his charge are long gone," Read said gravely. "It's likely they were already en route when Brooke called. You really think you can intercept them?"

"It's seventy miles to the coast. That's ten hours' travel. A lot could happen in that time. They might have shed a wheel."

Ignoring the sarcasm, Read looked at him. His voice softened. "My dear fellow, I completely understand your anger and you have my deepest sympathy. I know you want revenge for the kidnap and injury to Mrs Teague, but are you willing to sacrifice your position as a Bow Street Officer in order to pursue a personal vendetta?"

"He's a murderer. I'm supposed to bring murderers to justice, aren't I? The way I see it, I'd be killing two birds with the one stone, which means you have a question to answer. Are you willing to help me or not? Because while we're standing here arguing, he's getting further away. He boards that vessel for Jersey and we've lost him for good."

The magistrate's eyes flickered at the now openly combative tone in Hawkwood's voice and the use of the word "killing". "Why do I sense that, were I to refuse you, you would take the law into your own hands, anyway?"

"Because it's something I have to do."

"There is no way my counsel can dissuade you?"

"I think you know the answer to that, too."

James Read regarded him levelly. "You do realize I no longer have the authority to protect you. You will be on your own."

"It wouldn't be the first time."

"And you know that vengeance is not justice."

"I do," Hawkwood said, "but it's a bloody good place to start."

332

Read stared back at him, holding his gaze.

Finally, he nodded. "Very well, what is it you require?"

Dusk had almost fallen when Hawkwood arrived at the Black Bull livery yard on Swallow Street, where Jago was waiting.

"Good timing," Jago said. "Just got here ourselves."

Micah stood at the former sergeant's shoulder, along with Del and Ned, who both nodded a sombre greeting. All four men were dressed for warmth. Knapsacks, similar to the one Hawkwood had slung across his back, lay at their feet.

"Officer," Del said, without his usual levity, and then his gaze moved to a point beyond Hawkwood's right shoulder. "Jesus," he muttered, unable to help himself. Ned's eyes widened, too.

Hawkwood turned as a greatcoated, bare-headed figure strode out from an open stable door behind them.

"Gentlemen," the newcomer said.

Neither Jago's nor Micah's expressions altered. They had known what to expect. Del and Ned's reaction was understandable.

"Sergeant," the man greeted Jago warmly. "Good to see you again."

"Major."

The man nodded at Micah in silent recognition before addressing Del and Ned. "You'll be the new recruits, then." He looked at Hawkwood.

"Del, Ned," Hawkwood said. "Major Gabriel Lomax, Bow Street Horse Patrol."

It was Lomax's face rather than his uniform that drew the attention first, usually eliciting a look of either horror or sympathy, depending on the constitution of the observer and whether or not the eyepatch was present, which it was now, though the inadequate covering didn't make a lot of difference. It wasn't as if a scrap of leather could hide the disfigurement to any great degree, for the damage was extensive.

Lomax had been a soldier before he'd been recruited into the Horse Patrol; an officer with the 23rd Light Dragoons, part of Anson's brigade. He'd fought his last military engagement at Talavera. It had been the second day of the battle and Lomax had been part of the charge launched against the French in a bid to halt the enemy's advance against the British left flank. When his horse was shot from beneath him, Lomax had found himself trapped beneath his mount's dead weight with the grass fire caused by a stray spark and fanned by the summer breeze closing in around him. Ironically, it had been a Voltigeur officer who'd witnessed his plight and gone to his aid, dragging him clear before beating a hasty retreat to the safety of his own French lines.

Despite his saviour's actions, Lomax had not emerged unscathed from his brush with death. The fire had grazed him to the extent that the right side of his face looked as if it had been clawed by an irate bear and cooked over a low heat. Beneath the eyepatch, the socket was criss-crossed with scar tissue.

The flames had also affected his right hand, transformed it into something resembling a claw, though he could still ride. Invalided from the army, the former cavalryman had put his skills and experience to good use. These days, as a commander with the armed horse patrols, he protected travellers on the king's highways.

His and Hawkwood's paths had occasionally crossed while in the pursuance of their respective duties and Hawkwood had called on Lomax's help in the past, including during the Hyde case when, in the hunt for the grave robbers, the major had joined Hawkwood, Jago, Micah and Constable Hopkins in tracking down and eliminating the resurrection crew. A good man in a fight, with no sympathy for criminals of any persuasion, Lomax was an ally Hawkwood was glad to have at his back. It also helped that the Horse Patrol operated under the aegis of the Bow Street Public Office and made use of a number of livery stables around the capital. The Black Bull yard was one of them.

"Major," Del said hesitantly, his gaze switching to Lomax's blue jacket and scarlet waistcoat, visible beneath the greatcoat. As Lomax led them towards the stable, he turned to Jago. "A Runner *and* a Redbreast? You realize what this'll do for our reputation?"

"You'll get over it," Jago said, murmuring in a quiet aside to Hawkwood, "I know he's proved his worth, but you did explain to the major this ain't exactly an official pursuit, right?"

Hawkwood looked at him. "Says who?"

"You, for one."

"Things change," Hawkwood said.

"Since when?"

"Since Magistrate Read gave me signed authorization."

"To do what?"

"Anything I see fit in the pursuance of my duty as a representative of the Bow Street Public Office."

Jago stared at him. "And how the hell did you manage that?"

"Not me; it was His Honour's idea."

The authorization was handwritten on Public Office notepaper, complete with an official letterhead; stationery which Read still held in his library at home. It stated that the bearer of the document was on police business and was to be granted any and all assistance in the pursuance of his duties. Failure to render assistance could result in prosecution under the Law. The document was signed James Read, Chief Magistrate, Bow Street Public Office. The wax seal added authenticity.

"It's likely my resignation is too recent for the news to have been circulated to all counties outside the metropolitan area," Read had told Hawkwood as he'd pressed the seal into the molten wax. "If fortune is with us, this will open doors. My advice, though, is to use it sparingly."

"I always liked the man," Jago murmured softly. "I ever tell you that?"

At which point, as they entered the stable block, Lomax said, "You want me to lose the uniform?"

"Up to you," Hawkwood said. "We move fast enough, you'll still be within your jurisdiction."

Another reason why Hawkwood had sought Lomax out: the Horse Patrol didn't just protect the roads within the city; it was also responsible for guarding all routes in and out of London to within a radius of twenty miles from Charing Cross, which meant Lomax had an intimate and therefore useful knowledge

335

of the Portsmouth Road or, as it was also termed because it was the primary overland route for transporting navy personnel between the Admiralty and the Portsmouth Dockyard, the Sailor's Highway.

Lomax flicked an oblique glance at Jago then threw Hawkwood a jaundiced look. "Why do I sense a 'but'?"

"There's likely to be serious opposition. We may have to bend the rules."

"By how much?"

"It's unlikely the men we're chasing will want to surrender peacefully."

Lomax put his head on one side. "Seems to me we've been here before, haven't we? Ah, well, so long as I know."

"You're with us then?" Hawkwood said.

"Too bloody right. Think I'd let you requisition this lot without me being there to keep my eye on 'em?"

Lomax nodded to where six horses stood saddled and waiting patiently.

Before Hawkwood could think of a reply, Lomax's mouth formed a cruel grin. It made Vaughn's grimace look positively angelic. "Any case, it's not as though I had anything else planned for the evening."

It was when they'd left Bart's Hospital that Hawkwood had informed Jago of his intention to pursue Vaughn to the coast. "Not on your own, you bloody won't," Jago had snapped before Hawkwood had a chance to draw breath.

Hawkwood had shaken his head. "Not your fight. Not this time."

"What's that mean: 'this time'? 'Course it's my bloody fight! Comes under the headin' 'unfinished business'."

"My business, not yours."

"The hell you say!" The former sergeant's eyes glittered then narrowed as he said, more calmly, "I heard Ridger tell you your man had left with an escort. That could mean three, could be thirty-three. Either way, it means you'd be outnumbered. Not a wise strategy."

"Nathaniel . . ." Hawkwood began, only to be silenced by Jago's raised hand.

"Don't interrupt. I ain't finished. So, the way I see it, you're going to need someone to guard your back. And seein' as I've done that, and vice versa, more times than either of us cares to remember, you ain't got a say in it. Which means, in case the opposition *is* in double figures, we'll employ an escort of our own. You ain't got any pressin' plans, have you, Micah? No, there you go, then," Jago said, before his lieutenant had a chance to respond. "That makes it three against three, an' in case there are thirty more I'll have a word with a couple of others I know. Don't worry, they're a bit rough an' ready but they're good men and they won't mind their domino evenin' being postponed. Besides," he added, "they owe you a favour."

There had been no humour in Jago's voice when he'd said it. Hawkwood knew then that further resistance was futile.

Returning to the Blackbird, Hawkwood had taken Lily and Cassie aside to give them the news that Maddie was safe, though injured and in a surgeon's care. Instinctively, Cassie had moved to him and buried her head against his shoulder, paying no mind to the state of his attire and the bloodstains that smudged her dress. Hawkwood had held her gently until her tears of relief had subsided.

After reaffirming to Lily that she was to remain in charge pending Maddie's return, Hawkwood had gone to his rooms, emerging in a change of clothes with his knapsack in hand. Lily had been the only one to see him leave. No goodbyes were exchanged and when the door closed behind him he had not looked back.

"Figured it'd save time, so I took the liberty of getting them ready."

Walking up to a bay stallion, Lomax patted the animal's neck. "This one's Garth. He's mine. The others you can divide amongst yourselves. Won't matter which is which. They're all trained mounts so they'll be no problem." He looked at Hawkwood. "You did say they can all stay upright, yes?"

Hawkwood nodded at Jago. "So he tells me."

Jago threw him a look. Despite a professed distrust of all things equine, the former sergeant was a more than competent horseman. In his youth, before his fateful meeting with the recruiting sergeant, he'd ridden with the Romney smuggling gangs that operated along the Kent coast. And in the Peninsula, when he'd followed Hawkwood to fight alongside the *guerrilleros*, travelling on horseback had been the only means of traversing long distances. It had also proved useful when leading hit-and-run raids against French units.

Micah could ride, Hawkwood knew that from previous experience. Del and Ned were the wild cards, but Jago had assured Hawkwood that both men were more than capable of holding their own, having been ranking members of Jago's smuggling fraternity and thus well versed in evading the Revenue on horseback at speed across terrain that would have had the staunchest Cossack quaking in his boots. Jasper, the last of the trio, would have been available, Jago had informed Hawkwood, had he not been sent on another, earlier errand out of town.

"Long as mine's not called Thunderbolt," Hawkwood heard Del mutter as items were transferred from knapsacks to saddlebags.

Lomax made no comment as his good eye caught the lantern light glancing off a metal gun barrel.

Equipment stowed, they led their horses out into the yard.

"All aboard, gentlemen," Lomax said as he hoisted himself into the saddle, casting a glance towards Del and Ned as he did so. Nodding in quiet satisfaction as they made themselves comfortable, he turned to Hawkwood. "We'll be pushing, I take it?"

Hawkwood nodded. "I don't know how much of a lead they have, so yes."

Lomax absorbed the reply. "Aye, well, remember: we try to maintain a full gallop any longer than a mile or so without slowing and it won't be long before they give out beneath us. Keeping them to a canter's best. Might not seem as quick, but we'll make better time in the long run. We'll see how they fare.

If we do give 'em their heads and they start to falter, my advice is we pick up fresh mounts at Kingston."

"Just so long as we catch them," Hawkwood said.

"You still reckon they'll be travelling by carriage?"

"Almost positive."

"So we've double their speed," Lomax grunted. "Gives us more than a fighting chance, I'd say."

"If the weather holds off." Hawkwood raised his eyes to the sky, from which the thin drizzle had at last ceased to fall.

"From your lips to God's ear," Lomax said.

25

Vaughn let go a muttered curse as he scraped the mud from his boot and prepared to climb back into the coach. It was the third time he'd been called upon to step out since they'd left Putney Heath and the novelty had soon grown tiresome, as had the discomfort brought on by his rain-dampened breeches and the silent, unsettling presence of his fellow passenger, who had never once volunteered to follow suit.

They'd been on the move for a little over three hours. Progress had been frustratingly slow due to the road's uneven and, in parts, treacherous surface. Travelling by coach was a god-awful experience at the best of times. The rain had made the going even worse. The hills were the main problem. The combination of anything approaching a gradient along with the sucking mud and ruts gouged over the passage of time by an assortment of horse-drawn coaches, farm vehicles and livestock meant that very often passengers were obliged, at the behest of the coachman, to vacate their vehicle in order to give the horses a fighting chance of making it to the top of the incline without the wheels becoming stuck or the coach sliding back down or toppling into an inconvenient ditch.

The fact that this particular coach was a two-horse vehicle was both an advantage and a hindrance. It meant it was light when compared to the bigger conveyances such as the Regulator and the Perseverance, which made it easier to manhandle out of a muddy furrow, but a pair tired quicker than a four-horse team, necessitating a greater frequency in the changeovers, the next of which was due to take place less than a mile further on, at the Bear Hotel in Esher.

The reason they'd had to alight this time was because the coach's wheels had become so mired in mud after traversing Ditton Marsh that by the time they reached Ditton Common, less than a quarter of a mile further on, all traction had been lost. A similar occurrence had taken place on the stretch of road running between Combe Wood and Richmond Park. Then, as now, Vaughn had called upon the escorts to dismount and put their backs to the wheel, literally. It was small wonder, as they climbed back on to their horses, that they were starting to look more than a little ruffled.

There were six of them, all told, excluding Vaughn. Four were mounted: one pair of riders on point, the other pair bringing up the rear. Two men, one of whom was the driver, were seated up top. All were former soldiers who'd served with Vaughn at one time or another and so were used to hardship and taking orders – and not averse to taking up arms when the situation demanded it. All six carried weapons.

Vaughn was taking no chances. Complacency, he knew, was as much a risk to an enterprise as any physical threat and he was not prepared to gamble with the safety of the person he'd been contracted to protect. His orders had been specific: his charge's welfare was paramount. Nothing else mattered.

Not that the individual in question appeared to appreciate the effort being taken to ensure his uninterrupted passage south. It grieved Vaughn that he hadn't even been trusted with the man's name. He knew only that he was French and a cleric – the black cassock and the black and white splayed collar were self-evident – and for that reason he was to be addressed as *Mon Père* or *Monsieur l'Abbé*.

There hadn't even been an acknowledgement when Vaughn had shown him to his seat inside the coach. By the time the vehicle was in motion, the priest's head was already bent over a small leather-bound volume, the title of which, after an unobtrusive glance, Vaughn had identified as *L'Office de la Semaine Sainte*, though that description left him none the wiser as to its content. He suspected the book had been chosen as a convenient prop, enabling his charge to avoid unnecessary conversation. This suited Vaughn very well, small talk with members of the cloth not being his strongest suit.

He had been informed that the priest did have a command of English, but attempting to conduct what was likely to be a very stilted conversation had held no appeal, so Vaughn had been content to pass the journey in silence, though he'd watched furtively as the book's pages were turned, noting not for the first time the cleric's long fingers and the neatly trimmed nails. In fact, everything about the man was neat, from his garb to his thinning grey-blond hair, which was combed back from a high, pale forehead. His eyes were small and dark and framed by a pair of black-rimmed eyeglasses. His movements when handling the missal's gold-edged leaves were unhurried, even during the coach's more erratic jolting.

Their first encounter had taken place at the Committee's headquarters in Queens Street in Sir Edmund Saxby's chambers. Considering the man's supposed importance, Vaughn had been unimpressed by the cleric's unexceptional appearance – until the dark eyes turned towards him, at which point his opinion changed. The combination of the severe black garb, the reptilian gaze and skin that looked as though it was unused to bright sunlight, had given Vaughn an unexpected jolt. Transfixed by the lack of expression in the priest's eyes, Vaughn had the feeling that he was looking into some sort of dark void. There had seemed to be no life in them whatsoever.

There had been times in his career as a soldier when Vaughn had come across men who, upon first meeting, had appeared mild and unassuming but had subsequently shown themselves to be devoid of all morals and possessed of a venal nature that went beyond the bounds of what could be termed civilized behaviour and in whose company he had felt tainted and uneasy. So it was whenever he was in the priest's vicinity.

As Saxby's chief trouble-solver, Vaughn had been called upon to perform a variety of unsavoury jobs, many of them unlawful. The majority had entailed clearing up someone else's mess. Whether it was chasing down an indiscreet mistress or a potential blackmailer, or persuading witnesses to a crime that they should alter their testimonies in the interest of self-preservation, Vaughn had proved himself an adept facilitator, able to act without conscience or fear of apprehension and arrest. But there was something about the cleric that had Vaughn questioning his own capacity for rendering harm and retribution. The black robe and mild looks may have implied that the priest was a righteous servant of God, and thus immune to enticements, but to Vaughn, whose own moral compass had often led him down roads no virtuous man would follow, that cold, hard stare was evidence of a creature that only a man like Vaughn would have recognized: a fellow traveller.

As the escorts remounted and as he reached for the door frame to lift himself aboard the coach, Vaughn glanced up towards a tall spindle shape outlined against an unexpected patch of moonlit sky visible through a gap in the trees that bordered the road. To the uninitiated, it might have looked like a towering cross that had been deprived of its ascending arm, or a tree trunk shorn of branches. A more observant passer-by, however, would have noted that the stem was far too smooth and too uniform for it to be part of a natural phenomenon, which confirmed that the object was in fact a gibbet post.

It was one of several that had been erected along the Portsmouth Road, though it had been a while since the last corpse had been raised aloft in its iron cage as a deterrent to wrong-doers. The most notorious of the structures occupied the summit of the aptly named Gibbet Hill, south of the Devil's Punch Bowl, near Hindhead. The last bodies to have been suspended there had remained in their cages for three years before being taken down and buried in unmarked graves. Grisly as the sentence had been, however, over the fifteen or so years since then there had been no marked decrease in the number of hold-ups along the road, which was still a favoured haunt of

highwaymen, especially in the more isolated stretches of countryside. Not that Vaughn was expecting trouble. One glimpse of
the escort and no knight of the road in his right mind would
consider trying to waylay this particular party.

Even so, when the coach lurched to a creaking halt shortly
after they left the common, Vaughn experienced more than a
mild frisson of uncertainty until he peered out of the window
and realized they had arrived at the Esher turnpike.

A sturdy five-barred gate blocked the road. Adjacent to
the gate was a small, thatched cottage. The scene was illuminated by a lantern hanging on the wall next to the cottage
door and by two more, suspended one on either side of the
gate, to give warning to oncoming vehicles. As Vaughn
watched, the cottage door opened and a thickset figure
shambled into view. Vaughn resumed his seat as the coach
driver dredged his pocket for the required toll. His fellow
passenger glanced up briefly at the interruption to their
progress but then dipped his head once more. Ignoring him,
Vaughn settled back and waited for their journey to continue.

"Captain Vaughn, sir?"

Vaughn recognized the voice as belonging to Babbage, one of
the rear escorts. He turned to where a shadow blocked the coach
window.

"What is it?"

"Toll-keeper says there's a message for you."

Vaughn frowned. "Message?"

"Says to tell you it's urgent."

"Step away," Vaughn ordered and waited until the escort had
backed his horse before opening the door and stepping down.
He looked for the toll-keeper and found him standing next to
a second, younger man, dressed in a pea jacket, woollen cap
and muffler.

"Eyes open, Babbage," Vaughn said quietly as he summoned
the toll-keeper and his companion forward. Vaughn addressed the
toll-keeper. "I'm told you've a message."

"Not me, him," the toll-keeper said. He forced his gaze away
from Vaughn's scar, and indicated the younger man by his side.

"And you are?" Vaughn said brusquely.

The target of Vaughn's enquiry cast a wary glance at the escorts, all of whom, he noticed with some trepidation, had their pistols drawn. He drew himself up. "Croft, sir. You *are* Captain Vaughn, yes?"

"I am he."

Croft reached into his coat and then paused as several pistol barrels swivelled towards him. The hand withdrew, slowly.

"I mean you no harm, Captain. It's like Mr Tarp said: I've a dispatch for you."

"From whom? From where?"

"Cabbage Hill."

Vaughn looked blank. "Where?"

"The shutter station; over Claygate way?" Croft nodded to a point over Vaughn's shoulder, as if by turning around, Vaughn would be able to pinpoint the exact location.

Vaughn did not turn but, suddenly, he understood. "The telegraph?"

"Yes, sir," Croft nodded. "Message came in about forty-five minutes ago, relayed from the Admiralty."

"You couldn't have intercepted us sooner?" Vaughn snapped. "There are stations before this one, are there not?"

There were ten stations, Vaughn recalled, strung out between the Admiralty and the Portsmouth dockyard. Developed and operated by the Admiralty itself, and based on an earlier system conceived by the French, the line had been established in order to send messages speedily to and from Royal Navy Headquarters and the Channel coast. Other chains linked the Admiralty to Yarmouth, Plymouth and Deal, respectively.

The system had revolutionized the sending of dispatches. Previously, the quickest way for a message to be delivered had been by horsemen. At the very best, the journey between London and Portsmouth had taken between four and five hours. Under the new signalling system – sections of which skirted the course of the road – a message could be passed in a matter of minutes.

Responding to Vaughn's question, the messenger shook his head, trying not to wilt under the accusing glare. "Wasn't practical,

Captain, sorry. The station before us is Putney. Kingston's the nearest you'd have been to them, but it would have been a longer ride and I don't believe they'd have had horses available, or could be they were short-manned and couldn't spare a messenger. Either way, it's likely you'd have been out of reach by the time they got themselves organized. Cabbage Hill's a mile and a bit east of here, which makes it the closest station to the coach route, so there was more chance of the message arriving ahead of you. I live the nearest and I've my own ride so I was sent." Croft nodded towards the shadowed end of the cottage where, for the first time, Vaughn saw there was a grey gelding tied to a hitching post. "We reckoned I'd make the turnpike in good time. All I had to do was wait 'til you came through."

Bored with the explanation, Vaughn clicked his fingers. "All right, let's have it."

"Yes, sir." The horseman reached into his coat once more, brought out a folded piece of paper and handed it over. Vaughn opened it out but it was too dark to see so he stepped away and held the paper up to the lantern slung on the side of the coach.

The message was short:

We are betrayed. Additional escorts on their way. Rendezvous Bear Hotel, Esher. Await instructions.

Vaughn looked for a reference. A single letter denoted the identity of the sender: *S.*

Saxby. God damn it.

He addressed the messenger. "No possibility of a reply?"

"Sorry, sir; this was our last received message of the day. It's too late. Can't signal at night; not enough light for the next station to read the shutters, even with a glass."

Ask a damned fool question. Shit.

He placed the note in his pocket and looked up the road. He could see tiny lights twinkling like fireflies through the trees; Esher village.

The Bear it was, then. Not that they had a choice. On the positive side, though, there'd be food available and it wouldn't hurt to rest up after the time they'd spent being jolted around. The horses were due to be swapped out anyway, and it would keep the escort happy, too; give them a chance to dry off.

Vaughn nodded to the messenger. "Very good." To the escort he said, "All right, move out."

Ignoring the messenger's relieved look and instructing the toll-keeper to open the gate, Vaughn returned to the coach, where the priest put down his book.

"There is a problem?"

It was the first time the man had spoken anything approaching a meaningful sentence. The accent was noticeable, as was the lack of inflection which had made the utterance sound more like a statement than a question.

"A minor amendment to our schedule. Nothing untoward."

"Amendment? What does that mean?" Behind the spectacle lenses, the dark eyes narrowed probingly.

Savvy enough to know that the word meant the same in French as it did in English, Vaughn assumed the enquiry was meant in the wider context. He kept his voice calm. "We're due a change of horses at our next halt. I've been advised that we're to wait there for an additional escort and new instructions."

The priest's eyebrows lifted.

"I know no more than that," Vaughn said. "I'm assuming it's a precautionary measure."

"Precautionary?"

"Necessary."

The priest considered the word. "We will lose time."

"Some," Vaughn conceded, "but we'll still make the morning tide. In the meantime, I suggest we make use of the opportunity to avail ourselves of some supper. It's been a long day. A square meal wouldn't go amiss. If that meets with your approval," he added, unable to keep the dry note of sarcasm from his voice.

There was a pause before the priest nodded and said, "Very well, as you wish."

Yes, I do bloody wish.

The coach started off once more and Vaughn watched as

the priest, making it perfectly apparent that the discussion was over, wrapped his cloak closer about him and returned to his book.

Ten minutes later, the inn loomed out of the darkness.

Vaughn would have preferred his own company but the inclement weather had persuaded other travellers to linger in the warmth over the menu, which had led to a shortage of space in the inn's dining room. As a result, he'd had to resign himself to sharing the priest's table while the escorts had been accommodated closer to the door. The priest's continued reluctance to engage in anything approaching even a casual exchange implied that the resentment was mutual.

Watching the cleric bow his head and murmur grace beneath his breath was a profoundly disquieting experience, knowing, as Vaughn did, that behind the sickening display of piety there lay concealed base appetites of a magnitude far beyond those understood by rational men. That such diverse pursuits – the act of meditation and the commitment of murder – could be reconciled within a single individual, especially one in holy orders, seemed incomprehensible to Vaughn, who was the first to concede that he was no candidate for the papacy himself.

He watched with mounting distaste the way the Abbé dabbed the napkin fastidiously across his thin lips. It was a rare occasion that Vaughn allowed personal prejudice to take possession of his thoughts. In his line of work, there was little room for such indulgences. There was only the execution of business; the rendering of a service for an agreed remuneration. But when it came to the priest he was prepared to make an exception. The man's aloofness was irksome, certainly, but the thing that provoked Vaughn was the total absence of anything approaching humility or, given the cleric's sadistic predilections, contrition.

Had the priest been made aware of his – Vaughn's – knowledge of his crimes and the extreme steps that had been taken to ensure that no trace of his extra-curricular activities should see the light of day? Perhaps he was merely indifferent, which

348

made Vaughn wonder if that wasn't the defining reason for his contemptuous feeling towards the man seated opposite.

Vaughn had made it his policy never to question the motives of his employer. His was not to reason why or to question or delve. His was merely to serve. But on this occasion he had found himself wondering what made the priest so damned special. The more he thought about that, the more he had begun to realize that in all likelihood he would probably never know.

Dragging his thoughts back to the moment at hand, Vaughn consulted his pocket watch. They had been at the inn for just over an hour. In that time the surrounding tables had begun to empty as journeys were resumed. One other coach party, composed of three men and two women, remained at a table at the back of the room, while a smattering of other diners – all male – made up the remainder. Vaughn assumed they had all chosen to stay the night.

He thought about the signal from Saxby and the time it had begun its journey. Additional men were on their way, the message stated; from London, presumably. Vaughn thought about that. They wouldn't be coming by carriage. That would take too long, which meant they'd be arriving on the hoof which, in turn, meant, if they were on their way by the time the message was sent, their appearance could well be imminent. There had been no mention of numbers but it stood to reason that Saxby would be sending enough bodies to counteract the threat that had been perceived, whatever that was. Best, Vaughn, thought, to prepare for their arrival.

Catching Babbage's eye, he beckoned the escort to him and spoke softly. "Station someone outside. They're to inform me when our friends turn up. We'll move out soon after."

Babbage nodded. "I'll send Croker. He can prepare the coach at the same time."

Babbage went to relay the instruction and Vaughn watched as the driver rose from the table and left the room. The quicker they were on their way, the better. The priest could go back to his book and, come the dawn, they'd be shot of the bastard for good. He'd be someone else's problem.

The priest placed the napkin on the table and looked about him.

"If you're looking for the pisser, it's through there," Vaughn said and lifted his chin towards an alcove in the corner of the room to the left of the imposing hearth in which a log fire burned brightly. "Follow the smell."

He'd enquired about the privy himself, earlier. It was round the back, next to the stable yard. He watched the priest depart and thought again about the content of Saxby's message.

Betrayed by whom?

He was given no time to speculate. Babbage was back.

"Croker's just signalled," he said softly. "They're here."

Bloody typical, Vaughn thought, cursing the priest's bladder as he accepted the news with a curt nod. "Very good; his holiness is taking a piss. Soon as he returns, we'll settle up. I don't want to delay our departure any longer than necessary."

"Sir."

Babbage went to move away. As he did so, Vaughn looked beyond him to the entrance to the dining room and the individual now blocking it.

Clad in a long coat, it was clear from the figure's mud-splattered appearance that he'd been travelling hard. With the coarse-grained features of a man used to giving orders, he caught Vaughn's eye and ran a rough hand across a close-cut scalp. "Hell of a bloody ride, that was."

Vaughn rose from his seat. "Good to see you. Welcome."

"Weren't talkin' to you," Jago said; his face breaking into a broad smile as he stood aside.

The disbelief on Vaughn's face as Hawkwood moved into the room was palpable. He looked like a man who'd just swallowed a mouthful of sand.

"I wouldn't," Jago warned, as Babbage, uncertain, went to reach beneath his jacket. Jago's right hand rose into view from behind his coat, forefinger curled around the trigger of the Bingham pistol. "You can tell that to your pals, as well."

The remaining escorts, seated at their table, looked to Vaughn for instruction and at the quick shake of his head froze.

"Captain," Hawkwood said evenly.

As the shock receded, Vaughn straightened, acknowledging the Barbar held in Hawkwood's right hand. "Well, now, didn't think I'd be seeing you again." He fixed Hawkwood with an astute look. "I assume Mudd and Ridger are no longer with us."

"You assume correctly."

"Shame. I was hoping they'd have given me more time."

"You mean you hoped they'd give *me* more of a problem," Hawkwood said.

Vaughn's lips twitched. The scar crinkled. "Since you put it like that, yes."

"Good help's not always easy to find," Hawkwood said.

Vaughn let the napkin drop and threw a speculative glance towards the man standing at Hawkwood's shoulder. "Can't disagree with you there."

"But then you knew I wouldn't wait," Hawkwood said, "that I'd find them."

Vaughn shifted his gaze back. "I'd have been amazed if you hadn't."

"It's what you were hoping," Hawkwood said. "Right?"

Vaughn stared at him for several seconds and then smiled. "What can I say? *Mea culpa.*"

"Two against one; chances were, they'd be the ones left standing."

Humour showed in the dark eyes. "Nothing personal."

"No," Hawkwood said. "It never is, is it? Either way, you thought that by chasing *them* instead of tracking *you*, I'd be giving you all the time you needed to run."

"Something like that."

"Sorry to disappoint."

"Ah, well, can't be helped. I tried. Fact is, you did me a service; they *were* becoming something of liability."

"Not knowing their right from left and picking a disused Frog chapel to stage Flagg's suicide? I'll say. If I'd wanted to draw attention away from an émigré priest, it wouldn't have been the first place I'd've chosen. Whose bright idea was that?"

"Hah!" Vaughn gave a mirthless laugh. "Y'know, I asked them the same question. Funny thing was, they'd no bloody idea that's what it had been. All they knew was that it was an abandoned building on a watchman's route. I only discovered the history of the place *after* the deed was done. All I could hope for then was that when you did find Flagg and the whore you'd consider that to be the end of it and the location wouldn't get you thinking too hard about the whys and wherefores. As coincidences go, it was a dandy, right enough, but that's all it was. Even so, I did wonder if they shouldn't just have written you a damned note."

Hawkwood shrugged. "I wouldn't be too hard on them. It did get us thinking, but we were already heading in that direction. Once we knew Flagg's suicide was staged, it was one more ingredient tossed into the mix – a strange one, admittedly. If it makes you feel any better, I'd no idea it'd been a chapel either. I'd still be none the wiser if one of my constables hadn't had a vicar for a father."

"God damn, the world does move in strange ways, and there was I . . ." Vaughn shook his head in amusement and then frowned. "I'm curious, though, as to how you found us. I wasn't aware they knew where we were heading."

"They didn't."

Vaughn stared at him. "Don't tell me; another coincidence?" His eyes narrowed speculatively. "No, wait, it couldn't be. You had assistance."

"You're not the only one with friends in high places."

Vaughn eyed Jago. "Low, too, it would seem. Both do serve their purpose, though, don't they? I suppose I should have given you more credit. Still, what's done is done. I trust Mrs Teague was returned to you in good health? Her abduction was, as you rightly say, merely a delaying tactic to keep you occupied."

"Not exactly. She was shot."

Hawkwood's voice had carried further than he'd intended, as had the cold anger in his tone. Around the room, conversations, already interrupted as other diners became attuned to the confrontation, began to dwindle away.

Vaughn rediscovered his own voice. "Dead?"

The word sounded dry and hollow. In the hearth, the fire crackled loudly, cascading sparks across the hearthstone. From somewhere off to his right, near to where the women were sitting, Hawkwood thought he heard a low gasp.

"No. Fortunately your man's aim was off."

Vaughn stared back at Hawkwood. "They were under strict orders that no harm was to befall her. I made it clear."

"Not clear enough."

Hawkwood watched as the permutations garnered by that statement seeped into the recesses of Vaughn's brain.

"I regret that," Vaughn said eventually. "I do, truly; believe me."

"So, where is he?" Hawkwood raised the Barbar, causing a murmur of consternation to ripple round the room and Vaughn to suck in his cheeks.

Vaughn let out his breath. "He?"

"Jeannot."

"Is that his name? I didn't know. Well . . ." Vaughn spread his hands. ". . . not here, as you can see."

"He was, though," Hawkwood said, nodding towards the black cloak draped over the back of the empty chair, "According to that and your man outside."

"Croker?"

"Is that his name? I didn't know."

Vaughn acknowledged the riposte with a wry smile which faded when Hawkwood drew back the Barbar's hammer and, with his right hand gripping the butt, cradled the barrel along his left forearm.

"He's nursing a cracked skull, by the way, in case you were wondering about his welfare. He might not come around. Strikes me you're running out of foot-soldiers faster than I can count." Hawkwood threw a glance towards Babbage, who hadn't moved but who was looking exceedingly tense. "You might want to bear that in mind."

Vaughn lifted his head defiantly. "You know I can't give him up."

"Can't or won't?"

Vaughn gazed back at him.

"You really don't have a choice," Hawkwood said.

Vaughn looked about him again and then back at Hawkwood, his mouth crimping. "You do understand that he's protected?"

"Not by me."

Vaughn's head came up. His gaze hardened. "And you think that entitles you to take him by force, here, with all these civilians around? All this" – the dark eyes flashed mockingly – "sharp cutlery?"

"Major," Hawkwood called over his shoulder. His eyes did not stray from Vaughn's face.

There was another collective intake of breath from the people seated around them as Lomax moved into view. One of the female diners put her hand over her mouth and turned her head away in horror. From the expressions on other faces, more than one person had suddenly discovered they'd lost their appetite. Those with stronger stomachs, realizing that something even more untoward might be about to happen, had their eyes firmly fixed upon the unfolding drama. A lot of attention seemed focused on the open front of Lomax's coat and the sight of the blue and scarlet uniform visible beneath it.

Unperturbed by the reaction his appearance had provoked, Lomax allowed his one good eye to traverse the scene before switching its attention back to Vaughn, whose own eyes had widened at the sight of the ruined face. Immediately, Lomax forged one of his gruesome trademark grins. "Call that a *scar*? Why, it ain't hardly a graze."

"You think this will do you any good?" Vaughn said. "You're outgunned, and I have more men arriving."

Where the hell was the priest? Taking a shit instead of a piss?

"I wouldn't be so sure about that," Hawkwood said.

"Really?" Vaughn said confidently, his gaze shifting to the trio of long-coated figures who'd appeared at Hawkwood's back. "Then who are these gentlemen?"

Hawkwood did not turn. "I think you'll find they're with me."

Vaughn frowned, but then, when it became obvious that the

354

new arrivals were making no move to intervene, realization dawned. It took another two seconds before a bitter smile roughened the edge of the scarred mouth.

"Well, ain't we the clever one? It was you who sent the signal. And just before last light, too, so there'd be no chance of a reply, yes? Masterly."

It had been James Read who'd used his influence with a contact at the Admiralty to gain access to the telegraph. In formulating the ruse, the magistrate had remained tight-lipped when asked about the person's identity and Hawkwood had known better than to press for information. It had been Twigg, of all people, who, in a later private aside, had murmured that it was unlikely to be a coincidence that, as a young lawyer, Read had been a contemporary of the First Sea Lord, Robert Dundas, who'd also studied law and who'd begun his career as an advocate attached to a chamber at Lincoln's Inn, during which time, Twigg had revealed, certain indiscretions had been discovered, which, were they to be made public, had the potential to damage the First Sea Lord's growing reputation.

Twigg, remaining steadfastly loyal to his former superior, had clammed up at that juncture, leaving Hawkwood none the wiser as to the precise nature of the debt that James Read had called in. It also left him wondering how much longer Read could rely on the assistance of former allies before the establishment declared him persona non grata. In continuing to provide assistance to Hawkwood, the magistrate had taken a huge risk with his own, already precarious, position. Addington and his cronies would be after his blood. That's if they weren't already.

"When you're ready, Major," Hawkwood said.

Lomax took a pace forward. "Ladies and gentlemen, permit me to introduce myself. I am Major Gabriel Lomax of the Bow Street Horse Patrol. These are my associates. I apologize for the intrusion but we are here on police business. I'd be obliged if you would vacate the room in an orderly fashion. All except you gentlemen," he added, throwing a lop-sided glance at the men occupying the table by the door. "You stay exactly where you are."

Not one person moved. They stared at Lomax as if transfixed.

"Now," Lomax said, casually moving aside the hem of his coat to reveal the hanger at his right hip. "If you please."

If the gloved hand on the hilt of his sword was not a sufficient hint that compliance was the most sensible option, then the look on Lomax's ravaged face was clearly the deciding factor, though Jago and Hawkwood's weapons were helping to exert a not-inconsiderable influence, too.

A chair scraped back as the first diner got to his feet – a plump man who'd been seated by himself near the fireside. Dropping his napkin on to the table and glaring at Lomax over his shoulder, he turned for the doorway.

Directly into the path of an incoming waiter.

The collision was unavoidable. Tray, plates, bowls, a metal soup tureen, condiments and assorted serving utensils clattered on to the floor, spilling victuals in all directions. Diners, already made nervous by the appearance of armed men and an officer of the law, jumped out of their seats in alarm, dislodging drinks and toppling glasses and carafes on to the already debris-strewn floorboards below.

Whereupon, all hell broke loose.

26

Hawkwood heard Jago let go a curse behind him but did not turn because all his attention was riveted on Vaughn's right hand and the pistol that had suddenly appeared within it; an Egg or a Manton, maybe; the barrel not much more than five inches long, allowing for easy concealment within a coat pocket and for the weapon to be cocked using just the thumb. The sound of the crash had covered the click as the hammer was drawn back.

There was no time to think or aim. Hawkwood fired from the hip. The roar from the Barbar eclipsed the sound of the pistol shot, which came a split-second later; so close together that they sounded like a single report.

Despite the flared muzzle, a Barbar's load did not spread when it left the barrel, not at close range, anyway. Vaughn was less than five feet away when Hawkwood fired and at that distance there was nowhere for him to go. The shot took him in the chest, shredding his heart in an instant.

Hawkwood felt the wind from the pistol ball as it flickered past his ear.

A woman screamed as Babbage hauled the pistol from inside his coat. The crack from Jago's Bingham was as loud as a thunderclap and as the powder swirled around him, Hawkwood saw Babbage fall back with a screech, his jaw shot away, the gun dropping from his fingers.

A resounding crash came from behind as Vaughn's men up-ended their table to give themselves cover as they reached for their weapons. Another pistol cracked and Hawkwood thought he heard a low grunt but the exhalation was drowned by two blasts in quick succession from Del and Ned's Barbars, accompanied by the sound of breaking glass and more cries of panic as terrified customers scrambled for cover; the more agile among them rushing for the nearest doorway, while the rest sought shelter beneath the tables. A vision of the fight in the Hanged Man speared its way into Hawkwood's brain as another scream sounded.

I've been here before.

Over by the alcove, the diner who'd backed into the waiter had his hands around his head and was trying, unsuccessfully to curl into a ball, while the waiter was crabbing through the spilled crockery towards the shelter of a second table that had been overturned in the confusion. The room was wreathed in powder smoke. A candle that had been dashed to the floor but which had remained miraculously alight had caught the drooping corner of a tablecloth and small flames were beginning to lick along the edge of the grease-stained material.

Another loud report came from somewhere near the door and Hawkwood saw one of the women throw up her arms and pitch forward, the side of her dress blossoming red.

"Right!" Lomax bawled, his sword drawn.

Hawkwood turned in time to see one of Vaughn's henchmen come lunging out of the smoke, knife and pistol in hand. His charge ended in a wild shriek as Lomax's blade slashed down across a bared wrist. Blood spurted. In the gloom, Hawkwood saw Micah step forward and finish the man with a shot to the head. Flame lanced from the pistol barrel.

And then, eerily, as the echoes from the shots died away, there was stillness, swiftly broken by the sounds of people crawling out from their hiding places. A woman began to sob loudly.

As the smoke cleared, Hawkwood saw Ned rise shakily to his feet, the spent Barbar in his right hand, his left hand clamped against his right shoulder. Blood showed between his fingers. Behind him, Del, down on one knee and breathing hard, was surveying the chaos.

The air reeked of sulphur.

"Christ," Lomax swore, his one eye gazing spellbound at the bodies of Vaughn's men, the sword trailing in his hand. "What a bloody mess. Why the hell didn't they yield?"

No one replied.

Then Micah said, "This one's alive."

Hawkwood crossed to the man seated with his back against the wall, legs apart and the shirt over his belly stained dark with blood. A discharged pistol rested on his right knee.

Hawkwood bent over him. "Where's the priest?"

The man blinked, placed a trembling hand over his wound and then groaned in pain.

"God damn it! Where's the bloody priest?"

Lifting his chin weakly, the wounded man nodded towards the doorway at the back of the room.

"Go," Jago said. "We've got this."

Hawkwood straightened. He looked at Lomax. Lomax, sheathing his sword and drawing his pistol, nodded. Handing Jago the empty Barbar, Hawkwood drew the Bingham from the loop on his belt and turned away. He was halfway across the room when he heard the pistol shot behind him. He did not look back.

A narrow, candlelit corridor lay beyond the doorway. Hawkwood drew back the pistol hammer. As he did so, a shadow moved before him. Bringing the pistol up, he found himself staring into the frightened eyes of a pot-boy. The look on Hawkwood's face was enough. The pot-boy turned to run and squirmed like a tadpole when Hawkwood seized his arm.

"I'm not going to hurt you. I'm looking for a priest. I'm told he came this way."

The boy stared up at him, his lips drawn back in fear. Hawkwood lowered the pistol and held it down by his side. "Priest; likely dressed in black, yes or no?"

The pot-boy's lips moved but no words came out. Then, quivering, he twisted and pointed his free hand back over his shoulder.

"Where's it lead?"

The boy swallowed. "B-back yard 'n' outhouse."

Hawkwood released the arm. "All right, get out of here."

The boy went to run. "No, wait." Hawkwood stopped him. "Is there a doctor in the village?"

The boy gaped.

"A physician, damn it!"

The boy hesitated then nodded dumbly.

"Find him; bring him here. Tell him there are people hurt. They need his help. Understand?"

Another jerky nod.

"All right, off you go. Run!"

Hawkwood watched the boy disappear, then took a deep breath. Behind him, diners who'd been caught up in the skirmish, along with those of the inn's staff who'd plucked up the courage to come out of hiding, were calling for assistance, some voices sounding marginally more excitable than others. Lomax was going to have his hands full; the doctor, too, if the boy had done as Hawkwood asked and not gone screaming into the night. Hawkwood wondered if the woman he'd seen go down was alive, and from whose weapon the shot had come.

A vision of Maddie collapsing into Jago's arms rose before him. Gripped with fresh rage, his hold on the pistol tightened.

A flushed and frightened face, framed by curls peaking from beneath a mop cap, appeared in an open doorway.

"Stay inside!" Hawkwood snapped.

The head ducked back out of sight. Hawkwood followed the gun's muzzle into the room. Half a dozen kitchen workers cowered in the corner. They shrank back further as Hawkwood swept the area, the pistol held before him. "Don't leave here until you've been told it's safe. Understand?"

Six heads nodded in unison.

Hawkwood moved on. There was an open door at the end of the corridor. Through it he could see part of a slatted wall: the outhouse mentioned by the pot-boy. He approached cautiously. The smell of piss and faeces grew ever stronger. Even dampened by the cold and wet, the stench still managed to cast a wide shadow, completely masking the aroma from the kitchen behind him.

Inspection of the privy revealed there were no occupants secreted inside. Emerging from the stink, Hawkwood took stock. Obviously, the priest had heard the fire-fight – he'd have to have been deaf not to – which was why he'd taken evasive action. But where the hell was he? Where would a priest run to escape his pursuers?

Then, turning, Hawkwood saw it: a squat, stone-built structure; ivy-draped with a sharp, sloping roof framed by trees and bushes. It had been at the periphery of his vision and its construct had failed to register. In the moonlight, it could have been mistaken for a barn or a large storehouse, or perhaps an annex to the inn's stables, until the shape of it suddenly took on a firmer substance and its purpose became clear. There was a square, wooden turret, Hawkwood saw, with louvered sides and a pyramid roof supporting a weathervane. Set into the wall below that was a dark, diamond-shaped object, which materialized into a clock face. Beneath the clock was a small lancet window and below that a pair of long, narrow windows in the same style.

He stared hard, not quite believing what he was seeing.

A church?

It couldn't be that obvious, could it?

And then a moving shape caught his eye; a bat-like shadow silhouetted against the limestone; there one second, gone the next. So fleeting had the sighting been that he might have imagined it. Though he knew he hadn't.

Hawkwood ran.

As he drew near he saw the weathered path and the scattering of tombstones, set amid clumps of ragged gorse and un-mown grass. There was a covered porch on the right side of the building beneath which a stout wooden door stood slightly ajar. Approaching cautiously, Hawkwood eased it open a little further. The hinges groaned faintly as he did so. He froze and waited. Then, sensing there was no immediate threat, he moved inside.

The interior took him by surprise, for it was far more spacious than the unprepossessing exterior had suggested. Moonlight filtering through the windows revealed pale, whitewashed walls and a high, beamed roof. Rows of dark wooden pews led the eye towards a massive three-decked pulpit to the left of the main aisle that looked as if it should have been gracing a ship's prow rather than the inside of a country church. Beyond the pulpit, at the far end of the nave, a large three-panelled reredos formed an imposing backdrop to a small cloth-covered altar separated from the chancel by a low wooden baluster. Hawkwood's eye moved to the black-clad figure scurrying down the aisle towards it.

"Stand where you are!" Hawkwood raised the pistol. "*Arrêtez!*"

At the sound of Hawkwood's voice, the figure paused, spider-like, in a half crouch and then straightened and turned.

"*Ne bougez pas!*" Hawkwood spat out the words. "You Frog bastard. Not one bloody inch."

Spreading his arms, his hands held at hip level, the figure displayed his open palms, in what was almost a Christ-like pose. Behind the spectacle frames, the dark eyes were without expression.

"There's nowhere to go," Hawkwood said. "*Il n'y a nulle part où aller.*"

The cassocked figure kept the pose as Hawkwood approached and showed no fear as he looked Hawkwood up and down. Eventually he spoke.

"You are the one they told me about. *Le chasseur.*" The words delivered in English were accented but fluently spoken.

Hawkwood said nothing, struck by the inconsequential-looking individual who stood before him.

This is what I've been chasing?

"You mean to arrest me?" A mocking half-smile accompanied the enquiry. "They will not permit it."

"They?" Hawkwood said.

"Your superiors." The priest's head lifted defiantly. "I am on a diplomatic mission for your government. Your Minister, Adding*ton*, has granted me protection."

The Gallic stress on the last syllable sounded almost deliberate, as if to add emphasis to the name.

"Is that right? Well, Addington's not here; neither is your friend, Saxby."

At the mention of Saxby's name, the priest's gaze shifted to a point beyond Hawkwood's shoulder before moving back again.

"And if you're looking for Captain Vaughn, he won't be riding to the rescue, either."

"The captain is dead?"

"He was the last time I looked."

The priest eyed the pistol. "And you intend to kill me also?"

"I'm considering the possibility."

"You would shoot a priest: one of God's servants?"

"Like I said, I'm considering the possibility."

"Here? In *this* house? That would be a sacrilege. Your soul will be condemned to eternal damnation."

Hawkwood pointed the pistol at the priest's head. "If I were you, *mon père*, I'd be more concerned with my own chances of salvation. The things you've done, I've a feeling you'll be knocking on Satan's door long before I get there."

The dark eyes glittered. "I am a servant of our Lord. I do His bidding."

"God told you to kill and carve up women, did He? Even if I was a believer, I'd consider that a little far-fetched."

"They were harlots, adulteresses!"

"And that made it right?"

"They were abominations in the eyes of God! Their kind lurks on every corner! On the streets and in the squares! Their lips drip with honey; their words are smoother than oil!"

"Abominations?" Hawkwood drew closer. "I was wondering when we'd get to the Scriptures. That's usually the first port of refuge for bastards like you. What was that? Old Testament? It usually is. I had it drummed into me as a boy by Pastor Slocum. It might have impressed me then, even frightened me a little. Not so much now. So you can rant all you like. It won't wash. You say you do the Lord's bidding? You're no more a servant of the Lord than I am. You're naught but a twisted bastard masquerading behind a frock and a dog collar. Tell me, *Monsieur l'Abbé*, what's the Almighty's view on fornicating clerics? If that doesn't warrant a visit from Beelzebub, I don't know what does. But you know something? I don't care. I don't give a damn why you did what you did. What matters is that you won't be doing it any more."

The priest's eyes flickered. A look of doubt crossed his face and then his features assumed a more artful expression. "I have gold."

Hawkwood nodded wearily. "Now why did I know that was going to be your next move?"

"Fifty English guineas. They are yours."

For incidental expenses, Hawkwood supposed. It was substantially more than Brooke had advanced when the Alien Office had dispatched him into France. Not far off a Runner's wages for a year, as near as made no difference.

"Fifty guineas if I let you go?"

The priest placed a hand on the crucifix. "I have them with me."

"Do you? Well, it's a tidy sum right enough, and all I have to do to earn it is walk away; is that right?"

"Yes."

Hawkwood saw the possibility of a reprieve hovering behind the priest's eyes. "No."

"No?" the priest said, puzzled.

"Five hundred; five thousand; makes no difference; it'd still be no. Not in this lifetime."

The light in the Abbé's eyes faded to black.

Hawkwood extended the pistol once more.

And saw the hope in Jeannot's eyes suddenly rekindled when a voice from the darkness behind Hawkwood's left shoulder enquired tentatively, "Who goes there?"

Keeping the pistol trained on his quarry, Hawkwood half-turned to see an elderly man dressed in a grey cassock shuffle into view from a side door towards the rear end of the nave. The candle he was holding aloft illuminated a bald pate bordered by a fringe of snow-white hair, a round face enclosing a pair of small, watery eyes that blinked in myopic alarm.

"If you've come to rob the collection box, young man, I fear you'll be leaving empty-handed."

Drawing nearer, the old man caught sight of the Abbé. As his

364

gaze took in the black cassock and the crucifix, he halted abruptly, indecision writ large across his face. "What is this?"

Hawkwood kept the pistol trained on Jeannot's chest. "You're the vicar?"

The old man turned. "I am the rector. My name is Diggle. And you, sir?"

"Officer Hawkwood, Bow Street Public Office."

The rector started. "Bow Street? Why . . .?"

"Is there anyone here with you?" Hawkwood snapped before the old man could complete his sentence.

The rector frowned at the abrasive tone. "There is not. I am quite alone. I've a baptism first thing tomorrow and I wanted to prepare my notes. The quiet helps me think." The rector's eyes dropped to the pistol. "You dare bring *that* into my church?" His voice shook with anger. "Have you no regard for the sanctity of this place?"

Without giving Hawkwood a chance to respond, the old man switched his attention to Jeannot and frowned in the realization that, while their raiment might have been similar, the two-toned neckwear marked the possibility that here was a person of a different faith. "Father, is it?" he asked hesitantly. "Perhaps *you* would explain. I don't believe I—"

And the Abbé seized his chance.

Before Hawkwood could stop him, Abbé Jeannot turned and rushed headlong toward the altar, almost tripping over the hem of his cassock as he did so. Pulling open the balustrade gate, he threw himself across the cloth-covered slab, seized the gold cross that was the altar's centrepiece and clasped it to his chest before raising his eyes to the cross beams above his head.

"I am the Abbé Pierre-Vincent-Jeannot de la Basse! I cast myself upon your infinite mercy, oh Lord, and I claim the right of sanctuary!"

It took a second for the astonished rector to recover from the shock at witnessing the Abbé's headlong dash and hearing what was clearly a foreigner calling out in English. He stared at the Abbé in confusion. "Sanctuary? I don't . . ."

Hawkwood didn't wait for the rest. As he stepped forward,

the Abbé turned. Brandishing the cross before him, he sank to his knees, his features twisted into a triumphant grin. "I told you! I am protected! By God's holy grace!"

Hawkwood raised the Bingham. "The hell you are!"

"No!"

Rector Diggle moved remarkably fast for a man of his advancing years. Making a desperate grab for Hawkwood's gun hand, he went to push the pistol barrel aside. "For pity's sake, this is the house of God!"

Raising the lit candle with his other hand, the rector thrust the flame towards the altar screen. "Are you blind to His words?"

Hawkwood looked past the kneeling Abbé and saw for the first time, in the grey moonlight and by the light of the flame, the significance of the reredos' panels, each of which bore an inscription in ornate lettering. The panels to the left and right bore the Lord's Prayer and the Creed respectively, but it was to the larger, central panel that the rector directed Hawkwood's gaze, to the heading: Exodus Chap: XX, and below it the list of Roman numerals and the text inserted between each one.

"You see?" Rector Diggle said desperately. "God's holy writ! The Sixth Commandment! 'Thou shalt do no murder!'"

Hawkwood shook the rector's hand away. As the old man staggered back, Hawkwood raised the pistol. "Who said anything about murder? This is justice."

And fired.

The ball struck Jeannot an inch above the bridge of his nose and exited through the top of his skull in a mist of blood and shattered bone. As his corpse toppled sideways, the cross clattered on to the floor.

Frozen to the spot, the rector stared at the Abbé's lifeless body, his face suffused with horror that not even the gloom could conceal.

The door behind them slammed back with a crash. The rector jumped, causing the candleholder to fall from his hand and the candle to go out as Jago ran into the nave and pulled up short before walking forward cautiously, reloaded pistol in hand.

"Heard the shot. Everythin' all right here? Major's calmed everyone down and the lads are cleanin' up the mess."

"He killed him." Rector Diggle stared at Jago in fraught appeal. "He killed him!"

Jago stowed his pistol and stared down at the corpse, which had come to rest against the base of the altar. Blood had pooled on the ground beneath the head, as black as the cassock into which it was soaking.

"This the bastard?"

Hawkwood returned the Bingham to the loop on his belt and nodded.

Rector Diggle's legs began to buckle. One hand over his mouth, as if still unable to comprehend what he'd just seen, he groped his way towards the nearest pew. Seated and moaning softly, he began to rock back and forth, hands clasped tightly together.

Squatting down, Hawkwood ran his hands up and down the corpse and around the cassock's hem.

"What the hell?" Jago said as Hawkwood withdrew the stiletto from his boot.

The coins were contained in two leather sleeves, formed into tight rolls and sewn into a seam in the cassock's waistband.

"I'll be damned," Jago murmured as Hawkwood slit the material to expose them. "Wasn't expectin' that. How much do you reckon?"

"Fifty guineas."

"That a wild guess, or do you know something I don't?" Jago enquired.

"It's what he offered me to let him go." Hawkwood nodded towards the altar cloth. "Grab that."

Frowning, Jago went to comply. As he did so, the rector looked up. But there was no more protest left in him. Ashen-faced, his lips moved soundlessly as he watched Jago remove the blood-splattered linen sheet.

"We're taking the bugger with us?" Jago enquired doubtfully as Hawkwood tossed the coins on to the altar slab before taking the cloth, spreading it on the ground and rolling the body on to it. "That's a first."

Hawkwood knotted the ends of the cloth. "I'd say we've left enough of a mess, wouldn't you?"

Jago threw a glance towards the money and then the rector, who had not moved from his seat, and smiled grimly. "Aye, well a new altar cloth ain't likely to run cheap."

He stared again at the body, wrapped in its makeshift shroud. "Don't look much, now, does he?"

"Always the way with murderers," Hawkwood said tiredly. "Once they stop breathing, they never do."

27

Henry Addington stood before the rain-streaked window, hands braced against the sill, gazing into the square below him. When the door opened behind him, he took a deep breath and turned.

"Well?" Saxby said, without pleasantry. "What news?"

Addington crossed the room to his desk. "A warrant's been issued. The man is to be arrested on sight."

"You said the same thing two days ago. I was hoping for a little more progress."

Addington frowned at the accusing tone. "He knows the city and he has friends. Clearly he's gone to ground."

"You've spoken to Read?"

"I left that to Brooke. He says that Read has no idea of his man's whereabouts."

"*His* man?" Saxby said sharply.

"A slip of the tongue. His former subordinate."

"Is he telling the truth?"

"Read? He's a magistrate. I take him at his word." Pausing, he then said, "There are men watching his residence. If Hawkwood does turn up there – which is unlikely – we will know."

"Not Bow Street personnel?" Saxby said quickly.

Addington sighed. "No, Great Marlborough Street: men commanded by Conant before his appointment to Chief Magistrate."

Saxby nodded. "You're aware Artois and Louis are calling for more than his arrest."

"I am. They relayed their displeasure, in no uncertain terms."

"Can you blame them?" Saxby brushed a speck of soot from his knee. "Not only did he put paid to the entire enterprise, he also slaughtered their chief agent."

"Slaughtered?" Addington said archly.

"There was a witness."

"You're referring to the rector of St George's."

"I am."

"Yes, well, I'm not sure how reliable his testimony will be. I understand he's still suffering night spasms. According to his physician, he might never recover. Frankly, I'm not sure any of us will. The man left a trail of chaos in his wake."

"That's an understatement," Saxby said, ignoring Addington's sharp look. "After what he did with Jeannot's body? The man's clearly unhinged!"

"He was sending a message," Addington said heavily.

"He left the corpse hanging from a gibbet!" Saxby snapped. "For the entire world to see! And the ring in the mouth? What kind of message was that?"

Addington shook his head.

"Were the princes informed of the circumstances in which their man's body was found?" Saxby asked.

"They were not. We didn't think it appropriate."

"What about the killings at the inn? Vaughn and his men were cut down."

"Witnesses say Hawkwood and his associates did not start the fight. They said it was Vaughn who drew his weapon first. Hawkwood and his associates were forced to defend themselves."

"Leaving seven dead, including a woman?"

"Once battle was joined, there was a great deal of confusion; a lot of smoke and noise. The witness statements were not exactly consistent, though on the whole they did corroborate the account given by Major Lomax. The woman's death was clearly a tragedy. She was in the wrong place at the wrong time."

"I'm sure that's a comfort to her family," Saxby said. "And what do we know of this Lomax character?"

"I'm advised he is a former cavalry officer with a distinguished record," Addington threw Saxby a flinty look, "both as a military man and as a current member of the Horse Patrol."

"And he was with Hawkwood, why?"

"He was in pursuit of *your* Captain Vaughn, who was implicated in the abduction and murder of Mrs Madeleine Teague."

"Hawkwood's woman."

"So I've been informed."

"How convenient," Saxby muttered. "Did Lomax have anything to say about Hawkwood leaving the priest's body on display?"

"Major Lomax's report makes no mention of a priest. His sole concern was the apprehension of Vaughn and his men. After they were subdued . . ."

"*Subdued?*"

"Following the altercation," Addington continued stiffly, "Major Lomax remained in situ to assess the extent of injuries sustained and contain the damage done. According to his report, Hawkwood's services were no longer required, so he left the scene."

"And the others?"

"Others?"

"The *associates*."

"According to Lomax, they were concerned citizens who went to his assistance with no regard for their own safety. Once they'd established he had no need of further help, they too went their own way."

Saxby stared at the Home Secretary. "And do you believe him?"

"Whether I believe him or not is irrelevant. The witness statements confirm his account."

"It's clear he and Hawkwood were – are – in league together."

"So you say. And if they are, what do you propose we do? From where I'm standing, I would suggest that Vaughn's demise works to our advantage."

Saxby's chin rose. "How so?"

"It means there's nothing to connect him to you and, by association, to this office. It would be best to remember that. It eliminates any awkward questions that might arise."

Saxby said nothing for several seconds. Finally, he sighed. "Is there any possibility we can retrieve the situation?"

Addington shrugged. "Brooke thinks it unlikely, at least for now. Jeannot was integral to the cause. He won't be easy to replace. They lay the blame for the mission's failure entirely on our heads, of course."

"Have they been made aware of the reason Hawkwood went after their man in the first place?" Saxby grunted. "They do know the trouble I . . . *we* . . . went to?"

"They do now."

"And still they protest? Methinks they should be reminded that they are guests in this country. Permission for them to remain could be revoked at any time."

"Do that and we'll lose all Royalist support on the continent." Addington rose from his desk. "It's a double-edged sword. Every liaison we've nurtured would be lost. It would be foolish to jeopardize that relationship now that Bonaparte's on the defensive."

"How long before we can try again, do you think?" Saxby asked.

"Hard to say. Brooke's in consultation with the princes. Artois is dispatching Correspondence agents from Jersey to assess how much disruption Jeannot's death has caused. If we *can* contain the damage, it might be within a month or two, hopefully less."

"So long as Wellington can pick up the advance through Spain," Saxby said.

"According to dispatches, now that the Army's rested, he'll strike camp as soon as the weather breaks and head for the border."

"Which will show we're still committed to the fight *and* to the Bourbon cause."

"Indeed," Addington said.

There was a note in the Home Secretary's voice that made Saxby frown. "Are we?" he asked.

372

"Are we what?"

"Committed to the Bourbon cause?"

"We'd like *them* to think so. The fact is, we need the Royalists' support as much as they need ours."

"So the sooner we show willing and locate Hawkwood and make an example of him, the better."

"An example?" Addington said.

"At the very least, he's guilty of murder. One could also make a case for him having committed high treason. Either way, they're capital offences. If punishing him doesn't send out the appropriate message, I don't know what does. You don't agree?"

"You're implying there'll be a trial. I'm not sure that's entirely wise."

"Meaning what?" Saxby demanded.

"I'm simply pointing out that there are aspects of this debacle that would be best kept from the public domain: Jeannot's crimes, this government's harbouring of a murderer, your man's involvement . . ."

"The interest of the nation has always been our first priority."

"I'm not sure the public would appreciate the distinction. Plus, there's the émigré community to consider. There is a great deal of goodwill still felt towards those who have settled here. They've integrated into society extremely well. If the Abbé's activities were to be aired during a trial, well, who knows what might happen? What we don't want to see are mobs on the street attacking émigrés or their property."

"So if there's to be no trial, then what about Hawkwood? The arrest warrant still stands, yes?"

"It does," Addington said firmly.

"So?"

"So, as long as it does, that makes him a fugitive. Knowing his background, it's unlikely he'll surrender without a fight."

The room went quiet.

"You mean there's the distinct possibility he could be shot while resisting arrest?" Saxby said after a lengthy pause.

Addington placed his hands behind his back and stared into the fire.

"Well, that would certainly solve the problem," Saxby mused.

"Quite so," Addington said.

A light rain was still falling when Saxby emerged from the Home Department entrance on to Downing Street, where his carriage was waiting. A footman holding an umbrella aloft accompanied him to the vehicle and opened the carriage door.

"Boodles," Saxby ordered as he climbed inside.

The driver, hat pulled low against the drizzle, acknowledged the directive with a nod. Closing the door, the footman stepped away, receiving no acknowledgement for his service. Brushing errant raindrops from his shoulder, Saxby settled into his seat.

Under normal circumstances, the journey to St James's Street was a brief one, but the roads were more congested than usual due to the weather, people preferring transport in the dry to trudging in the wet. Whitehall was wide enough to allow ready movement but as the carriage neared Charing Cross, traffic began to slow as converging vehicles vied for space. It was a route Saxby had taken many times before, so when the carriage took a right turn past the Charles I statue and on to the Strand instead of bearing left into Cockspur Street, he frowned. He was about to hammer on the roof to attract the driver's attention when the carriage rocked and the door swung open.

Before Saxby could protest, a pistol barrel was levelled against his forehead. Even as he stared at the man wielding the pistol, at the saturnine features, the powder burn and the scars on the left cheek, the coldness in the grey-blue eyes, he knew. His insides turned into gruel. He eyed the door.

"Don't," Hawkwood said, closing the door behind him.

The pistol moved away as Hawkwood took the seat opposite. Saxby threw a quick glance towards the carriage roof.

"Won't do you any good," Hawkwood said. "Your driver was called away."

Trying to control his fear, Saxby glanced sideways through the window. The view told him they were still on the Strand, travelling eastwards. He debated making a bolt for freedom, despite the warning, but the expression on the face of the man before him told him it would be a foolish move.

"You know who I am," Hawkwood said.

"Yes," Saxby said huskily. The door clasp was within easy reach, only a few inches from his hand. If he moved quickly, maybe . . .

"Trust me," Hawkwood said, "you'd never make it."

Saxby swallowed bile, tasting the sourness at the back of his throat. They were still on the Strand. Somerset Place came into sight through the right-hand window. Bluster, he decided, might be the best policy. "What is it you want?"

"Maddie Teague probably asked the same thing," Hawkwood said, "when the scum you hired took her off the street."

Saxby felt his stomach drop. His palms felt suddenly damp. "That was not my doing."

"Really? Vaughn was *your* lackey, following *your* orders. *That* makes it *your* doing. There's a saying: shit slides downhill. I'm here to tell you: not any more."

There followed several seconds of tense silence, save for the rattle of the carriage wheels and the noises issuing from the busy street outside.

"You didn't even ask me who Vaughn was," Hawkwood said, and saw the light die in the other man's eyes.

Saxby, thoughts tumbling through his brain, found his voice. "Where are you taking me?" He eyed the pistol warily, noting the drawn-back hammer.

"Not far."

Saxby felt a fresh coldness spread through him. The thought that he should try calling for help flashed through his mind, but he knew help would not be forthcoming. He sensed that the man opposite was waiting for him to try something as an excuse to attack or restrain him. There was no pity in the grey-blue eyes, only steel.

The coach continued past St Clement Danes and into Fleet Street. Crossing the junction at New Bridge Street, they rattled on to Ludgate Hill. Less than two minutes later, they turned north, allowing Saxby a glimpse of St Martin's church tower and beyond that the dome of St Paul's, dimly visible through the overcast. A short time later, he became aware of the smells seeping into the carriage, the pungent aroma of livestock and shit.

When the grim façade of the Old Bailey appeared in the right-hand window, Saxby realized the smell had to be coming from Smithfield. Hardly had the realization dawned when the carriage made a sudden left turn on to a cobbled street, and then a sharp right on to smoother ground, before coming to a halt.

"Out," Hawkwood said.

Saxby rose unsteadily and stepped down into thin rain and mud. He looked around. They were in a yard. The gate to the yard was open, allowing partial view of the faded sign scrawled upon it which revealed they'd arrived at the premises of one *Thomas Reilly, Slaughterman & Purveyor of Fine Meats.*

Frowning and hesitant, Saxby turned. "What is this place?"

A figure materialized at Hawkwood's side. Saxby took in the coat and hat and realized it was the driver he'd addressed back at Downing Street. As he watched, the headwear was removed, revealing a tough-looking man with short, gun-metal grey hair and a hard face. After looking Saxby up and down, Hawkwood's companion turned towards a doorway a few yards away. "Tommy Reilly! Get your arse out here!"

The man who answered the summons was short and thick with thinning red hair, a broad chin and lumpy ears. He wore no shirt, only a filthy waistcoat that might have been grey at one time, along with a leather apron over a pair of dirty brown breeches and knee-length boots reinforced with leather straps. He squinted suspiciously. "That you, Jago?"

"Course it's me, you ignorant Mick. Sent a message telling you we were coming. How're the boys?"

"Ain't been fed for a few days," Reilly said, casting a speculative look in Saxby's direction.

"They still out the back?"

"Aye."

There was a wary look on the slaughterman's face. Aaron Mudd's yard wasn't more than half a dozen streets away and word of

Jago's visit there had spread. Not that there was any danger of Reilly alerting any of Mudd's friends or of telling Jago to sling his hook. The latter's reputation and his past dealings with Reilly ensured complete discretion. Besides, it wasn't as though the Irishman had an unblemished record when it came to servicing the requirements of his community, which had more to do with the disposal of unwanted items than with the butchery trade, often necessitating methods too grisly to be discussed in polite company. The man had a reputation, not to mention secrets of his own to protect.

Saxby felt the muzzle of the pistol press against the middle of his spine.

Reilly took his cue, turned and without further comment disappeared through the doorway from which he'd emerged.

"Walk," Hawkwood said.

Saxby, gripped by a profound sense of trepidation, remained rooted to the spot.

"You heard the man," Jago said.

"No." His hair wet and sticking to his scalp, Saxby tried desperately to keep the tremor from his voice. "I demand to know where you're taking me!"

Hawkwood shrugged. "Your choice."

Saxby failed to see the kick coming. He felt it, though, in the middle of his buttocks, the force sending him on to his knees and into the slurry. Before he had a chance to push himself upright, he was hoisted under both armpits and hauled forward. Struggling violently, legs kicking, yet unable to break free, Saxby's vocal protestations turned with increasing urgency from anger and threats of reprisal to desperate pleas for mercy.

He had no awareness of the direction in which he was being dragged, only that by the time he was eventually flung to the ground, he had lost the strength to resist. Humiliated, chest heaving, he lay sprawled in the mire, his clothes mud-splattered and damp against his flesh, his nostrils clogged with the stench of shit and offal . . . and something else, a musky odour that he couldn't quite identify, unlike anything he'd smelled before; something . . . malignant.

He looked up. He'd been deposited before a crude wooden fence some six feet high and constructed from rough-sawn planks fashioned into horizontal slats, each one separated from the one above and below by a three-inch gap, giving a fractured view of the pen's interior. As Saxby's brain took in the sight, his eye was drawn to a dark, heavy, indistinct shape moving on the other side of the screen. The motion was accompanied by a heavy snuffling noise. The smell as the thing drew closer was appalling. Saxby felt the hairs lift along the back of his neck.

As he watched, a second shadow appeared a few feet further along the fence and then a third. The stench grew stronger as the snuffling grew louder, settling into a series of rasping grunts. Saxby recoiled as the guttural emanations intensified. It sounded like axe heads being sharpened against a grinding stone, magnified a thousand times. The noise went right through him. He stared as a portion of bristly black hide appeared in a gap less than two feet from his face. The fence panels let out a groan and for one heart-stopping moment, Saxby thought they were about to give way. But then, the sounds receded as whatever it was that had caused the fence to vibrate retreated to another part of the pen. The yard fell quiet.

For all of five seconds.

Saxby let out a near-hysterical shriek as a black snout suddenly thrust its way into the opening. To Saxby's horror the snout was replaced by a set of slavering jaws, jacked open to reveal a gaping maw and a set of vicious, ivory-coloured, five-inch-long tusks which began to rip and tear at the edge of the slats. Ravenous growls and snorts accompanied the noise of wood being shredded.

The grey-haired man grinned. "Impressive buggers, ain't they? Seven 'undred pounds apiece, if they're an ounce. Not from round here, of course. Word is their daddy was a boar brought over from Poland for display in an animal emporium, until some bright spark decided it might be an idea to breed the old boy with some of our English hogs. Worked, too, 'ceptin' when they 'ad the litter, there was no one who could handle the bloody things. That's how Reilly was able to get 'em cheap.

"Plan was to fatten 'em into sausages – 'til he realized they were quite the attraction. Figured he could make more money charging folk to come an' see 'em than he would turnin' 'em into crackling. Started out at a penny a throw; two pence if you wanted to watch 'em feed. Wasn't long before people started bringin' in their own swill. Our Tommy's never looked back since. Thing is, y'see, they'll eat anything. Cabbages, cauliflowers, dead cats – makes no difference. Stalks 'n bones, they'll go through the lot. Knew someone who saw them eat a dead cart-horse once. It was cut up, mind; it wasn't all at one go. Told me I should've seen 'em fighting over the scraps. Said it fair turned his stomach."

The grey-haired man chuckled. "An' they do look anxious to make your acquaintance, don't they?"

Saxby gazed at Jago in horror as the reality of his plight took hold. "No!" he said weakly, shaking his head. "You can't . . .!"

The fence shook again as the hog tore at the wood. Shadows expanded as it was joined by its companions. The sounds coming from within the pen tore into Saxby's soul. He tried to climb to his feet but only got as far as his knees. He turned to Hawkwood. "I'll do whatever you want! I can pay you! Please! You can't do this! For pity's sake!"

"Get up, you snivelling sack of shit!" Grabbing Saxby's collar, Hawkwood hauled Saxby upright and nodded to Jago. "Gate."

Saxby tried to pull away but again lost his footing. Hawkwood dragged him up once more.

Jago walked over to the fence, to the gate fastened by a rope and a heavy metal clasp. Saxby tried to slither out of Hawkwood's grasp. His breeches were black with mud and dung from his fall. His face was streaked with dirt.

The enraged hogs had now turned all their rabid attention to the gap at the base of the barrier. The noise rose to a crescendo, by which time Saxby's cries had descended into a series of breathless, heaving sobs. "Please," he implored. "Please!"

Jago undid the clasp on the gate. He looked at Hawkwood.

Saxby, finding fresh strength, began to squirm like an eel.

"Do it," Hawkwood said.

Jago, his face set, nodded. Taking a strategic step to the side and bracing his feet, he pulled the gate open.

"Ple—" Saxby said. That was as far as he got.

As Hawkwood pushed him through the opening, the noises inside the pen erupted into an ear-splitting clamour.

The gate secured behind them, Hawkwood and Jago turned away as a chorus of high-pitched squeals rose into the air.

It was hard to tell which were animal and which were human.

Thirty minutes had passed when Jago said, "How long you reckon?"

"Until?" Hawkwood said.

"He twigged."

"A while, probably," Hawkwood said. "The state he was in."

Jago grinned crookedly. "Let's find out."

They retraced their steps to the pen.

It had taken a long time for the noises on the other side of the wall to melt away; the squeals and snarls subsiding into more harmonious rooting sounds as the hogs gradually calmed down and wandered away to another part of their enclosure. It was only as Hawkwood and Jago approached that the animals' mood changed and the volume of their grunts and snuffles began to intensify as they turned once again to resume their assault on the perimeter.

Drawing close and ignoring the commotion, Jago opened the gate.

"Ah, Jesus," he muttered.

Seated in the muck, knees drawn up to his chin, arms held tight together, elbows folded before his face and with his hands raised to protect his skull, the terrified Saxby had managed to cram himself into the corner of the wall. There was not a part of him that was not coated with mud and ordure; a good deal of the latter, Jago guessed, having voided from Saxby's own bowels. A low keening sound issued from the tiny gap between Saxby's forearms and he remained motionless as Jago stared down at him. Jago wondered if the man was even aware he was still alive.

No more than five feet square, the inner pen was the means by which Reilly was able to keep his pets fed. There was a stout inner gate that gave access to the main run, but even Riley wasn't foolish enough to risk entry through that, so he used an adjacent hatch as the means by which to satisfy the beasts' voracious appetites. The inner gate was kept for special occasions, there being no safety barrier beyond it. For those souls who did venture through it, either via their own misguided volition or by involuntary persuasion, there was not the slightest chance of a return to safe ground.

The scream that rose from Saxby's throat when Jago touched his shoulder was almost as shrill as the tumult issuing from the other side of the wall.

"Going to need a hand here," Jago called.

Arms swinging, legs kicking, such was Saxby's terror at being manhandled that it took an effort for both men to drag him back through the outer gate. In the end, Jago had to pin his arms while Hawkwood delivered a backhanded slap across his face before he calmed down enough to realize that it wasn't the hogs that had a hold of him.

As his eyes lost their glazed look, he stared up at the men standing over him. It took a further second for recognition to set in. Throwing up his hands, he recoiled in fear and let go a scream as his collar was held. Spittle ran down his chin as he shook his head from side to side. His body stank of excrement and fear. "Please," he whispered. "No more . . ."

Hawkwood put his lips close to Saxby's ear. "Don't worry, you're not dead . . . yet."

Saxby blinked uncomprehendingly. Tears had left snail tracks down his cheeks.

Hawkwood tightened his grip. "Tell Addington to call off his dogs. He doesn't, I'm coming for you; Gaunt and the Rain woman, too. And know this; you let me down and I *will* feed you to the pigs – and by Christ I'll gut you first, to make it easy for them to take a hold. Do you understand?"

A whimper trickled from Saxby's quivering lips.

"I didn't hear you," Hawkwood snarled. "Say it again."

"Ye-yes! Yes!"

Hawkwood released his grip and watched stone-faced as Saxby fell back. "And don't think you can hide. Cross me and I *will* find you and I *will* see you dead."

"An' if he doesn't," Jago growled. "I will."

Stepping away, Hawkwood gazed down at Saxby in disgust and wiped his hands on his coat. "Let's get the hell out of here. The stench in this place is starting to get to me."

"They're bleedin' hogs," Jago said. "What d'you expect?"

"I wasn't talking about the hogs," Hawkwood said.

"Still can't believe you didn't top the bastard," Jago said. "If it'd been me . . ."

"There's been enough killing," Hawkwood said.

Jago fixed him with a speculative look. "Reckon you'd feel that way if Maddie weren't still with us?"

"Probably not," Hawkwood conceded.

It was late evening and they were in the Hanged Man, seated at the table in front of the window. The room was filled with low chatter and the click-clack of dominoes from an adjacent table.

"Thought as much," Jago said, and then sighed. "She was bloody lucky."

"We all were . . . considering."

Jago nodded ruminatively. "Lass is doing well, though. To look at her, you wouldn't know what she's been through."

"She'll still need time," Hawkwood said, "but she's strong."

"That she is." Jago paused then said, "You think they talk about us behind our backs?"

"Every waking moment, I shouldn't wonder."

Jago grinned. He'd been referring to Maddie and Connie Fletcher.

Maddie was out of hospital, thanks to James Read's tame doctor. Under Surgeon Gillray's assiduous supervision, she was recuperating at Connie's Cavendish Square house. The two women had been introduced a long time back and had become firm friends. Connie had been quick to make the offer of accommodation after visiting the hospital with a hamper and, more importantly, a welcome change of clothes.

Maddie had resisted the idea at first. But Connie had refused to take no for an answer and so, upon the advice of Surgeon Gillray, and knowing the Blackbird was safe in Lily's more than capable hands, she'd allowed herself to be persuaded. Despite Connie's protestations, she was now back on her feet and anxious to return to her own bed.

"You think Saxby'll persuade Addington to lift the warrant?" Jago asked over the rim of his mug.

"Hard to say."

"If he doesn't?" Jago pressed.

"He was warned."

Jago looked thoughtful. "Aye, well, Reilly's hogs ain't goin' anywhere."

Hawkwood gave a grim smile.

"Even though you said there's been enough killing?" Jago mused.

"A man's entitled to change his mind. And I'd have nothing to lose. They can only hang me the once."

"That's if they catch you," Jago pointed out. "But if they don't, it means you'd be lookin' over your shoulder the rest of your natural. That ain't no way to live."

"No, it's not."

"Even if the warrant is lifted, there's no guarantee they won't come after you. People like that don't care for bein' humiliated, an' they tend to have powerful friends."

"I'm aware of that," Hawkwood said.

Jago looked at him, lips pursed. "Aye, well, There's transport standin' by, if you do need to run. I can get you across the water."

"Water?"

"The Channel. It's that bit o' sea off the south coast."

"France?"

"Hell, why not? You speak the lingo like a native, an' it's the last place they'd think of lookin'. Gravelines is close to home. You could hide out among the free traders. There's plenty owe me a favour. Or you could always send a message to our pal Lasseur. He'd help you out. Probably offer you a roof, play your cards right."

"Sounds like you're anxious to get rid of me."

"Just lookin' after your interests." Jago took a sip from his mug.

"Yes, well, I appreciate the thought, but it might not come to that."

"It might, though."

"True, it might," Hawkwood agreed.

Jago paused then said, "You thought about what Maddie'd say, if you did disappear again?"

"After all that's happened? She's probably better off without me."

Jago played with the handle of his mug. "You do know she doesn't blame you?"

"I keep hearing that."

"Then maybe you should start believin' it," Jago said pointedly.

For a moment neither of them spoke. The situation was diffused when a call came from one of the domino players.

"What about you, big man? Fancy a wager? Ned's about to get the drinks in."

Jago took a calming breath before turning and glancing towards where Del, Ned and Jasper were turning over the tiles in preparation for a fresh game. "An' I thought miracles only occurred in the good book."

"Oi, I heard that," Ned said.

Jago smiled and placed his empty mug aside. "Thanks, lads, but I reckon I'll pass. Nothin' personal, but I've a sudden hankerin' for some home comforts. Besides, it's getting late."

"Never too late when there's hankerin' involved," Del said, grinning.

"An' a man needs 'is beauty sleep, right?" Jasper gave a knowing wink.

"You can sit in, Officer," Del offered, "if'n you don't mind losin' a few bob."

Jago eyed Hawkwood. "Don't let me stop you."

Hawkwood emptied his drink. "Not for me. I'm away, too." Pushing back his chair, he rose. Jago did the same.

Seated at the table at the top of the stairs, Micah looked up. Jago waved him back down. "We're callin' it a night. Finish your book."

Micah nodded and watched both men's backs as they made their way downstairs. On the ground floor, the one-eyed fiddle player was at his usual place by the fire, his instrument held loosely in one hand, a mug of gin in the other. His dog was stretched out at his feet, gnawing on a bone. Around them were the usual regulars who didn't have homes to go to. Their families consisted of the molls, leg-men, mutton-mongers, chippers, dummy-hunters, pads and priggers seated or sprawled among the adjoining tables.

Acknowledging the nods of recognition and, in some cases, deference, they pushed their way through to the street outside. The noise faded behind them.

Jago slipped on his woollen cap, turned his collar and thrust his hands into his pockets. "Think they'll be waitin' up for us? Be the last bleedin' straw if they are. There's only so much domesticity a man can take."

"I'll tell Connie you said that."

Jago grinned.

The rain continued to fall steadily as they made their way along the darkened street in companionable silence.

Until Jago said softly, "You saw what I saw, right?"

"I did," Hawkwood said.

"Two?"

"Two," Hawkwood confirmed.

Jago removed his hands from his pockets and blew on them before unbuttoning his jacket.

It was difficult to make out details through the rain, but the moving shadows of the men he'd seen ducking back out of sight down the alleyway fifty paces ahead of them had seared a warning into Hawkwood's brain. Jago's observation confirmed that the sighting had been real and not imagined.

"Saxby's hirelings?" Jago murmured.

"I'd say we're about to find out." Hawkwood unbuttoned his coat and reached inside it.

"Heard footsteps behind, too," Jago said. "At least one, maybe two."

They were thirty paces from the entrance to the alleyway when the shadows shifted and two men stepped out from the darkness. Dressed in long coats and caps, it was hard to make out features as they split apart to cover both sides of the narrow street. Each held what looked like a heavy cudgel in their hands.

"Here we go," Jago murmured.

As the scuff of a boot on the cobbles sounded from behind them.

"Watch your front," Jago whispered, turning in time to see a tall, thin figure, hunkered down, shoulders tucked in, hat pulled low coming towards them. By the posture, this was no threat, merely a fellow pedestrian hurrying to get out of the rain.

Letting go a sigh, Jago was about to turn back when a sixth sense made him glance over his shoulder again, to find that the figure had slowed.

"Nathanial Jago?"

The voice came out of the gloom.

"Who's askin'?"

"I am."

The figure drew closer, head lifting to reveal a gaunt face and a ferocious look in the eyes.

"An' you are . . .?"

"Name's Michael Shaughnessy."

As the speaker straightened further, his left hand swept the front of the coat open, revealing the gun in his right hand, the flared muzzle instantly recognizable. "You knew my boys."

Out of the corner of his eye, Jago saw the other two men bringing up their weapons – not cudgels, he realized, but Barbars – and Hawkwood drawing the Bingham from the loop on his belt.

"Ah, shit," he said wearily, as another darting shape appeared over Shaughnessy's right shoulder – Micah, coming in fast, pistol levelled. "So much for a quiet night in . . ."

Historical Note

Readers who have been following Hawkwood's adventures will recognize La Congrégation and the part it played during his mission to Paris in October 1812 and the failed attempt to seize the capital – and, indeed, the Empire – by the resourceful but ultimately doomed General Claude-François Malet.

The organization is not a figment of the imagination. Founded around 1800 by a former Jesuit priest, Jean-Baptiste Bordier Delpuits, and governed by the rules of the Society of Jesus, La Congrégation was made up from cells of students with whom Delpuits had previously engaged in spiritual discussions. It conducted its business in the ways outlined in the novel until it was suppressed by Bonaparte in 1809.

Les Chevalier de la Foi – the Knights of the Faith – also existed, the majority of the members being drawn from La Congrégation's ranks. Formed around 1809/1810 by three brothers – Ferdinand de Bertier de Sauvigny, Anne Pierre de Bertier de Sauvigny and Louis Bénigne – its aim was to unify and consolidate all royalist forces within the French Empire. Fascinated by Freemasonry, which they believed lay behind the causes of the French Revolution, its founders wanted to transpose the Masonic system into the service of the Church and the king, so they infiltrated masonic lodges to study their operation and organization.

As they worked to a secret agenda – the overthrow of Bonaparte – most of their activities took place in the shadows, so how effective they actually were has been open to interpretation. In the main, they saw their role as preparing public opinion for the return of the Bourbons, and in that regard they were certainly instrumental in arranging the royalist coup in March 1814 which helped to convince the Allied governments of the feasibility of restoring the old dynasty, a move which enabled the British to capture both Bordeaux and Toulouse later that same month. They continued to work closely with British agents during the Hundred Days, an alliance which eventually aided the second restoration of King Louis XVIII, in July 1815.

Given that timeline, it's clear that Saxby and Home Secretary Henry Addington were being more than a tad optimistic when they discussed the possibility of Wellington advancing from his winter quarters in the early part of 1813. I confess to taking some liberty (some would say played fast and loose) with the dates involved. In fact, Wellington did not set off from Ciudad Rodrigo until May. In June he defeated Joseph Bonaparte's forces at the battle of Vitoria and the British laid siege to San Sebastian later that same month. The city was eventually taken in August. Wellington crossed the Bidassoa River into France in October.

The Committee – *Subscribers to a Fund for the Relief of the Suffering Clergy of France in the British Dominions* – was founded and managed by John Wilmot from its offices in Queen Street – now Museum Street – which at one time over-looked St Giles & St George's Charity School.

Margery Weiner, in her very readable account of émigré life in London, *The French Exiles 1789–1815*, states that the circumstances of John Wilmot's sudden resignation from the Committee in 1806 were puzzling.

She writes: 'In 1805 there was a sharp series of letters from the Audit Office, querying the accounts of the Committee. There is neither evidence nor suggestion of peculation, only a bald entry in the Minutes chronicling the resignation of the chairman.' She goes on to add that Wilmot might have been 'tired and glad to be relieved of his task . . . perhaps the Treasury goads and pricks had enervated him. History does not say.'

By all accounts, John Wilmot was an extremely honourable

man, refusing a peerage for his charitable works. Pleading historical licence, I thought it would be more interesting to suggest that he may have discovered that Committee funds were being misappropriated for clandestine purposes, with the blessing of certain members of the government, and therefore took the honourable way out rather than risk compromising both his good name and that of the Committee he founded.

Certainly, Home Secretary Henry Addington was no stranger to intrigue and took great interest in the workings of Britain's very effective intelligence service, which at the time the novel is set operated out of the Alien Office under the guidance of Superintendent Henry Brooke.

The Office should have been dissolved after the Peace of Amiens but with great foresight it was kept going by the Duke of Portland, who'd been Home Secretary under William Pitt and who remained in situ for several months under Addington when the latter took over as PM.

The understanding between Portland and William Wickham, head of the Alien Office prior to Henry Brooke, was that only a small number of men would know what the Office got up to. Under Portland's direction the department became even more secretive, his directive being that such was the clandestine nature of the work undertaken no other government office should know of the Office's activities, not even the Prime Minister.

Wickham, however, wanted Pitt to be in the know. He believed that once the latter saw how the Office functioned he could not fail to grasp its importance and that, operating away from the public's gaze, it was 'the most powerful means of Observation and Information that was ever placed in the hands of a free government'.

Which prompts the immediate question, two centuries later: now where have we heard that one before?

In 1802, after succeeding Pitt as Prime Minister, Addington did set up a secret committee of the House of Commons to investigate all aspects of foreign and domestic secret service. He decided that there needed to be more accountability with regards to the distribution of funds. He was, however, a supporter of the Alien Office and saw its full potential as a tool against Bonaparte – especially with regards to fermenting insurrection within France – using Bourbon sympathizers, which the British would fund.

La Correspondence was a secret network of agents operating under the command of Admiral Philippe d'Auvergne from its base at Mont Orgueil in Jersey. In the course of her research for her hugely informative volume: *Secret Service: British Agents in France 1792–1815*, the author and historian Elizabeth Sparrow had occasion to interview a former agent of SOE (Special Operations Executive), the wonderfully named Bickham Aldred Cowan Sweet-Escott. He gleefully advised Sparrow that shortly after he joined SOE back in 1940 the organization's Chief of Staff, George Taylor, told him that the intention was 'to do to Europe what Pitt did to France before 1807'. He was referring to the work of the Alien Office, which worked closely with La Correspondence during the Napoleonic Wars.

Given that the Alien Office was involved – both directly and indirectly – in a number of sabotage missions on the French mainland, which included several officially sanctioned attempts to assassinate Emperor Bonaparte, I can't think of a better analogy, as it echoes what Churchill himself is known to have said, that the remit of the SOE was 'to set Europe ablaze'.

Charles-Philippe – the Comte d'Artois – and his brother Louis Stanislas – the future Louis XVIII – each commanded his own independent network of royalist agents. Of the two, Artois was probably the most effective, as his organization operated out of Jersey with the British Prime Minister's blessing.

Anyone who has occasion to pass through the village of Esher will know the Bear Hotel. As one of the main coaching inns on the Portsmouth Road, it has been providing shelter and sustenance to travellers for the best part of three centuries.

St George's Church, which is open to visitors, is located a stone's throw behind it. The church's Tudor-built architecture has changed little over the intervening years. The interior, with its three-tiered pulpit and the reredos inscribed with the Ten Commandments and the Lord's Prayer, is as it was during

Hawkwood's time, when Reverend Wadham Diggle served as the rector.

James Read held the post of Chief Magistrate at Bow Street from 1806 to 1813. He was succeeded by Nathaniel Conant, formerly of the Great Marlborough Street Public Office, who received a knighthood upon his appointment. Ironically, when Conant resigned from the post in 1820 he did so due to failing health.